Fiona was born in a youth hostel in Yorkshire. She started working on teen magazine *Jackie* at age 17, then went on to join *Just Seventeen* and *More!* where she invented the infamous 'Position of the Fortnight'. Fiona now lives in Scotland with her husband Jimmy, their three children and a wayward rescue collie cross called Jack.

For more info, visit www.fionagibson.com. You can follow Fiona on Twitter @fionagibson.

By the same author:

Mum On The Run
The Great Escape
Pedigree Mum
Take Mum Out
How the In-Laws Wrecked Christmas: a short story
As Good As It Gets?
The Woman Who Upped and Left
The Woman Who Met Her Match
The Mum Who'd Had Enough

The Mum Who Got her Life Back

FIONA GIBSON

avon.

AVON
A division of HarperCollins*Publishers*
1 London Bridge Street,
London SE1 9GF
www.harpercollins.co.uk

A Paperback Original 2019

1

First published in Great Britain by
HarperCollins*Publishers* 2019

Copyright © Fiona Gibson 2019

Fiona Gibson asserts the moral right to
be identified as the author of this work

A catalogue record for this book is
available from the British Library

ISBN-13: 978-0-00-831096-7

Typeset in Sabon Lt Std by Palimpsest Book Production Ltd,
Falkirk, Stirlingshire

Printed and bound in Great Britain by CPI Group (UK) Ltd,
Croydon CR0 4YY

MIX
Paper from
responsible sources
FSC
www.fsc.org **FSC˚ C007454**

This book is produced from independently certified FSC™ paper
to ensure responsible forest management.

For more information visit: www.harpercollins.co.uk/green

With thanks . . .

To the amazing Jackie B, who manages a Mary's Meals charity shop and let me spend a day nosing around, talking to volunteers and rummaging in the back room. I couldn't have written this book without your help, Miss Brown! To Kath Brown and Miranda McMinn at Woman & Home *magazine for getting me thinking about Happy Empty Nesters (HENs) and inadvertently inspiring this book. To Jen, Susan, Laura, Wendy and Lisa (Kath, you were missed!) for celebrating with me in Ibiza when this book was done. To Wendy (again) for a detailed description of a certain type of pokey facial, which I used almost verbatim. To my brilliant editor Rachel Faulkner-Willcocks, publicist Sabah Khan and the whole fantastic Avon team. To my super-agent Caroline Sheldon for being the best in the business. Finally, all my love to Jimmy, Sam, Dexter and Erin, my lovely family who put up with me working crazy hours and very often talking to myself.*

For my fabulous friend Miss Jackie Brown
Queen of Fife

Part One

Things that happen when your kids first leave home

- You keep checking to see if they've texted to say they're managing without you. They haven't . . . because you've only just moved them into their student halls and are still sitting in your car, in the car park.

- You realise it's no longer necessary to buy those two-kilo bags of potatoes. They just go green and start sprouting.

- You also stop buying The Big Milk and switch to the smallest carton. *How tiny you are!* you think, the first dozen times you spy it in the fridge.

- Friends say things like, 'You might miss them at first. But when they come home on visits they'll trash the place, and you'll be relieved when they go back to uni.' *How harsh*, you think. *I love my kids. I'll never think of them in that way.*

- You realise you could now have sex in your own home without worrying about the kids overhearing. Or perhaps you're thinking more along the lines of, *Shall I redecorate to mark this new chapter?* Perhaps your mindset is less 'shag pad', more 'upgrading of cushions'. Either way, it's pretty thrilling.

- Towels remain on the towel rail and the loo roll sits, unmolested, on its holder.

- The washing machine goes on about twice a week. You start to feel proud of your tiny carbon footprint.

- No one criticises your home-cooked lasagne. You don't even have to make lasagne, with all the chopping and stirring it entails. Dinner can be a pot of hummus and a boiled egg if you feel like it.

- No one crashes in, switching on all the lights and frying things at 3.30 a.m.

- After a while you stop thinking, *My God, this is weird! Where is everyone?* You're not missing the days when it looked as if wildebeest had stampeded through the kitchen, whenever someone made toast. Gradually, you become used to them not being there, and – it almost seems criminal to admit this – you don't completely hate it.

This signifies that you have transitioned, relatively painlessly, into being a HEN: a Happy Empty Nester. Yes, you're still a doting parent, but no longer in the day-to-day sense, which suggests that your new life has begun.

So, what *now*?

Chapter One

Nadia

Since my children left home, nothing terrible seems to have happened. There has been no evidence of malnutrition or the taking of shedloads of drugs. No one has phoned me, crying, because they couldn't get a crumpet out of the toaster. At eighteen years old, my twins Alfie and Molly seem to have coped perfectly well during their first semester at university . . . which means I've done a decent job as a parent, right?

Naturally, their father, Danny, should take some of the credit. But the moving-out part was down to me. Danny is an independent film-maker and he was away shooting down south when I took Molly to her student halls. In the seven years since we split, his career has blossomed; he is pretty famous in film circles, and incredibly busy. At least, too busy/famous to drive Molly from our home in Glasgow to her university halls in Edinburgh.

'Well, this is it,' I remarked with fake jollity as we lugged her possessions into her stark little room.

'Yeah,' she said casually, tossing back her long dark hair.

3

'You will be all right, won't you?'

''Course I will!'

I cleared my throat. 'Any time you need me, I mean if you need *anything*, I'll come straight over.'

'Mum, I won't need—'

'No, I know, but . . .' I stopped. My daughter has always given the impression that she rarely needs anything, from anyone.

'I'm not dying,' she said, smiling. We hugged tightly, and I was immensely proud of myself as I hurtled out of the block, shoving my way past more new arrivals with their stoical parents and desk lamps and mini fridges and, in one instance, a gerbil in a cage, which I was pretty sure wasn't allowed in halls. Only when I was safely back in my car did I allow the tears to spill out, and had to mop my face on a waterproof umbrella sleeve.

Two days later, I drove Alfie to his own halls further north, in Aberdeen. The city felt chillier and greyer than it had when we'd come up for the open day (his father had been too busy/famous to go to that too), and I reminded my son several times that he might start wearing a vest.

'You can just leave my stuff here, Mum,' he said, indicating the floor on the landing.

'Really? Can't I come in?' But he'd already scooted into the flat to find his room, and so I stood there, waiting, like a FedEx delivery person.

Moments later Alfie reappeared, and we fell into a pattern of me fetching stuff in from the car, lugging it up three flights of stairs and handing it over at the designated spot on the landing. He grabbed the final box in which I'd assembled an emergency rations pack of tinned soups, pastas and – rather optimistically – fruit. 'See you then,' he mumbled, gazing down at his feet.

'Er . . . okay, love. Look after yourself, won't you?' In truth, I was more worried about him than Molly. He'd always been rather shy and disorganised, and a klutz when it came to practical matters. I wasn't convinced he'd be up to boiling spaghetti without somehow setting it on fire.

'Of course I will,' he insisted. I forced a hug on him and left the building, passing a woman carrying an enormous tropical plant (does anyone really need a *tree* in their uni halls?), and wishing that Danny was here too, but that night he was in London at his wrap party.

Good for him, I thought. Good for my ex and his girlfriend and those miles of canapés and champagne sloshing everywhere. No, this was all *great*, I told myself as I drove back to Glasgow, then stepped back into my second-floor flat. Danny is a caring dad – I've never disputed that. However, he's never been too hot on the practical matters of parenting.

We were thrilled when we found out we were having twins, but from the word go we fell into pretty traditional roles. While Danny toiled all hours to get his career off the ground, I threw myself into the hurly-burly of toddler groups. We've been lucky to have always lived in a decent area of Glasgow: a little shabby, but friendly and safe. We stretched ourselves to upgrade to a four-bedroomed flat so the kids could each have their own rooms, and Danny could have a much-needed study.

For a few years I worked from a desk in our bedroom. I am a freelance illustrator, and had accumulated a small roster of clients before the twins came along. During my early years of motherhood, I'd tackle any commissions after the kids had gone to bed. I also did some occasional life modelling – i.e. with my clothes off – for

5

local art classes, to bring in extra cash. In a weird sort of way, they offered a bit of respite from family life. Reclining nakedly on a sofa was pretty soothing compared to chipping hardened Weetabix off the floorboards – and I assumed the kids would never find out what it really involved. Anyway, I was around so much after nursery and school that Alfie and Molly didn't actually believe I worked at all. Their primary school teacher laughingly told me that, when she'd asked Molly what her mum did for a living, she'd replied, 'She colours in.'

In contrast, Danny did go to work – not in a nine-to-five sense, but for weeks at a time if he was away filming, or to his study at home where he'd hide away to work on edits or scripts.

'Nadia, the kids keep coming in!' he'd yell.

'They just need to see you for a minute, Danny. Alfie wants to show you something he made at school . . .'

'Honey, *please*. Can't you just keep them at bay?' he'd say, as if they weren't his six-year-old children, but wild bears. But then, Danny's work was all-consuming, and it was my job to thwart the kids' access to He Who Must Not Be Disturbed.

'Daddy's busy being Steven Spielberg,' I'd explain, ushering them away.

'Who's Steven Spee—' Alfie would start.

'A very important film man like Dad,' I'd say. Alfie always needed more reassurance than Molly, and I was conscious of over-compensating for Danny's unavailability: painting with the kids whenever they demanded it, and indulging Alfie's lengthy baking craze. The more cakes he made, the more I felt obliged to scoff ('Sounds like a feeble excuse to me,' Danny had sniggered), my once-slender body expanding and softening, my skimpy knickers making way for sturdy mummy-pants.

Meanwhile, Danny remained his gangly, raffishly handsome self, all messy dark hair and stubble. He seemed to experience no guilt whatsoever on turning down one of Alfie's Krispie cakes: 'They look great, Alf, but I'm not really into that breakfast-cereal-confectionery hybrid.' He didn't intend to be mean, and the kids still adored him. However, Danny had always done whatever he wanted and he didn't really worry what anyone else thought.

I'd known, when I got together with a film-maker, that I might be signing up for an unconventional sort of life. However, I also knew that other film-makers – friends of Danny's – managed to be reasonably functioning adults, able to maintain healthy, happy relationships. To my knowledge they never left their partners stranded in restaurants because they'd gone to a lecture on Hitchcock and the Art of Cinematic Tension instead (on aforementioned partner's fortieth birthday). Nor had they blown a small inheritance from an uncle by drunkenly bidding on one of the actual suits worn in *Reservoir Dogs*. Of course it wasn't just about the suit or the missed meals; it was loads of stuff, piled up year after year.

Although it was me who finally decided we should split – Danny and I had never married – he didn't exactly beg me to reconsider. I think we both knew we'd reached the end of the line. And so he moved out, to a rented flat half a mile away, and we both did our best to present our break-up in a non-dramatic manner. 'We're still friends who care about each other,' I told Molly and Alfie – which was actually true.

A year or so later, Danny started seeing a make-up artist ten years his junior. I was fine with that, truly;

Danny and I were managing to get along pretty cordially, and I was enjoying teasing him about his new liaison. 'So how are things with Kiki Badger?' I asked during one of our regular chats on the phone.

I heard him exhale. 'Nads, why d'you always do this?'

'Do what?'

'You know. Use both of her names.'

I smirked. 'It's one of those names you have to say in full . . .'

'Why?'

'Because it sounds like a sex toy. "The batteries in my Kiki Badger have gone flat!"'

'You're ridiculous,' he exclaimed, laughing. Then, after a pause: 'It's nothing serious, y'know? We're just . . . hanging out.' Yeah, sure. 'How about you?' he asked. 'Is there anyone . . .'

'You know there isn't,' I said quickly.

'No I don't. You might have someone squirrelled away—'

'Hidden in a cupboard?'

'Maybe,' he sniggered.

'Chance'd be a fine thing,' I retorted, but in truth I wasn't too interested. It's not that Alfie and Molly would have kicked off if I'd started seeing someone; at least, I don't think they would have.

As it turned out, their dad and Kiki have stuck together over the years, and the kids have always seemed fine with that. However, they lived with me, and perhaps that made me more cautious. I wasn't prepared to endure some teeth-gritting, 'Alfie, Molly – this is Colin!' kind of scenario at breakfast with some bloke I wasn't particularly serious about. There were a couple of brief flings, conducted when Molly and Alfie were at their dad's, and a significant one, eighteen months ago; well, it was significant to me. But since then? Precisely nothing.

It's fine, honestly. It really is. It's just *slightly* galling that the kids have left home and I'm free as a bird – yet I've found precisely no one to tempt into my nest.

Chapter Two

And yet . . . celibacy has its advantages. It really does!

I'm not even saying that in a bitter tone, with my teeth gritted. I can happily wander about with hairy bison legs beneath my jeans, if I want to. I can orgasm perfectly well by myself, and have plenty of friends to knock around with. Corinne and Gus are two of my closest; we've all known each other since our art college days in Dundee, and these days we share a studio pretty close to the city centre. As my children grew up, and I managed to establish myself properly, I reached the point where I could finally afford to work outside of the flat. It feels like a luxury sometimes, as now Alfie and Molly have left I can hardly complain about the lack of space at home. But I love working here. Our studio is the top floor of a tatty old warehouse, currently decked out with decorations and a sparkling white tree, as Christmas is approaching.

'So your present to yourself is to get online,' remarks Gus, as he makes coffee for the three of us.

'I'm not joining a dating site,' I say firmly.

10

'Why not just give it a go?' He glances over from the huge canvas he's working on.

'I've told you, Gus. It's just not my thing.'

I turn back to the preliminary sketches that are littered all over my desk. I'm illustrating a series of study guides covering English, maths and history, and possibly more subjects, if the client is happy with the results. As I start to sketch, I'm aware of Gus and Corinne exchanging a look; both of them reckon I have been single for far too long.

It's a year and a half since I last slept with someone, and that person happened to be Ryan Tibbles, who was also at art college with us, although I hadn't known him very well when we were students. I'd just experienced a little frisson whenever I glimpsed him mooching around, with his mop of black, shaggy hair and languid expression, a smouldering roll-up permanently clamped between his sexy lips.

After we'd graduated, everyone had scattered all over the country in pursuit of work or to further their studies. I returned to Glasgow, to do admin for a small design company, hoping it would lead to greater things. Ryan, who'd been the star of his year, whizzed off to do a post-grad at St Martins in London. I heard nothing from him for all those years until he turned up out of the blue at a party at Corinne's.

She hadn't even invited him; he'd been in Glasgow on some work-related mission, and someone had brought him along. We sat together all night, reminiscing about college and, eventually, indulging in a little furtive hand-holding and kissing. 'Be good, you two!' Corinne had chuckled as we left together.

I took him back to my place where we crept in gingerly

at 6.30 a.m. There was no real need to creep – Molly and Alfie were away on a school trip to France – but still, I'd half expected them to jump out from behind the sofa yelling, 'Ah-a! So here's our filthy mother, drunk and with a man!' Even when Ryan and I went to bed, I was still on edge in case they charged in, flung down their rucksacks and clicked on the dazzling overhead light.

In the four days that followed, it felt as if we were teenagers, getting it on as much as humanly possible before my parents returned. When the kids phoned home, it was an almighty effort to put on a normal voice as I asked about their trips to Parc Astérix and the Camembert factory, which Alfie especially loved (ironic, given that he is now a vegan and regards cheese as the devil's work: 'No, I don't miss it, Mum. Why's everyone so obsessed with cheese?' Because it's heavenly! I always want to retort).

During that whole time, Ryan and I barely left my flat. We had pizzas delivered – *cheese-laden* pizzas – and drank wine during the day. We had long, languid baths together, with Ryan graciously occupying the tap end. It was terribly decadent but then, it had marked the end of yet another lengthy sex drought for me. It was as if I'd been on a juice fast – not just a weekend 'cleanse', but for *two bloody years* – and had then been presented with a mountain of profiteroles. I started to think we might have a 'thing', albeit of the sporadic, long-distance variety, as Ryan was still based in London. Like an idiot, I pictured him nipping up for weekends, and me standing there – blow-dried, make-up immaculate – at Glasgow Central station, waiting for him.

Then my kids came back, by which point Ryan had already loped off back to London, where he runs a successful leather accessories company, promising to stay in touch. But his replies to my texts were curt – he was 'manic with work', or 'out of the country' – then they stopped altogether. Some frantic googling revealed that, for many years, Ryan had been having an on-off thing with a model-stroke-personal-trainer with an ash-blonde pixie cut.

I felt pretty foolish, I suppose, as he'd claimed he hadn't been seeing anyone for ages. I'd trusted him; perhaps that's another reason why I refuse to join a dating site, despite Gus and Corinne badgering me to do so.

'There must be someone you'd consider having a drink with,' Corinne remarks now, when the three of us break off for coffee on our squashy corner sofa.

'Yeah, there are about 800,000 people in this city, Nads,' Gus adds with a smirk.

'Yes,' I say, 'but once you take away everyone who's too young, too old, married or crazy, that probably leaves about three, and what would be the chances of us fancying each other?'

'There's every chance,' Gus insists. 'You're a very gorgeous woman, Nads.'

I laugh and look at Corinne. 'And he's not even drunk!'

He snorts in mock exasperation. All three of us are single but, unlike Corinne and me, he has no shortage of dates. A good-looking artist with bags of charm, apparently he has no desire to meet 'the one'. While his lifestyle would be a little hectic for me, I envy him sometimes.

'Don't you ever look at a man and think, *oooh*?' he asks.

'It's very, very rare,' I say truthfully. In fact, I reflect as I get back to work, I've wondered if that part of my biological make-up has died, like a flat car battery. But

13

that very lunchtime, when I pop out to buy a few last-minute presents, it becomes clear that that hasn't happened after all.

The city centre feels jolly and festive, and I look around, feeling grateful to be part of this big, vibrant city where I grew up, and which I still love very much. In a few days' time I'll be installed at my sister Sarah's on the Ayrshire coast, with Molly and Alfie and Sarah's family for Christmas, and it'll be lovely. We'll all eat too much (Sarah is a wonderful cook, the self-appointed Queen of Christmas), play board games and kick back and relax. But for now I'm enjoying the festive build-up, the seasonal music blasting out from the shops, and the sense that quite a few shoppers have enjoyed a few drinks already.

Feeling the chill now, and regretting not putting on a jacket, I step gratefully into the warmth of a bustling shop. I'm perusing the shelves, looking for stocking fillers for Molly, when a dark-haired man – wearing jeans, a black jacket and a grey sweater – walks in. I know it's weird to stare so blatantly, but I can't help myself. Despite the marauding hordes, and 'Winter Wonderland' blaring out of the speakers, I cannot tear my gaze away.

Apparently, my ability to find another person wildly desirable hasn't died after all. It has just *jump-started*.

He is tall and lean with a strong, proud nose and the kind of generous mouth that suggests he smiles a lot. From my vantage point some way across the shop, I can't tell what colour his eyes are. But actually, it's not just his appearance that's stopped me in my tracks.

Normally, the word 'aura' makes me shudder, but this man has one. It's one of quiet courage and calmness – the way he strolled into the melee without flinching. Clearly on a mission, a bold pioneer fearlessly navigating the

14

store, apparently untroubled by people clamouring for highly scented goods. He wanders from one display to the next, then stops and looks around, as if assessing the terrain before deciding how best to proceed . . .

A man, in a branch of Lush, five days before Christmas: he deserves some kind of national bravery award for that.

I try to focus on what I came in for, but all thoughts of body lotions and bath oils have evaporated now. I edge past a boy with mauve dreadlocks who's demonstrating some kind of product in a bowl of bubbly water. Girls cluster around him, squealing excitedly as if he might be about to pluck a live unicorn from the foam.

I'm closer to the man now, pulled towards him by a powerful magnetic force. Although he seems to be alone, I still scan his immediate vicinity for evidence of an accompanying female – daughter, wife, friend. There appears to be no one. This man looks like someone I absolutely have to speak to; all I need to do is figure out how.

Don't be a lunatic, I tell myself. He's probably married or gay or . . . my God, he made eye contact and smiled at me! It was a proper smile – warm and wide and perhaps held for a couple of moments more than you might expect from a stranger. Heat surges up my neck as I smile back, briefly, before turning away. Now I'm gazing around the shop as if I have never been to Lush before, and am considering writing a thesis on it. (I'd start it: How trustworthy are those labels on the products, depicting the person who made them? Can we be sure that Daria really created that massage bar, or could the labels be randomly generated?)

Pushing away such disturbing thoughts, I edge my way towards the man, pretending to examine the hand-cut

15

soaps along the way. There's just a display table between us now, bearing an outlandish rockery of pink and yellow spheres. He's peering at bowls of gloop that are displayed on crushed ice, like fish. Feeling terribly stalkerish, I sidle around the table and position myself next to him. Now I'm close enough to register the colour of his eyes; they are a clear, piercing blue.

I am literally bursting to say something to him – but what? I no longer feel like a fifty-one-year-old menopausal mother of two. In fact, I seem to have reverted to my adolescent self, who gleaned her talking-to-boys tips from *Just Seventeen*. I try a conversation opener in my mind: *D'you think the smell in here is just from the products, or do they pump something out of secret vents?*

As he picks up a macaroon-shaped bubble bar, inspiration hits me. 'You're not planning to eat that, are you?' I blurt out.

He looks momentarily shocked, then smiles. 'Ha, no, don't worry. They do look pretty edible though, don't they?'

'They really do,' I reply, sensing my face simmering. *Thanks, plummeting oestrogen levels. Fine time for a hot flush.* I press a hand onto the crushed ice in an attempt to cool myself.

'So hard to choose, isn't it?' I add, trying to establish common ground: i.e. *we both find Lush confusing. Therefore, we must leave and go for a coffee together immediately.*

'To be honest, I don't know where to start,' he says.

'Can I help at all?' I ask eagerly.

'Er, yes, maybe you can.' Another disarming smile. 'That would be brilliant, actually . . .'

'So, um, is it Christmas presents you're after?'

Of course it is, idiot. Why else would he be in here on December 20th? 'Yeah.' He rakes back his shortish hair. Noting the absence of wedding ring, I plough on: 'Who for?'

'My daughter.' Yes! Not *my incredibly sexy wife.* 'She's kind of addicted to this place,' he adds.

'Ha, yes, mine too. So, has she given you any hints of what she'd like?'

'Not really. Just bath stuff, I think. And maybe, uh, some creams and things for her face?'

'You mean skincare?' I offer, expertly.

'Yes, skincare – stuff like that.' He pauses. 'She's fourteen. Could you tell me what girls of that age tend to go for?'

I'm about to feign insider knowledge and say yes, of course – when I realise: *he thinks I work here.* Lush staff don't have uniforms, a quick glance confirms, and in my black sweatshirt and jeans I could probably pass as a sales assistant (apart from being roughly thirty years older than these exuberant boys and girls, and having no interesting piercings or tattoos).

I press my hand further into the ice, reluctant to correct his mistake, as he'd probably hurry off to find someone to help him. 'You could start with some bath bombs or bubble bars,' I suggest.

'Right.' He looks at them thoughtfully. 'So . . . what do they do, exactly?'

'Er, well, they're pretty spectacular,' I start, trying to exude the enthusiasm of a genuine salesperson. 'You drop them in, and there's this *explosion* . . .'

'Explosion?' He flashes a wide grin, and something seems to effervesce right here, thrillingly, in my stomach.

'Like a sort of sherbet grenade,' I charge on, 'and it

17

fizzles and turns the water pink or blue or whatever . . .'
He nods, apparently taking this in. 'It doesn't stain the
skin, though,' I add reassuringly.

'Well, that's good.'

'But some are glittery. Perhaps avoid those, unless you
want to look like a disco ball after your bath.' His eyes
glint with amusement. 'I know they're for your daughter,
but the glitter clings to the tub, believe me. My daughter
loves them. I always tried to choose her the non-glitter
kind, but then there'd be *secret* glitter, lurking inside . . .'
I catch myself and laugh self-consciously. 'That's one thing
you don't miss when your kids leave home. The sparkly
bath! Hours I've spent, picking it off myself . . .' *Stop
ranting, idiot . . .*

'I'll bear that in mind,' he says, picking up a small
brown nugget shaped like a Christmas pudding.

'That's a bubble bar,' I explain, authoritatively, as Molly
has had dozens of these too. 'They're more, er . . .'

'Bubbly?'

'Yes, that's right.'

'And glitter-free?'

'Yep,' I reply, hoping that's correct. Whilst I'm managing
to wing it so far, I'm dreading questions of a more complex
nature. But of course, he's a man – a terribly attractive
man with his lovely, warm, slightly wonky smile – and
he's hardly going to quiz me about the nourishing prop-
erties of cocoa butter.

Realising my hand has gone numb, I extract it from
the ice and surreptitiously wipe it on my jeans. Under
my protective gaze, he starts to select various items from
the display. 'I'll get you a basket,' I announce, flitting off
to fetch one and zooming back before he can get away.

'Thanks.' He piles everything in. 'Oh, what do these

18

do?' He indicates some candy-pink boulders piled up on a slate.

I speed-read the explanatory label. 'They're jelly bombs. They're, um, supposed to surprise and bewilder in the bathtub . . .'

He laughs. 'Is that what people want?'

I smile. 'Personally, I'd rather just relax in the bath.' *Preferably with you in it with me* . . . As this scenario flits into my mind, I sense my cheeks blazing again, as if he might have read my lewd thoughts. 'So, you mentioned skincare?' I prompt him.

'Yes, if you possibly could help me with that . . .'

'Of course,' I say, escorting him now to the cleansers and moisturisers where I manage to suggest several potions his daughter might like, simply by dredging my memory for Molly's preferred products. As I blabber on about aloe vera and mallow extract, dropping in words like 'brightening' and 'invigorating', I realise I'm starting to enjoy myself. 'Fresh dove orchid helps to plump up the cells,' I explain, thinking, hang on: his daughter is only fourteen, so, presumably she doesn't want her cells plumping . . .

'Sounds ideal,' he says, dropping a tub into his basket.

'Could we talk about blackheads?' I venture.

'Sure!'

And so it goes on, this stranger amazing me with his willingness to purchase a toner, a purifying face mask and something called a 'spritz'. I'd never realised it was so easy to flog beauty products. Perhaps I should apply for part-time work here, instead of supplementing my earnings by posing naked for the art class. At any rate, he seems impressed by my knowledge and passion for the brand, and obediently selects everything I recommend.

19

Glancing down at his laden basket, I try to ignore a twinge of guilt as I wonder how much it's going to cost him. Still, if I am outed as fake employee, at least I've boosted the day's sales.

'You've been so helpful,' he says, eyes meeting mine. 'Thank you.'

'No problem. Anything else I can help with?'

'No, I think I'm all done.'

'I'm sure your daughter will be pleased . . .'

'Yeah, I hope so. Well, thanks again.' He turns and navigates his way through the crowds towards the till. If I wasn't afraid of my cover being blown, I'd accompany him, just to make sure he doesn't get lost en route. Instead, I just dither about, feeling oddly light-headed, and make my way towards the door.

Outside, I inhale the crisp December air and stride along the busy shopping street. The sky is unblemished blue, the sun shining brightly. Veering off into a side road, I stop at a nondescript sandwich shop that I never go into normally. I emerge with my lunch, wondering now what possessed me to grab a cheese and onion sandwich, made with industrial white bread, like the 'Toastie' loaf Danny used to buy occasionally in an act of rebellion against my preferred granary. I'm clearly not thinking straight.

I walk briskly back to the studio and canter up the concrete stairs to the bright and airy top floor. 'How'd you get on?' Corinne asks, picking at a Danish pastry at her desk.

'The shops are rammed,' I reply.

'That's a surprise!' Gus chuckles, tweaking his neatly trimmed beard.

'I'll have to go out again tomorrow,' I add, perching on the chair at my own desk.

'Why didn't you do it all online?' Gus asks. 'It's the modern way, you know—'

'Yes,' I cut in, a swirl of excitement starting up again in my stomach, 'but there are benefits to going to the real shops.'

'Such as?'

I'm smiling ridiculously, and now there's no way I can resist filling them in on my impersonation of a Lush employee.

'*You* should try that,' Gus tells Corinne as they convulse with laughter. 'Running to the aid of a confused and helpless male in a soap emporium—'

'But did you get his number?' she asks, looking at me.

'No, of course not!'

Gus turns back to Corinne and smirks. 'Yet she was absolutely fine, flogging him bubble bath under false pretences.'

'Why didn't you just give him yours?' Corinne wants to know.

'Because I was serving him. It would have been *unprofessional* . . .' This sets them off again.

Okay, I decide, as I start to tuck into my unlovely Eighties-style sandwich: so I'll probably never see that man again. However, something important happened today, in that I discovered I *am* still capable of fancying someone, after all. I am Nadia Watkins, a fully functioning woman with a working libido and everything. Which makes me think: maybe I will try to meet someone, and perhaps even find myself naked in the presence of another person, and not just the students at the life drawing class.

Chapter Three

Jack

Well, I messed up there all right. I completely forgot that Lori had asked for 'that squidgy bath stuff' and not bubble bars or face wash or any of the other stuff I ended up buying. It was just, the woman who'd helped me . . . I'd been so mesmerised. I'd completely forgotten what I'd gone in for. How could I focus on shopping efficiently when I was transfixed by the golden flecks in her greenish eyes? She'd been so patient and friendly, I'd just grabbed everything she suggested.

I know she'd only been doing her job, but . . . had she been flirting a tiny bit?

No, that's just called 'being friendly to customers', you fool. They probably have training days about it, with role-play and everything. Still, it had worked a treat. On my way out, I'd noticed a soap the size of a dustbin lid propped up on a shelf. I'd have bought that, too, if she'd recommended it.

Back at work now – I'm the manager of a charity shop a few streets away – I realise I forgot to pick up any lunch. But no matter. Iain, one of our volunteers, offers to grab something for me while he's out. I ask for a chicken sandwich; he returns with a duck wrap and an enormous cheese scone.

'That's what you wanted, wasn't it?' he asks, ever eager to please.

'Yeah, it's fine, thanks,' I say quickly, sensing a 'situation' brewing now as Mags, another volunteer, has emerged from the back room where donations are sorted, and is now slotting paperbacks onto the bookshelf.

'Leave the books alone,' shouts Iain, a keen reader of dated how-to manuals, who regards the book section as 'his'.

'I'm just putting new stuff out,' Mags retorts, pink hair clip askew, lipsticked mouth pulled tight. Although it's hard to put an age on her – our volunteer application forms don't require a date of birth – I would guess mid-forties. She favours stonewashed jeans and floaty tops, usually made from cheesecloth, encrusted with beading around the neck. 'You're not the boss round here,' she adds, glaring at Iain.

'I'm deputy manager,' he announces.

'Says who?'

'Says everyone, actually. Says Jack!' He turns to me for confirmation, and I shrug. Although no such position exists, I – along with most of the volunteers – am happy to go along with his self-appointed elevated status, just as we willingly accept Iain's instant coffees made with water from the hot tap. He works hard, coming in virtually every day, with utter disregard for the rota; he was visibly unsettled when I reminded him that we'd be closed for the days between Christmas and New Year.

During the couple of years he's been volunteering for us, I've been to his flat several times. The last time involved

23

escorting him home when he'd had 'a turn' whilst steam-cleaning some trousers in the shop's tiny back room. As far as I've been able to gather, his only regular visitor is Una, the elderly lady upstairs who helps with his dog and tricky matters he struggles to deal with, like filling in forms and making calls on his behalf (Iain doesn't like using the phone). Like with Mags, it's hard to guess at his age, although I've surmised early thirties. He lives with his ageing mongrel, Pancake (''cause he likes to lie flat'), and has a liking for what he calls 'found furniture': i.e. the stuff people have left out on the pavement to be taken away by the council. Bookshelves, occasional tables and a wooden coat stand: Iain has dragged them all home, given them what he calls 'a good sanding down' (he means a perfunctory wipe) and then puzzled over where to put them.

The last time I was at his place, several shabby, mismatched dining chairs were lined up against a living room wall; it looked as if some kind of support group meeting was about to happen. 'I'm going to sell them,' he explained, with enviable confidence.

'Piss off, Iain!' Mags snaps now, swiping at him with a Galloping Gourmet cookbook. I stride over and suggest that she reorganises the plundered shoe section. 'C'mon, Mags,' I say. 'You've got a real eye for it. No one makes it look as good as you do.' As she beams with pride, Iain 'straightens' the books unnecessarily in order to re-establish his territory.

All afternoon, I keep thinking of the beautiful woman in Lush and wishing I'd asked her name or something. Christ, though – I don't know what made me behave like some idiot male who'd never heard of a bath bomb. Lori's been demanding the things every Christmas and birthday since she was about eight. I could probably sketch an accurate floor plan of that shop, the amount of times she's dragged me in there. I'd never seen the woman who helped me, though. Maybe she's new.

As closing time rolls around, I lock up and step out into the street, making my way through the revellers, many who've tumbled straight from all-afternoon Christmas lunches, by the look of it. We had our own last week, at an old-fashioned Italian in Merchant City. Mags demanded that the balloons be removed from the vicinity (she fears balloons). Iain shunned all offerings from the dessert menu and was finally appeased with a slice of Madeira cake adorned with squirty cream.

As Lush comes into view – happily, it's still open – I decide, what the hell, I could just nip in buy the squidgy stuff Lori asked for, which I forgot all about. I clear my throat, smooth back my hair as if about to go in for a job interview, and stride in.

The heady scent engulfs me as I scan the store for the gorgeous dark-haired woman. But there's no sign of her now. With the help of a shiny-faced teenage girl, I locate the product. It's called 'Fun' and, as the girl explains its many uses, I put on a fine show of listening whilst conducting one final scan of the shop.

Nope, she's definitely not here. And anyway, I reflect as I travel home on the packed subway, what would I have done if I'd seen her again? Lurched over to thank her one more time, when she'd probably attended to fifty more customers after me and would have assumed I was just some random nutter? *Hello again! You probably don't remember me, but a few hours ago you patiently explained the purposes of Tea Tree Gel . . .* I imagine her at home now, with her attractive, fully functioning family: handsome husband, delightful kids, wrapping presents and putting the final touches to the Christmas tree . . .

Get a grip, Jack McConnell, I chastise myself silently, *and possibly try to get out more.*

Chapter Four

Over the next few days, I venture nowhere near the overly scented store. It's not that I want to avoid looking like a weirdo stalker. Okay, it *is* partly that – but, perhaps handily, there's no time to take lunch breaks anyway. A deluge of donations has arrived at the shop, suggesting that the whole of Glasgow is clearing out its old tat ahead of Christmas.

If the shop is going to be able to function, then all of this stuff has to be sorted. Despite the sign in our window reading 'We welcome your *sellable* donations', we're gifted an alarming amount of skanky underwear and used tooth-brushes with bristles splayed (sometimes harbouring 'bits'). Because naturally, such items will bring in the money we need to build and support our network of animal sanctuaries. In fact, I think people sometimes forget that we are a charity at all, and regard us as a gigantic bin. *Thank you kindly for your ancient knitting pattern that might possibly have been used to line a budgerigar's cage!* But then, happily, there is the odd pearl among the dross, and we actually do a tidy trade.

As the volunteers and I separate the good stuff from the ripped lampshades and filthy sandwich toasters, I find myself wondering why my lovely helper in Lush chose to work in what seems like a particularly youthful environment.

It's not that she's old, not at all; I'd put her at around the same age as me, and I don't *feel* old. At least, sometimes I don't (when I plucked a cracked glass dildo from a box of donated goods I did, admittedly, feel about ninety-six – and on more than one occasion my ex Elaine has 'jokingly' asked if I ever worry that being surrounded by so many old things might somehow seep into my consciousness and accelerate the ageing process). It's just that she didn't seem to quite fit with the other, multiply pierced and tattooed assistants in there. It's bizarre, the way this stranger keeps sneaking into my thoughts. Perhaps it's the time of year; it always unsettles me a bit.

'Are you sure you're going to be okay over the holidays?' I ask Iain, who's stayed on to help on our last day before we close until the new year.

'I'll be fine,' he says breezily, carefully checking that all the components are present in *Home and Away: The Board Game*.

I glance at him. 'You're going to your mum's, right?'

'Yeah.'

Together, we begin to stack up the boxes of donations we haven't yet sorted, in order to leave the back room in a reasonably orderly state. 'What about the rest of the time?' I ask. *Who will you see,* is what I mean, *and what will you do to fill the days?*

'I'll be fine,' he says again.

'Yes, but . . .' I pause, wary of sounding patronising. 'You won't be on your own the whole time, will you?'

'Of course not,' he says with a trace of defensiveness. 'I'll be with Pancake . . . and I'll finally have time to read,' he adds, with a note of triumph, as if his life is too hectic normally.

'Well, that's good,' I say as I lift a basket of hairdryers, their cables entangled, onto a shelf.

'Yeah.' He beams at me. 'I'm going to learn some new stuff. Expand my mind . . .' He indicates the scruffy hardbacks he's stacked on the fridge, set aside for him to take home.

'What kind of stuff?' I ask, now wiping down the worktop of our tiny kitchen area.

'All kinds of stuff!'

I turn and look at him. Whenever Iain's in the shop, he's never far from my side. Today he's wearing one of his customary V-necked sweaters – tufts of chest hair are poking out – and his curious old-mannish trousers that always look a little too tight for his belly. Dropping the sponge wipe into the sink, I check the books he's chosen. '*Vehicle Maintenance for Beginners*,' I murmur.

'Yeah!'

Whilst I am not au fait with Iain's various conditions, I'd be surprised – and frankly alarmed – if he was ever capable of driving a car.

Small Plot Gardening in Full Colour is another of his choices. But Iain doesn't have a small plot, or even a balcony. I check more of his books – which he'll insist on paying for – hoping to find something that might be of use to a single man living alone with a dog. *Picture Framing Made Easy, Creative Crafting With Yarn* . . .

'That's what I'm going to do,' Iain says eagerly.

I frown. 'What, make macramé pictures of owls?'

'No,' he sniggers. 'I mean this one. I'm going to learn

29

to cook.' He plucks the relevant book from his pile, and I recognise it immediately: a once-popular guide to a savagely punishing dietary regime.

'We get this all the time,' I remark. 'If there was a prize for the most handed-in book, this would win it. It's because no one can actually stick to it, Iain.'

He pushes back his wonky, possibly self-cut fringe: 'But it's full of healthy recipes. Weren't you saying I should start eating better?'

I shrug in bafflement, having no memory of saying anything of the sort. 'I don't think so.'

'Yeah, you did. At the Christmas lunch . . .'

'Oh, that. All I meant was, we'd seen the menu before-hand, and you said you were fine with the full turkey dinner. And then, on the day, you decided you didn't want veg . . .'

'I don't eat veg,' he says indignantly.

'You wanted chips,' I remind him, 'instead of roast potatoes, and baked beans in place of the sprouts . . .'

Iain beams at me. 'Yeah, well, like I said, I'm going to read this and be healthier, like you're always on at me about . . .' This is so not true. I'm never 'on at' him about anything, although sometimes I suspect he'd like me to act like a sort of dad-type figure, dispensing advice. Although he mentions his mum occasionally – I gather she struggles with a raft of mental health issues – he's given the impression that his father was never around. It's Una, his upstairs neighbour, who seems to keep an eye on him.

'Well, um, I think that's great,' I say, 'but, y'know, that book was written quite a long time ago, and people don't really go for her methods anymore . . .'

'But she's a *doctor*,' he insists, jabbing the author's name on the cover.

I pause, wondering whether to break it to him. 'The thing is, she's not actually a real one.'

'But it says it on the book!' His eyes flash with indignation.

'Yes, but there's been some debate about whether her qualifications are real, or if she's just a bit of a charlatan . . .'

'A charlatan?'

'You know – a cheat, a fake . . .' I'm reminded now of a difficult conversation I had with Lori a few years back, when she asked me to tell her straight – no messing – whether Father Christmas really exists.

'People can't do that,' Iain retorts. 'Not when they write books.'

'They can, if they have the nerve. I mean, I could call myself a doctor . . .'

'But you'd be lying, wouldn't you?' He glares at me as if I might be considering it as a possibility.

'Well, yes. I'm just saying—'

'How did she write a book then?' Iain snaps.

'By sitting at her computer and hammering it out, I'd imagine.' I catch Iain's crestfallen expression and regret being so blunt. 'Look,' I add, 'I don't know for certain, but I do know there was a TV show years ago where she used to examine people's poos . . .'

'Ugh!'

'And you don't want to spend your Christmas doing that,' I remark, but my attempt at a joke seems to appal Iain even further.

'No, I do *not*.'

'It wouldn't be very festive,' I add, at which, thankfully, his eyes glimmer with amusement as he finally realises I'm having him on.

'I don't want to *ever* look at people's poos,' he adds, 'unless they're Pancake's. And I don't like it, y'know – I just do it, with the little plastic bags, because you can't just leave it lying there, can you? Not if you're trying to be a good citizen.'

'No, you can't,' I say, glancing at the clock now. It's almost seven p.m., and Iain and I have spent an extra two hours past closing time, sorting donations. I'm paid an okay-ish salary to manage this place, and for the most part I enjoy it. But now I'm seized by an urge to head home, maybe go for a run or meet up with friends, anything rather than be trapped in our dingy back room.

I can tell Iain's still feeling rattled as he stuffs his books into a carrier bag. In regular shops, where everyone's paid, you can pretty much expect your team to come in and do their job, and go home; it's a straightforward exchange of money for labour. A charity shop works differently. While some of our helpers – mainly the elderly ladies – simply enjoy the company and want to make a difference, others are more emotionally entwined with our little emporium.

I started out here as a volunteer myself. I needed something to keep me busy after the Glasgow-based book publisher's I worked for went bust. It was gutting, really, when it happened. Gander Books had been a tight-knit operation with just the MD, two editors, a couple of admins and myself. After a media course at college, followed by a smattering of casual jobs, I'd been taken on at twenty-three as an admin assistant. Keen and hard-working, I seemed to fit in well, and pretty soon I was promoted until I was taking care of Gander's publicity, marketing and events. It was a brilliant job, and as book publishing jobs are few and far between in Glasgow, I was happy to stay put.

Gander won literary prizes and Independent Publisher of the Year, and all seemed to be going swimmingly for many years until authors started to complain of advances and royalties being delayed, then not paid at all. The permanent staff were put on 'emergency measures' (i.e. drastically cut pay) and finally, after months of uncertainty, the whole place sunk.

We were all bereft. I'd worked there for fifteen years, and the place had felt like a second family. There was no payout for staff, and by then Elaine and I had a four-year-old daughter so I couldn't hang around, perusing job ads until the 'ideal' position came up. For a few years I worked for an events company, building up a second strand in freelance proofreading on the side. When redundancy happened again I decided, to hell with it; the next job I took would really matter to me and what the hell if I took a big pay cut. I'd kept in touch with the manager of the charity shop, and when she decided to move on it felt kind of right to apply.

Iain turns up his jacket collar against the sharp wind as we step outside. 'It's great that you want to learn to cook,' I tell him. 'But how about you forget that cranky cookbook, and try something simple that doesn't need a recipe?'

He folds his arms over his substantial stomach as I lock up the shop. 'Like . . . *salad*?'

'No, not salad,' I say quickly. 'How about soup? Something simple like that?'

'But I just buy my soup . . .'

'Okay, but if you're going do some cooking over the holidays, it's a good place to start. It's the easiest thing. Even Lori can make it.'

'What d'you do, then?' he asks as we fall into step.

'Fry up some leeks or onions, then chuck in any other veg, and water. Throw in a stock cube . . .'

'Is that all soup is?'

'Yep, that's it.' We fall into companionable silence as we make our way towards the car park. On the days I drive in, Iain tends to accompany me to my car, as if I might be incapable of finding it without his help. 'Well, enjoy your Christmas,' I add as we reach it. 'And good luck with the cooking—'

'Aw, shit!' he says as his carrier bag splits, and his books tumble to the ground. As we don't have another bag for him to carry them home in, he agrees to leave them in my car. Apart from the dog-eared diet cookbook, which he insists on taking home – 'in case I need it.' And I watch him, clutching it to his chest as he marches off, leaving waves of indignation in his wake.

Chapter Five

The next day I take Lori for our Christmas Eve lunch. As it's her mum's turn to spend the big day with her, this is our festive treat together. My daughter chose the sushi restaurant – because naturally, what you really want in Glasgow in December is chilled rice and raw fish, shunting towards you on a conveyor belt. 'Shivery food,' her mother calls it, but in fact, I'm quite happy to be here. Although Lori usually spends a couple of weeknights at mine – plus every second weekend – it still feels kind of special as we perch on our stools and tuck in.

'So, did you go to the school dance?' I ask as she swipes her third plate from the belt.

She shakes her head. 'Decided not to.'

'Oh, why was that?'

Lori twirls a noodle around her chopstick. 'You know what they're like.'

I can't help smiling. 'Not really, Lor. I mean, our school dances had Scottish music, and this awful situation of the boys all lined up on one side of the hall, and the girls on the other, and you were expected to walk over and pick someone . . .'

'You mean the boys always picked? How is that fair?'

'It's not fair. It's just the way it was . . .'

'The girls never picked?'

I laugh and shake my head. 'I wasn't responsible for the system, Lor. That was a long time ago . . .' I break off, realising she's dodging my question. 'Anyway, why didn't you go?'

She shrugs. 'I wasn't allowed.'

'By who? By Mum?' I frown at her. It's unlike Elaine to lay down the law about anything. She let Lori have her ears pierced at ten years old, which I wasn't delighted about. But what could I have done when I only found out after the event?

'Mr Fletcher said I couldn't go,' Lori says airily, referring to her form teacher. She flicks back her fine light brown hair and studies the conveyor belt. 'I wish there were those little pancake things. You know the ones with the duck?'

'Lor, why weren't you allowed to go?' I prompt her.

'Just stupid stuff . . .'

'Okay, but what exactly? It seems a bit severe—'

'I didn't want to go anyway,' she says firmly, wrinkling her lightly freckled upturned nose.

She snatches a dish of tuna sushi and spears it with her chopsticks. At fourteen, she wears her long hair pulled back in a ponytail, virtually lives in jeans, T-shirts and baggy sweaters, and shows zero interest in make-up. All of this makes her look, if not younger than she really is, like a girl of her actual age. It's a relief, frankly. Her best friend Shannon has spray tans and wears terrifyingly thick false eyelashes, like fluttering canopies. She is well into boyfriend territory – livid love bites have been spotted on her neck – whereas, thankfully, Lori still seems to regard boys as mates.

'It's not really anything,' she adds firmly.

'C'mon, just tell me. I promise not to go on at you, okay?'

She sniffs. 'Just behaviour and things.'

'Right. So what kind of—'

'Dad,' she says impatiently, 'just being late for lessons, stuff like that.' She sighs, and I decide to let it go for now as we tuck into our lunch. 'So, where are we off to next?'

'Fancy seeing a film?'

'Yeah! What's on?'

Consulting my phone, I run through the list. It's a madcap comedy we go for, and as Lori and I snigger our way through it – at one point a piece of popcorn shoots from her mouth – I sense my worries about her ebbing away. Never mind her lateness, the school dance, or whatever might be going on in her mother's life ('Everything's fine, Jack! Why wouldn't it be?'). I have friends whose teenagers would never deign to go to the cinema with them, and it's one of my greatest joys that Lori doesn't yet find my company repulsive.

Back at her mother's pebble-dashed terrace on the Southside, Elaine oohs and ahhs over the presents I've bought Lori, which she insisted on opening immediately, littering the living room with torn paper.

'All that Lush stuff!' Elaine marvels, arms folded across her dark green sweater. 'You're a lucky girl. It's not cheap in there, you know.' Behind her, a miniature fake Christmas tree is sitting a little askew on a side table. 'Get me some henna next time you're in, will you?' she adds. I smile;

Elaine is the only woman I know who still hennas her hair. Sometimes it's a startling orangey colour, at other times a deep shade of rust; as a colouring agent it seems rather hit and miss.

Now Lori is enthusing over further gifts of new jeans, a top (incredibly, she still allows me to choose clothes for her), a voucher for trainers and a small wad of cash.

Lori hugs me goodbye, and disappears back into the living room as Elaine sees me out. 'You're so good to her,' she says. 'Thanks, Jack. So, are you off out tonight?'

'Maybe. No plans as yet. How about you?'

'Nope, just a quiet night in for us two.' She pauses, and as I glance across the garden I can't help noticing that one of her wheelie bins – the one for glass – is crammed to the point where its lid won't shut.

'Look at the state of that,' she retorts, catching my gaze.

'It's pretty full,' I concede.

She steps further out into the garden, her breath forming white puffs in the chilly air. 'That's people dumping stuff in as they walk past.'

I look at her incredulously. If Elaine wanted to lie, couldn't she have blamed the bin men for failing to empty it? 'You mean passers-by lean over your wall, open your bin and drop their empties into it?' I almost laugh.

'Yeah,' she exclaims. 'Can you believe it?'

'Not really. Not when there's a perfectly good council bottle bin down the road . . .'

Elaine purses her lips. Her partying days are long over, she's always keen to assert; now, it's just a glass or two of wine in the evenings, and what's wrong with that?

'I've told you about this before,' she adds, frowning, although she hasn't; last time it appeared to be overflowing, she insisted it was 'mainly olive oil bottles and pickle jars' (Christ, it sounds as if I've created a hobby of monitoring the fullness of Elaine's bin!).

'Maybe you should put a lock on it?' I suggest, at which she regards me coolly.

'Jack, what are you trying to say exactly?'

'Nothing.'

'Obviously you are. Why not just come out with it—'

'No need to be so defensive,' I say lightly. 'It's Christmas Eve, let's not start bickering now . . .'

'If I'm defensive,' she shoots back, 'it's because you're bloody sanctimonious!'

Hell, why did I touch on the matter of her drinking now? I should have known better – it achieves nothing – and if we were going to talk about it properly, then it wouldn't be in her front garden with Lori just a few feet away, inside the house. 'I don't mean to be,' I say levelly. 'I know I'm not perfect, and I'm not trying to judge—'

'Not trying to judge?' she splutters. 'Well, you are judging. You always have and you're even worse now, with your *running* . . .'

'What? I jog up and down the river about three times a week . . .'

'. . . with your personal bests and your fancy sports watch . . .'

'Can we leave it please, Elaine?'

She glares at me. 'Or we could empty the bin if you like, and count the bottles?'

Oh, for crying out loud, why did I let us get into this? 'Jesus, just forget it okay?' She blinks at me and, alarmingly, her eyes have filled with angry tears. 'Are you okay?' I ask, stepping towards her.

'I'm fine, thank you,' she mutters, and I glimpse Lori,

39

briefly, at the living room window before she disappears again.

'But you don't seem—'

'Just go, Jack,' Elaine adds, turning away, 'and enjoy your Christmas. Have a fantastic time, tanking into your dad's Italian wines with your brother . . .'

'*Elaine* . . .'

'But that doesn't count as drinking, does it?' she snaps. 'Not when it's good stuff. It never does.'

That went well, I reflect bleakly as I drive home, hoping that Lori didn't overhear any of it, and reminding myself that Elaine is an adult woman of forty-five, who can make her own choices in life – and is a pretty good mother by all accounts. Lori is apparently well cared for, adequately fed and sent off to school on time. She never has any untoward stories to tell. I've tried to quiz her – gently – about whether everything's okay with her mum, but Lori just snaps, 'She's *fine*, Dad. Why're you asking?' I've even made it clear that, if my daughter ever wanted to live with me full-time, that would fine with me, we could make it work – but she's dismissed it. 'Mum's just been a bit unlucky,' she admitted recently, and maybe it's true.

When Elaine recently lost her administrative job at a community project, it was apparently due to cuts, and not the copious sick days she always claimed were due to her asthma, and never hangovers. When she fell downstairs and broke her arm last summer, it was apparently due to her tripping over the laundry basket on the landing. Lori backed up her mum's explanation, and I didn't want to go on about it. Anyway, without installing CCTV in Elaine's house, it's impossible to know exactly what goes on.

40

Back home now, I let myself into my tenement flat in the part of town that's being flaunted as 'the new West End', which just means cheaper than the West End, and less desirable. I like it though, with its muddle of individual shops with their mysterious vegetables piled up in boxes outside.

In my living room, I open a couple of Christmas cards from cousins down south and place them on the mantelpiece with the others. I, too, have a Christmas tree; Lori would be appalled if I didn't. And while I can't claim to have had 'tons' of festive nights out, there was a jovial pub gathering with a few of us who've knocked around together since I was nineteen, when I first moved here from out in the sticks, up in Perthshire. And now – Mr Popular! – my phone pings; a text from my mate Fergus, reminding me that a bunch of them are meeting for drinks in town. It's tempting to join them right now but, with the drive up to Mum and Dad's tomorrow morning, I decide to delay the pleasure of a few beers by going for a run first.

A short while later I'm pounding along beside the river. The Clyde shimmers beneath the dark sky, and traffic nudges slowly over the bridge. I keep close to the railings, wondering now about Mags and Iain, and how they'll fill their days until the shop opens up again after New Year.

I had considered opening up for those in-between days so they'd have somewhere to go. 'That's a bit bonkers, Jack – you need a break too,' Dinah the area manager had said, and she was probably right. Now it's Elaine who's snuck back into my thoughts. Will she remember to defrost her turkey and not try to nuke it in the microwave as she did a couple of years ago? *Of course she's capable of cooking a bird,* I tell myself, annoyed with my inability to switch off and 'get in the zone', as proper runners are supposed to do. I jog on, all of this stuff whirling in my head like a gigantic stew, and then it all stops – suddenly – when I see her in the distance.

I'm sure it's her – the woman who helped me in Lush. Yes, it's definitely her. With her creamy skin and abundant dark brown hair, there's something incredibly striking about her. She is strolling towards me, head slightly dipped. I slow my pace, wondering if she'll recognise me and thinking perhaps it's best if she doesn't, given I'm wearing my ratty old running gear and slathered in sweat. Of course she won't; she's on her phone, seemingly deep in conversation. She stops and rakes a hand through her hair. I stop too, and pretend to check the sports watch I bought in the hope that it would turn me into a bona fide athlete, but which serves only to plague me with its mysterious vibrations and bleeps.

We're closer now – close enough for me to catch her conversation. 'Are you sure this is what you want?' she exclaims, phone clutched to her ear. 'It sounds like you're being pressurised, love . . .' I fiddle with my watch, wondering why a picture of a weight lifter has appeared on the screen. 'For God's sake, Alfie,' she blurts out, 'what about the nut roast?'

There's more muttering, and just as I'm thinking, *What d'you think you're doing, eavesdropping on a stranger's personal conversation?* she finishes the call and shoves her phone into her bag. She stands there for a moment, staring out over the river as if trying to gather herself together, then strides on.

My watch bleeps again. I look down, still catching my breath but cooling rapidly now. Inexplicably, the word

'Move!' is flashing on the screen. It's so bossy, this hideously expensive gadget. I couldn't make head nor tail of its functions as I squinted at the instructions with the ant-sized print. But now I'm thinking: perhaps it *is* useful after all? Maybe, on top of monitoring my pulse rate and pace, it can sense my indecision and give me some indication of what to do next?

'Move! Move!' my watch commands me.

I move.

Chapter Six

Nadia

Well, that's just great. Alfie, who has already delayed his homecoming by some days, isn't spending Christmas Day with me after all. 'You don't mind if I spend it at Cam's, do you?' he just asked me, when I was expecting him to be rattling towards Glasgow on the train. Cam – Camilla – is his new girlfriend with whom he appears to be smitten.

Do I *mind*? Of course I bloody mind!

'So when will I see you?' I asked, feeling horribly needy as I marched along by the river. I only came down here because he called, otherwise I'd have headed straight home on the subway. Now I'm so agitated I'm just stomping along, trying to calm myself. But there's no point in getting angry; I know that. He doesn't care about the nut roast I've already made to take to my sister Sarah's tomorrow.

In truth, I'm not entirely happy about this vegan business – especially as he let slip that Camilla happens to be vegan too. 'Don't make yourself anaemic just to impress her,' I wanted to say when he declared his new dietary principles a few weeks ago – but I had the good sense not to. Instead, I merely suggested that he should read up on nutrition and treat it seriously. *Of course I will,* he retorted. *I'm doing it properly, y'know. I'm not an idiot . . .* Hmmm. I still wasn't overly delighted. I'm sure veganism is fine, if you're motivated enough to swot up on all the food groups and soak things for billions of years. I just couldn't quite imagine my eighteen-year-old son, who used to virtually faint with delight at the sight of a steak, involving himself with pulses.

'Aw, Mum, I'll see you the day after Boxing Day, okay?' he muttered a few minutes ago.

'The day after Boxing Day?' I exclaimed.

'Well, there are no trains till then.'

'I could come up and fetch you. How about that? Have Christmas with Camilla, and then I'll drive up and—'

'Yeah, but they have a massive party on Boxing Day,' he continued blithely, 'and Cam says it's brilliant. Everyone brings musical instruments, there's a whole jamming thing going on, it sounds mental. There's so much food and drink, her dad saves his special wine for it and I really wanna be there for that.' Ah, right. How fantastically fun. Clearly, the thought of us lot sitting around eating Twiglets and playing Pictionary can't compare to Camilla and The Special Wine. 'Your nut roast'll keep, won't it?' he added, trying to placate me now.

'I'm not sure,' I huffed. 'I'll probably have to freeze it. It's this gigantic boulder made from ground hazelnuts and about sixty-five other ingredients and it'll take about three weeks to defrost.'

Alfie chuckled. 'Sounds awesome, Mum . . .' No, it didn't. It sounded as if it'd have him hurtling to the lavatory. 'So, I'll see you on the 27th, all right?' he added. 'We'll have a nice time then.' Which felt like being offered the flat gold-wrapped toffee from the Quality Street tin after all the best ones have gone.

Never-fucking-mind, I think tearfully as I stride onwards now, my breath forming clouds as I exhale fiercely into the crisp evening air. I'm being silly, I know. It's only Christmas, and Molly is home with me already; she arrived yesterday. But then so have her friends, so I've just seen her as a blur who's darted in and clogged up the loo with an avalanche of paper before rushing back out again. She found me later, trying to unblock it with a wire coat hanger. 'What're you doing?' she asked.

'Panning for gold,' I replied.

'You're pretty handy, Mum,' she said, grinning. 'Let me know if you find something we can sell.'

The thought of my daughter's audacity lifts my spirits as I glance across the shimmering river. Christmas *will* work out okay, I tell myself. Perhaps I should be more like Danny, who never gets in a state about stuff like this; to him, the festive season merely represents an interruption to his work schedule. He spends time with the kids, and sometimes he even pops round to see me – minus Kiki, with whom I have a polite-but-distant relationship. She's fine, actually. I only tend to see her occasionally, in passing, and apart from her obvious gorgeousness there's absolutely no reason to feel iffy about her at all.

Anyway . . . sodding Christmas. It's up to Alfie where he spends it, I guess, and I just want to kick back and enjoy the holidays with my family. I've been working flat-out lately, finishing jobs in the early hours, sometimes tumbling into bed when the birds had started to tweet outside. On top of the textbooks, I've completed a series of greetings cards, a travel guide to Scotland and a department store's stationery range recently. When I finally

46

cleared my workload, and with Molly and Alfie's home-coming imminent, I scrubbed the flat from top to bottom (as if they'd notice and praise my efforts!). I even bought them new bed linen, as if they've been at sea for six months. I don't plan to spoil our precious time together by moaning about their toast crumbs or tendency to lie in till noon, or constantly demand to know where they're going and what time they'll be home—

'Hi! Excuse me?'

I stop and glance around. At first I'm not sure who called out, assuming it wasn't directed at me anyway. But then I see a man in running gear striding towards me. As I pat my pockets instinctively, thinking I must have dropped something, and he's kindly picked it up, it dawns on me that it's *him*: the man I encouraged to buy numerous unnecessary products for his daughter.

Oh, God, he's going to say he knew all along that I was a phoney! And he'll ask me if I have any other hobbies, apart from impersonating the salespeople in Lush . . .

'Hi,' he says again, smiling hesitantly now as he approaches.

'Hi,' I say brightly.

He stops in front of me and wipes his brow with the back of his hand. 'Erm, you probably don't remember me, but you helped me in—'

'Yes, I do remember,' I cut in quickly as various thoughts dart around my brain, such as: Shall I admit I don't work there, and how can I do so without sounding mad? And: How is it possible for a man to appear so attractive in jogging bottoms and a running top, all claggy with sweat?

'Well, um,' he says, 'I just thought I'd say hi. Nice to see you again.' He shuffles from foot to foot. 'Guess you're looking forward to your break?'

47

'Er, yes. Yes, I really am.' *Because it's exhausting, being trapped in the back room, slicing up soaps!* I'm aware that my smile has set.

'Pretty hectic in there, isn't it? In the shop, I mean . . .'

'It is, yeah.' I laugh in a tell-me-about-it sort of way.

He looks up and down the riverside walkway and clears his throat. 'So, erm, anyway, I just wanted to say thanks for helping me choose all those—'

'Oh, it's fine, really . . .'

'Just doing your job, of course . . .'

'Yes!' I beam at him, wondering how my cheeks can possibly burn so hotly on a cold December night.

There's a moment's pause. 'Er, so, are you heading straight home now?' he asks.

'Erm, yes, I s'pose I am.'

'To wrap presents?'

'All done . . .'

'Well done you!' We laugh awkwardly and look at each other, and now I'm thinking rather hopefully: yes, I am going home, but I don't have to stay there all evening. I could come out later as Molly's bound to be out again, and my son has chosen to be with his girlfriend whom he has known for all of five minutes instead of his family, and—

'I hope you don't mind me saying,' he adds, 'but you seemed a bit upset just then.'

Christ, he noticed? 'Oh, that was just my son,' I say quickly, 'telling me he won't be coming home for Christmas with me after all.' I shrug.

'Really? That's a shame.'

'The lure of the girlfriend. I suppose I don't blame him really . . .'

'Yeah. Hard for you, though . . .'

48

'I'll just have to manage without him.' I smile, aware of that flat-toffee feeling ebbing away rapidly.

The man grins, rather shyly, and I sense that neither of us wants to move on. 'Um, I don't suppose you'd like to meet for a drink sometime?' he asks, pushing back his sweat-dampened hair.

'Oh.' I realise I am beaming now, and wonder if he's noticed the absence of a wedding ring – or perhaps it's the way I said 'Christmas with me' and not 'us'? 'Yes, that'd be lovely,' I say, even as I'm wondering what on earth I'm going to do about the Lush issue. How would I keep up the pretence, if he we did meet up? But what the hell – it's just a drink he's suggesting, and if the subject comes up, I'll swerve him off it . . .

'You're not free later this evening, are you?' he asks.

'It's Christmas Eve,' I remind him.

'Yes, it is.' He gives me what I can only interpret as a hopeful smile.

'Don't you have plans?' I say.

'Um, well, my daughter's at her mum's tonight. Some friends of mine are meeting up later, but it's nothing definite, nothing *important*, I mean . . .' He pauses. 'I'm Jack, by the way . . .'

'I'm Nadia.'

So we agree to meet. I sense a surge of delicious anticipation as we exchange numbers and say goodbye, with me heading for the subway and Jack jogging home.

Back at the flat, I shower and blow-dry my hair, then rake through my wardrobe, dismissing pretty much everything as being either too scruffy or try-hard. Why don't more outfits fall into the 'middling' category? Now, I'm wishing Molly was here, to vet my outfit (she just knows when things are right). But she's out on the lash, as far as I can gather – she's pocket-dialled me twice. All I could make out was a load of exuberant people shouting.

So I end up fishing out a dress that must be eight years old; mid-blue, bias-cut, hovering just above the knee and perhaps a tad dull – but at least it doesn't scream 'date' and is infinitely flattering across my ample bottom and hips. Make-up is applied – twice, as I mess up my first attempt due to being in a fizzle of nerves. Finally, cutting it fine time-wise now, I am ready.

Christ, I reflect, checking my reflection once more: I am meeting a man I wasn't set up with by my friends. He wasn't picked for me in a well-meaning attempt to coax me 'out there' again; I chose him by myself. I have texted Corinne, who replied, simply, *Yesss!!* And then Gus, who sent me a selfie with an enthusiastic thumbs-up, captioned GET IN.

I virtually skip out of my flat and into the waiting taxi. And when I step into the thronging pub and see Jack waiting at the bar, all my hurt and upset over the nut roast seems to have miraculously disappeared.

Chapter Seven

Jack

My God, but she's lovely. I'd thought she was gorgeous in her work clothes, all casual, but in her simple blue dress she really is something else.

'Are you sure your friends won't be missing you?' Nadia asks as – miraculously – we find a tiny table tucked away at the back of the pub.

'I'm sure they'll cope without me,' I tell her as we sit down. 'So, what else would you have been doing tonight?'

She smiles. It's a lovely smile: generous and open, but a little hesitant. Her eyes are an incredible shade of green, her skin glowing, her hair long, dark and shiny, falling around her shoulders in soft waves. 'If Alfie had come home, we'd probably have watched some Christmas movies together,' she explains. 'We'd have cracked open the snacks – the nuts, the Twiglets, all the festive delicacies.' She chuckles, and her eyes seem to actually sparkle, which does something peculiar to my insides. 'We really know how to have a good time,' she adds.

'Alfie's your son?' I ask, unnecessarily.

'Yes – he's a twin. Molly, his sister, is home already,

51

but I've hardly seen her. And Alfie's spending Christmas at his girlfriend's parents' hunting lodge up in the wilds of Aberdeenshire . . .'

'A hunting lodge?' I repeat.

Nadia sips her white wine. 'That's kind of misleading. You'd think it might mean a little wooden shack out in the hills, wellies piled up at the front door . . .'

'That's *exactly* what I'd think,' I agree, although I can't say the subject has ever crossed my mind before.

'Yes, well that's what I assumed. Alfie keeps insisting they're not that posh, but I managed to coax him into telling me the name of their place – this *lodge* – and of course I googled it immediately . . .'

'Of course! Who wouldn't?'

She chuckles. 'Yep, well, it's actually a Baronial mansion with twenty-four rooms and a dedicated annexe for falcons.'

'Falcons. Wow.'

'Someone's specifically employed to be the falcon keeper. I mean, that's all they do.'

'They probably involve quite a lot of care and attention,' I suggest.

She laughs and pushes a strand of hair from her face. 'Sorry. I'm really going on. It's the time of year, y'know. It's all a bit . . . heady.'

'I know what you mean,' I say, thinking: heady is precisely the right word, and I want this kind of headiness to stretch on and on. I do hope she's in no hurry to go home.

'So, what are you doing for Christmas?' she asks. 'You mentioned your daughter . . .'

'Yeah, Lori's fourteen – she's my only one – and me and her mum take it in turns to have her on Christmas Day.' I grimace. '*Have her.* I mean, enjoy her delightful company . . .'

'And this year?' Nadia asks with a smile.

'I'll see her on Boxing Day when I'm back in town. I'm off to my parents' first thing in the morning. They're up in Perthshire, near Crieff but out in the country. They have a dairy farm . . .'

'Is that where you grew up? You're a farmer's boy?'

'That's right.' I smile, reluctant to bore her to death with my entire life history – although her interest seems genuine. 'But I moved here when I was nineteen,' I add.

'Desperate to get to the big city,' she suggests.

'God, yes. No doubt I still smelt of the farm . . .'

Nadia flashes another smile. 'Do your parents still have it?'

'Yes, incredibly – they're both seventy this year.'

'Pretty young parents,' she remarks.

I nod. 'Yeah – they were still teenagers when Craig, my big brother, was born. He and his wife handle a lot of the day-to-day now.'

'And there's just the two of you? You and your brother, I mean?'

'Erm, we had another brother,' I murmur, 'but there was an accident . . .'

'Oh, I'm so sorry!' Nadia exclaims.

'A long time ago now,' I say briskly; Christ, the last thing I want to do is heap all that stuff on this beautiful woman whom I've only just met. I mean, for fuck's sake, it's Christmas Eve, she is utterly lovely and I've somehow swerved onto the subject of death . . . 'So, how about you?' I ask quickly.

'Um, you mean . . . my background and stuff?'

'Yes.'

'God, where to start?' She laughs, and her eyes meet mine, and there seems to be a kind of . . . moment between us. An understanding, perhaps, that we will talk about other, deeper things; not tonight, but later on, when we know each other better. Because there will be a later on, I'm sure of it already, and I sense she feels it too.

'I grew up in Ayrshire,' Nadia is telling me, 'and we moved to Glasgow when I was a teenager. There's just me and my sister, Sarah – she's the truly grown-up one. A fully formed adult by the age of ten. Then I moved to Dundee, went to art college . . .'

'You're an artist as well as working at the shop?' I cut in.

She colours slightly. 'Well, um, I kind of . . . *dabble*.'

'Right. I have to say, I can't even draw stick men. So, how long've you worked in—'

'Would you like another drink?' she asks quickly.

'Oh, erm – yes, but I'll get them . . .'

'No, it's my round.' She has already leapt to her feet. 'Same again?'

'Yes please.'

I watch her as she wends her way through the crowds towards the bar. Fair enough, I decide; she probably doesn't want to be quizzed about her shop job right now. Maybe she's just picked up some seasonal shifts.

'Whereabouts d'you work, Jack?' she asks as she returns with our drinks.

'I manage a charity shop,' I reply.

'Really? Which one?'

'We're just a small operation really – half a dozen shops across Scotland, but just the one in Glasgow. The charity's called All For Animals, we fund sanctuaries – it's a bit of an unfortunate name as it's often referred to as AA . . .'

She chuckles. 'I know your shop. I've been in a couple

of times, actually. It's lovely. I mean, I know charity shops have raised their game, displaying things nicely, organising the clothes in colour groups – but yours is a cut above.'

'Thanks,' I say, surprised and flattered by her enthusiasm.

'I bought Molly a Biba-style top and some vintage magazines for myself,' she continues. 'I was chatting to the guy who was manning the till – a tall man, very chatty, said he's in charge of the book section . . .'

'That's Iain . . .'

'He seemed lovely.'

I smile. 'He is. He has his issues but he really does care about the shop, and the other volunteers. Makes everyone coffees . . .'

'How kind of him.'

'. . . with water from the hot tap,' I add with a smile.

Nadia laughs kindly. 'So, it's not *all* volunteers, then? I mean, you're not one?'

'Nope, the managers are paid.' I smile. 'Honestly, it is a proper job. I also do some freelance proofreading for publishers and authors . . .' I pause. 'I'm sure you're wildly impressed,' I joke.

'I am. I really am.' And so the evening goes on, with both of us covering vast swathes of ground, personal-history wise, and the-state-of-our-lives-now wise: our families, our work (she happily tells me that she models occasionally for life drawing classes, but still seems reluctant to talk about her job at the shop). There is barely a lull, and every now and then, one of us breaks off to apologise for 'going on'.

'You don't really want to know about dairy herds,' I tell her, noticing now that we have pulled our chairs closer and are leaning towards each other, across the table.

'I do,' she says. 'All the books I loved as a kid were set on farms. I longed to sleep in a hay barn and collect eggs. Did you have sheepdogs?'

'Well, yes, because we had sheep too . . .'

'The ones with black faces?'

I can't help smiling at that. 'Yes. We still have them. Scottish Blackface . . .'

'Is that what they're called? I love those!' She grins at me. 'Any other kinds?'

'Um, a few Shetland and Hebrideans. They're good if you want to do things organically. They're smaller, very hardy, coming from the islands originally—' *obviously* '—so they're not as reliant on feed, they can graze on rough ground, on heathers . . .' I break off and chuckle. 'I'm telling you about the dietary needs of sheep.'

'But only because I asked.' We laugh, and she touches my hand across the table, which has the effect of shooting some kind of powerful current through my body. I want to lean over and kiss her beautiful mouth right there. I don't, of course, because you can't just swoop on a woman like that, can you? I catch her studying me with an amused glint in her eyes, and there's a small pause in conversation that feels anything but awkward.

Because we know, I think, that this is definitely the beginning of something. I don't think I've ever felt so sure of anything in my life.

Of course I've dated women in the nine years since Elaine and I broke up. There was Amanda, who was a regular customer to the shop, but it never really felt as if it was going anywhere, and eventually she moved away down south. My thing with Zoe last year was more fiery – she collected Mexican death masks and painted pictures with her menstrual blood. She was striking, passionate and unpredictable; one minute, she'd be insisting that we should move in together and the next, that I wouldn't see her for six weeks as she was off to some Pagan drumming thing on a remote island. When we broke up, she egged my car. 'What a waste of eggs,' Lori chuckled as we sluiced the windscreen down.

For a brief period, I succumbed to my mate Fergus's nagging that Tinder was the way forward. It wasn't just for young people looking for casual hook-ups, he insisted. 'Old fuckers like us use it too now,' he enthused. Although I met a couple of perfectly lovely women, it felt terribly random, and I couldn't be doing with all that swiping business. I know everyone meets online these days – Elaine's had a couple of relationships that started this way – but it wasn't for me. I started to think that perhaps *nothing* was for me.

But now, as the evening rolls on, I wonder if *this* was what I was holding out for: just a lovely, normal night in a pub with a gorgeous, sparky woman.

'What about your kids' dad?' I ask, having given her a brief summary of the Elaine business.

'We get along fine,' she replies. 'Even the break-up wasn't that traumatic, not really. It was my decision, finally, but he didn't fight it. Danny said he almost felt cheated that no clothes had been torn up, no prawns stuffed in curtain poles, not a single incident of screaming.'

I smile. 'So, you've divorced now?'

'Oh, we weren't married. But we were as good as, of course. The kids were eleven when we split . . .'

'And their dad really was okay about it?' I ask.

'It seemed like it at the time,' she replies. 'I mean, he started dating fairly soon, and he met his current partner a year or so after we broke up. They're still together –

very happy, by all accounts. But maybe . . .' She shrugs. 'Later on, Danny told me he'd been devastated. I said, "Really? I didn't think you minded that much." And he said, "You make it sound like you just put an old armchair out for the council collection men."'

I can't help laughing at that.

'Have you heard of Danny Raven?' she asks.

'Yes, of course . . .'

'Well, that's him.'

'Really?' For some reason, this feels like a punch to the gut. Her ex is Danny Raven, fêted film-maker, for Christ's sake. So why's she spending her Christmas Eve in the pub with the manager of a—

'Jack?' Her voice cuts into my thoughts.

'Yes?'

The smile seemed to illuminate her face as she leans more closely towards me. 'It's very, *very* over between him and me. We get along fine, and we raise our kids together. But I am most definitively on my own now. I mean, there's no one . . .' She pauses. It feels as if my heart has stopped. Even closer she comes, her beautiful face before me now. As she kisses me lightly on the lips, I feel as if I might topple off my chair.

We pull apart and look at each other. Somehow, our hands have entwined under the table. There's so much I want to say to her, I hardly know where to begin. 'I'd really like to see you again,' is all I can manage, 'if that's all right with you.'

Nadia nods. 'I'd really like to see you too. But, um, there is something . . .'

Oh, shit – here it comes: the 'but'.

'Uh-huh?' I say, feigning nonchalance.

'There's, er . . . a thing I need to tell you.'

58

I inhale deeply, various possibilities already forming in my mind: she's in love with someone. Or something's wrong – maybe she has an illness? Or an issue with her kids? – and she doesn't want to get involved with anyone right now. Fine, it's been a lovely evening; but maybe I really should get home, seeing as I still have a pile of presents to wrap for my parents, my brother and sister-in-law . . .

'What is it?' I ask lightly, draining my glass.

She looks down. 'I have to tell you . . . I don't actually work in Lush.'

'*What?*'

She reddens and nods with a closed-lipped smile. I'm baffled now; so why did she spend twenty minutes chatting to me about bath bombs? 'I'm so sorry,' I murmur, shaking my head. 'I just assumed . . .'

'Yes, of course you did.' She is laughing now.

'But I accosted you and asked you all those questions about skin stuff! Why didn't you just tell me to leave you alone?'

'Because I didn't *want* you to leave me alone.'

'But what must you have thought?' I laugh, mortified by my mistake.

'You didn't *accost* me,' she insists. 'Look – it's me who should be apologising . . .'

'Why?' I am genuinely bewildered.

'Well, I, er . . .' She looks down at her hands, and then, as her gaze meets mine, something seems to somersault in the pit of my stomach. 'I let you *think* I worked there,' she says, smiling. 'Actually, I sort of pretended . . .'

'You pretended? Why?'

She pauses and pushes back that wayward strand of hair. 'Because,' she says simply, 'I just wanted to talk to you.'

Part Two

Sex and the Empty Nester: Things to Know

- Your friends will go on about how you can 'swing from the chandeliers' – or your IKEA 'Maskros' pendant lamp – now the kids have left home. There may be an expectation that you are doing it constantly. You might feel obliged to say you are.

- Even ordinary sex is better now that you don't have to be silent.

- You might find yourself being super-noisy and shouty – more than you ever were pre-children – just because you can.

- Being able to wander about in the nude feels like a wonderful novelty of which you will never tire.

- It's important to enjoy this stage while it lasts – because it might not.

Chapter Eight

Four months later

Nadia

Molly once explained to me how a microwave works, how its radio waves 'excite' the atoms in food, causing them to jiggle about in a frenzy, making everything hot. I feel this way whenever I'm with Jack, even several months in – not hot in a menopausal sweat kind of way, but sort of shimmery and super-charged.

At certain times my setting switches to FULL POWER: e.g. during sex. To think, I'd almost forgotten what the point of it was, apart from making babies. Like knowing who's number one in the charts, I'd begun to assume it belonged to a previous era of my life; something I could get along without quite contentedly.

The full-power thing kicks in even whenever Jack just happens to stroll nakedly across my bedroom. I should be used to him now, as we have been seeing each other regularly since Molly and Alfie headed back to uni after the Christmas break. But I wonder if the novelty aspect will ever wear off, as I still want to shout, 'There's a beautiful naked man wandering casually across my bedroom!' And I want to take a quick snap of his luscious rear view with my phone and beam it onto a huge building. Yep, I want to objectify him, plus lots of other things, because the truth is – although he'd deny this to the hilt – he has a lovely body. It's not intimidatingly buff, and that's a plus, in my book, as I've always found the idea of a six-pack disconcerting (especially as, size-wise, I am a generous fourteen). Jack has more your casual runner's-type physique: fairly slim, although he insists that's just the way he's built – 'A bag of bones when I was kid' – rather than due to his endeavours on the fitness front.

I have to say, his bottom is especially lovely. Corinne has a word she uses, to describe an attractive male rear: *biteable*, adjective, meaning 'evokes lust'. It suits Jack's perfectly. I do have a few pictures of him on my phone – not of his bottom, but his lovely face, and of the two of us together; selfies taken when we've been out and about, doing the kind of things newish couples do: strolling through parks, visiting galleries, having picnics and walks along the river. When no one's looking I'm prone to browsing through them. *My boyfriend.* It feels weird, using that term at fifty-one years old, but nothing else seems quite right. Jack is the kind of man I'd imagined, occasionally, might be out there somewhere: the one I'd kept missing as we went about our business in the same city all these years.

The long, cold winter has blossomed into a glorious spring, and by now I have met his friends and the volunteers at his shop. Iain claimed to have remembered me from when I popped in, and I was treated to one of his hot-tap coffees before Jack could dive for the kettle himself.

This coming weekend, significantly, I am meeting Lori. He's been suggesting it for a while now, but I've been nervous. He'd also told me about his ex Elaine's litany of boyfriends, and how they've tended to just appear at her house, to be presented to Lori, and then in a few weeks they'd be gone.

'It's not like that with us,' Jack has insisted, 'and she knows all about you. She really wants to meet you and thinks I'm hiding you away – or making you up.'

'What, even though you've shown her pictures of me?' I asked.

'Yeah. She's starting to think her dad's a sad bastard who's taken pictures of some random woman off the internet and is pretending she's his girlfriend.' He laughed, then turned serious. 'She also knows your kids are academic types, at uni, and she said, "You're not ashamed of me, are you, Dad?"'

Well, that did it. We agreed that I could go round to his place one Saturday, when Lori was there, and he'd make lunch.

Naturally, I've been to Jack's place countless times, but when the day rolls around my mouth is parched, my hands sticky with sweat, as I emerge from the subway station and make my way to his flat. Determined to make a good impression, I'm wearing a summery cotton dress, plus cardi and minimal meeting-the-boyfriend's-offspring-type make-up . . . at least, I hope that's what it is. I've never been in this situation before. Jack has already filled me in on the fact that, whilst Lori isn't terribly keen on school, she does love her drama club – which seems appropriate as I feel as if I am on my way to an audition.

In fact, it's Jack who seems the edgiest when I arrive, and he fusses over serving our lunch: a big bowl of

65

spaghetti puttanesca, slightly over-boiled, which is unlike him; Jack's pasta is usually cooked to perfection.

I like Lori immediately. For one thing, she looks so like him; I knew that already, from photos he'd shown me, but it's even more apparent in real life. As she tucks into her lunch, she's relaxed and chatty, answering my questions about her drama club. And as I watch them together, I'm overcome by a surge of love for Jack.

'Lori's an actress who doesn't want to be famous,' he remarks, and they catch each other's expressions and smile.

'I so don't,' she declares. 'But some of them do.' She looks at her father. 'Shannon does . . .'

'That's Lori's best friend,' he explains.

'Yeah.' Lori spears her spaghetti and smirks. 'I love her but, you know. She's kinda . . .' She glances back at her dad, as if checking for confirmation. 'Shall I show Nadia what she's like?' She nudges her phone, which is parked right at her side on the table, and he nods.

'Go on then.' He grins.

'I feel mean,' she adds, wincing. 'She's a really sweet person . . .'

Jack chuckles. 'But.'

'But,' Lori repeats, smiling now as she flips to her friend's Instagram account and shows me a series of selfies. She is deeply tanned, displaying colossal false lashes and those extreme brows that tend to look too defined: sharp-edged, as if cut from black fabric and stuck onto the face.

'Wow,' is all I can say.

'I know,' Lori murmurs, continuing to scroll through her friend's pictures.

'Those lips,' I exclaim at one point.

'They're fillers,' she says sagely, and I notice she's edged her chair closer to mine.

'Lip fillers? I mean . . . how old is she?'

'Fourteen, same as me. And yeah – loads of girls are having them . . .'

'But . . . how much do they cost?'

Lori shrugs. 'About three hundred quid.'

'Three hundred quid?' I exclaim, hoping I don't sound like some buttoned-up aunt.

Lori nods, and she and her father start laughing, clearly enjoying some shared joke. 'She had them done for an audition,' Jack tells me.

'*Oliver*,' Lori adds. 'She's into musical theatre. Wants to go to London . . .'

'Or work on cruise ships,' Jack cuts in.

'Right,' I say. 'And how about you?' I catch myself. 'Sorry. I know people always do that, ask what you'd like to be—'

'. . . when I grow up,' Lori says with a grin. 'Don't know really. I just like my drama club. We do improv, we write little plays – it's just . . . good.' She shrugs and smiles. 'I don't want to be up on some stage, belting out ballads, doing the big-eyes-and-teeth thing . . .'

I nod, and because it seems okay to do so, I tell her all about Danny, and how some of the actors in his films were discovered working in cafés, or in school plays. She's vaguely aware of his better-known films, and I'm happy to share what I know about the film-making process. Then once again I am privy to her Instagram feed – specifically pictures of Lori and her drama club friends involved in various acting workshops.

'That's Shannon?' I ask, picking her out from a group picture, and Lori nods.

'Lor,' Jack says as he clears away our bowls, 'tell Nadia what happened last time the two of you were left alone at your mum's . . .'

'*Dad*,' she groans, feigning horror, although I suspect she wants me to know. She turns to me. 'Shannon threw up all over the living room carpet.'

'Oh no!'

'Orange sick,' Jack adds with a grimace. 'Lori's adamant that Shannon brought the booze . . .'

'She did, Dad! Where else would it've come from?'

Jack eye-rolls, clearly enjoying playing the part of the disapproving dad.

'She has a fake ID,' Lori tells me, 'so she can buy anything . . .'

'Plus, she looks way older than she is,' Jack remarks, at which Lori nods.

'I'd never get away with it, even with a fake ID. I don't drink anyway. I don't like it.'

'Well, you're only fourteen,' I remark, hoping that doesn't sound patronising – and I'm fully aware that lots of kids of that age *do* drink. There were certainly a few incidences where both Alfie and Molly had tottered in, clearly tipsy well under-age.

'I don't think I ever will,' she adds lightly, and I catch a quick look between her and her dad, before she blurts out, 'I forgot! I made brownies for you coming.'

'Really?' I am extremely touched by this. Without wishing to read too much into the gesture – perhaps she just enjoys baking, like Alfie used to? – I decide to interpret it as a sign that she really was looking forward to meeting me today.

The afternoon flies by, and when it's time to leave I am almost sorry to go.

'Great to meet you, Lori,' I say, as I pull on my jacket.

'You too,' she says with a smile.

Jack sees me out. 'Did that go okay?' I ask.

'What do you think?' He pulls me closer and kisses my hair.

'I think she's lovely. She's a real credit to you.'

He smiles and shrugs off the compliment. 'She's very much her own person. But thanks, darling. We, um, had a quick word, when you were in the loo . . .'

I feign a terrified face. 'What about?'

He laughs now, brushing away a strand of hair from my face, the way he does sometimes. 'She just said you were lovely too. And normal!'

'She said I'm normal?' I remark, laughing now.

'Yeah. "Not weird", she said. You know how everything's "weird" these days? I mean, someone only has to scratch their ear in public to be classed as "weird". She said I was weird, the other day, for singing while I was cooking—'

'Did she? Christ – I sing all the time . . .'

'Apparently you're not weird, though,' he says, kissing my lips. 'But you *are* very gorgeous.'

I smile, fizzling with happiness. So I've passed the test, I reflect, as I stride towards the subway. I am filled with the most delicious, chewy brownies (top marks to Lori), and a feeling that Jack and I have somehow moved along another small but significant step.

So his daughter thinks I am actually all right. I know I am grinning madly – I literally cannot stop – as I descend the escalator to the train. And I also know that if Lori could see me now, she'd think I was *far* too weird for her beloved dad.

Chapter Nine

It's Jack's turn to be vetted a couple of weeks later, when my sister invites us for Sunday lunch. Jack offers to drive us to her renovated farm on the Ayrshire coast. I glance at him as we near her place, reflecting that a newish relationship presents a series of these 'firsts', these meetings during which everyone pretends there's no 'checking out' going on (when of course there is). Anyone who cares about you wants to appraise the person you've fallen in love with.

Jack and I have already had drinks with a couple of old schoolmates of mine, plus other friends I've got to know through the children, their various activities and the life modelling circuit. He's handled it well, being his natural, extremely likeable self, despite his slight shyness and the fact that he might have started to feel like a new puppy being given his first tour of the park.

Naturally, he met Corinne and Gus early on. Corinne enjoys referring to him as Mr Lush, even to his face, which Jack always takes in extremely good spirit. A terrible flirt, she made a huge fuss over him that first time we all went out, and insisted on a selfie with him, crammed into the corner of our booth in the pub, later to be captioned: 'Stole Nadia's new boyfriend for five minutes, took him round back of pub and God he was GOOD.'

Jack pretended to be mortified when I showed him her Instagram post, but I could tell he was secretly amused. 'Always nice to get a positive review,' he chuckled. Meanwhile Gus, who seems to find it hilarious that Jack is all of two years younger than me, refers to him as my 'toyboy', a term I'd assumed had fallen into obscurity a long time ago. One lunchtime, when we nipped out for a sandwich together, Gus spotted a portly young man sauntering towards us wearing a T-shirt bearing the charming slogan: 'MILF-CHASER.'

'Get one for Jack?' he whispered, swerving to avoid my punch to his arm. Later, we spotted another guy – bearded and lanky, sporting a wiry man-bun – whose T-shirt read: I'M RAISING A TRIBE. And that, we concluded, was far more offensive as slogans go. Gus took a candid picture of the man with his phone and sent it to me.

'Look at this,' I said later, showing it to Jack.

'Oh, God,' he groaned. 'The smugness. It should be banned under some kind of offensive clothing bylaw.'

'Yeah. We wanted to tear it off him and pelt him with rusks.'

He spluttered.

We just 'get' each other, Jack and I; and if we had raised a tribe, I'm pretty sure he'd have just got on with the job rather than wearing a T-shirt to advertise the fact.

And now, as the Ayrshire coast opens up before us on this clear-skied May afternoon, I allow myself a moment to reflect that perhaps this wouldn't have happened if

71

Alfie and Molly still lived at home. At least, it might not have seemed quite so easy. As it is – particularly as Lori spends at least half the week at her mum's – Jack and I have been able to spend time together without being answerable to anyone. There was no one else hovering around in the morning the first time he stayed over at mine. I've been able to stay at his place without letting Alfie and Molly know I wouldn't be home until morning. At first it was something of a novelty, waking up in Jack's light-filled, airy bedroom, and sipping his far superior coffee while he pottered about warming up croissants and festooning me with his extensive selection of jams. ('I have such a sweet tooth,' he admitted. 'The palate of an eight-year-old. It's embarrassing really.')

Of course, I do miss my kids, in that I'd love to see them more often. But I have to say it has also been extremely *liberating*, living my life unpoliced, in this way.

'It's the next turn-off to the right,' I tell Jack, as we pass a familiar row of ancient stone cottages, then a farm shop and a B&B.

'It's lovely out here,' he remarks. 'I don't really know this part of the country at all.'

'We used to come here all the time when we were little,' I tell him. 'We loved the coast. It was only a half-hour drive from home but it seemed like a real treat. Sarah's always stayed in the area.' I wonder now when Jack might tell me more about his childhood; specifically, about his younger brother, Sandy, who died. Obviously, whatever happened must have been horrific, but whenever Sandy's name has been mentioned, I've sensed Jack shutting down, as if sending out the clear message that he really doesn't want me to ask about it.

Fair enough; I'd never want to pry. But I'd like to think

that, at some point, he might feel able to tell me what happened.

I glance at him. 'You okay?'

'Yeah, of course.' He smiles.

'Like I said, Sarah's lovely – but we're very different . . .'

'I'm ready for my interrogation,' he teases.

'She won't interrogate you. She does enough of that at work.' Although not remotely intimidating off-duty, I suspect that my sister can come over as pretty scary when in professional mode; she is in charge of a team who inspects care homes and children's nurseries. Meanwhile, Vic, her husband, is a car auctioneer, which I'm sure Jack would never have guessed, as they come out to greet us and, after warm hugs and handshakes, my brother-in-law struts around Jack's battered old Fiat, as if sizing it up for sale.

'This is your motor, Jack?' he asks with a smirk.

'It is, yeah,' Jack says with a nod.

'Ha! Surprised you got here in one piece . . .' He crouches to poke at a corroded wheel arch.

'C'mon, Vic,' Sarah says tersely, 'leave Jack's car alone.'

Vic grins at Jack. I'm fond of my brother-in-law; he's a caring and generous husband of the traditional type. He barely cooks, but gardens enthusiastically, and their cars' tyres will forever remain at the correct pressure whilst there is breath in his body. Plus, he's a fantastic father to Scott and Ollie, who are in their mid-twenties and still live locally. Both boys are immensely practical; Scott rewired his parents' house, and Ollie fitted their new kitchen. Sarah and Vic couldn't hide their horror when, on a visit to my place, Alfie seemed utterly confused when I asked him to replace the bulb in the table lamp.

'You've got a rust issue there, Jack,' Vic observes, frowning.

73

'Yeah, it is a bit of a wreck,' Jack concedes.

'You want to catch that before it goes any further. Got an abrasive wheel?'

'Erm, I don't think I have,' Jack admits, as my sister and I exchange glances.

'Well, you want to get one, or at least some sandpaper. Rub it down nice and smooth until it's shiny metal. Get your primer on, then your paint and your topcoat . . .'

'Yep, I'll do that,' Jack murmurs, and I'm overcome by an urge to hug him for playing along with this blokes' talk.

'I take it this old wreck's just a stop-gap,' Vic remarks.

'Erm, well, not really,' Jack admits, as Sarah tugs on Vic's arm, coaxing her husband away from the car like a mother pulling her child away from the chocolates in the checkout aisle.

'Maybe Jack's perfectly happy with it,' she retorts as we all head inside. Vic shrugs good-naturedly and fetches us drinks, and soon Scott and Ollie arrive, plus Ollie's girlfriend Morvern, whom he lives with. I hadn't expected such a gathering. Sarah had merely said the boys 'might drop by'. But there are enthusiastic hellos and hugs, and it feels like quite a houseful as numerous dishes are brought from the oven, and we all settle around the huge kitchen table.

Occasionally, during my seemingly endless years as a single person, Sarah would call to ask, 'Are you . . . okay?' *All by yourself* is what she meant. Of course I was. In fact, I slightly resented the implication that I might be falling apart without a man to look after me. But then, Sarah has always been protective, and since our parents died, eight years ago now, she has edged herself into a sort of motherly mode with me, despite being only four years older.

As I chat to the boys and Morvern – whom I've met several times before – I become aware of my sister gently quizzing Jack about his life. 'A charity shop? That sounds interesting. Oh, animal sanctuaries! That's fantastic. Does all the funding come from the shops, or d'you have bene-factors, or . . .' On she goes, wanting to know all the details in the way that, when she inspects a care home, she leaves no stone unturned.

Vic turns to me with a grin. 'So, Nads, is your Alfie still seeing that posh bird?'

'Yep, they're planning to go travelling together this summer,' I reply, at which Vic looks at Morvern.

'He ditched us at Christmas for the aristocracy. Our own nephew!' He laughs. 'Our roast potatoes aren't good enough for him anymore.'

'Have you met them, Jack?' Sarah asks. 'Alfie and Molly, I mean?'

'No, not yet,' he replies.

'I, erm, thought we'd wait till the summer break,' I remark, sensing that an explanation is needed. 'They've been home on visits but it's always seemed so rushed. Anyway, they're back in a couple of weeks . . .' I don't add that I've felt slightly apprehensive about that first meeting, having never been in this kind of situation before. Easter had felt a little too soon to introduce them, even though Jack and I had been seeing each other regularly – spending at least half the week together – since the Christmas holidays had ended.

Vic turns to Jack and grins. 'Well, good luck with that, mate. They're bloody terrifying, that pair . . .'

'Vic!' I splutter. 'No, they're not . . .'

'They'll have you strapped to a rack, thumb screws on, dazzling light shone in your eyes: "And what are your

75

intentions with our mother?"' He sniggers and takes a big swig of wine.

'Dad,' Scott exclaims as Jack laughs off the comment. 'Jesus . . .'

'Sounds like I'll have to start revving myself up for it,' Jack says with a smile.

'Yeah,' Vic asserts. 'I mean, singly, they're quite a force, but *together* . . .'

'First the rust, and now this,' Sarah groans, rolling her eyes.

'What's that about rust?' Morvern asks.

'Vic was haranguing poor Jack about his car,' Sarah explains with a shake of her head. She turns to me. 'Are the kids coming back for the whole summer?'

'Yes – at least, Molly is. She's been offered work at her friend's dad's garden centre. You know what she's like. Loves to earn a few quid and doesn't mind grafting.'

'So that's your fun spoiled, Nads,' Vic remarks with a grin.

'It'll be fine,' I say, aware of my cheeks flushing as I laugh.

'And what about Alfie?' Sarah asks.

'He'll only be around for a few days, then his girlfriend's coming down to our place, and they'll head off. They're going Inter-railing around Europe . . .'

'Oh, I'm glad he's met someone nice, Nads.'

'Me too.' My sister and I exchange a look across the table. She knows how much I worried about Alfie as he went through secondary school. Whilst he had a couple of close friends, he was always quiet and studious, a sensitive type who enjoyed drawing and baking and had no interest in sport. Unfortunately, this made him a target for bullying in his early teens, and the fact that his father is a film director only seemed to attract more unwanted attention (Molly exuded such self-assuredness, no one ever dared to hassle her about it). On one occasion Alfie was hurt pretty badly in a fight after school. The school tried to deal with it, and the problem seemed to abate, but since that time Alfie has always been rather awkward socially. He'd never had a girlfriend until he met Camilla at university, so I suspect a new start, in a different city, has helped to boost his confidence.

'It's been good for Nadia, you know,' Vic observes as he fetches Jack, the only non-drinker at the table, another ginger beer from the fridge. The rest of us are knocking back the wine with some enthusiasm. 'Getting the kids off her hands, I mean,' he adds. 'I don't mean that in a *bad* way, do I, Nads? It's not like you were counting the days till the buggers were off your hands—'

'No, you're right,' I concede. 'It has been good for me.'

'We'd started to think ours would never leave home,' Sarah tells Jack with a smile. 'Scott was twenty-three when he finally moved out . . .'

'And Ollie hung on in there till he was twenty-bloody-five,' Vic exclaims.

'That's nice, Dad,' Ollie exclaims with a snort.

'Too bloody comfortable, that's why,' his father adds.

'Ollie still says he misses your gravy, Sarah,' Morvern says, grinning, and it strikes me that this scene isn't so different to that lunch at Jack's, when I met Lori: an easy gathering, with friendly and generous people who are happy to welcome in someone new. I find myself hoping that I can create a similar atmosphere of relaxed jollity when my own offspring return home.

There's a clattering of crockery as everyone helps to clear up, and afterwards the TV is put on far too loudly, as per Vic's wishes, with everyone talking above it, and over each other.

'Go on,' Morvern urges Jack, flushed now from the wine, 'what's the worst thing you've ever had handed in at your shop?'

'There have been so many,' he says, pausing, perhaps to choose an example that's not too disgusting. 'Um, last week someone brought in an ancient pressure cooker that still had soup in it. All fuzzy with mould . . .'

'Ew!' Morvern shudders.

Jack is further quizzed until, finally, I suggest that we really should be going.

After promises to visit again soon – and Vic's parting shot of 'Remember to catch that rust, Jacky-boy, before it catches you!' – we drive home to Glasgow, chuckling over the rust issue, and how weird it is that some men find it impossible to comprehend that not every other male shares those typical masculine interests (i.e. cars).

'They're lovely people, though,' Jack adds.

'Yes, they are.'

I think about how Sarah thought I was crazy to split up with Danny; or, rather, she reckoned I should 'hang on in there', as she put it, until our kids left home. It served only to crank up my guilt, because wouldn't a break-up have hurt them at any stage? And what was the alternative: to sit tight, pretending, until our facade of togetherness crumbled in front of our children? A failed relationship is nothing to be proud of, I know, but I'm not so sure it was a failure really, when we have Molly, who excels at her studies despite her hectic social life, and Alfie who, despite his shyness, seems to have found his niche in Aberdeen.

'So, d'you reckon you're ready to meet them, then?' I ask, studying Jack's expression.

'Molly and Alfie?' He glances from the driver's seat. 'Yes, of course I am.' He grins. 'Although, if it's easier, you could just pretend I'm a friend . . .'

'Yeah,' I say, smiling. '"This is Jack, my new friend, who I'm not *remotely* attracted to . . ."'

'"I'm very fond of your mum,"' he chips in, '"but don't worry, there's no physical attraction whatsoever . . ."'

'They do know I'm seeing you,' I remind him.

'And they were okay about that?'

'Of course they were,' I say firmly, 'although I'm not sure they were listening. Whenever we talk, it's always, "yeah-yeah", like they're desperate to get off the phone . . .' I look at him. 'They're nice kids, Jack. Alfie can be a little awkward like most boys of his age – but they're decent, well-mannered people . . .'

He touches my knee, which sends a ripple of pleasure right through me. 'I'm sure they are.'

'You do know Vic was winding you up, don't you?'

''Course I do.'

We fall into silence as we join the motorway, then I ask, tentatively, 'Are you nervous about meeting my kids?'

There's a beat's silence, and he glances at me with a teasing smile. 'Absolutely crapping myself,' he says.

Chapter Ten

The following weekend, it's one of Jack's rare Saturdays off work. Lori is with her mother, and Glasgow shimmers in the bright May sunshine beneath an unblemished blue sky.

Jack and I have already browsed the shops in the West End, and strolled through Kelvingrove Park. We should stay out, we both know it, but after a quick lunch we end up back at my flat, kissing on the sofa. That was something else I used to assume had shut down permanently: my ability to enjoy kissing as a thing in itself. But God, no. Proper kissing, I've realised since meeting Jack, does not come under the same banner as crocheted bikinis and novelty hair accessories; i.e. it's *not* just for the young.

We are lying there together, entwined and naked now (at some point during the proceedings our clothes have come off). 'We probably should go out,' I murmur dozily, making no move to go anywhere.

'D'you feel like we're wasting the afternoon?' Jack teases.

'Totally,' I say with a smile as he pulls me closer. And

so we waste yet more time, delighting in our indulgence and the fact that no demands are being made upon us whatsoever. My heart soars as it did on Christmas Eve, on our first date, when Jack and I kissed in the pub, and then outside the subway station before we said goodbye. I replayed that evening over and over, all through the next day when Molly and I went to Sarah's. As I tucked into turkey and all the trimmings, a single thought looped around my head: *I kissed Jack last night! We snogged in the street, like young things, even though we both possess reading glasses and have a combined age of a hundred!* That evening, my head was so full of Jack, and our kiss, I didn't manage to answer a single Trivial Pursuit question correctly.

Now our perfect Saturday has somehow tipped into late afternoon, the light turned golden now. 'Jack,' I start, 'would you like to go away somewhere this summer? Just the two of us, I mean?'

'I'd love to,' he says. 'Any ideas where?'

I rest my head in the crook of his arm. 'You know that series of Barcelona maps I've been asked to do?'

'Uh-huh?' While Danny seemed to regard my job as a hobby, Jack expressed a keen interest right from the start. All his questions, and requests to browse through my work; it almost made me squirm, the way he was so complimentary and enthusiastic.

'Well, I *could* do them without actually going there,' I continue. 'That's what I usually do. But I thought it'd be more fun to really immerse myself in the city – so why don't we go together?'

'On a sort of research trip, you mean?'

'Exactly. We could get to know all the different neighbourhoods, so each map would have its own distinct feel . . . Could you get some time off work, d'you think?'

'I'm sure I could,' he replies. 'Helen used to manage the shop, and she's usually happy to come back and do my holiday cover. I'm not taking Lori away until August, so . . . when were you thinking?'

'As soon as possible, really – after Alfie's headed off on his travels . . .'

'But won't you be busy sketching and making notes? I don't want to get in the way of your work. I shouldn't *distract* you . . .'

I laugh and kiss him lightly on the lips. 'You can distract me anytime you like.'

'And what about Molly?' he asks. 'She's here all summer, isn't she?'

'Jack, she's *nineteen*. She's lived independently for nearly a year now so she's perfectly capable of looking after herself.'

He nods. 'So she wouldn't mind us nipping off to Spain together . . .?'

'Of course not,' I say, grinning now. 'She'll probably be glad to have the place to herself for a week or so . . .' I squeeze Jack's hand. 'Neither of my kids particularly care what I get up to these days,' I add, 'and even if they did . . .' I tail off and kiss him again. 'Well, I'm a fully grown adult . . .'

'Of course you are,' he says firmly.

I beam at him. 'Anyway, it's a research trip, remember?'

'Oh, yes,' he says. 'A vital part of your work—'

'Actually,' I cut in, smiling, 'I just want to go away with you.'

I get up, and fetch our dressing gowns from my bedroom – my boyfriend keeps a dressing gown here! – plus my laptop and diary (I still use a proper paper one; I've never managed to switch over to digital). Back on

82

the sofa now, wrapped up in our gowns, we peruse dates and apartments in Barcelona. We shortlist three in El Raval, a district close to the Ramblas that was once, apparently, a bit on the shady side but is now peppered with cool coffee shops, bars and galleries. Jack texts his friend Helen, who agrees to cover the shop for the dates we'll be away. We book flights, having our first minor tussle over money – Jack is insistent about transferring his share of the cost to my account immediately – and that's all done.

'That was simple,' I remark, setting my laptop on the coffee table and snuggling back into his arms.

'Eerily simple,' he says. 'I guess it is, when it's just the two of us.'

'Yeah,' I agree, still thrilled by the novelty of it all. 'God, the debates we used to have, when it was Danny and me and the kids. He didn't believe in package holidays. Said he'd rather have sawn his hand off than go anywhere with a kids' club . . .'

Jack chuckles. 'Those terrible kids' clubs with all their toys and games and enthusiastic staff . . .'

'"I'm not parking our kids in a facility," he used to say. A facility!' We laugh, and then we are kissing again on the sofa, our gowns tossed onto the floor as he holds me closer and— he stops abruptly and pulls away.

'What is it?' I ask.

'I thought I heard something?' He frowns.

'Just someone on the stairs,' I remark, unconcerned until I hear another, more distinct sound: that of a key being poked into a lock. No, not *a* lock, but *my lock*. And now my front door is opening . . .

I shoot a look of alarm at Jack. 'Is that someone coming—' he starts.

'Who is it?' I call out. Thoughts shoot through my head: I'm being burgled. No, burglars don't have the Yale key for my door. Is it Danny? Has he held on to his keys all these years, and if so, how can he possibly think it's okay to let himself in?

Jack and I scramble up. 'Hello?' I call out, more forcefully now as footsteps sound in the hallway. The front door closes with a heavy clunk, and Alfie's voice rings out: 'Hey, Mum, are you there? It's *me*.'

Chapter Eleven

For a single, mad moment, I consider pretending we're not in. We could duck down behind the sofa in the hope that Alfie might dump his stuff here, then go out. But where would he go? He's only just arrived – *a whole week early*. And our clothes are strewn all over the floor . . .

'Mum?' Alfie calls out again, his footsteps growing closer in the hallway.

Miraculously, Jack has already tugged his dressing gown back on.

'Just a minute, love!' I call out in an oddly tight voice as I snatch mine from the floor and clutch it in front of myself.

He appears in the doorway and stares at us. 'Oh God. Sorry!'

'Alfie, um, this is a surprise . . .' Our eyes lock and I force a smile.

'Yeah.' His gaze flicks towards Jack, an unfamiliar six-foot male, then he looks down at the knickers I'd flung off in lust, which are lying, a wanton scrap of black lace, in the middle of the floor.

'This is Jack,' I blurt out.

'Er . . . hi,' Alfie mutters.

'Hi!' Jack says brightly as I study my son's face.

I grip my dressing gown more tightly. 'Is everything . . . okay, Alf? I thought you were coming next—'

'I'm good,' he cuts in, his mouth set in a firm line. Then, like an elderly person: 'I'll just go and put the kettle on.'

I exhale loudly as he wanders off to the kitchen, and Jack and I stare at each other like teenagers caught copulating in a parental bed.

'Bloody hell,' he says under his breath, gathering up his clothes and pulling them on: boxers, jeans, T-shirt.

'I'm *so* sorry. Christ, Jack, I don't know what's going on . . .' I snatch my knickers and pull them on, then struggle into the bra, jeans and T-shirt that were also scattered all over the floor. I'm aware of my cheeks burning hotly as I smooth down the sofa and arrange the cushions tidily, as if a little light housekeeping will make everything okay.

Jack's expression is unreadable as he sits heavily on the sofa and pulls on his socks.

'I'm sure it was meant to be next weekend,' I add. 'That's what he told me . . .' Is it me who's got it wrong? I'm wondering now. Have I been in such a funk of lust that I've made a mistake over Alfie's homecoming date?

'He's not going to . . . mind, is he?' Jack murmurs.

'Of course not,' I reply, and try to reassure myself that he won't. After all, I'm a fully fledged, consenting adult, entitled to do adult things. Christ, I waited long enough. And what else am I supposed to do: take up crochet, or cultivate bonsai trees?

I glance at Jack, who is up on his feet now, smoothing

down his hair and possibly already spiriting himself away to another kind of Saturday – the kind he used to enjoy before I launched myself at him and forced him to buy an unnecessary lip scrub.

As Jack laces up his faded Converse, I try to find more ways to apologise, but I can't seem to find the words. It's not that I don't want to see my son – of course it's not. As an empty nester, you build up your kids' homecoming to a massive event; you run around the shops, locating their favourite peanut butter and breakfast cereal, buying The Big Milk again and cramming the fridge with so much food you can hardly shut the door. With a mixture of excitement and mild fear, you start anticipating the flat being full of noise and people again. It's a little like waiting for your own party to begin.

But no one wants a party guest turning up a whole week early.

Aware of Alfie clattering about in the kitchen, I check my reflection in the mirror on the living room wall. My mascara is smudged, my hair matted at the back and bushed up around my face. With no brush to hand I try to flatten it down, but it springs up defiantly. I throw Jack a grim look.

'I really am so sorry,' I say. 'I didn't imagine you'd meet Alfie like this.'

Jack looks at me and clears his throat. 'Well, it's happened now. C'mon, you go through and see him – and don't worry. I'm sure everything'll be okay.'

And it is okay-*ish* . . . on the surface, at least, by which I mean that it might have been worse. Alfie could have barged in and caught us actually doing it, which would have meant I'd have had to throw myself out of the window, which would have caused a terrible scene in our street, and he and Molly would be motherless. As it is, Jack and I sort of glide out of the living room, all affected serenity as if we'd merely been watching TV. Thoughtfully, he swerves into the bathroom, presumably to give Alfie and me a few moments alone together.

In the kitchen, I find my son studying a box of high-fibre cereal in the cupboard as if that might cleanse his mind of the horror he's just witnessed.

'Hi, darling!' I arrange my face into a semblance of normality as I go hug him.

'Hi.' Our embrace feels awkward, as if we have too many arms.

I step back and clear my throat. 'Honey,' I start, 'I'm really sorry about that, but I actually thought it was next weekend you were coming. Did I get the date wrong?'

He shrugs. 'No, I just decided to come home a bit early.'

'Oh, right!' I pause. *Couldn't you have warned me? Couldn't you have communicated this fact?* 'Is everything okay?' I ask, frowning. 'I mean, I thought you'd want to be there until the final weekend, before everyone headed off—'

'Nah,' he cuts in with a dismissive shake of his head. 'I kind of changed my mind . . .'

'Did you? Well, it's *great* to see you. And, um, that was Jack, obviously . . .'

'Um, yeah. You already said.'

Alfie looks at me, and I take in his face, which looks rather gaunt, his cheekbones sharper than usual; he has definitely lost weight since I saw him a few weeks ago. 'I did tell you about him,' I add.

'Er, yeah, I think you mentioned him,' he replies vaguely.

88

I definitely did, I want to add, wondering now if I mentioned Jack by name, or merely dropped in that I'm 'seeing someone'. Not that Alfie ever seems particularly interested in what I'm up to. On the rare occasions I call him – rather than texting – he tends to bark, 'Mum?' as he answers, sounding startled, as if phone calls are only for announcing that someone has died.

An awkward silence descends, punctuated by Jack flushing the loo, and now Alfie has opened the fridge and is staring into it as if expecting a full vegan banquet to materialise. At what age does it stop, this need to check on provisions immediately on arrival, as if food doesn't exist in Aberdeen? I don't recall that I ever did it myself as a student – flinging open cupboards and staring at my parents' baked beans and Ambrosia Creamed Rice whenever I returned home to Glasgow from my various student hovels in Dundee.

'Are you hungry, love?' I ask. 'Have you eaten?'

'No. I'm starving.'

'I'll make you some pasta or something . . .' I lurch for a pan.

'I'm not really in the mood for pasta.'

'Some pie then? I made a feta tart yesterday, there's plenty left in the—'

'I don't eat cheese,' he reminds me, frowning now, as if on top of rolling about with my boyfriend – in the living room, *in the day* – I am now trying to force my dairy products onto him. 'I'll make something myself,' he adds, adopting a lofty tone now.

'Okay. And we can do a proper vegan shop as soon as I'm, erm, more organised.'

Alfie observes me levelly. 'That'd be good.'

Another silence descends as he sets about making

himself a sandwich, perhaps to give him something to do in preparation for Jack's inevitable appearance. Or, more likely, to underline the shabby standard of facilities around here. He delves into the bread bin and flops two slices of not terribly fresh granary onto the worktop. The fridge is peered into once more, accompanied by a heavy sigh, and a flaccid cucumber is extracted.

I watch as he fashions himself a rather bleak-looking cucumber sandwich – no butter, obviously – and bites into it. 'So, does Dad know you're home?' I ask, setting about making a pot of tea now as Alfie didn't get around to putting the kettle on.

'No, not yet.'

'Right . . .' I pause. 'Well, he'll be glad to see you.' Alfie nods and munches silently. 'I've got quite a bit of work on,' I continue, 'but if I make early starts, we can still do some nice things together until you go away . . . you're still going travelling, aren't you?'

'Um, yeah. At least, I think—' He stops abruptly as Jack wanders in.

'Hi!' I exclaim as if his appearance is a delightful surprise.

'Hi.' Jack smiles tightly. 'Um, hi, Alfie . . .'

'Hullo,' my son says glumly, pushing the rest of his sandwich into his mouth.

'So, um, was your journey okay?'

Still chewing, he nods. 'Yeah-it-was-fine-thanks.'

'Great. Erm . . .' Jack pauses, as if trying to think of something interesting to say about the Aberdeen-to-Glasgow train journey: the catering facilities, maybe, or the scenery en route?

'Have you ever been to Aberdeen?' I ask Jack, ridiculously.

'Uh, yeah,' he replies, eyebrows shooting up as he leans against the fridge. 'Mum and Dad took us to a B&B once, when we were kids. Rained the whole week. The B&B lady chucked us out after breakfast and we weren't allowed back until teatime.' He snorts. 'Saw the same matinee at the cinema three times . . .' I see his mouth twitch with tension as I place three mugs of tea on the table and add milk.

'Mum, that's cow's milk!' Alfie yelps.

'Oh God, love, sorry.' We all stare at the unwanted tea as if it might be radioactive. 'I don't have any soya milk in yet,' I add. 'Will you have a black one?'

I catch him glancing at Jack, who's standing awkwardly, seeming even taller than usual in his creased T-shirt and jeans. 'I won't bother,' Alfie says.

'Oh, okay! I'll have it.' I smile. 'I'll have two, I'm quite parched actually . . .' *Christ, shut up. What* are *you going on about?*

'So, d'you like Aberdeen?' Jack asks my son.

'Yeah, it's okay,' Alfie replies airily.

'I'm sure it's not always raining,' Jack adds, as if worried that he might have caused offence.

Alfie glances towards the window in confusion.

'Jack means in Aberdeen,' I say quickly, as if my boyfriend is incapable of expressing himself. 'Actually,' I add, 'I think Glasgow's rainier, being, um, in the west . . .'

Just when it looks as if we're about to lurch into a fascinating discussion about the varying precipitation in Scotland, Jack remarks: 'Aberdeen's the most northern city in Britain, isn't it?'

'Or is that Inverness?' I muse, picking up a mug of tea and blowing across it.

'Or Lerwick?' Jack frowns. 'I suppose it depends on

91

how you define a city – like whether it's based on population or if it has a cathedral . . .' He smiles brightly at Alfie. 'Is there a cathedral in Aberdeen?'

Alfie narrows his eyes at Jack as if he asked, *Do people crap in the street in Aberdeen?* 'I'm not really sure,' he says levelly.

'We should look it up,' I suggest, because that's what I always used to do when Alfie was little: get the laptop out, turn a question into a learning experience, which he seemed to enjoy back then – discovering which planets are made of frozen gas, how earthworms reproduce.

As my laptop's sitting there on the kitchen table, I flip it open and google *cathedrals Aberdeen.* 'There are three,' I announce, realising I'm sounding quite mad.

'Really, Mum?' Alfie asks dryly.

'Yes. I never knew that,' I say. My son looks blank. I look round at Jack, hoping that at least he will show interest, but his mobile trills in his jeans pocket, and he snatches at it.

''Scuse me,' he mutters, striding out to the hallway to take the call.

I clear my throat. 'So, love. What made you decide to come back early?'

'Uh, there didn't seem much point in staying on after the last exam,' Alfie says, looking shifty now as Jack conducts a mumbled call.

'But I thought you had plans for this weekend?' Alfie had mentioned a party before everyone headed off for the summer. I'd been delighted to hear that he'd formed friendships fairly quickly in his uni halls. I've even met a couple of his new mates when I've been up for visits; they seemed far more confident than I remember being at their age. I have yet to meet Camilla, whose dad has

92

kindly offered to pick up Alfie's stuff from his room, and store it at the family pile, until the start of next semester when he moves into a new flat with a couple of friends.

I will meet her soon, though. Apparently, the plan is for Alfie to show her the highlights of Glasgow before they head off on their trip.

'Just fancied coming home and chilling out,' he replies now, idly fiddling with the sugar bowl.

'Right.' I pause, considering this. 'Has something happened, Alf? I mean, is everything really all right?'

Before he can answer Jack reappears, shoving his phone into his pocket. 'Well, I'd probably better be off . . .'

'Really?' I ask.

Jack nods. 'Stuff to sort out . . .'

Although their exchange is perfectly polite – 'Good to meet you, Alfie'; 'Yeah, you too' – I can't help feeling relieved when Jack says, 'Bye, then!' from the kitchen doorway, as if he's a BT guy who's come around to investigate a faulty line.

With Jack gone now, Alfie checks the cupboard for vegan biscuits – apparently, there are none – while I sweep up the crumbs he dropped all over the floor. I know I should ask him to do it, but now's not the time; something's wrong, I'm sure of it. There must be a reason why he's shown up like this, unannounced.

Picking up the second mug of now-tepid tea, I sit down and look at him across the table. 'So, love,' I start, trying to meet his gaze, 'can you please tell me what's going on?'

Chapter Twelve

Jack

What the hell was I thinking, quizzing Alfie about the architectural features of Aberdeen? Does it have a cathedral? What did I expect him to say, 'Yes, Jack, and I believe it's one of the best-preserved examples from the pre-Reformation era'?

Jesus wept . . .

I drive home from Nadia's, trying to shake off the lingering image of Alfie gawping at us from the living room doorway: a tall, gaunt boy with a shock of messy dark hair, horrified at the sight of me in my dressing gown and his mother clutching hers in front of herself. Still, it's happened now, and maybe it's one of those things Alfie and I will chuckle about, once we've all got to know each other, perhaps when he's around thirty-seven years old. I try to summon up an image of us all together at some kind of gathering, our families merged and Alfie wandering over to me, beer in hand – because, naturally, we'll be firm friends by then – and saying, with a smirk, 'Remember that time I walked in on you and Mum? Nearly scarred me for life, that did!'

And I'll reply, 'Sorry about that. You can send me your therapist's bill.'

Oh, how we'll laugh. At least, I hope we will. In the meantime, I try to reassure myself that surely things will be better with Molly, when she comes home next weekend. Even if it is a bit awkward, Nadia's told me that Molly has a full-time summer job lined up, and Alfie is planning to go travelling with his girlfriend pretty soon. So things should soon settle back down.

Is that awful of me to wish Nadia's kids out of the way, to want to spirit her son off to another country? Oh, I don't really. They're part of her life, of course they are – and it's up to me to be pleasant and patient and, hopefully, get to know them at least a little. However, rather selfishly I suppose, I have loved these past few months with Nadia, and, well . . . things are going to change, aren't they?

Jack hates change. That was a favoured declaration of Elaine's, when we were together, because she loved to 'switch things around', as she put it. On one occasion she came home pissed after a boozy lunch with her mates via a shop that sold tile paint. Because of course that's what you do after a bucket-load of Prosecco. You totter into a home decor store and buy tile paint – 'It was on offer! Weren't you saying we should try to save money?' – and instead of waiting until you'd sobered up, you cart it home and start slapping it on right away, because won't murky green tiles look fantastic?

'You know what Jack's like,' Elaine chuckled to her friend Ginny, when I came home to find her balancing precariously on a stepladder, waving a dripping paintbrush as she finished off the highest bits. 'He hates change!'

'All men do,' Ginny agreed.

95

'Well, I don't,' I insisted. 'Really, I don't. But I'm not crazy about dark green, and actually I thought the white tiles were perfectly—'

'Aw, look at his face, bless him,' Ginny giggled. 'Oh, Jack. You are *hilarious* . . .'

When you're with someone like Elaine, who's always the first up dancing – often on tables and bar-tops, knocking over glasses – there's only one direction you can go in, really, and that's down Boring-Fucker-Avenue. Oh, she was fun all right, which is one of the reasons I'd been so attracted to her in the first place. We'd met at a music festival near Dumfries. She was twenty-five; I'm four years older. I'd gone with a bunch of mates, hoping for a distraction from the worst thing that had ever happened to my family. The guys had been brilliant with me, up to a point: ever-patient, even though I was a drunken belligerent mess at the time. However, things had boiled over and there'd been a stupid row.

I really shouldn't have gone to the festival at all, but they'd persuaded me. 'It'll be good for you,' my friend Fergus had insisted, adding that I needed to kick back and have a laugh, to try and get over what had happened.

I'd never get over it; I knew that. What had happened was all my fault, and no one would persuade me otherwise. But I allowed myself to be dragged along by Fergus, Tam and Paul, and to reward my friends for being so understanding, I'd behaved like a real arsehole.

When stuff was nicked from our tent, I blamed them. 'You said you were going for a kip,' I snapped at Paul.

'He went for a walk instead,' Tam reasoned. 'We can't expect anyone to stay here, guarding our stuff all the time.' It escalated into a full-on argument, with me trying to lob a beer can at Tam's head (fortunately my aim was poor), telling everyone to 'just fucking leave me alone' and storming off pissed. I woke up hours later, in a soggy patch of field, minus a shoe, with a mysterious gash on my shin, and this fragile, pretty, red-haired girl gazing over me like a kind spirit.

Elaine sat with me and stroked my hair while I blabbered on about my friends' perceived crimes, our stolen rucksacks and the fact that I had no money.

And my little brother. I found myself telling her all about him, our Sandy – short for Alexander, although no one ever called him that. He was thirteen years younger than me, fifteen younger than Craig: 'A surprise,' as our mum always put it. 'My last gasp,' Dad often joked, to which Mum feigned shock. But they were delighted, apparently, when they'd discovered Mum was pregnant, and it was brilliant having this cheerful little kid around the place. Sandy was a giggler, so joyful and fun. Everyone adored him.

As he grew a bit older, he became quite a handful, but he was so damn cheeky and adorable, he got away with stuff that Craig and I never would have. We'd been pretty easy, by all accounts, doing our share of the chores without too much grumbling, helping with milking and lambing and the tons of other jobs people rarely think of when you mention you grew up on a farm. We fixed fencing and dry-stone walls, and filled in the pits in the half-mile of unmade lane that led from the main road to our property.

We didn't love it, but we didn't exactly hate it either; there were plenty of other farm kids at our school, and it was just what we all did. But Sandy was different. Although he loved animals he had no interest in working with them. In fact I suspected he disapproved of them being born and raised for a specific purpose – i.e. for their milk, in the case of our dairy herd, or to be sold, when it came to our lambs. I often reminded him that it was our family's livelihood, but once Sandy had made up his mind about something, that was that.

He befriended the hens, the calves and especially the dogs. They were pets to him, not workers. One year we found out he'd donated all his Christmas money to a small charity that funded animal sanctuaries (although it no longer exists, it was a sort of prototype for the charity I work for now). He was only eight years old. We were all amazed by that, as none of us kids ever had much money. Dad would sometimes despair of the way in which Sandy pampered Bramble and Kit, our collies – sneaking them kitchen scraps, encouraging them to sleep on his bed, very *un*-farmy things to do with your dogs. But Sandy got away with it.

He got away with tons of other stuff too. The one kid who mooned out the coach window on the way back from Scouts' camp? That was him. The one who nicked Dad's brandy and straddled the horse statue in our nearest village, and fell off and ended up in A&E with what he laughingly referred to as a 'riding injury'? Him again. He was a little sod really, full of backchat and cheek, and no one had ever made me laugh so much.

That afternoon at the festival drifted into a warm, heady night, and Elaine listened as I told her everything. She didn't interrupt, and nor did she argue that it hadn't been my fault: she just sat there and held my hand, and somehow, she helped me to heal, a tiny bit.

It was the first time I'd properly cried since it had happened. Elaine seemed so kind, so gentle and good.

I spent that night in her tent. Filled with a quiet confidence, she'd come to the festival alone, although she kept bumping into people she knew. We didn't have sex. We didn't even kiss properly. It was the last thing on my mind back then. Instead, she just covered me in a multi-coloured striped blanket, which smelt of dust and some kind of hippie perfume, and was oddly comforting. She held me until I fell asleep.

The festival ended, and although there'd been a shaky kind of truce with my mates, I travelled back to Glasgow with Elaine, both of us knowing we were together now. And we stayed together: me, the quiet guy who worked for a small book publisher's, and her, the free spirit who flitted from job to job, never seeming to worry about anything.

Gradually, our differences became more apparent. We moved into a tiny rented flat, where Elaine would arrange parties with two hours' warning. She'd send me out for tons of booze and 'just a few crisps, no one cares about food'. Once, after one of these errands, she laughed herself senseless when I returned home with the requested beverages and Kettle Chips, plus a large quiche.

'Who provides quiche at a party?' she hooted when the do was in full swing. Her friends gathered around it and laughed as if it were a full roast dinner. 'Hey, who wants a slice of Jack's quiche?' I fixed on a big grin and drank too quickly, in an attempt to propel myself to the level of tipsiness that everyone else seemed to have reached already. 'Jack, you're drunk already!' Elaine laughed. 'How did you manage that?'

'He can't hold his booze,' someone sniggered.

Elaine beamed at her friends. 'It's all your fault, guys, for mocking his quiche!'

This was pre-Lori, and I have to admit, life was never boring with Elaine. It was expensive, though, having the kitchen redone when she finally admitted that her gloomy green tiles gave the impression of 'living in a swamp'. It was stressful when, a year or so after Lori's arrival, Elaine accused me of 'only seeing her as a mother', to which I'd replied that of course I didn't, that was only part of who she was. 'Everything changed,' she raged at me, 'after you saw me giving birth!'

What was I supposed to have done, sat out in the hospital corridor, like the dads of yesteryear, doing the crossword until they called me in to hand me a cleaned-up, swaddled baby?

Meanwhile, we struggled on, pretending to the outside world that everything was okay between us. There were still laughs, of course, and we socialised as much as we could manage. You wouldn't believe how much mirth could be wrung out of a single quiche, but the joke went on and on. One time, at her friend Ginny's birthday party, someone actually brought one and plonked it on the top tier of a cake stand, still in its box for added comic effect.

Still, Elaine was a devoted mum, delighting in Lori's latest developments, and maybe I should have relaxed more and worried less. One night, I happened to mention that perhaps we shouldn't have such full-on gatherings at the flat anymore.

'Why not?' she asked.

'Because we have a small child,' I reminded her, 'and she keeps being woken up at night, and being all cranky in the mornings and falling asleep at nursery . . .'

'She's fine!'

'She doesn't *seem* fine.'

Elaine regarded me across the kitchen table with what I could only interpret as deep disappointment. 'You never used to be like this,' she muttered. 'You used to be fun . . .'

'I am still fun,' I countered, somewhat unfeasibly.

'Really? Are you? Because sometimes I think you forget we're still people . . .'

'Of course we're people! What else would we be?'

'And you seem to think that becoming a parent means sacrificing everything, and losing the very essence of who we are. Can't you understand that, Jack? *Can't* you?'

Charlie Gillespie understood. Charlie-bloody-Gillespie wouldn't have protested about the tile paint, or tried to sober everyone up at a party with a quiche lorraine. No, Charlie understood Elaine; he really 'got' her, apparently. He was *fun*.

And now, as I drive home from Nadia's, I try to quell a niggle of worry that I blew it today, the first time I met Nadia's son. Cathedrals and rainfall! What was I thinking? Still, there'll be plenty of chances to make a better impression, and to convince Alfie that his mother isn't going out with a twerp.

Chapter Thirteen

Nadia

I tried to wheedle out what was happening in his life, but Alfie wasn't having any of it last night. Too traumatised by the sight of me and Jack in a state of undress, probably, and of course I understand his disgust that I might enjoy anything resembling a sex life. But curiously, neither he nor Molly is remotely judgemental where their father is concerned. Danny's so cool and relaxed, so damned successful and in demand, he can do anything he likes.

After he'd been seeing Kiki for a few months, Danny introduced her to our kids. She 'seemed really nice', both Molly and Alfie reported back, when I'd casually asked for a full and detailed description, hoping for reports of terrible personal habits or appalling dress sense. But no, she was 'so nice', allegedly: friendly and pretty ('like a model,' according to Molly), with 'long, flowing, really *lovely*' reddish hair.

'Ginger?' I asked.

'More of a really nice red,' Alfie said. The four of them had gone out for a curry together, and it had all been very grown up and congenial, apparently.

'That's great!' I said, perhaps a shade too brightly.

'Dad said Kiki's curries are better,' Alfie remarked.

'Yeah, she told us she makes her own paneer,' Molly added. 'You know, that Indian cheese . . .'

'I know what paneer is, yes.'

'And she says she'll make some for us sometime.'

Wonderful! But at least Danny was happy, I conceded – and a happy Danny meant a better dad.

Of course, Alfie's first meeting with Jack wasn't such a success. I decided not to text or call Jack last night; no point in apologising again, or going over and over it. But later, just as I was getting ready for bed, he sent me a customary *Night, darling xxx* text.

Night, darling, I texted back. *See you v soon. Just need to spend a bit of time with Alfie, see what's going on, ok?*

Ok xxx, he replied.

When Alfie emerged from his room this morning, I tried again to find out the real reason he'd come home early – because there had to be one. I know something's up, by the way he is avoiding talking about Camilla, or their travel plans. All he seems fit for is lazing about in the matted oatmeal onesie my sister bought him years ago and munching dry toast (admittedly, he has spoken to me a little, if only to inform me that 'butter furs up your arteries' and ask, 'When can we get some non-dairy spread?').

I also apologised again for what happened yesterday, adding, 'Well, I'm glad you've met him anyway. He means a lot to me, Alfie. He's a lovely guy – really caring, and a great dad to his daughter. He's a hard worker too. He looks after the volunteers at his shop, like a kind of father figure to some of them—'

'Yeah, okay, Mum,' Alfie cut in, turning his attentions to the raggedy paperback he'd brought with him. And now, seemingly exhausted, he has loped off back to his room for a nap – on this bright, sunny Sunday – taking his battered old rucksack with him without unpacking it. So I can't even try to redress the good-mother balance by attending to his dirty laundry.

Pathetic though it may seem, I want to perform menial tasks for him, to prove that I'm still his sock-washing, dinner-making mum. It's terribly feeble of me, I know. However, even as I sit at the kitchen table and sketch out some ideas for a new stationery range, I keep picturing that seething mass of dirty clothing in his rucksack.

I've been asked to come up with a forest theme, incorporating various animals, birds and a tangle of branches and foliage. But the ideas just aren't coming today. It's almost impossible to focus on owls and squirrels when I'm battling an urge to tackle Alfie's mouldering laundry and hand it back to him, all fragrant and folded with a casual, 'There you go.'

I feel cheated, actually; cheated out of making his homecoming special. I'd planned to fill the fridge with delicious treats, and to scrub the flat from top to bottom (like they'd notice and compliment the absence of dust!). Instead, still feeling out of sorts, I grab my phone and message Jack: *Hey, all ok? xxx*.

To which he replies: *Good thanks, just been running, doing some house stuff. Think you need time alone with A today?*

Hmmm, I'd love to see Jack, especially as Alfie seems to have no interest in communicating with me, but then, it'd seem pretty churlish if I went out. What if my son decided he wanted to talk, and I was unavailable?

Yes, I reply, *but see you v soon. I love you x.*

I love you too x, he replies, which settles me a little. With time to myself, I try to switch my focus back to the forest wildlife theme, and by mid-afternoon, I have at least sketched out several possibilities for the notecard designs. I have also come up with a sort of plan regarding Alfie. Of course, no teenager wants to be quizzed outright by his mother, especially about 1. Feelings; 2. Relationships; and 3. Plans for the future, and I suspect that whatever is going on in his life involves all three.

Over the years, I found that a far better way to communicate was to approach a topic more in the way of a casual chat, whilst something else was going on. When their dad and I were about to break up, I mentioned it when the kids and I were pottering about in the kitchen together. Molly was painting and Alfie was making cookie dough. I made sure I was beavering away, too – topping and tailing green beans – hoping that all of this industriousness would somehow dilute the enormity of what I was about to say.

'Erm, I have something to tell you,' I started hesitantly. 'I know it's not going to be easy and I'm really sorry. But the thing is, me and your dad have decided we're going to separate . . .'

Of course they were shocked, the painting left unfinished, the cookies never baked – but it was still better, somehow, than 'sitting them down' and blurting out the terrible news to their faces.

When Molly was seventeen, and it became apparent that her 'friend' Bryce was actually her boyfriend, I broached the subject of contraception when I'd picked her up in the car from a party across town. Of course, it wasn't the first time I'd mentioned it, but now it felt

105

as if some urgent revision of the subject was needed, and if she was having sex with this boy then surely she could handle a short chat about condoms? Although I can't say she relished it, at least she couldn't run away – not from a moving car – it was less painful than me eyeballing her across the kitchen table.

And now I'm employing that tactic with Alfie too. Despite his reluctance, we are actually leaving the flat, stepping out into the bright May sunshine (he blinks on emerging, like a vole) and into my car, with the promise that we're going 'somewhere nice'.

'Where to?' Alfie asks, gazing out of the passenger window.

'Just a little place I thought you'd like.'

He exhales loudly. Of course, he's too old for a mystery trip; I'm just trying to inject a bit of fun into the occasion. Also, going out has meant that he's had to get dressed – in daytime clothes – rather than shuffling about in that onesie like someone convalescing. Although maybe he is, in a way. Naturally, I have already noted that his eyes are dull, his complexion sallow, his dark hair lank and outgrown. Twenty minutes later, having arrived at a part of town I never visit normally, we pull up at a kerbside parking space.

Alfie turns to face me. 'Arnold Clark? Are you buying a new car?'

'No,' I reply, 'we're going to Planet Earth.'

He frowns. 'But that's what we're on, Mum. We *live* on Earth.'

'I mean that Planet Earth,' I say with a smile, pointing across the road. 'It's a shop. Look. It's just opened; it's all organic and mostly vegan. Fancy a browse?'

'Yeah!' he says, perking up now as we cross the street.

Having so far been denied the pleasure of laundering his skanky underpants, I took it upon myself to speed-learn about veganism this morning. My son might have witnessed me and my boyfriend in the buff, all dignity vanished – but I can still prove that I am a proper mother, provider of nourishing fare.

We step into the cheery, light-filled store. Its walls are the orangey-yellow of a pampered hen's egg yolk.

'Whoa, this looks good,' Alfie observes approvingly.

'Yes, isn't it great?' We gaze around at the spankingly fresh vegetables and gnarly loaves. Eager sales assistants with radiant complexions are busying about, wholesome-ness radiating from their pores.

'What are we getting?' Alfie asks.

'Whatever you like.'

'Really?' He grins. 'You mean . . . anything I want?'

'Yes,' I say. 'Just go ahead and choose.' It had been a risk, hoping to delight a nineteen-year-old boy with what is essentially a trip to a food store, but so far, as we grab a basket each and he starts to browse the bottles and jars, it seems to be paying off.

Admittedly, it's pricey, but simply by being here, amongst all these glowing customers with their wicker baskets and brown paper bags, I start to feel purer inside. By the time Alfie and I browse the fresh juices, it has started to feel as if yesterday never happened. Perhaps my session with Jack on the sofa was just a figment of my fevered fifty-one-year-old mind?

'Look at all these milks,' I exclaim, gazing at various products derived from rice, soya, almond, hemp – it seems that *anything* can be made into a whitish liquid.

'Mmm, yeah.' Alfie drops a carton into his basket.

'You don't get this choice with normal milk,' I add,

hoping to convey the fact that I am wholly supportive of his dietary choices. 'It's just skimmed, semi or full fat. How boring is that? I mean, oat milk! How d'you think they milk an oat?'

He smiles briefly and moves on to the maple syrup, which is so ruinously expensive I wonder if there's been some kind of mistake. But who am I to quibble? Nope, I am *embracing* this stuff, even though a dinky bottle costs roughly the same as a small family car. Into his basket it goes, along with a slab of dark chocolate, crackers like roof tiles and a packet of sausages in an unsettling shade of grey.

I feign enthusiasm over slabs of off-white matter, their brand names giving no hint as to what they actually are. 'I suppose you can get used to this stuff,' I say cheerfully, 'and stop even *wanting* normal cheese.'

Alfie gives me the side-eye. 'Could you stop saying "normal"?'

I frown. 'What d'you mean?'

'Well,' he says as we wander onwards, 'you're implying that eating animal products is normal and choosing not to is not . . .'

'That's not what I meant at all.'

'It's your generation,' he adds loftily. 'You're the ones who still think there has to be meat on a plate for it to be a proper meal.'

'Alfie, that's so not true!' I say, trying not to laugh because, really, has he forgotten how, just a few short months ago, he and his friends used to shun hummus? 'Fart paste', they called it, backing away fearfully whenever I offered them some, as if I were about to splat it in their faces. Greasy burgers and fried chicken were more their kind of fare; until fairly recently, my son could be found chomping on some kind of animal part at least twice a day. That was before Camilla, of course – pre Alfie's reinvention as a chickpea devotee.

Now three tubs of hummus are loaded into his basket. 'I guess that's good for protein,' I remark.

'That *protein thing*,' Alfie remarks, a trace of amusement in his voice.

'What d'you mean?'

'That's what everyone says.' He rolls his eyes. '"How d'you get your protein?"'

'Well, how do you get it?'

'Protein's so over-rated . . .'

'Alfie, how can you say that?' I say, laughing. 'It's essential for building your hair, your nails, repairing your skin cells – everything really. We're *made* from it.'

'Yeah, but you're overplaying its importance,' he retorts.

Overplaying it? I only asked where he was getting it from! It's not as if I've tried to force-feed him a pork chop. But then, I'm determined for us to enjoy our time together, especially after him spying my sex-knickers lying on the living room floor. *Yep, silly old protein. Pesky amino acids. It's all about flax seeds now.*

At the checkout, I manage not to choke when the total appears on the till. Never mind, I decide, as we load our bags of produce into the boot of my car. The afternoon has brightened, and Alfie is sitting beside me, noisily wolfing some kind of savoury snacks. The mood has definitely lifted, and I glance at my boy who was once devoted to Prawn Cocktail Quavers, and is now snacking happily on shards of baked beetroot from a brown paper bag.

'I'm glad you're getting into healthy food,' I remark as we drive home.

'Yeah, it's really important, I think,' he muses, still crunching away.

I give him a quick glance, relieved that my transgression seems to have been forgiven, that he has apparently recovered from that awkward exchange with Jack yesterday. Who knows, maybe the two of them will get along after all? There's no reason why they won't. Jack's hardly allergic to young people; he's a wonderful dad to Lori, and if things are going to change slightly for a while, with Alfie and Molly being around, then maybe it's for the best. For the past few months, Jack and I have existed in a kind of blissed-out bubble. But we can't continue like that, and being a mum is a huge part of who I am. I smile, looking forward now to a few days together with both of my kids around – such a rarity these days – before Alfie sets off with his girlfriend for a thrilling summer of adventures.

Lucky bugger, being nineteen. Well, Jack and I are going away too, I reflect; a week in Barcelona awaits us. It's a city I've never been to, and of course, the 'research' thing was just an excuse. I've illustrated numerous maps before, using existing city maps as my guide, plus Google Images, with no reason to venture further than my studio.

Back home now, although it's only just gone four and I'm not especially hungry, I give Alfie free rein to make dinner for us. He is keen to show off his newly acquired vegan cheffing skills, and also 'starving', apparently. Generally, having been chief cook around here for nineteen years, I regard watching someone else engaged in food preparation as a fantastic treat. Like with Jack, for instance. The first time he invited me round for dinner, my expectations weren't high. Single guy, living mostly alone – shamefully, I'd anticipated a few random items

110

chucked into a wok. A stir-fry kind of man, I'd surmised; quite wrongly, as it turned out. As I perched on a stool in his well-ordered kitchen, I was quietly impressed as he chopped and stirred, all the while chatting away and topping up my wine glass while he knocked up an impressive prawn curry.

It was obvious, too, that he hadn't put on a show to impress me, that he wasn't trying to seduce me by way of his herb-chopping skills. You can always tell by the way a person handles themselves in the kitchen whether they are comfortable with being there. And Jack clearly was, in the way he'd made the fragrant paste, *and* cleared up after each stage; I was wildly impressed.

Watching my son cooking is a different experience. For one thing, there's no sipping of wine as he attacks a beef tomato with a serrated knife. I wouldn't dream of drinking alcohol right now, in case I am required to apply a tourniquet, or drive him to A&E.

'What are you making?' I ask.

'A Lebanese thing,' he says airily, in a tone that suggests, *You wouldn't have heard of it, Mother.* I've noticed this loftiness creeping in since Alfie started university: he's assumed a sort of 'I am the brainy one' attitude, explaining basic politics to me whenever we watch the news together, and using the phrase 'your generation' a lot, the implication being that 'we' (i.e. the old duffers) are solely responsible for Brexit, Trump, rising child poverty, the bigger gaps in Toblerone and pretty much everything else that's gone wrong with the world. Basically, I am helping to fund my son through further education so he can patronise me.

However, I am prepared to tolerate all of this because he is young, and right now I am gripped by the spectacle of him preparing a meal. For instance: who knew that a single tomato could emit so much juice? I'd almost forgotten the god-awful mess he'd make whilst baking, but it's all flooding back to me now. A puddle of tomato juice has formed on the worktop, and it's dripping slowly down a cupboard door. Meanwhile, Alfie rummages around for other ingredients and utensils. I watch him, unsettled by his haphazard approach as he opens drawers and bangs them shut, perhaps intent on breaking our kitchen, and burrows in cupboards as if he's not my son, who should be utterly familiar with our flat – having lived here from the age of two to eighteen – but a police officer searching for stolen goods.

Without wiping them first, he starts to chop our Planet Earth mushrooms, each as costly as a natural pearl, then a red pepper, green beans and a ton of other vegetables. Frankly, it's rather alarming, watching him battering away with various knives – but I'm so stunned to see him interacting with an aubergine that I can't bring myself to interfere.

'Are you sure you don't need any help?' I ask.

'No, it's all right.' He tips a jar of passata into a pan, and the chopped vegetables into another. With what feels like unnecessary clattering he manages to locate the grater in a cupboard and starts to grate a small pile of carrots vigorously, straight onto the worktop. Steeling myself, I resist the urge to warn him not to grate his fingers.

Now various packets are being torn open, with tofu sliced haphazardly and fried in a pan. A fistful of saffron is added. This had better be good. I'd estimate that the ingredients used so far have cost in the region of £675.

'Can you handle one of these?' He waggles a fat red chilli in my face as if I have never encountered one before.

'Of course I can, Alf. I'm fifty-one, not seven . . .' My

112

phone rings and I pick it up. It's Jack, who I'd love to speak to, but not right now as a minor emergency seems to have occurred.

'Hi, honey,' he starts.

'Hi—'

'My eye!' Alfie yells. 'Agh, Mum—'

'Jack, sorry, there's something happening . . .'

'Agh, my fucking eye!'

'Is everything okay?' Jack asks, sounding concerned.

'Yes, it's just . . .' I'm distracted by Alfie, who is hopping around me, left eye bloodshot and streaming.

'I have to go,' I say quickly. 'Alfie's managed to get chilli in his eye—'

'Bloody hell,' Jack mutters. 'Is he all right?'

'Yeah, I think so . . .'

'Can he slosh some water in from the cold tap?'

'Erm, I'm not sure . . .'

'No,' Jack corrects himself, 'it shouldn't be water. Tell him to get some milk . . .'

'Milk?' I repeat, more sharply than I intended.

'Yes, milk. This happened to Lori once. Tell him to get some kitchen paper or a tea towel, wet it with milk, use it as a pad to—'

'Alfie,' I cut in. 'Jack says wet a towel with milk, dab it on your—'

'*What?*' he snaps, clearly unkeen on taking advice from my boyfriend.

'Here, I'll get it . . .' Still clutching my phone, I lurch for the fridge.

'I don't have dairy,' Alfie barks.

'We can use plant milk then . . .' Christ, there'd never have been this kind of drama if he'd settled for a baked potato . . .

113

'I think it should be cow's milk,' Jack says. 'It's to do with the proteins. They neutralise the chilli oil—'

'Please stop mansplaining,' I say, regretting it instantly as Jack replies, 'Okay, sorry – I'll leave you to it.' And then he's gone.

As I tend to Alfie's eye, I start to wonder how things will pan out with my son and boyfriend. Perhaps they just need time to get to know each other when we're all relaxed and uninjured. But maybe now's not the time, with Alfie just having arrived home, with things clearly not quite right in his own life.

'That better?' I murmur.

'Yeah, a bit.'

I pour a little more oat milk onto the kitchen roll and hold it gently over the affected area.

'Thanks, Mum,' he mumbles.

'That's okay, love.' Filled with a surge of affection for him, I tell myself that everything will work out okay. After all, normal service will be restored soon. Camilla will arrive – that'll cheer him up – and off they'll trot on their European tour.

Is it wrong of me to want to know precisely *when* my son will be leaving the country?

Chapter Fourteen

Alfie's Lebanese Thing isn't too shabby at all, for a pile of variously raw and over-cooked veg, plus fried tofu, all splattered – apparently from a great height – with runny tomato sauce. Okay, if you were served it in a restaurant and had the balls to do so, you might send it back. But our son made it, so we are all tucking in enthusiastically.

Yes, *our* son. Danny showed up, with Kiki in tow, just as Alfie's eye had stopped weeping and he was able to dish up. Alfie had texted his dad to announce his arrival – which was fine, of course. But due to all the cheffy activity he had neglected to read Danny's response, which was to say that 'they' would pop right over to say hi.

'They' are parked at my kitchen table now, enthusing that the meal is 'sensational' (Danny) and 'an unusual combination of flavours and textures' (Kiki).

'It's great, Alf,' I agree, finishing up my small heap (as we've had to stretch it to feed four, there hasn't been much to go round).

'Glad to see you've learnt something in a year at uni,' Danny chuckles, scraping his plate clean.

'So it's not all Pot Noodles then,' chips in Kiki, her fine copper hair flowing around her tiny freckled face, her skin perfectly smooth and apparently pore-less. At forty-two, she is only nine years younger than me, but she could easily pass for mid-thirties.

'Haha, nah,' Alfie says good-naturedly. I know I should be pleased that he puts on a good show for his dad's girlfriend; that he has manners and welcomed her with a hug. However, given the events here over the past twenty-four hours, I can't help feeling a little short-changed.

'So, have you made plenty of friends at uni?' Kiki asks.

'Yeah, quite a few,' he replies.

'A right motley bunch from what I've seen,' Danny adds with a grin.

I blink at him. 'Who have you met, then?'

'Oh, I haven't *met* them,' he explains. 'Just seen them on Facebook.'

'Hang on,' I cut in, glancing from my son to his father. 'You mean you two are Facebook friends?'

'Yeah. So I get to see all those pictures of them out on the lash, clinging to each other, glitter all over their faces,' Danny continues, chuckling.

I realise I am staring at Danny now, across the table. Danny, whom Alfie has *friended on Facebook*. When I asked why he hadn't accepted my friend request, Alfie guffawed as if I had requested to move into his halls to keep an eye on him. Yet it would seem that his father is privy to his every antic and piss-up.

'I bet your uni mates will be friends for life,' Kiki observes as I get up to make coffee for everyone.

'Yeah, they're a good lot,' Alfie says, like a proper mature person.

'Oh to be young and free and surrounded by like-minded people.' She beams at Danny. 'Does it make you jealous, hon?'

'Seethingly,' he remarks with a smirk.

'Me too,' she says, laughing indulgently. I grit my teeth, observing my destroyed kitchen post Alfie's dinner preparation, knowing I shouldn't feel rattled by how jolly they're all being (no toe-curling debate about Aberdeen's rainfall this time!). And I despise myself even more for minding that the cooker hob is liberally sprayed with red juice and slimy bits, as if a violent crime has taken place, and that the tofu packet is lying on the floor.

'Coffee?' I say brightly, to which everyone says yes, but rather distractedly, as they are engaged in a proper conversation about Kiki's job.

'Are you working a lot?' Alfie asks.

'Oh God, yeah – too much,' she says with a self-deprecating chuckle.

'Well, that's good,' my son remarks, actually taking an interest in the life of an adult. The working life, even. The *career*. When I landed a commission to illustrate a prestigious series of travel guides, he merely enquired, 'How much are you getting for that, then?'

As I hand out coffees, which are barely registered amongst the congenial chatter, I reflect for about the billionth time how attractive Kiki is. Granted, it's a handy quality to have when you're a 'skincare guru' (that's what her website says; I think it's a posh term for a beauty therapist). Maybe that's something else I could try, as a sideline, given my success as a moisturiser pusher at Lush. However, unlike Kiki, who has the glowy freshness of the child-free, I doubt if I'd replicate her success.

She and Danny have been together for six years, and

he seems to be a totally different kind of partner to her than he was with me. Although he was always a kind, sweet dad – brilliant at reading bedtime stories, with all the funny voices – he was pretty useless on the practical side. It sounds a little pathetic now, but I stopped asking him to pick up milk or bread when he was out; when I had, he'd come back with a packet of cigs and a newspaper ('Sorry, love – I forgot'). And he'd have died if I'd ever suggested having a dinner party. Yet he and Kiki seem to 'entertain' regularly; she has him charging all over town, not just for forgotten essentials (potatoes, tonic water) but more exotic ingredients such as sorrel and blackstrap molasses. If I'd asked him for blackstrap molasses he'd have sniggered that he didn't have time to find a sex shop. Although I don't envy Kiki – I mean, why would I covet her taut stomach and toned thighs? – it still galls me slightly that Danny has morphed into being Mr Perfect with her. But then, Danny and Kiki have only existed as a couple unencumbered by small people and their endless demands. Perhaps that's why Alfie and Molly accepted her so readily (not that they *shouldn't*, of course): she has never been a tired, grouchy mum.

'So, how's your work going, Nadia?' Kiki asks, turning to me now.

'Really well, thanks,' I reply. 'I've been asked to do a series of maps for—'

'Oh, you work so hard,' she interrupts. 'I don't know how you've done it, fitting it in around the family all these years . . .'

'You just get on with it, I suppose,' I remark.

Kiki smiles. 'You look a bit stressed, if you don't mind me saying.'

'Do I?' I say lightly. 'Oh, I'm not really. Just, you know, busy . . . but I have a trip coming up.' I look at Alfie. 'I've booked a week away in Barcelona with Jack, love.'

'Oh, that's good,' he says distractedly.

'You and Jack are going away?' Danny asks, finding this amusing for some reason – but of course, I have only holidayed with my female friends, plus Gus, in all the years since we broke up. It's unheard of for me to have a boyfriend to go away with.

'Just for a week,' I say, wondering now what possessed me to tell Alfie when Danny and Kiki are here. I look around the table. Alfie shuffles in his chair and pushes back his unkempt dark hair.

'You okay, darling?' I ask, at which he nods.

'Yeah, I'm fine.' A silence descends. Surely he's not upset by the thought of me and Jack having a few days away?

'Alf?' Danny prompts him. 'What's up?'

Alfie looks down and picks at his nails. 'Nothing.'

'What is it, love?' I ask with a frown. He looks around at us, mouth pressed tightly shut. My heart seems to have speeded up alarmingly. It can't be anything major, I re-assure myself, or he'd tell me – and his dad – in private. He wouldn't come out with it with Kiki sitting here, gazing at him—

'You're going away this summer, aren't you, Alfie?' Kiki asks pleasantly. 'Your dad mentioned . . .'

'Actually, I'm not,' Alfie blurts out.

'Why not?' I exclaim.

'Um . . . plans have sort of changed.'

'But . . . why?'

He shrugs, as if it's nothing. 'I'm just not going, okay?' I stare at him, uncomprehending. He's looked forward to it for months, grafting away in a shabby club which, as far as I've been able to make out, has mostly involved him being accused of pouring short measures and mopping up vomit. He has planned his itinerary: an extensive tour of Paris, Berlin, Prague, plus numerous other teen-pleasing cities . . . it's been a *huge* deal to him.

'Mum, I don't really want to go into all the reasons, okay?' he mumbles.

'You've just decided it's not what you want to do,' Kiki observes, which only serves to rile me again: what's wrong with me today? I breathe deeply and look at his dad.

'Well, that'll save us a packet,' Danny observes.

'He was paying for it himself,' I remind him. 'That's why you've been working in that club, isn't it, Alf?'

'Yeah, on top of all the hand-outs you give him.' Danny rolls his eyes. 'So, Alf, I'm guessing you're not going because—'

'It's just stuff, Dad,' he says curtly.

Danny nods. 'Is it all over with the posh bird, then?'

Another pause as Alfie studies his hands. 'Sort of, yeah.'

'Oh, Alfie.' I reach across the table to squeeze his arm, but he pulls away. 'I am sorry, love,' I murmur.

'It's all right.' He picks up his mug and takes a noisy slurp of coffee. 'So, anyway, I've sold my Inter-Rail ticket . . .'

'Can you do that?'

'Well, yeah. I have!'

I catch Danny glancing at Kiki, and then back to our son. 'Seems like your mind's made up, then,' he remarks, as if it's no big deal at all. 'So, what're you doing this summer? Not planning to lie about scratching your arse, I hope?'

Kiki chuckles, and I sense my jaw tensing as my back

120

teeth clamp together. Why is she parked at my table, sitting in on this family discussion? And why couldn't Alfie have explained all of this as soon as he came home? He tells me precisely nothing – apart from the fact that I 'overplay the importance of protein'.

'I'll get a job in Glasgow,' he says with a shrug.

'Okay, Alf,' I mutter, figuring that perhaps Molly's friend's dad might have something at the garden centre for him too? It'll all work out, I try to reassure myself. His sister is planning to be here pretty much all summer anyway, and if it turns out that Alfie is too, well that's fine; he can get to know Jack properly, they can have jovial conversations about Pot Noodles, maybe even become Facebook friends . . .

'The other thing is,' Alfie starts, 'I've decided I'm not going back to uni after the summer.'

I stare at him. We all do – even Kiki – as if waiting for him to burst into laughter: *Haha, only kidding. That got you all started, didn't it?*

'What?' is all I can say.

Alfie gets up and proceeds to tidy up the mess he made whilst cooking. If he was doing it just to be helpful – and not just as a diversionary tactic – it would be nothing short of miraculous. But right now, I couldn't give a stuff about the state of the kitchen.

'I'm quitting,' he says, gathering up all the vegetable matter into a tidy pile.

'You're not serious, are you?' I ask weakly.

He picks up the tofu packet from the floor and grabs a sponge wipe from the sink. 'Yeah, I am.'

'Are you sure about this?' Danny frowns.

'Yes, Dad, I'm sure.' He starts to mop up the puddle of tomato juice.

'Alfie, you don't need to do that,' I start to protest.

'I'm just clearing up—'

'I don't mean that! I mean quitting uni. I know you've been stressed without exams, but don't make any rash decisions without taking the time to think it through—'

'It's not rash,' he interrupts. 'I've been thinking about it really carefully.' He squeezes out the sponge at the sink.

'Well, Christ, if you've decided,' Danny says, shaking his head. I shoot him a sharp look.

'Alf, please,' I say firmly. 'If this is because of Camilla, because you're upset—'

'It's not that.' He bends to wipe a dribble of juice from the cupboard door.

'But I thought you were enjoying it?'

'I'm not,' he says sharply. 'I'm not enjoying it at all.'

'I thought you loved English Lit!' I exclaim.

He straightens up, turning his attentions now to the splattered cooker hob. 'I don't love it, Mum. I mean, who does, really? I chose it 'cause it's something I'm reasonably okay at . . .'

'You're very good at it, Alf. You know you are!' I look at Danny, willing him to back me up here, but he is merely gazing at our son, as if Alfie has mooted the possibility of opting for a slightly different kind of haircut. 'Alfie, could you please stop cleaning the cooker and just sit down and talk to us?' I say sharply.

He frowns. 'You're always telling me to clear up my mess.'

'Yes, but not now, when you're telling us something really important . . .'

He stares at me, then looks at his father and Kiki as if to say, *See what she's like? See what I have to put up with, with a mother like this?* Rather dramatically, he

122

flings the sponge into the sink, rubs his hands on the front of his jeans and sits back down.

'Okay, son, so what's going on?' Danny asks.

'Yes, tell us what's on your mind, love,' Kiki offers, even though this is nothing whatsoever to do with her.

Alfie fiddles with his coffee mug. 'I suppose it's just not what I thought it'd be. The whole academic thing, I mean.'

'Could you think about changing courses?' I ask. 'Or maybe take a year out, do something different, then see how you feel after a—'

'It's just not what I want, Mum,' he says.

Silence falls. 'Are you homesick, honey?' Kiki asks, tipping her head to one side.

'No!' he exclaims, as if that's a crazy suggestion. 'No, I'm never homesick . . .'

'And you've definitely made up your mind?' Danny asks.

Alfie nods. 'Yeah, Dad, I have.'

I rub at my face, not getting it at all. 'Couldn't you have said something to me, if this is how you've been feeling? We could have talked it over, Alf.' *Why won't you ever talk to me?* is what I mean.

He shrugs. I feel utterly desolate, not because he wants to leave university – Christ, I know it's not for everyone, and anything Alfie wanted to do would have been fine by me. Maybe he could become a tradesman. His cousin Ollie is a kitchen fitter, and Scott is an electrician. Both are such grafters, and making real lives for themselves. All I want is for Alfie to be happy.

'So, what're you going to do now?' Danny asks.

'Get a job, like I said,' he replies, as if it's that simple. 'And what about all your stuff, if you're planning not

123

to go back? I thought Camilla's dad was going to pick it up for you?' I try to make eye contact, to get a grip on what he's feeling, but his gaze remains focused on his lap.

'Jez is going to store it for me. We can pick it up from him sometime . . .' He means one of his mates from his student halls.

'I thought you, Jez and Ned were all set to share a flat?'

Danny looks rather blank at this. He never seems to remember any of Alfie's friends' names.

'Well, that won't happen now,' Alfie murmurs. 'Someone else'll take my room. That won't be a problem . . .' He rubs at an eye, and for a moment I think he's going to cry.

'Oh, son,' Danny says, reaching out to squeeze his arm, at which Alfie manages to muster a faint smile.

'It's all right, Dad. Really, it's the right decision . . .'

'Good for you,' Kiki cuts in. 'I think it's very brave, following your heart instead of what's expected—'

'Kiki, if you don't mind,' I cut in.

'I mean, *I* never went to university,' she announces, 'and I've managed to scrape my way through life.'

'Neither did I,' Danny concedes with a shrug.

'Yeah,' Alfie exclaims, turning to me. 'Look at Dad, how successful he is, how he made his whole career out of, well, *nothing* . . .'

'Cheers, Alf,' Danny says with an infuriating chuckle.

'Yes, I know,' I bluster, 'but that's different.'

'D'you think it would've made any difference to Dad if he'd got, I dunno, a history degree or something?' Alfie asks with a raised brow.

'Probably not,' I start, sensing my cheeks flaming now as I will Danny to chip in with something useful.

'I've always believed that life experience is more valuable than qualifications,' Kiki cuts in, smoothing back her sleek hair. *Yes, but that's because you stroke people's faces and encourage them to buy creams!*

Incensed now, I sip my tepid coffee in silence, aware of my son studying me.

'Mum, you're the only one here who went to uni,' Alfie observes, although I don't quite know what he's implying.

'It was art college actually,' I remind him.

'Yeah, well, that's pretty much the same thing,' he says gruffly.

I can sense my eyes prickling as a silence descends. Never mind that I've managed to rake in enough work to contribute significantly to our family for nineteen years. The implication is clearly: *And look at all the good that did you.*

Ridiculously, as Alfie falls into a chat with his father and Kiki about possible work options, I start to feel tearful and ganged up on. I even pretended to enjoy the Lebanese thing, for crying out loud. I allowed Alfie to choose crackers that were £8.50 – and *there were only five in the box!*

Danny stands up, followed by Kiki. 'Well, I guess we'd better be going,' he says lightly. 'We've got a thing to go to—'

'What kind of thing?' I ask, not really caring.

'Just a boring old industry event,' he says with a sigh.

'Yeah.' Kiki beams at my son. 'We'd better dash off. Great to see you, Alfie. Let's get together really soon . . .'

'That'd be nice,' he says, hugging each of them in turn. 'You'll see me a lot over the summer, now that I'm back home for good.'

'Fantastic!' She beams, turning to me as she and Danny

make for the door. 'Great to see you too, Nadia. But you *are* looking stressed. Please try and take care of yourself, because if you don't, no one will!' And with that, she grabs Danny's hand and off they scoot, as if Alfie's shock announcement hadn't happened, and I'm being ridiculous for worrying about anything at all.

Chapter Fifteen

Jack

After our hasty phone call on Sunday with the chilli incident, I decided it was best not to call Nadia back. So I just texted: *Hope all ok with chilli/eye,* and she replied, *All fine, sorry I snapped at you. Bit stressed.* Then she called to tell me, in murmured tones, about Danny and his girlfriend turning up, and Alfie announcing that he wasn't going travelling or – more importantly – returning to uni after the summer.

'Maybe he'll change his mind?' I suggested.

'Um, I don't know. He seemed pretty certain. I can't believe he's throwing away this chance, Jack. He won't even consider changing courses, or taking a year out . . .'

I wasn't sure what to say to that. Anything I could think of – like: 'I'm sure it'll work out' – would have sounded so trite, so I added, 'Maybe it's good that he's home now and you can talk it over . . .'

'He won't talk to *me*,' she lamented.

I hesitated. 'Well, look, I'd love to see you, but no pressure. I know you'll probably want to be around for him . . .'

'Can we play it by ear?' she asked, and naturally I said that was fine. I've grown used to us spending as much time as possible together; in fact, I see Nadia most days when Lori's not with me. But this is a temporary thing, and it's only right that she's there for her son. 'I didn't mean what I said,' she added, 'about you mansplaining.'

'Oh, I probably was.'

'You were only trying to help . . .'

I couldn't help smiling at that. 'It's just, the proteins in milk help to neutralise the—'

'Jack,' she cut in, and I knew she was smiling too, 'protein's a sensitive issue around here.'

'Why's that?'

She chuckled. 'I overplay its importance, apparently.'

And now it's Monday morning, and my working day has kicked off with a call from Dinah, the area manager. 'So, what we're doing,' she announces in her strident tone, 'is asking all of the managers to source a high-value item, so we can put it on social media and email out a press release, drum up some publicity to our cause. What d'you think, Jack?'

'Sounds good,' I reply, aware of a heated discussion between one of our volunteers and a middle-aged woman who drops off donations from time to time. The woman's wispy hair has been dyed an odd shade of burgundy with, I have to say, limited success.

'But I need the trousers back,' she says, looking quite distressed.

'They must have been sold,' Mags says plainly. Like Iain, she assumes a superior role around here.

'Are you sure? Might they still be in the back room?'

'Well, *I* don't know, do I? Once you've handed stuff in, that's that . . .'

'Jack?' Dinah says sharply.

'Er, yes, I'm right here . . .'

She exhales. Despite working in the charity sector, Dinah tends to behave as if she is CEO of a global bank. 'The idea is, we'll auction off these items at a special event. You know how competitive things are these days. Everyone's being badgered to donate left right and centre, and the bigger charities have enormous support, all the high-profile backers—'

Mags waves to attract my attention, and I mouth *just-give-me-a-minute*. 'Yep, no problem,' I say. 'So, how will we get these high-value items?'

'Well, they'll be donated,' Dinah states, as if it's obvious.

'Right . . .' I glance down at a box of assorted bits that's just been brought in. Amongst what looks like mainly crockery, I spot a box of 'strong and hygienic' paper knickers and a knitted Womble.

'But we can't just sit back and wait,' she goes on. 'We have to approach people who have clout and influence – be *proactive*. D'you hear what I'm saying?'

Yes, loud and clear. She doesn't seem to realise that you can speak at a perfectly normal volume whilst on the phone. 'Okay, but who d'you have in mind . . .'

'Celebrities!' she announces. 'It all started with Jessie at the Edinburgh shop. She's a right little terrier, that one.'

'Really? I haven't met her yet . . .'

'Oh my God, the balls on her,' Dinah raves on. 'Fired off something like two hundred emails to various agents and publicists . . .'

My attention wavers. The customer is still haranguing Mags about the trousers. 'Could I call you back, Dinah? I just need to—'

'Jack, can I count on you to get on board with this?'

she asks. 'This is what we need to focus on now – boosting publicity. Making a big splash. Something like this will send our profile through the roof.' I glance up at our mottled polystyrene ceiling tiles. 'So,' she adds, 'Jessie's managed to make contact with Miranda Ford . . .'

I try to summon up an appropriately enthusiastic response, when in fact I haven't the faintest idea who she is.

'Miranda Ford!' Dinah reiterates. 'C'mon, Jack. You must have heard of her.'

'Um, the name rings a bell,' I fib.

'She won best newcomer at the soap awards last year?'

'I don't really follow the soaps, Dinah . . .'

'What, none of them?'

'Well, er, I remember *EastEnders* in the Den and Angie years . . .'

'Oh, get you,' Dinah says, laughing now, possibly in despair at my ignorance. 'Too low-brow for you, are they? She's in that Mackie's potato waffles advert as well. You must've seen that . . .'

'I think I might have.' Another lie.

'Yeah, well, she's the face of Mackie's Waffles and she's hot as anything right now, and Jessie's persuaded her to donate some gloves . . .'

'What kind of gloves?' I ask.

'Uh, well, technically they're mittens – just ordinary ones, dark brown sheepskin . . .'

'Amazing,' I say as Mags jabs me sharply on the arm.

'Jack,' she mutters, 'this lady says she brought in some trousers, dark blue bobbly material. D'you remember seeing them?'

'Sorry, no.' I shake my head distractedly.

'So you need to match that,' Dinah announces. 'I've

130

got all the managers onto it. We're after celebrity-owned items, okay?'

'Er, right!' Hmm, now which of my many celeb buddies should I contact first?

'Great. I know I can rely on you, Jack. Make sure it's something *really* special . . .'

'George Clooney's underpants?' I say dryly.

'If you can get hold of those, that'd be great.'

'Maybe I'll just break into his house and steal them?' She laughs. 'Dedication – that's what I like to see. Anyway, I can tell you're busy, Jack. Good luck!'

Call finished, I turn to the woman who's been haranguing Mags, alarmed to see that her light grey eyes are wet with tears. 'Can you talk to me now?' she asks gruffly.

'Yes, of course. What's the problem?'

Her mouth is trembling as she fills me in on the situation: 'I'm sure my wedding ring was in the pocket of those trousers. I've looked everywhere else.'

Who would put their wedding ring in a trouser pocket?

Of course, I don't say that. I just express concern and promise to keep a lookout for it.

'Is there any way of tracing who's bought things?' she asks.

'Not unless we know the customer personally. I'm sorry.' I smile my thanks as Iain emerges from the back room and hands me a chipped mug of Nescafé.

'Can you ask all your customers if they've seen it?' the woman wants to know. Her face is heavily crinkled, like the crepe paper Lori used to use for making flowers to stick on her bedroom wall.

'I will,' I assure her, 'and I'll put up a note on the wall too. Could I take your name and number, in case it turns up?'

She nods, tight-lipped, as I grab paper and a pen. 'Jean Cuthbertson . . .' She breathes over me as I write down her number. 'If someone's found it, they're just going to keep it, aren't they?' she remarks.

'Not necessarily. I mean, what would you do, if you found something in a pocket?'

'Return it, of course,' she says crossly.

'Well, I think most people would do that too.'

'Oh, I don't think so,' she retorts. 'Not these days . . .'

'Let's just see, shall we?' I say, trying to convey optimism. 'Let's hope for the best.' And off she goes, still seemingly upset and disgruntled, as if the loss of her wedding ring is somehow *our* fault.

There's still no joy on the ring front next day, despite us all searching high and low for the trousers. I also gather from Nadia during our quick catch-up at lunchtime that things are still tricky at home. 'Are you working just now?' I ask.

'Trying to,' she murmurs.

'Am I interrupting you?'

'No,' she says quickly. 'Not at all.'

'Are you at the studio?'

'No, I'm at home. I'm working at the dining table. Hang on . . .' There's a pause, and I gather that she's gone to another room. 'Alfie's here,' she says.

'Right. So . . . how's he doing?'

'Hmm.' I hear her inhale. 'Let's just say he's taken to cooking in a *big* way . . .'

'Well, that's good, isn't it?'

She laughs dryly. 'I s'pose so, but his methods are a bit . . . chaotic. It's kind of hard to concentrate on work when he's blitzing things in the blender and the lid shoots off . . .'

'Oh, God.' I pause. 'Any news on the . . . you know. The uni situation?'

'Nope. That's why I'm here, instead of at the studio, in case he decides he's ready to talk things over . . .'

'But you need to work,' I point out.

'Yes, I know,' she says, rather tetchily. 'Oh, I'm sorry, Jack. You know how it is just now.'

'Of course I do. Don't worry.'

'I'd love to see you but I feel like I need to be here for him at the moment.'

'Yeah, I know. That's fine. I really do understand . . .'

'What're you up to this evening?' she asks.

'I thought I'd see Fergus and the lads,' I reply.

'Oh, that'll be nice. Have fun.'

Things feel a little different, I reflect, as we finish the call still with no definite plan to meet. But naturally Alfie has to take priority and, if I'm starting to feel a little uneasy, then I really should grow up.

The shop is busy enough for the afternoon to fly by, and soon I'm installed in the pool club with Fergus, Tam and Paul. It's hard to get everyone together these days. Fergus still lives locally – he manages a restaurant – but Tam lives in Liverpool, and Paul's high-flying job as a geologist involves him spending chunks of the year in the Far East.

'So how's the big love thing going?' Tam asks, chalking up his cue at the pool table.

I smile. Neither he nor Paul have met Nadia yet. 'Pretty good.'

'You keep posting pictures of the two of you on Facebook,' he adds with a smirk.

'Yeah, well,' I retort, 'what d'you want me to post? Photos of me sitting at home, staring at a radiator?'

Fergus laughs. 'Tam's just jealous.'

'You've met her, right?' Tam remarks.

'Yeah.' Fergus nods. 'She's lovely. He's punching well above his weight.'

My phone starts trilling, and I snatch it from my pocket, aware of a twinge of disappointment that it isn't Nadia.

'Hi, Elaine,' I say, wandering over towards a quieter corner.

'Hey, where are you?' she asks.

'At the pool club . . .'

'Ew, that dingy dive,' she teases, although she's never been here. I can tell immediately that she's a bit pissed, but I know there's no point in commenting on the fact. She'd only accuse me of being sanctimonious. 'Surely that's not where you take Nadia?' she remarks in a sarky tone.

'No, I'm with Tam, Paul and Fergus,' I reply, refusing to rise to the bait.

'Aw, the old gang, all together. That's sweet!'

'Hmmm. Yeah. So, uh, is everything okay?' Elaine and I never just call each other for matey chats.

'Er, yeah. Could Lori head straight over to you after school tomorrow, instead of on Thursday? Something's come up . . .'

'That's fine,' I reply, and it is. We have our regular weekly pattern, but it's never set in stone. 'Doing anything nice?' I ask, curious now.

'Erm, well, I've sort of started seeing someone . . .'

'Oh, that's good . . .'

She laughs. 'Yeah. Well, it's early days, he hasn't met Lori yet, but it's his birthday tomorrow and we're both pretty broke. I thought he could come over here, we'll order in a take-away . . .'

134

'Sounds great,' I say, keen to get off the phone now.

'Thanks, Jack. You're a star. Speak soon—'

'Elaine?' I cut in.

'Yeah?'

'Is Lori there?'

'Oh, yeah, but she's in her room – homework, I think. Better not disturb the creative flow . . .' She chuckles.

'Okay,' I murmur, thinking: that's pretty unlikely. The homework element, I mean. I am aware that quite often Lori doesn't get around to doing it, and that Elaine probably wouldn't have a clue either way. A short while later, after the lads and I said our goodbyes outside the club, I text Lori.

Hope all's good? Mum says you're coming tomorrow. All ok? Naturally what I really want to ask is: *How drunk is Mum?* It's a Tuesday night, after all – not that the day of the week is that significant as Elaine isn't working.

All fine, Lori replies, and I'm loath to pester her further. Instead, I make my way to the subway just before ten, thinking how sensible we've become – Tam, Paul, Fergus and me. 'Work tomorrow,' Paul announced, and I resisted the urge to suggest one more round.

And I have the audacity to worry about Elaine's drinking?

I emerge from the subway, almost home now, and stop to check my phone again. *Miss you,* Nadia has texted. *I know you're out tonight but feel free to come over and stay if you like. Doesn't matter if it's late. I'm sitting here working but thinking about you.*

I smile and call her as I walk. 'Hey, that was sweet of you, to send that.'

'Just missing you,' she says. 'Are you still out?'

135

'Almost home actually.'

'Well, if you fancy coming over . . .'

Hmm, the prospect of being alone in my chilly bed, or curling up with Nadia in hers? Tough choice . . . 'What about Alfie?' I ask. 'Is he home?'

'Yes, he's here,' she replies lightly, 'but he'll need to get used to us being together, won't he? It's fine, Jack, honestly. No one expects me to live like a nun.'

Chapter Sixteen

Is it awful of me to hope Alfie will be tucked up in bed, like a nine-year-old, by the time I arrive? Of course he isn't. He's stretched out on the sofa with various devices close to hand: phone, iPad, laptop. But at least he says hi, and sort-of smiles, as I breeze in.

'Hi, Alfie,' I say, with a big, relaxed grin, wondering now if my affected casualness has caused me to swagger, like a cowboy entering a saloon. Aware of Alfie returning his attentions to his gadgetry, I perch on one of Nadia's rather hard, unyielding chairs that forces me to sit unnaturally upright. Sure, I'm relaxed enough around here to take a seat, without prior invitation – but I'm not quite brave enough to sit next to him yet.

'Like a beer, Jack?' Nadia asks, having given me a chaste kiss on the cheek.

'Better not, I've had *loads* tonight.' I smile tightly, realising that sounds as if I'm inebriated, and wondering whether Alfie will assume I make a habit of this: going out on the piss with my mates, then bowling up here to shag his mother.

'So, how was everyone?' Nadia asks, squishing next to Alfie on the sofa (this requires him to edge up – grudgingly – to make space for her). Still, at least the TV is on, helping to defuse the awkwardness as I regale her with thrilling tales of my friends' recent adventures: Paul's plane home from Hong Kong being diverted due to a passenger brawl and, less thrillingly, Tam's camping trip to Arran, and Fergus's badminton injury.

On and on I prattle, thinking how lovely Nadia looks in her lounge-type outfit (could you even call black leggings and a snugly fitting vest top an outfit?). Anyway, she looks gorgeous, and I'm wondering now when I can stop wittering on about my friends' lives and we can just go to bed.

Alfie glances up again. As well as poking at his devices he seems to be at least partially watching TV. It's a panel show featuring one of those angry chefs – Kevin-someone – who's primarily known for his own programme, where contestants are given a limited budget and three hours to prepare a dinner party for ten. I only know it because Lori enjoys it. He shouts, he mocks his contestants' dishes and frequently reduces them to tears. But now, the panel show reveals that he has the wit of a sloth.

As my conversation with Nadia stalls, I glance at Alfie, knowing that I should at least try to talk to him – to show him I'm perfectly capable of communicating with a nineteen-year-old boy. The situation starts to feel especially urgent when Nadia gets up and wanders off to the kitchen, having persuaded me that I'd like tea, but possibly for some respite from my ramblings about Fergus's groin strain. But what should I talk about? As Alfie's gaze flicks between TV, laptop, iPad and phone – it's admirable, his ability to multi-view – I run through a mental list of things to *not* mention, such as:

1. Religious architecture of any kind.
2. Rainfall in Aberdeen.
3. His academic course.
4. In fact, anything Aberdeen-related given his recent announcement that he's not going back.
5. Politics (too risky).
6. Anything to do with my own life, as why should Alfie be interested? He hasn't chosen to spend time with me. From his perspective I've just been foisted upon him, out of the blue.

So what does that leave? *What kind of music d'you like, Alfie?* I can imagine the withering look that would trigger. Or: *Heard any good jokes?* No – people of his age don't tell jokes (are jokes becoming obsolete?) and I'm not about to tell him one of mine, not even the one about the guy answering the door in his pyjamas (handy place for a door, haha!).

I'm contemplating whether to broach the topic of veganism – in an all-ears, tell-me-all-about-it sort of way, as if I might be considering veering down that route – or suggesting I 'give Nadia a hand with the tea'. But then, he'd know I was fleeing, and I don't want him to sense my fear.

'So, any plans for this week?' I ask, blandly.

'Not really,' Alfie replies.

Silence. 'Nice to be back in Glasgow?'

Alfie nods. 'Yeah, I s'pose it is.'

I nod too, as if contemplating what he's said. 'Bet it is.'

Understandably, Alfie doesn't bother responding to this. I'm tempted to add, *Bet it's great being looked after*, but this might imply ineptitude, and that his mother's role is that of a serf. Instead, I run my tongue over my teeth, willing Nadia to reappear – not to rescue me, no, but to rejoin the happy throng here.

Finally she comes back, looking a little stressed around the eyes and brandishing three mugs, which she sets on the coffee table.

'Thanks!' I beam at her.

'That's okay.' Her smile tenses as she settles back down next to Alfie, and we find ourselves discussing the TV programme half-heartedly. At least Alfie is actually conversing now, and who knows, I think, my patience fraying a little now, a few more nights like this, and perhaps the three of us will be booking a holiday together (Heaven fucking forbid!). At least Nadia and I are going away, I remind myself. It's still a few weeks away, by which point things are bound to be more relaxed with her son.

'I'm shattered,' Nadia announces finally, looking at me. 'Shall we get some sleep?'

She yawns ostentatiously, which sets me off too. Look at the two of us, yawning away, clearly exhausted and going to bed for a good night's sleep, and nothing else! Nadia stands up and stretches, rotating her shoulders in a way I've never seen her do before, and I get up from the rigid chair and say goodnight to Alfie.

'Night,' he mutters, eyes glued to the TV.

'Turn the TV off when you're done, love,' Nadia murmurs.

''Course I will.'

'Well, you didn't last night . . .'

'Didn't I?' He affects the look of the wrongly accused, and she laughs indulgently as she makes for the door. Affecting a shambling walk now, as if I'm looking forward to nothing more enticing than assembling a flat-pack bedside table, I follow Nadia out of the living room.

Of course, once we're in bed, sex isn't an option, not with her son in the flat. To even contemplate it would be ridiculous, and to actually *do it* – or even to engage in any kind of foreplay – would be far too risky to even think about.

So I lie there, thinking about it, as Nadia curls up by my side.

The trouble is, she is naked: beautifully, perfectly naked, her soft, warm body next to mine. So of course I can't just lie there and think about going to sleep, or the fact that my kettle is broken – I need to order a new one – or indeed any other pressing domestic issues. Numerous scientific studies have proved that it's impossible for your average straight male to contemplate housekeeping matters in such a situation. Add the fact that Nadia is the most desirable person I have ever been to bed with since – well, ever – and I find myself taking her in my arms, and kissing her, and of course things start to happen.

'Just relax,' she whispers, sensing my slight hesitation. I try to, in the way that I tried to 'relax' as instructed just before my dentist hoiked out one of my molars, with pliers. But it's impossible. Never before has our sex life required some kind of risk assessment, but now it must. Her bed is rather creaky, I know this from numerous previous occasions, and we've laughed about the fact that some of those rivets could probably do with tightening up. I also know what teenagers are like, feigning deafness whenever you ask them to wash up, for instance – but with hearing as keen as a whippet's whenever the situation requires it.

We are kissing again now, and naturally, I want to *do*

things. I can feel her heartbeat against mine, and sense her quickening breath. But we mustn't do it, because things have got off on a shaky enough start with Alfie and I don't want to make things worse. And now I'm remembering the time I took Lori on a 'bat watch' at a wooded nature reserve, and the ranger led us to a clearing, armed with a sonic device that could pick up the tiniest sounds the bats made, which were inaudible to the human ear.

Could Alfie have installed such a device in here?

'Jack,' Nadia whispers again, 'you seem so tense.'

'I'm fine,' I fib as she starts to stroke my inner thigh.

'Worried about Alfie?' She casts a glance in the direction of her bedroom door.

'It's just . . .' I wince. Her hand is slowly working its way upwards and I'm finding it extremely difficult to be articulate.

'It's okay,' she says. 'He's still watching TV . . .'

'Yeah, I know . . .' But didn't she imply that he's prone to leaving it on when he's gone to bed? I'm aware that his bedroom is just across the hallway, and although I haven't been aware of any footsteps out there, he could be *prowling*.

We lie side by side in silence for a few moments. 'Remember the bathroom's between us and the living room,' Nadia adds.

'Yes, I know.' She rests her head on my chest, and then she starts kissing my neck and my chest and my stomach, and I am powerless to stop her as I lie there, my head swirling from her loving attentions. Now she's sort of nuzzling at my ear, and it's wonderful . . . She stops and looks at me, smiling as she pulls me close.

'Come here, you.'

Just three little words, but their effect is something like the starting gun at the Grand National. We are on each other, and a few moments later my head is spinning to that place she takes me to, where I can't think about anything but how good she feels – how *it* feels with her. We're actually doing it now – albeit quietly but, Christ, I'd never realised near-silent sex could be so, well, erotic, possibly even more than the noisy kind, because—

Bang!

Nadia and I leap apart. It was only the bathroom door shutting, but I'm aware now that Alfie is closer; my mind seems to have turned into a radar device, capable of tracking his movements as if he's an enemy battleship. We start kissing again, but it's impossible to get back into that zone. Every sound Alfie makes seems terribly amplified: the flush of the loo, some ostentatious coughing, the sound of a tap being turned on at full force. I can actually hear him washing himself now, the slapping of hands on wet skin. It sounds almost . . . violent. Perhaps he's trying to knock himself out, in order to escape the horror of what he's imagining is going on in here?

And now, as we continue to kiss and touch, I am aware of the battleship exiting the waters of the bathroom and into the otherwise serene straits of the hallway.

Brrrrrr! A shrill whirring sound seems to fill the flat. 'What's he doing now?' I hiss. 'Drilling for oil?'

She pulls away and sits up, stifling a laugh with her hand. 'Oh, God. I am sorry.'

'What is it?' My mind is actually boggling.

'It's his electric toothbrush.'

'Are they usually that loud?'

'His is,' she whispers, grimacing.

'He cleans his teeth in the hallway?'

143

Nadia nods, clearly finding the situation hysterical. 'He likes to pace about.'

'But . . . why?'

She shrugs. 'Exercise?'

I splutter, and we hold each other, trying not to laugh and gradually building to silent hysteria – she is actually *crying* with laughter – at the sound of the whirring and pacing. God, 1 love this woman. But needless to say, neither of us gets any more exercise that night. And next morning, when I find her son clad in a fleecy onesie, guarding the kitchen like a malevolent bear, the whole Alfie-back-home issue doesn't feel quite so funny after all.

Chapter Seventeen

Nadia

There's nothing like a homecoming adult child to throw a spanner into the workings of your love life – but what can I do? Of course Alfie doesn't require me to be here constantly, tending to his needs. However, I also know that Lori is at Jack's from this evening – Wednesday – probably until the end of the weekend. I could stay at his place when she's there; Jack has always said there's no reason why I can't. But so far I haven't, as I know he values their time together. I'm also aware that he's concerned about his ex's situation (specifically, Elaine's tendency to sound as if she's had a few whenever they speak on the phone), and apparently she has a new man on the scene. So perhaps a few days apart will give us the chance to focus on our own lives?

Anyway, I'm due to pick up Molly from Edinburgh on Friday, and once she's home, I'm hopeful that her presence will defuse things. Naturally, I have tried to talk to Alfie some more, and reassure him that his dad and I will support him whatever he decides to do. But still, he has to make the *right* decision (i.e. the one I want him to make!). He's a bright boy, and he really wanted to go to uni; I hate to see him wasting an opportunity like this.

Eventually, I've had to leave Alfie alone to his moochings, and focus on my work. I've managed to finish the woodland illustrations, plus an illustrated menu for an upmarket burger chain. It's a well-liked company, with admirable ethics – the Lush of the burger world, all smiley and grass-fed – and I was delighted to be commissioned. Although work's going well, it can be a precarious business sometimes.

Danny contributes to the kids' living expenses, of course. He's not tight where they're concerned, but he doesn't believe in showering them with cash (quite rightly). Plus, he's not crazily rich; at least, not nearly as much as some might imagine. As for me, he would help me out, if I asked him to, but I never would. We agreed that, once Molly and Alfie had turned eighteen last year, he'd funnel his contributions straight into their bank accounts instead of mine. Luckily, we've never needed any lawyer-type shenanigans to sort this stuff out. However, on the emotional support front, he still doesn't get it sometimes.

'What are we going to do about Alfie?' I ask, grabbing the chance to call Danny as soon as Alfie has gone out to meet up with a couple of old friends.

'Can I call you back?' Danny asks. 'We're checking out locations . . .'

'At this time?' It's just gone nine p.m.

'Yeah. Bit of a mad day.' I should know by now that Danny doesn't adhere to anything resembling working hours, so I call Molly – not to offload, but to check that everything is at least all fine in her world, and that there won't be any shock announcements when I see her on Friday.

'I know about Alf,' she says, in her usual breezy way. 'I called him. He's mad. I can't believe he's doing this, because of her!'

'Because of . . . Camilla?' I venture, wary of fishing for info.

'Um, yeah.' I sense her guard going up.

'Molls . . . what's actually happened with Alfie and her?'

She hesitates. 'Oh, Mum. You'll have to ask him. Anyway, about Friday—'

'Yes, please be all packed up and ready, darling. I'll be with you by about ten. I meant to tell you, I've booked a week away in Barcelona. I hope you're okay with that. I'm going with Jack . . .'

'That's great,' she enthuses. 'Yeah, 'course it's okay.' She pauses. 'Could you bring boxes and some really strong bin bags?'

'To Barcelona?' I ask, baffled.

'No, on Friday, to help me move out—'

'Molly, how can you be packed if you don't have anything to put your stuff in?'

She sniffs. 'I thought it'd be easier if you could get some . . .'

'Whenever I moved, I'd go around all the local shops, asking if they had any old boxes kicking about . . .' I tail off. Molly is laughing.

'You want me to go around begging for boxes?' she snorts.

'It's not begging exactly,' I insist, realising there was no point in going on as we finish the call. *Ruddy millennials,* is one of Danny's favourite retorts, *with their sense of entitlement; falling apart if the Wi-Fi goes down. What they need is a bloody war!*

147

A joke, of course, and he's hardly been Tough Dad over the years. We've just muddled along, in our terribly modern way, constantly wondering whether we've been too stingy or generous, with fingers firmly crossed that everything would turn out okay. With my own parents, things were more cut-and-dried, with firmer boundaries. Mum, a primary school teacher, was kind but rather distant (she 'suffered with her nerves', as she put it). Dad grafted long and hard as a welder, but always had time for Sarah and me; we were very much 'his' girls, delighting in the stories he read us, and the long summer days when we hung out at his allotment. But there were rules, certainly, and a firm structure frameworked our young lives: dinner at six, a ten p.m. curfew once we'd reached our teens, chores allocated between us. I'd never so much as heat up soup without thoroughly deep-cleaning the kitchen afterwards. Mum would have had a meltdown if I'd attempted to make that Lebanese dish of Alfie's.

Dad died of a heart attack at seventy, and Mum had a stroke shortly afterwards, from which she never recovered. Admittedly, Danny was a rock during this time, even though we were no longer together. Along with Sarah and Vic, he helped us to clear out their home, a shadowy Victorian terrace still swathed in the patterned net curtains and ornament-laden sideboards of a previous era. But he had time back then; his career hadn't quite reached the level it has now.

When Danny finally calls back, just as I am about to go to bed, he sounds weary. 'Nads, you worry too much about Alfie,' he tells me.

'You always say that. There's usually been a justifiable reason . . .'

'Like what?' he asks.

'Well, the bullying, for one thing. That time he was attacked by those boys. Didn't you see how that knocked his confidence—'

'Yes, but that was years ago, and it's always been your default response,' he insists. 'You worried whenever the kids fell out with a friend, if they got a bad school report, a wonky haircut, when Alfie wouldn't practise the tuba—'

'This isn't about the tuba now,' I retort.

'No, thank Christ. What a god-awful racket that made – those blasts and honks, like warnings of impending nuclear attack . . .'

'I think the way they teach music in schools is all wrong,' announces Kiki in the background. Christ, he must have us on speakerphone.

'Sorry?' I manage to choke out.

'All those scales and exams and classical pieces,' she says shrilly. 'Shall I tell you what it does?'

I frown, momentarily lost for words.

'It takes all the fucking joy out of it,' Danny agrees. 'That's what it does. But Nadia was adamant because he'd signed up for lessons and we'd bought him the goddam instrument . . .'

'Who are you talking to here?' I bark.

'Er, you,' he says sheepishly.

'Well, the tuba was on loan from school,' I mutter, frustration bubbling up in me now. 'We didn't buy it.' This is what drove me mad when we were together; not a single incident, like the *Reservoir Dogs* suit, but constantly being forced into a position where I was regarded as the joyless parent, while Danny was the fun, spontaneous one. It was me who insisted on proper dinners, with vegetables, eaten at a reasonable and regular time of day; routines, homework, the writing of thank-you letters, the practising of musical pieces.

But actually, I didn't give a shit about the tuba! Alfie had *wanted* to learn, just as he'd wanted to study English Lit at Aberdeen University. He could have picked the guitar or piano or a tinny plastic keyboard, for all I cared, but no: he went for the biggest, brassiest instrument that would be a fucker to transport back and forth from school. And now his dad is inferring that I loomed over him, with a whip, while he struggled through Bach.

'Kiki's only trying to help,' Danny adds.

Well, just bloody don't, I want to snap. Instead, I inhale deeply. 'Okay. So, can you suggest anything helpful, Danny? Like, how Alfie might think about filling the summer, for instance?'

Of course he can't, and as I climb into bed once we've ended the call, I send Jack a customary goodnight text, and sense a wave of nostalgia for the time Jack and I had together, before my son came home (crazy, I know, as it was only a week ago). Does this make me a bad mother, to find it hard to just slip back into Alfie and I coexisting in this flat? To miss the peace and space that I had, and be seized by an urge to bin that damned onesie? Jack responds to my text with a call; we commiserate with each other about our barely communicative teens, as Lori keeps on insisting that 'everything's fine' with her mother, and all Alfie will offer is that 'everything'll work out, Mum. Stop going on about it.'

'I've told Alfie and Molly about our Barcelona trip,' I add.

'Are they okay about it?' Jack asks.

'Of course,' I say, my spirits rising now at the thought

150

of it. 'I'm sorry things have been a bit . . . different lately.'

'Hey, that's okay,' he says quickly. 'Things happen. Our lives are busy. Just know that I'm thinking of you all the time, and that I love you with all my heart, okay?'

'Oh.' I blink, overcome with a rush of love for him. We've said I-love-you before, many times. But his declaration was so spontaneous and heartfelt, it makes me think: everything *will* work out, like Alfie said. 'I love you too,' I murmur.

I sense him smiling. 'Well, we're agreed on that, then.' He pauses. 'What're you up to tomorrow?'

'I'll have to do a long day's work, I think, and then Sarah's staying over. She's in a town for a training day, so we thought we'd get together.'

'And Friday?'

'I'm driving over to Edinburgh to move Molly out of her halls. She and her friends have found a flat but the tenancy doesn't start until late August. So we need to bring her stuff here for the summer . . .'

'I wish I could help you with that. If I wasn't at the shop—'

'We'll be fine, honestly,' I say firmly.

'Couldn't Danny do it?'

'He's working – and anyway, I really can handle it myself. If I needed an extra pair of hands I could've asked Alfie, but I'd rather have the space in the car . . .'

'Yes, that's probably more useful,' Jack remarks.

I frown, wondering what he meant by that. 'You mean Alfie's not useful?'

'I didn't say that—'

'He would help, you know, if I asked him to.' There's an awkward pause, and I'm aware of over-reacting and how unreasonable that is; I've grumbled about Alfie's

151

laziness plenty of times, but then, I'm his mother. It's *allowed*.

'Yeah, I know,' Jack says, with a trace of defensiveness. 'I just meant—'

'You can't imagine Alfie lugging boxes?' I ask, hating the coolness that's crept into my voice.

Jack sighs. 'Well, perhaps not.'

I prickle with irritation, even though Alfie has hardly demonstrated himself to be a handyman around the house in Jack's presence – or anyone's presence for that matter. 'You haven't seen much of him really,' I mutter. 'He's not quite as helpless as he might seem.'

'Yes, okay,' he concedes.

'He just needs time to get himself together,' I add.

'I realise that.'

'Mmm.' Another pause hangs between us.

'Well, I'd better let you get some sleep,' Jack adds.

Something seems to twist inside me, and I wish I could rewind time and start this call all over again. 'Look, Jack,' I say, 'I know I probably mollycoddle Alfie. His dad's always telling me I do. Maybe I'm just a little sick of being criticised—'

'I'm not criticising you,' Jack exclaims.

'No? Well, anyway, he's going to start working. He just said this evening, "I'll start earning as soon as I can. You won't need to look after me . . ."'

'Really?'

'Yeah.' I frown, waiting for a response, but none comes. 'Jack,' I start, 'are you okay? Are *we* okay, I mean?'

'Um, yes, of course we are.' He sounds surprised. 'Why d'you ask?'

'It's just . . . things seem different, don't they? Just a little bit?'

'A little, yes. But you have a lot on your plate,' he says quickly, 'and we're fine, Nads. Look, I'd better let you get some sleep . . .'

'Oh. Goodnight, then . . .'

'Night,' Jack says. I'm about to add, 'sweet dreams,' but he's already finished the call.

Chapter Eighteen

Jack

You won't need to look after me.

That's what my little brother Sandy said when he'd asked if he could come down and stay with me for a few days in Glasgow.

Of course Nadia doesn't know this. She's aware that something happened to Sandy but I haven't gone into the details, because . . . well, I'm not sure what she'd think of me if I did. I told Elaine, at the festival, when it was all so recent and raw and it just tumbled out. But it's not recent now. Over the years, I've decided it's best left buried in the past.

I reflect on the conversation Nadia and I just had, when she seemed to think I was criticising Alfie. I'd love to call her back, to explain that's not what I mean to do at all; we were only discussing her helping to move Molly out of halls! But maybe she needs a little space. Obviously, she's upset over Alfie wanting to drop out of uni. And his homecoming has changed things, certainly; her kids will always take priority, just as Lori does for me. That's just a fact, when you fall in love at our sort of age, and you already have lives. You have to respect that the other person might have stuff going on, and that you might not be a part of it. Isn't that in the job description of a bona fide adult – to put other people's needs before your own?

I *think* I was a decent brother to Sandy, when I still lived at home on the farm. He certainly loved being around me anyway. I suppose that's a natural younger brother thing – to want a piece of the older ones' lives. He liked being around our eldest brother, too, but Craig was already taking on more and more farm work and he didn't have as much time, or patience, for Sandy as I had. Sandy wanted to play my records and hang out in my room, bringing the dogs in with him; they'd all lounge on my bed in a damp, dirty heap. And despite the thirteen-year age gap we were incredibly alike, even appearance-wise, with our blue eyes and dark hair and rangy builds.

Admittedly, it did get on my nerves sometimes, Sandy always being around. Even when I'd left home, he'd still want to talk, calling from the landline in our parents' kitchen; this was way before everyone had mobile phones, and my parents were of the belief that they 'damaged your brain'. They refused to have a microwave for the same reason.

When he was old enough to travel by himself, Sandy started to nag about coming to stay with me in Glasgow. I let him visit a couple of times, picking him up from Queen Street train station and taking him for a huge bowl of spaghetti at the cheap Italian restaurant I liked with the red gingham tablecloths and an army of waiters who were curt and dismissive until you'd been about eight hundred times, and they'd finally decided you were okay.

Of course, they'd thought Sandy was 'okay' the first time I took him there, the wee bugger. 'Aw, treating your kid brother to the big city lights? Look after him, man! Don't go corrupting him!'

Then one time Sandy called asking to come and stay, and I wasn't in the mood for ferrying him about, taking him for spaghetti and to the cinema and all the stuff he liked. 'C'mon,' he wheedled from the phone in our parents' hall. 'I'll just do my own thing if you're busy. I won't get in the way.'

'I've got too much on at the moment,' I told him.

'But I'm sixteen! I'm not a kid. I won't be any bother. You won't need to look after me.'

I'd do anything to be able to look after him now. I mean *anything*. Stuff my weekend plans, my selfish twenty-something desire to go to a party because I'd heard some girl I liked was going to be there – a Spanish waitress I had a thing for, I can't even remember her name now. Never mind the fact that Sandy might have cramped my style a bit, or that I'd have had to keep a bit of an eye on him.

Selfish, selfish fuck.

While Sandy had pleaded with me, I'd heard Mum in the background, asking if everything was okay.

'I'm on the phone,' Sandy shot back, irritably.

'Say hi to Jack!' she called out.

'Mum says hi,' he said curtly, then he put the phone down. I just assumed he was having a teenage strop, so I didn't bother phoning back.

You won't have to look after me, my brother said.

Those words are tattooed onto my brain.

Chapter Nineteen

Nadia

Before the kids left home there were so many little annoyances – wet towels dropped on the floor, the freezer door left open with all the food defrosting – that I almost stopped noticing them. But now, I seem to be on high alert for every minor misdemeanour of Alfie's. And that, coupled with that rather tetchy conversation with Jack last night, seems to be making me rattier than usual.

For both Alfie's and my sake, I decide to get out of the flat and decamp to the studio. I spend the day working away steadily, breaking off only to tell Gus and Corinne about my son's ridiculously loud electric toothbrush, whirring away on the other side of my bedroom door as a remarkably effective sex deterrent.

'You shouldn't be doing it at your age anyway,' Gus teases. 'Sex is only for young people. Didn't you know?'

'Doesn't that son of yours ever leave the flat?' Corinne asks with a smirk.

'Now and again, yes – there are still some of his friends kicking around. But not when I *need* him to.' In fact, I don't just mean this in a getting-it-on-with-Jack context.

I've found it extremely challenging to relax in the flat with Alfie bashing around. He has melted the rice steamer in the microwave, caused my favourite china teapot to 'just fall', and somehow our shower seems to have come apart from its fitting on the wall. As a temporary measure I have gaffer taped it back into place. It's tantamount to vandalism.

'Couldn't you send him out on an errand?' Gus suggests with an arched brow.

'Like a Boy Scout, you mean?'

'I mean for bread, or strong alcohol . . .'

'He could get that from the corner shop. He'd literally be out for about six minutes.'

'You can achieve quite a lot in six minutes,' Corinne remarks.

'Though you'd better skip foreplay,' Gus adds, which sets the two of them off sniggering again. 'Or how about giving him money for the cinema? That way, you know he'd be out for, what, three hours minimum . . .'

'Maybe some cinemas still do double bills,' Corinne muses.

'You're saying I should pay him so Jack and I can go to bed together?'

'Desperate times call for desperate measures,' she remarks. 'Even with popcorn and a drink you're talking less than twenty quid . . .'

'Which sounds reasonable for sex,' Gus quips. 'Cheaper than buying a caravan to do it in anyway . . .' We all dissolve into giggles, but I can't help wondering: how will things pan out with Jack, now that Alfie seems to be back home for good?

'D'you think I should be having Jack to stay over anyway?' I ask. 'When Alfie and Molly are home, I mean.'

158

'Of course you should,' Corinne retorts, sipping her coffee. 'They're adults now. You can't be expected to put your life on hold.'

'But maybe you should think of other things to do with Jack instead?' Gus suggests with a grin.

'Like what?' I ask.

He shrugs. 'Board games?'

'Yeah, you were always the Scrabble whizz at college, Nads,' Corinne chuckles. 'Maybe it's time to dig it out?'

Back home, I'm thrilled to find Alfie hunched over his laptop, brushing up his CV. I'm even more delighted when he accepts my offer of help. It's a little patchy, admittedly, but at least he's done a few shifts in a club, plus a stint of cleaning hotel rooms, which we boost to the point where he appears to have substantial experience in the hospitality industry.

When my sister shows up later, having been in town all day for a training session, she, too, is keen to batter his CV into shape. By the time she's finished, it looks as if he'd be capable of running the entire chain of Premier Inns.

Alfie frowns at the heavily edited document on his screen. 'I'm not sure I want to do hotel work,' he calls through to Sarah, who is now rearranging the contents of my food cupboard: so much wasted space, apparently, with all these torn-open packets and everything bunged in willy-nilly! If anyone else marched in and started rooting about amongst my dried goods, I'd feel *violated*. But something about Sarah's brisk manner makes me accept that her way is probably better than mine.

'What do you want to do then?' she calls back to Alfie.

'Um, I was thinking of getting some work at a festival?'

159

'The Edinburgh festival?' she asks, reappearing at his side, clutching a bag of paella rice. She darts a look at me. 'This is four years out of date, by the way.'

'I thought rice lasted forever?' I remark.

Sarah shakes her head.

'I mean music festivals,' Alfie explains, at which she laughs.

'Getting paid to sit around getting stoned and watching the bands, you mean?' Sarah asks.

'No!' he exclaims, and she sniggers again.

'So what would it entail?'

'Anything. Bar work, stewarding, security . . .'

She glances at me. I have already warned her against mentioning his seemingly firm decision to drop out of uni, and I'm grateful for her jolly, no-nonsense presence. 'Well, good luck, honey.' She hugs him. 'Aren't you coming out for a bite to eat with us tonight?'

'Aw, nah thanks. There's not much I can have.' From our local pub's menu, he means.

Sarah frowns. 'Surely there'd be something meat-free? I thought it was virtually the law these days . . .'

'He prefers actual vegan places,' I explain, as the two of us head out on foot. 'More choice.'

She winces at the thought of it. I did consider the possibility, as – amazingly to me – Glasgow appears to boast more vegan restaurants per capita than anywhere else in the universe. Our reputation of being entirely fuelled by chips and deep-fried Mars Bars has always been nonsense, but it's especially laughable now. These days you're never more than ten feet from a chickpea.

However, before long, just the two of us are installed in the Hog's Head, tucking into prawn penne (me) and an Aberdeen Angus rib-eye steak (Sarah). Our talk focuses on the delightfully normal: Vic's plans to extend their house and funny tales from the world of the care homes she inspects. We touch on Jack, naturally, but I wouldn't dream of telling her about the whirring toothbrush sex interrupter, or Alfie marching in on us when we were virtually naked. I'm not sure she'd approve. Sarah and Vic have been together since she was sixteen, and she doesn't really discuss anything intimate. I can only remember one incident, when she remarked that they were having 'some issues in the bed department' – and knowing Sarah, that could have meant a tiff in John Lewis.

However, later that night, when I take a cup of tea to her in Molly's room, I have to admit it's comforting, having my sister around. Those glorious weeks of being able to wander about in my knickers, and to do things with my boyfriend at any given moment, might have dropped off the radar temporarily. But at least my kitchen cupboards are a beacon of respectability now.

Chapter Twenty

I set off for Edinburgh next morning, armed with the boxes I ordered, plus vast quantities of brown tape, bubble wrap and strong bin bags. Naturally, I don't mind helping Molly to move out of halls. But I would appreciate some assistance from Danny occasionally, when it comes to practical matters like assembling fifteen cardboard boxes.

'You're much better at it than me,' Molly says with a grin, when I point out that my box tally has reached twelve, while she has only managed to build one.

'Why am I better?'

She smirks, teasing me now. 'You're just . . . more efficient at repetitive, manual tasks.'

'Thanks!' I exclaim. 'Maybe I should put that on my CV, under "strengths", if I ever apply for a regular job . . .'

'It's a good skill to have,' she chuckles. 'Box builder. You'd go far with that, Mum.'

In fact, all the assembling and packing and carrying – *without her father's help* – is oddly enjoyable as, despite her aversion to brown sticky tape, Molly is a physically strong girl and not prone to moaning. Between the two of us we soon have her room emptied and cleaned, her flatmates bid goodbye to, and my car jammed to the hilt.

'I can't believe that's your first year over,' I tell Molly as we drive home. 'It only feels like last week when I moved you in.'

'Yeah, I know,' she says with a smile.

'D'you think you'll like your flat-share next year?' Despite her apparently happy state, I'm a little nervous that she, like Alfie, might have some dramatic announcement to make. When does it stop, this worrying?

'Definitely,' she says. 'Halls are great but, y'know . . . it's always going to be pretty mad and messy when you throw ten people together in one flat, including a few who've never cooked for themselves and someone who thinks you boil potatoes by putting them in a plastic bag in the oven . . .'

'You're kidding me,' I say, laughing.

'Unfortunately not. I mean, it was great – but now I'm ready to choose who I live with . . .'

I nod, sensing a swell of pride at how well Molly has adapted to student life. I know she gets up to high jinks; unlike Alfie, who's friended only his father on Facebook (and not me! The nerve of it!), Molly accepted my friend request years ago, *and* let me follow her on Instagram. She doesn't seem to feel the need to hide her life from me. So I've seen all the messy photos: she and her mates in a tangle at parties, lipstick smeared, booze being slugged and ciggies being smoked. But she's a grafter too, sitting up all night to power through an essay when a deadline requires it.

'So, was it sad saying goodbye to everyone?' I ask.

Molly nods. 'Kind of. We had a little do last night . . .'

'I thought I detected a hangover.'

163

She chuckles, and I glance at my daughter. She's bare-faced with her long dark hair worn loose and barely brushed, wearing a faded green T-shirt and old jeans. She is quite the beauty, even after a late night. 'We made our own drink,' she says, grinning.

'What kind of drink?'

Molly sniggers. 'Actually, we fermented a pineapple in an old bucket . . .'

'Where did you get the bucket? And can't home-made booze cause blindness?'

'Mum,' she exclaims, 'I'm okay, aren't I? My vision's fine, and we found the bucket lying in the street. Don't look like that. We *washed* it,' she adds, proceeding to describe the fermentation process in such detail that, by the time we reach Glasgow, I'm pretty confident that I could competently set up a fermentation plant of my very own. I could certainly do with a steady supply of booze at the moment.

But when she and Alfie greet each other with a heart-felt hug, I have a flash of how brilliant this is, having them home, our tight little unit together again. And soon Molly will meet Jack, and that's bound to go much better than when Alfie met him. For one thing, we'll be *clothed*.

However, I'm not quite sure when that will be, as when I call Jack that evening he sounds a little preoccupied with Lori, who's talking about spending more days at his place, apparently, and fewer at her mum's.

'Is something wrong?' I ask, perching on the edge of the kitchen table.

'It's hard to know for sure. Maybe she just wants a bit of a break from her mum. You know how Elaine is . . .'

'Well, yes, sort of,' I reply. Although I have never met

his ex, he's told me how chaotic she can be, with the wheelie bin overflowing with bottles, and the slurring on the phone. But I'd been under the impression that things had been pretty stable recently. 'Let's get together next week, then,' I add, trying to quell a surge of missing him.

'Of course, yes.'

I pause. 'And Jack?'

'Uh-huh?'

I'm about to say *I miss you*, and *surely we'll figure out ways of being together with everyone else around?* But Molly has marched into the kitchen and appears to be conducting a full inventory of our biscuits.

'Aren't there any Oreos?' she asks, seemingly unconcerned that I am on the phone.

'No, love—'

'I'm sure I saw two packets?'

'Alfie ate them,' I reply.

'All of them? *Two packets?*'

'Yes. They're vegan . . .'

'What a pig!'

'Molly,' I start. Then, to Jack: 'Sorry, she just wanted—'

'Biscuits?' he says wryly. 'Sounds serious.' We laugh about how the kids still rule our lives – hahaha – and agree to see each other very soon. *Perhaps for Scrabble,* I reflect as we finish the call.

However, the days roll on, with both of us keeping on top of family and work stuff, to the point at which I start to think, did Jack and I fully appreciate the acres of time we had to spend together before my offspring came home? He has spent the weekend with Lori, and I've hung out with my kids, trying to assess Alfie's wellbeing as well as suggesting numerous jobs he could apply for. Barista? He brushes this off as too humdrum and is more drawn to the idea of zooming around Glasgow, being one of those food delivery rider guys. But then, he doesn't possess a bike, and I'm loath to buy one for him in case he uses it precisely once, then leaves it forever chained to the banister downstairs. Which seems like a probable outcome, since he's already expressing concern over the size of the boxes those guys have strapped to their backs . . .

Molly starts working at the garden centre on Monday, and it feels important to be around in the evenings for those first few days, considering that she's putting in long shifts. I'm seized by an urge to feed my kids proper dinners, especially when I hear Alfie confessing to Molly that, actually, pasta lubricated with ketchup has been his main staple for several months. I'm wondering now whether so much as a single pulse was soaked during the entire academic year.

By mid-week, Jack and I still haven't managed to get together. He has a backlog of proofreading to plough through – a necessary sideline, as he would struggle to get by on his salary – and I'm cracking through my commissions as efficiently as possible, holding on to the vision of Jack and me together in Barcelona in just a few weeks' time. Meanwhile, after the brief flurry of effort in researching possible job options, Alfie seems to have slumped back into a fug of inactivity.

'What's with the onesie?' Molly asks, looming over him on Wednesday evening as she marches in from work.

He shifts on the sofa and looks down at it, as if he's only just remembered he has it on. 'It's just comfy to wear around the house.'

'For God's sake,' she scoffs. 'You're acting like an old man!'

'And it's not a onesie,' he protests.

'What is it then?' she asks.

'Footed pyjamas.'

I choke back a laugh. '*What?*'

Alfie turns to face me. 'That's what Auntie Sarah said when she gave them to me.'

'They're not a "them",' Molly retorts. 'They're an *it*. Just because it doesn't have a hood and little teddy-bear ears doesn't mean it's not a onesie. C'mon, Alf – it's only six o'clock. Too early for bed. Get some proper daytime clothes on, and then you can start thinking about getting a job . . .'

'I'm capable of thinking while wearing my pyjamas,' he says, chuckling now.

Molly snorts. 'Okay, then. Think of everyone you know who might be able to offer you some work, and start asking around. That's how I got *my* summer job.' She turns to me. 'Could Jack give Alfie some work in the charity shop?'

'It's all volunteers,' I reply, 'apart from the managers . . .'

'What about Dad, then? Or you?'

I smile and look at my son. 'You know, Alf – they're always looking for life models at the art class . . .'

'No way!' he exclaims as Molly laughs.

'Aw, c'mon,' she cajoles him. 'Mum's always said it's easy work, but . . .' She looks down at him, pursing her lips in disapproval: 'You wouldn't be allowed to wear your *footed pyjamas* for that.'

By chance, although my 'proper' job means I rarely have time these days, I find myself agreeing to model for a class the following evening. The booked model is ill, and so I head off to the community hall where

Stuart, the tutor, explains that I'll be changing poses every two minutes. As tonight's theme is 'dynamic drawing' he wants the students to work in a loose and speedy style.

'Does that sound okay, Nads?' he asks.

'Of course,' I reply. Stuart and I go back years; he knows I'm generally happy to do whatever's required. I undress behind the screen – that's a part of the process the students never get to see – and slip on my robe, casting a quick glance across the room to see if I recognise anyone here, as is my custom since I was 'outed' as a life model, many years ago.

One evening, when the children were ten and Danny was away for work, Alfie confronted me over the dinner table. 'Leon says you're a stripper,' he announced.

'*What?*' I exclaimed. He turned to Molly, and a look of disgust passed between them. 'Alfie, what are you talking about? If you mean the art class—'

'Yeah, Leon's dad went to it. He said you were the naked model!'

Christ, I didn't even know his friend's dad. At least, I certainly hadn't recognised anyone at the class. 'Look, Alf,' I said firmly, 'a model and a stripper are totally different things. *You* know that . . .'

'How are they different?' Molly eyed me defiantly across the vast dish of lasagne.

'Um, well, you know that strippers do it purely for entertainment, for men to look at, and, uh, find attractive . . .' I sensed my forehead prickling with sweat. 'It's a sexual thing, obviously,' I added, seeing Alfie turn pale. 'Whereas in a life drawing class, I'm not really a woman to them.'

'What are you, then?' she demanded.

'Just, um, a *shape*, really. A collection of angles and bumps and, er, other bits – like a kettle or a bowl of fruit.'

Alfie looked aghast. 'Do you stand, or sit, or what?'

'Whatever they ask me to do really. I change poses when they ask me to.'

'D'you lie on a sofa?' Molly enquired.

'Yes, if that's what they want. Sometimes I stand on a revolving platform.'

'Oh my God!' Alfie groaned.

I tried to reach for his hand. 'Look, love – you both know I do this. I've been doing it for years . . .'

'But with no clothes on,' Molly crowed. 'You never told us that part, did you?'

'No,' I conceded, 'and I'm sorry if you're embarrassed. But that's just what life drawing classes are like. You know how naked people are a big thing in art? Go to any gallery and you can't move for nude women—'

'But you're not a painting in a gallery, are you?' Alfie snapped. 'You're our *mum*.'

When Danny returned, he couldn't understand why I was so het up. 'They must've known what life modelling entails. Did they think you sit there wearing a duffel coat?'

'Probably,' I said with a hollow laugh.

'And now they know it involves fifteen people staring at your fanny.'

'Danny!' I exclaimed, trying to be outraged, but I couldn't help laughing. 'D'you think it's wrong, that I do this?' I added.

'Don't be crazy. Of course I don't . . .'

'I mean, it's just a few polite students in St Cuthbert's Community Hall. It's where the Embroiderers' Guild have

169

their meetings. How could anything sleazy possibly happen there?'

Danny barked with laughter.

'Seriously, d'you think I should give it up?'

'No,' he retorted. 'We can't let the kids control our lives like that, and anyway, if it wasn't that, there'd be some other reason why you're embarrassing . . .'

'Why *I'm* embarrassing,' I spluttered. 'Not you.'

'Hey, who's been parading about in her nuddy-pants around here?' he snorted.

And now, as I take off my robe and recline, sit and stand, I find myself wondering: is that what I'm doing, yet again – shaping my life around my kids, when it really is time to please myself now?

I have never felt embarrassed or shy doing this kind of work, perhaps because I was so used to the life drawing classes, and being around nudity, at college. A modelling session has always represented a time to think, as far as I'm concerned. You just assume poses that you hope are satisfying to draw; you really are just a 'thing' to the students. And now, as I'm being drawn, I finally have time to mull over recent events, and decide I really must stop fussing around Molly and Alfie, preparing their every meal as if they were twelve. Christ, the other evening I heard myself asking Alfie if I could run his bath for him, seeing as I was 'passing'. As if he might be incapable of operating the taps.

As for Jack, I know I've sidelined him since Alfie bowled up – and that will change too. The kids – well, Alfie in particular – will just have to come to terms with that.

As if he knows he's on my mind, Jack calls as I'm lacing up my shoes, having just got dressed after the session. 'Are you home just now?' he asks.

170

'Heading that way,' I reply. 'I was asked to do life class at the last minute, but I've just finished . . . is everything okay?'

'Um . . . sort of. I'm out with Iain from the shop. Lori's here too. We're only five minutes away from your place, actually . . .'

Jack, Lori and Iain, all out together? 'Really? What're you doing?'

He sighs loudly. 'Don't fancy joining us later, do you? Iain's dog bolted today – escaped from his flat. He called me at the shop in a panic, and we're all out looking for him, and we're not too far from you . . .'

It's wrong, of course, to feel happy about a dog being lost, but I'm *so* glad he called. 'Of course I'll join you. I'll be home in fifteen minutes . . .' I pause. 'You're so kind, helping him—'

'Huh.' Jack laughs dryly, 'I had no choice really. Seems like it was all my fault.'

Chapter Twenty-One

It's no surprise when Molly agrees to join the search party, but it takes a little cajoling to persuade Alfie that he could do something heroic (or at least, be involved in something heroic). However, eventually, he shuffles off to his room in his customary convalescence wear and re-emerges clad in not especially fresh jeans and a grey T-shirt. And before long we've found Jack, Lori and Iain, striding across an expanse of waste ground a few blocks away from our street.

'Thanks for coming,' Jack says, hugging me briefly. 'You too, Alfie . . .'

''S'all right . . .'

'Jack, this is Molly . . .' I start.

'Hi, Molly.' He smiles, and she beams at him as he introduces Lori and Iain.

'We really appreciate this, don't we Iain?' Jack prompts him.

'Yeah, thanks for coming,' Iain murmurs with a shrug.

'I can't believe Dad made you all come out,' Lori exclaims.

'Oh, we're happy to help,' I tell her. 'We can all split up and cover more ground . . .' I scan the expanse of scrubby grass bordered by run-down, mostly shut-up shops, and a partially demolished building with tangled grasses sprouting from its crevices.

'It all feels a bit hopeless,' Iain says glumly. 'Me and Una have looked all over already.' He glances at me. 'She lives upstairs from me. She walks Pancake at lunchtime when I'm at the shop.'

'Well, let's start searching,' I suggest.

'Yep, we have to be hopeful here,' Jack offers, agreeing that our 'plan' should be to split up and search the surrounding streets in order to cover as much ground as possible. But first, Iain is keen to impress upon me that Pancake's disappearance is Jack's fault.

'I was cooking,' he tells me as we start to wander along in a straggly line, 'like Jack's been telling me to . . .'

'That was at *Christmas*, Iain. Five months ago.' Jack throws me a quick look and shakes his head.

'Yeah, well, I'm a busy man,' Iain retorts. 'I've only just got around to it, and look how it ended up.'

'What happened?' I ask, frowning.

'I was making soup. That's what Jack's always saying. "Make soup! It's healthy! Even my daughter can do it!"'

'I *can*,' Lori says, a smile flickering across her pale face. 'I make loads at home. It's not that difficult.' I gather that Jack's daughter has met Iain on several occasions, and thinks he's 'sweet, but a bit sad'. Unlike her mother, who reckons that Jack gets 'far too involved' with the volunteers.

'All I said,' Jack murmurs, 'is that maybe it'd be good to learn to cook a few basic things, and not just live on cereal . . .'

173

'Nothing wrong with cereal,' Iain retorts.

'I just meant, perhaps you could have some meals that aren't spooned from a bowl,' Jack adds.

'Soup's spooned from a bowl,' Iain retorts, which causes Alfie to catch my eye and splutter. Christ, my son is actually laughing, in public, with people he doesn't even know. I'm glad that I dragged him along now.

'But not the soup he made today,' Jack says, addressing me now. 'Iain, tell Nadia what happened . . .'

'You tell them,' Iain huffs, as if to underline – once again – Jack's culpability.

Jack sighs. 'So, I told Iain that all you have to do is fry up some onions or leeks . . .'

'Which I *did*,' Iain says pointedly.

'Yes,' Jack continues, his hand brushing against mine as we walk, 'but I didn't say fry them to the point where they're stuck to the bottom of the pan, and burning . . .'

'Making the kitchen stink,' Iain adds pointedly.

'*Okay*, Iain . . .' Jack glances at me with an eye-roll, and my heart seems to shift. I've missed just being with him these past few days. I love being together, out in the world, just pottering, chatting and doing ordinary stuff. I love all those conventional date-type things, like wandering through a park or a museum, or stopping off for lunch on a sunny Saturday afternoon. But it feels just as right being here, in the desolate car park we're striding across now, the tarmac pitted, an overflowing bin surrounded by stacks of wet cardboard and cooking oil tins.

'So, Iain opened his flat door to let the smell out,' Jack explains.

'And the main outside door as well,' Iain interjects, ''cause I didn't want the hallway filling with cooking smells. Una wouldn't like that . . .'

174

'And that's how your dog got out?' Molly asks, catching my eye.

'*Nooooo*,' Iain exclaims. 'Pancake was lying in his basket, perfectly happy. I chipped off the onions and scrubbed out the pan, and then – because Jack had been on at me – I got the butternut squash . . .'

'I said any veg would do,' Jack cuts in. 'I didn't specify butternut—'

'So I put it in the pan with water,' Iain continues, 'and boiled it, *just* like Jack said . . .'

'Without peeling it or chopping it up,' Jack adds dryly.

Iain looks around at us. Somehow, we have all stopped and gathered around him, apparently keen to find out what happened next. 'And it exploded,' Iain exclaims with a swoop of his arms. 'I mean, a fucking *huge* explosion! Una ran down from upstairs. She's eighty-three. I'd never seen her run before—'

''Course it exploded,' Lori says, laughing in bewilderment now. 'You boil a whole butternut squash in a pan and what d'you think'll happen?'

'I wouldn't have imagined that,' Alfie remarks. 'I'd have thought—'

'The bang terrified Pancake,' Iain cuts in. 'He shot out of his basket and out of the flat, along the hall, then outside and . . .' He breaks off, eyes wide as he looks around at all of us. '*This* is what happens when I take Jack's advice to make soup.'

Having been shown a photo of Pancake on Iain's phone – a floppy-eared scamp, the colour of concrete – we split up into groups, comprising Molly and Lori, Jack and Iain, and Alfie and me.

175

'Poor guy,' Alfie says, giving me a look as soon as we're out of earshot.

'Jack seems to think he does okay,' I say. 'He's very attached to the shop, and he manages things at home—'

'As long as he's not cooking?' he asks with a smile.

'Well, yes.'

'So, why did he call his dog Pancake?'

'Because he likes to lie flat,' I reply, which seems to amuse Alfie hugely as we pass unprepossessing businesses in a neglected street: a picture framer, a dusty off-licence, and what I'd imagine is one of the last internet cafés in existence.

'Pancake!' we call out repeatedly, choking back giggles every time. '*Paaaaan*-caaayyyyk!' Naturally, the ideal result would be for us to find the renegade hound and bring him back to Iain and be heroes. However, despite the lack of a positive sighting, I find myself enjoying Alfie's company as we prowl the streets.

'Jack's all right, isn't he?' Alfie muses as we turn a corner.

I look at him, both delighted and surprised. 'Yes, he is. I'm glad you think so too.'

We make our way along a narrow lane filled with overflowing skips. 'I do.' Alfie nods. 'I mean, doing this for Iain, helping him out . . .'

'It surprised me at first too, the way he's so involved with the volunteers—'

'What, all of them?'

'No, not all,' I reply. 'I mean the ones who, you know . . . need a bit of help sometimes. Like Mags, who brings in forms when she needs help with filling them in. Or with some of the older ones, he's popped round to see them if they've been ill, that kind of thing.'

'That's kind of him,' Alfie concedes, and I catch him giving me a quick look. 'How did you meet him again?'

'Erm, just in a shop, love.'

'In a *shop*?' He peers at me.

'Yes, we just got chatting . . .'

'Chatting in a shop? How weird!'

'Why?' I ask, laughing now. Nothing weird about pouncing on a handsome stranger, impersonating a sales assistant and frantically up-selling bath bombs . . .

'It just seems kind of . . .' He pauses. 'Funny.'

'You mean, because we met in real life?'

'Yeah.' He grins as we start to head back towards the waste ground.

Sensing his defences down, I decided to broach the issue of his girlfriend. 'But you met Camilla in real life, didn't you?' I remind him.

'Yeah, but that's different – we're students . . .'

I hesitate before continuing: 'Hon, I hope you don't mind me asking, but is it really over with Camilla?'

'Mmmm, looks like it,' he mumbles.

Encouraged by his neutral tone, I decide to press on. 'Maybe you just need some time together away from uni? Could she come down to Glasgow for a bit?'

'Nah, I don't think so.'

'D'you want to get back together?' I ask tentatively, at which Alfie shrugs. 'Because if you do,' I add, 'and you've just had a falling-out or something, maybe you could write to her?'

He stops and stares. 'Write to her? Like, an email?'

'Well, yes, you could do that. Or you could, you know . . . write her a letter and put it in the post—'

'The *post*?' He laughs incredulously. 'I don't think so, Mum . . .'

'Why not?'

'Because it's, like, the twenty-first century!'

'Yes,' I say, 'but actually, receiving a letter is a brilliant thing.'

'Is it?' Alfie asks, smirking. 'Why's that, then?'

'Well, it's personal, obviously. It's taken time and thought, which suggests that the sender really cares . . .' He looks baffled now, as if I've suggested sending her a telegram.

'Yeah, but . . .' He scratches his ear. 'It all sounds a bit . . . complicated.'

'It's not,' I assure him. 'C'mon, honey, you're an English student and an excellent writer. And you used to write thank-you letters, remember?'

'Yeah, 'cause you made me.' He snorts. 'You nagged me to death. "Put in some detail," you'd tell me. "Say *why* you liked the present . . ." Christ, Mum, you virtually stood over me with a gun . . .'

Although we're both laughing now, I can't help wondering: was I really that bad? Tyrant of the tuba, thank-you-letter obsessive . . . it would seem that I was. 'Well, yes,' I concede, 'because you can't just put, "Dear Auntie Sarah. Thanks for the robot. Love Alfie."'

'It would've got the message across.'

I smile, wanting to put an arm around him now, but managing not to as he shuns physical affection from me these days. 'Well, okay, but compared to that, writing to Camilla would be a breeze . . .'

'But what about finding paper,' he bleats, 'and an envelope, and going out to post it?'

'There are postboxes, Alf. They're usually red, with a slot where you put the letter in—'

'And stamps!' he interjects. 'Where would I get a stamp?'

'Stamps are everywhere. Supermarkets have them, and corner shops. I even have some in my purse . . .' We continue like this, joshing and teasing, and by the time we rejoin the others it's almost like old times, when we could talk without perpetual eye-rolls and irritation, and he seemed to *like* me.

'No luck?' Jack says, striding towards us.

'Nope, no sign, I'm afraid . . .' I glance at Iain, and my heart twists at how disappointed he looks. 'I'm so sorry we haven't found him.'

'Thanks for trying anyway,' he murmurs, digging the toe of a shoe into the earth.

'How about phoning the rescue centres?' Molly suggests.

'Dad's done that already,' Lori explains.

Jack nods. 'I've left messages and posted on various Facebook groups too. There's a Pets Reunited page and loads of forums, and the council have wardens out picking up strays.'

'He's not a stray,' Iain corrects him. 'He's an escapee . . .'

'Yes, well, they have council kennels,' Jack goes on, 'but Pancake's definitely not there.' He looks around at all of us. 'After all that, I think we should all go for a pizza. What d'you reckon?'

'I've got no money with me,' Iain says.

'My treat,' Jack says firmly.

'That's not fair—' he starts to protest, but Jack is adamant.

'It's only pizza, Iain. C'mon . . .' He looks at Alfie, Molly and me. 'Have you eaten tonight?'

'No,' Molly declares, 'and I'm starving . . .'

'Me too,' puts in Alfie, 'but I'm actually a—'

'The place down the road does vegan pizzas,' Jack cuts

in. 'I've checked the menu online.' He waggles his phone.

Oh my God, he actually thought to do that. If we weren't in public, with our nearest and dearest in close proximity, I would grab this man and kiss him – passionately – on his lovely, entirely *kissable* lips.

Chapter Twenty-Two

So we gather around a communal table in the buzzing restaurant, where the pizzas are made from sourdough, as seems to be the law these days. Dog-hunting is hungry work, and we tuck in enthusiastically. 'At last, decent food!' Alfie announces, as if our bank-stripping trips to Planet Earth had never happened.

Iain, who seems to have forgiven Jack for the exploded butternut squash, is now explaining how he runs the charity shop, pretty much singlehandedly. 'Some of the volunteers don't care about how things are presented,' he retorts, flicking a crumb from his mustard cardigan. Although Jack reckons he's only around thirty, Iain's old-mannish, side-parted hairstyle and his clothing (corduroys and matted knitwear) confuse the issue somewhat. 'I have to keep an eye on the general appearance of things,' he adds.

'That's so important in a charity shop,' Molly remarks.

'Yep, Jack relies on me for that kind of thing. Some of the other volunteers don't have a clue, do they, Jack?'

'Everyone brings something different,' Jack replies, catching my eye with a smile.

Iain stuffs in the rest of his pizza, a daub of cheese clinging to his unshaven chin. 'You're nice, Nadia,' he blurts out, mouth full, turning to Jack. 'She's better than that mad Zoe, with the death masks—'

'Let's not get into comparisons,' Jack says quickly as Molly looks at Lori. They both try, unsuccessfully, to stifle sniggers. Clearly, they bonded a little during their search for Pancake. 'Oh, I forgot to tell you, Iain,' Jack adds, perhaps to change the subject. 'Dinah called again, wanting to know how many celebs we've persuaded to donate stuff. For the auction, remember?'

'Aw, do we really have to do this?' Iain groans.

'Seems like it, yeah,' Jack replies. 'She reckons it'll boost our profile and get us loads of press coverage . . .'

'Celebrity stuff?' Molly asks, interest piqued. 'What've you got so far?'

Jack drains the last of his lager. 'Nothing, unfortunately. We'll have to get our act together. Apparently the Edinburgh shop have some mittens donated by . . .' He tails off and frowns. 'Some soap woman. The face of waffles.'

'The face of what?' I ask, laughing.

'I can't remember. Miranda someone?'

'Miranda *Ford*?' Lori stares at her dad. 'They have Miranda Ford's mittens?'

'Uh, yeah. Dinah reckons we have to come up with something to match that . . .' He grins at Iain. 'So the pressure's on, mate.'

The talk turns to the world of celebrities, in which I used to nurture a passing interest. However, the people whom Lori, Molly and Alfie are gossiping about are famous solely from having appeared on some dating show, and I haven't a clue who they are. Somehow, without noticing it happening, I have graduated from *Grazia* to Pinterest.

Lori turns to me and smiles. 'Are you coming to our party, Nadia?'

'Oh, what party's that?' I ask, glancing at Jack.

'It's not really a party, Lor,' he says apologetically, turning to me. 'We've decided to have a little gathering for my parents. Only hatched the plan last night, didn't we, Lor?' She nods. 'They're going on a cruise to celebrate Mum's seventieth birthday,' he adds, 'and she refused point blank to have a party . . .'

'So we've decided to have one anyway,' Lori says, grinning. 'They *can* come, can't they, Dad?'

'Of course, if they don't mind being trapped for an afternoon with us lot . . .' He looks at me and smiles. 'We're just inviting a few of their friends and relatives who live around Glasgow. It's *really* low-key . . .'

'Oh, you don't want us there, then,' I say quickly, 'if it's just a family thing.'

'No, I'd love you to come,' he insists, and I try to figure out whether he means this, or was pushed into asking us by Lori.

'It'll be fun,' Lori announces, and I see her catching Iain's flat expression as he toys with a paper napkin. 'You should come too, Iain . . .'

'I'm probably doing something,' he says airily. 'When is it anyway?'

'A week on Sunday,' Jack replies. 'Just an afternoon thing. If you're free, we'd love you to come . . .'

'I could probably switch some things around,' he concedes quickly, at which Jack catches my eyes and smiles.

'Great. So, what d'you think, Nads?'

I clear my throat. The thought of hauling Alfie and Molly along to Jack's family gathering feels rather nerve-inducing. 'Are you sure?' I ask. 'I mean, I'd love to meet your parents but maybe it's not the best—'

'I'd like to go, Mum,' Alfie cuts in, placing his cutlery on his plate. I stare at him in amazement.

'Great.' Jack beams at him. 'How was your pizza, anyway?'

'Really good!' Ah, I see: my son's been won over by a vegan margherita.

'Molly?' Jack prompts her. 'D'you fancy braving our family en masse?'

'I'd love to,' she says. 'I don't work Sundays.'

'Brilliant,' Jack enthuses. 'I'm sure you'll like them—'

'Gran and Grandpa are great,' Lori exclaims with genuine warmth. 'They run everything, don't they, Dad?'

Jack nods. 'Yes, pretty much all the young farmers' activities – karaoke nights, parties, that kind of thing . . .'

With the matter apparently settled – and despite my protests – Jack insists on paying the entire bill.

As we make out way out into the damp and chilly night, I glance at Molly, unsurprised that she has agreed to come to Jack's do. But where Alfie's concerned, I'm still amazed. And as we part company, the kids and I walking the few blocks home, I am reluctant to mention it in case he blurts out that he doesn't really want to go, not to a thing with old people, whom he doesn't even know, who are holidaying on a *ship*. I know his father's take on such ventures: 'If I ever mention that I might want to go on a cruise, just shoot me. Or let me go, then shove me overboard.' Since when did we all become so judgemental about other people's holiday choices? However, it seems that Alfie really *is* fine about

184

going, and now I'm thrilled that we've all been asked along.

'Mum?' Alfie looks at me as I let us into our flat.

'Yes, love?' Ah, he's had a change of heart already. My stomach sinks a little.

'I was just, um, thinking. About Jack, I mean . . .'

'Oh, look,' I say quickly, trying to pre-empt what's bound to come next, 'it was nice of you to say you'd go to his do, but you really don't have to . . .'

'It's not that, Mum,' he interrupts. 'It's just . . . you know that celebrity sale thing he mentioned?'

'Yes?'

'Well, what about Dad?'

I can't help smiling at that idea. 'I know he's done pretty well for himself, Alf, but I can't imagine they'd get much at auction for one of his faded old T-shirts . . .'

'No, not *Dad's* stuff.' Alfie snorts at my idiocy. 'I mean, could he help out by asking around? He knows everyone in the business, doesn't he? I know he says he hates all that showbizzy crap, but he's connected . . .'

'Well, yes, of course he is,' I concede. 'D'you honestly think he'd help? I mean, he doesn't even know Jack.'

''Course he would,' Molly enthuses. 'It's for charity, isn't it? Dad's always giving money away. And remember when he allowed *himself* to be auctioned that time? "Win dinner with Danny Raven?"'

Alfie smirks. 'That young film student won it.'

'Yes, and your father was such a surly sod about it that the guy said he wouldn't bother with dessert, as he had to go home early . . .'

Alfie laughs. 'Ask him anyway, Mum. Bet he'll be able to get hold of something . . .'

I look at Molly, and then at Alfie, thinking: maybe this

185

is his way of showing he's accepted Jack, after that terrible first meeting. And now I'm wondering if Jack will be viewed as part of our family one day, and if we will be part of his. I know I'm jumping the gun here, but how lovely it would be if Jack became mates with my kids, and Lori started hanging out with them, in a little-sisterly role . . . she and Molly certainly seemed to get along well when they were searching for Pancake. Perhaps that's how it goes, when you start dating again as an empty nester? Maybe it just takes a little adjustment before everyone settles down and gets used to the new shape of things.

'I think it's a brilliant idea, Alf,' I say, winding an arm around him and managing to plant a kiss on his cheek, before he wriggles from my clutches and spins away.

Chapter Twenty-Three

Jack

While I wouldn't wish for anyone to lose their beloved dog, I am very slightly grateful that it happened. Before Pancake's disappearance, things had started to feel a little odd – sort of distant – between Nadia and me. We've certainly seen a lot less of each other since her kids – particularly Alfie – came home. This is normal, I know, and God, I'd hate to feel as if I'm being possessive over her time. I mean, I'm not a monster, the type to resent a woman's family when I've only been seeing her for a few months. Anyway, at least our pizza night enabled me to meet Molly in a non-mortifying way, and hopefully persuade Alfie that his mother hasn't involved herself with a jerk.

'Thanks for coming out last night,' I tell Nadia when we speak on the phone during my lunch break on Friday.

'Oh, I wish we'd found him,' she says. 'But I do have some good news for you. I spoke to Danny about your celebrity auction thing. I thought he might be able to help . . .'

'Really?' I say, surprised but delighted, as Dinah has just called me again, cajoling me about the darn thing.

'Yeah. It was Alfie's idea actually. I'm not sure if he'll come up with anything, but you never know . . .'

'I really appreciate it,' I tell her as I finish my lunch in the shop's back room. 'So, what're you up to later? Fancy meeting up, or coming over, or—'

'Could we just have a quick drink?' she asks. 'I'm at the studio . . .'

'Great, yes. You can come over to mine afterwards, if you like.'

'I'd love to but Alfie's full of the cold. I did say I'd bring some provisions home and rustle up dinner.'

'Right, of course . . .'

I hear her sigh. 'It's been a bit crap lately, hasn't it?'

'It's fine,' I say firmly. 'You have tons of stuff on, I get that . . .' I'm doing my utmost to not sound like a needy houseplant, requiring constant tending. However, when we meet after work I can't help feeling slightly disappointed that one drink is all we manage before her phone rings.

'Oh, Alf. Can't you get hold of Molly and use her key?' she asks tersely, mobile gripped to her ear. She exhales loudly and rolls her eyes at me. 'You don't have a jacket on? It's not that cold, love. Yes, I know you're ill . . .' The pub is busy, as it's Friday evening and there's a sense of bubbling good humour as the night is only just beginning. But not for us, as Nadia has to leave straight away. 'He went out,' she explains, snatching her jacket from the back of her chair.

'Really? Why?' *I thought he was ill,* is what I mean. But apparently, he was so desperate for Lemsip while Nadia's been in the pub – we've been here for less than half an hour – that he ventured out by himself, shut the door behind him and had forgotten his keys. 'And now,' she says with a grimace, 'he's locked himself out.'

188

She kisses me briefly on the lips, and rushes off to the rescue.

All weekend, Alfie's cold goes on. Oh, I know that's normal for any virus-type thing, and of course Nadia wants to look after him as now I gather it's full-blown flu. But it's a little disconcerting when I call her on Sunday evening – and the whole family (Danny included) are about to go out.

'We're going for dinner,' she says distractedly. 'Danny's been away location-hunting so he's hardly seen the kids. He really wanted to get us all together . . .'

'Oh, right,' I say, which must come out oddly as she says, 'We're just going to a cheapie little noodle bar.'

'I'm just glad Alfie's better,' I say, which doesn't sound right either; after all it was a cold/flu, not malaria. Did it sound like I was being facetious? I wasn't looking to meet up tonight anyway; Lori is here, with a couple of friends. As it's a school in-service day tomorrow I agreed that she could have a sleepover. However, as Nadia and I finish our call, and I wish her a really fun night out ('It's only a quick bowl of noodles, Jack!') I wonder if I have somehow made things worse, by not doing very much at all.

Perhaps that's why, later that night, I find myself doing the ridiculous thing of googling interviews with Danny Raven. These tend to be found in the broadsheet news-papers and specialist film magazines. He's not the kind of 'famous' that the *Daily Mail* goes for. As far as I can gather, no one's particularly interested in his love life (he's been with Kiki for years anyway) or wants to photograph him in his Speedos on a beach. No, he's more the highly respected kind of famous: thoughtful and clever, and a handsome fucker too, I decide, finding myself sinking into a cesspit of gloom as I read about his most recent film, a critical success, and 'an important comment on today's fragmented society', according to the newspaper's clearly besotted interviewer.

Were you surprised by the incredible success of Lavender Road?

DR: I was, yes. I mean, I always believed in the film, right from the start. I knew it had heart and I knew it was a story I had to tell. But the response – well, it's blown me away really, and I'm humbled by it.

Fuck, he's a talented bastard. A decent person, too, by all accounts. Although Nadia's told me some of the lunatic things he did when they were together – buying that *Reservoir Dogs* suit, and then getting pissed while he was wearing it and leaning against a lit candle at a party.

'Can anyone smell burning?' he'd asked, apparently.

'It's you!' Nadia had shrieked at him. 'You're on fire, you bloody nutter!' So that was the suit. There were loads of other incidents too, and eventually her patience just ran out. But not so much that she can't enjoy a Sunday night out with him now . . .

I fetch a beer from the fridge, then retreat back to my bedroom where I read on:

What's next in the pipeline?

I'm starting to cast for another film – a follow-up of sorts, although it'll be its own story. But there'll be characters from Lavender Road *who've moved on, and a new protagonist – a girl who's just come out of the care system as her birth mother has shown up after having disappeared for many years . . .*

You often cast untrained actors, don't you? Why do you favour that approach?

190

It's something that just seems to work for the films I make. There's a freshness there, an authenticity you sometimes don't find with trained actors who know the business; they have agents and a career plan and they're great, yeah, but when you find someone off the street, so to speak, it can be quite dazzling.

Interestingly, the big-name stars involved in your movies tend to have smaller roles.

Yes, well, we like them to know their place [laughs].

Like Seb Jeffries?

Yeah, Seb and I go way back, to my first film twenty years ago, when he was just starting out and not the big star he is now. For me to cast Seb in a main role would be a mistake, I think. He's brilliant, but for me it's more powerful to see him in a supporting role, to let the fresh, untrained actors sing out. It's more interesting. It's not what people expect.

What I love most about your films is that, despite the bleakness, there's always a strong sense of optimism – a belief in the importance of family ties . . .

God, yeah. At least I hope so. I mean, that's what drives us all, isn't it? What else is there, if we don't have that love that binds us? I can't imagine anything more—

'Dad!' Lori bangs on my bedroom door, interrupting my reading.

'Yeah?'

'Not in bed already, are you?'

'No, of course not.'

'Could you heat up the rest of those samosas, then? But don't come in my room. Just leave the tray outside my bedroom door.'

Chapter Twenty-Four

Nadia

Oh God, what a night. A catch-up over noodles ended up with Kiki telling me all the best places to go to in Barcelona – she has been numerous times with girlfriends – while Danny, Molly and Alfie settled into a far more satisfying conversation of their own. Why had she come along at all? I know she's fond of the kids, but this seems to be happening more and more; that she's just 'there', whenever we get together.

Thank goodness it's rare. Mercifully, Molly and Alfie usually spend time with their dad without me being there.

'You really must come to me for a facial before you go,' Kiki remarked. 'I can tell you really need one, Nadia.' She leaned a little closer across the table, gaze fixed upon my face. That's the thing with socialising with a skincare guru. Like falling into conversation with a dentist at a party – when you're convinced they're inspecting your teeth – I can't help feeling that Kiki is always assessing the state of my pores.

'I've never really been a treatment kind of person,' I explained.

'Oh, you should try it. You'll feel like a new person! A facial is the one thing that'll make a big difference to the way you feel . . .'

No, Kiki, I think darkly; the one thing that'll make a big difference is Alfie remembering to flush the loo instead of leaving his pee sitting there, worryingly dark in hue and stinking out the bathroom. Of course, I doubt if anyone *ever* flushes in student halls – and I suppose I'm less worried about his toileting habits than the recent announcement that he has chucked in his chance of further education. But still, it's starting to get to me, and what d'you do in that kind of situation? Ask the pee-leaver to please flush (around fifteen times daily) to no avail, or flush it yourself – or leave it, just to make your point, and endure the smell?

'Life's so stressful these days,' remarked Kiki, who I'd imagine has never had to involve herself with another person's wee, 'but honestly, a facial releases tension like nothing else on earth.'

Danny looked over and grinned. 'Apart from gin,' he said with a snigger.

'Well, that helps too,' she agreed with a tinkly laugh. 'Seriously, Nadia, would you consider it?'

'Oh, I'm not sure if, er, I have the right skin type for it,' I blustered, as I've heard about her 'treatments'. We're not talking the smoothing on of deliciously scented oils, oh no; apparently, Kiki massages the face from the *inside*, jamming her pokey fingers into the mouth. I'd worry, frankly, that she could do me serious harm. 'I'll think about it, though,' I added.

'Are you a bit sensitive, skin-wise?' she asked, toying with a spinach leaf on her chopstick.

'Very,' I said firmly.

'It'll be fine,' she asserted, flashing those bright white teeth. 'C'mon, my treat. Pop over sometime and I'll give you one . . .'

'Ooh, aren't we modern,' Danny said with a guffaw.

'Stop it, Dad,' Molly retorted, laughing.

Kiki beamed at me. 'Give me a ring and we'll fix something up, okay? Go on, Nadia – you do so much for everyone else. You really do owe it to yourself.' Then Danny, who is hardly strapped for cash these days, diverted our attention by making a big issue about the price of the green smoothie Molly had ordered.

'Blended spinach, basically,' he crowed, a bit tipsy by now. 'More fool us for falling for this shit!'

No matter how successful he becomes, and how many glittering red carpet events he's invited to, he can't stop waggling his 'working class' card; rough tough Danny Raven who drinks beer and wears ratty old jeans and T-shirts, forever the professional scruff. 'Didn't you tell me you'd love me to look smarter occasionally?' he asked when I baulked at the thousands he'd spent on that blasted *Reservoir Dogs* suit.

'Yes,' I replied, 'but I just meant, maybe you could get a nice suit out of Marks & Spencer's for when we go somewhere posh?'

He'd snorted at that. 'If you wanted a Marks & Spencer's man, then what the fuck are you doing with me?'

Anyway, the fuss about the green juice mark-up dampened the mood somewhat, and as result of all this, I came home tonight and studied my face for far too long in the bathroom mirror. Was the ageing process accelerating all of a sudden? Was that why Kiki had been so insistent about sorting out my shrivelling skin? And now I'm in bed – alone, naturally – reflecting that a short while ago, I felt so revived and youthful, relishing my new life as an empty nester. I could see Jack when I wanted, have sex in the daytime and eat my lunch standing up, wearing only my knickers if I felt like it, whilst thinking: Well, I realise I'm supposed to feel redundant now the kids have left home. I know I should be texting them every ten minutes and weeping over their childhood teddies and old family photos when they were so little, but actually . . . isn't this bloody *great*?

And now I have a pee-smelling bathroom and Alfie complaining loudly to Molly, directly outside my bedroom: 'See these vitamin capsules Mum got me? I've been taking them for three days and I've just read the ingredients and the casings are made out of milk!'

Well, excuse *me* for caring about his nutrition. Call the Vegan Police and shoot me dead.

Chapter Twenty-Five

Jack

Monday morning arrives, and with it Mags's announcement that a box of new donations contains what she describes as 'one of those dolls that does all the baby things to stop teenage girls getting pregnant'.

'Like what?' I ask, glancing round. We are in the shop's back room, sorting donations; Mags is clutching the rather sinister-looking life-sized doll whilst eating a Magnum ice cream at 10.30 a.m.

'*You* know. It cries all night and screams till you cuddle it and you have to change its nappy.' She pauses. 'Or it's meant to. I think this one's broken inside.'

'Ah, well, we'll probably still get a couple of quid for it,' I remark. 'Your Magnum's dripping, by the way.'

Without responding to my comment, she plonks the half-eaten ice cream on the worktop and bobs down to delve further into the box. 'Look at this!' Now she's brandishing a painted ceramic clog.

'Very nice, Mags . . .'

'And this!' She caresses a carved cherrywood elk. One by one, more items are lined up on the floor while she muses over their potential resale value.

'Maybe something'll just turn up for the auction?' she asks, finishing her Magnum, having left a sticky brown smear on the Formica.

'I doubt it,' I reply. 'But Nadia's asked her ex to put the word out, so that might help.'

'Nadia?' She frowns.

I nod. 'Yeah, you know. You've met her . . .'

'Her ex is going to put the word out? What can *he* do?'

'Well, he's a film director . . .'

'Is he now?' Mags mutters, and I can sense her mood darkening, a situation that lingers on as the morning progresses.

Out in the shop, I glance over at her as she dusts the bric-a-brac unnecessarily, wondering what's got into her now. I'd have expected her to be positively sparkling, with Iain not being around (he's still too busy looking for Pancake to come in at the moment). But the huff continues and, even though she is usually eager to help a customer, she pointedly ignores Jean Cuthbertson when she comes in for an update on the lost wedding ring situation.

'I've been through my whole house and it's not there,' she announces, looking pointedly around the shop as if it might be sitting on a shelf with a price tag attached.

'Jean,' I start, indicating the 'lost ring' note attached to the wall, 'we're doing everything we can . . .'

'How am I going to tell my husband?' she asks sharply. 'He keeps asking where it is. How am I going to tell him it was in the pocket of those trousers?'

'I really am so sorry . . .' Now, out of the corner of my eye, I see Mags crouching at Iain's bookshelf, which she seems to be 'rearranging' (i.e. wantonly muddling crime and romance with no other purpose than to upset him).

'Have you hoovered the shop lately?' Jean wants to know.

'Yes, of course,' I reply.

'It might've been hoovered up then. When did you last empty the bag?'

'Er, quite a while ago, I think,' I say, catching a waft of Jean's overly sweet perfume and taking a step back.

'Can you sift through the bag, then?'

'Not right now,' I say, with as much patience as I can muster.

'Could you do it later?' she asks.

'Jean,' I start, 'I'm pretty sure it hasn't been hoovered up. Someone would have noticed . . .'

'Not if it was that simple boy, they won't.'

I stare at her, hackles rising. '*Simple* boy?'

She nods. 'The one who's, you know . . .'

'I'm not sure who you're talking about,' I say curtly.

'Yes, you do,' she insists. 'The one with the funny flat hair. Sort of dirty blond, wears an old man's cardigan. You know who I mean. He's a bit . . .' She winces.

'Okay,' I say tersely, indignation welling up in me now.

'Two months' wages, that ring cost our Tony.'

'*Yes*, Jean, I do understand that it's very—'

'He had it engraved on the inside!'

I wait for her to catch breath. 'Yes, well, as I said before, we have your number and I'll be sure to call you if it turns up. Now, I'm really sorry but I have an awful lot of stuff to get on with.' I smile tightly, and as soon as Jean has shuffled out of the shop, Mags flutters over, wafting her heavily mascaraed eyelashes at me. 'Ooh, Jack,' she murmurs, clutching a cow-shaped butter dish, 'I love it when you're all masterful like that.'

I laugh uneasily. 'Thank you, Mags.'

She beams. 'I've had a brilliant idea . . .'

'What's that?'

'Maybe the wedding ring *was* hoovered up?'

'Oh, I really don't think . . .'

'I'll take care of it,' she exclaims. 'I did it at home when my diamanté earring flew up the tube. You know what to do?' I shake my head, baffled. 'You just get some newspaper and wet it, and you tip all the stuff from the bag onto it. Everything – all the fluffy, hairy stuff – kind of *settles* onto the wet paper . . .' God, she's making it sound almost relaxing '. . . and then you pick through it and find your thing.'

'Right.' I smile at her.

'I *am* helpful, aren't I?'

'You really are,' I say.

'Am I more helpful than Iain?'

'Everyone's helpful,' I say, which isn't *entirely* truthful, but that's how it is here. In the back room now, we flatten out a newspaper and douse it in water and, under Mags's watchful eye, I tip the contents of the hoover bag onto it.

'Keep looking,' she instructs, breathing over me as I pick through the mass of dirt and bits, the odd foil sweet wrapper or drawing pin catching my eye and giving me false hope.

'No ring,' I say finally, wrapping up the damp mass in the newspaper and dropping it into the bin.

'Worth a try, though, wasn't it?' she asks brightly.

'It's actually a really handy tip to know about,' I enthuse, at which she grins broadly.

199

'That's me. Full of handy tips.' And she beetles off back into the main shop, where she swoops upon a customer who's perusing the summer dresses. 'Try on anything you like. Changing room's over there, I'll guard it if you like . . .'

I watch Mags for a moment from the back room doorway, relieved that our rummaging session through the hoover bag seems to have cheered her up. It gets me sometimes, how much this shop means to some of the volunteers, and how important it is to feel useful and needed. Perhaps it's no coincidence that a lot of our regular helpers don't have children or families of their own – or even friends, in some cases. In a way, perhaps this place fills that void. Yes, we fund animal sanctuaries all over the UK, but it's more than that. Strangers walk past, and I know many of them think, 'It's just a charity shop full of junk.' And of course it is, but it also offers structure and the company of other people, those things that many of us take for granted, but which help to shape all of our lives.

Later, when almost everyone else has gone home, I spot a small box of chocolates sitting on the fridge in the back room. There's a note on the box, written in wonky capital letters:

DEAR JACK,

THOUGHT BLACK MAGIC BETTER THAN MILK TRAY, FOR A MAN. YOU DESERVE THEM! YOU WORK V V V HARD. THANK YOU FOR BEING MY FREIND. LUV MAGS XX.

I clear my throat to get my emotions in check. God, that was sweet of her. It's unlike a volunteer to show *me* any appreciation; quite rightly, it tends to go the other way, as they're the ones who show up day after day without pay.

200

It's only Sally, one of our older volunteers, and me who are left in the shop. 'Ooh, chocolates?' she remarks with a smile, popping her head around the doorway.

'Yes, would you like one?'

'Mmm. Don't mind if I do . . .'

'They were a present from Mags,' I add, whipping off the cellophane layer and offering her the box.

'Ah, that figures,' Sally says, her eyes glinting mischievously now.

'What d'you mean?'

She laughs as she pops a caramel into her mouth. 'You do realise Mags is in love with you, Jack?'

I splutter. 'Don't be crazy. She was just being sweet!'

'Believe that if you want to, but everyone knows.' She smiles wryly and squeezes my arm before heading for the door.

Oh, Jesus Christ. It's my own fault, of course; Elaine reckons I get too involved with the volunteers and customers, but then, who wouldn't in this kind of job? When I worked at Gander Books, my role was clear-cut. It was hard graft, and office hours simply didn't exist – but there were boundaries. I could walk out of our cramped fire hazard of an office, and that was that; there were no lost dogs or wedding rings, no hospital visits or besotted volunteers.

It's Mags I'm thinking about later when I pull on my trainers at home and set off in the light drizzle.

Like Iain, she lives in a flat on her own – only I know less about her living situation than I do about his. I suspect, though, that she has few genuine friends. She talks about her 'favourite lady', Karen, who works on the checkout at her local Sainsbury's, as if they're genuine mates: 'Karen fell off her bike yesterday on her

201

way to work.' 'Karen was saying yoga's really good. I might go along!' As if yoga is a new thing, virtually unheard of, when you cannot move through the streets of Glasgow these days for bouncy people carrying rolled-up mats.

It seems tragic, in this huge city of ours, in which hundreds of thousands of people are all going about their business, meeting friends and looking forward to the weekend, to live the way Mags seems to. Hoping it won't be interpreted in the 'wrong' way, I vow to make a special effort to be appreciative of her efforts in the shop over the next couple of days. And of course, I decide, as fine rain starts to fall and I loop back home, I'll thank her profusely for the chocolates.

As the week goes on, we are deluged with donations. Sales are healthy, and there's a spirit of efficiency and optimism in the shop. Still no celebrity donation, though, which is worrying – especially with Dinah's constant updates. Today – Wednesday – she texted me a photo of a stripy apron with the caption 'Can you match this??!' She then called to announce – gallingly – that the apron was donated by Kevin Masters, a certain celebrity chef/professional bully whom Lori enjoys on TV. Apparently the *brilliant* Inverness shop manager managed to persuade him to offer it up for auction.

'Haven't you managed to get anything yet?' Lori asks dryly, when she comes home from drama club that evening.

'No, not yet,' I reply, in a *but-I'm-working-on-it* sort of tone.

She gives me a look more befitting a disappointed teacher. 'What're you doing about it?'

202

'Well, I've fired off tons of emails to agents and managers,' I reply.

'Has anyone got back to you?' She arches a brow.

'Er, no, not yet.' I pause. 'Maybe I haven't prioritised it enough. To be honest, Lor, it always feels like there are far more urgent things to do.'

She gives me an unimpressed look over her bowl of pasta. 'Like what?'

'Like ploughing through the donations so we can get things on sale and actually function as a shop!' I pause and exhale noisily. 'Anyway, apparently Danny Raven is on the case about the auction. So maybe he'll come up with something . . .'

'Does Nadia still get on with him?' Lori asks.

'Seems like it,' I reply with a shrug.

'Hmm.' She sighs and dumps her fork in her bowl. 'You are still seeing her, aren't you?'

'Of course I am, love. Things have just been a bit hectic now her kids are back . . .'

'Definitely going away together?' she asks.

'To Barcelona? Yes, it's all booked.' I study her face as she pokes at her dinner.

'What is it, Lor?' I ask, sensing her ill humour.

'You've put broccoli in this sauce,' she mutters.

'Oh, I just thought we should be eating more vegetables.'

'I'm not five, Dad,' she says, sounding sharper than usual. 'You don't have to *hide* vegetables anymore.'

'I wasn't trying to hide them, I just didn't flag them up.'

At least this provokes a flicker of a smile as we clear the table. Lori insists that everything's 'fine' as I make us a pot of tea, and I know better than to keep asking and probing as we settle down to watch TV.

203

She never told me the real reason she wasn't allowed to go to the school Christmas dance all those months ago, or why she didn't even mention the history department's trip to the Highlands that most of her friends seemed to go on, and which I only heard about afterwards. Whenever I ask whether she has homework these days she tells me it's 'kind of optional', and she claimed she 'totally forgot' to tell me about the last parents' evening, or give me the letter about it (and no, she hadn't told her mother either, so neither of us had gone).

How the hell is a parent supposed to find out what's going on in their teenager's life? It's sodding impossible.

After copious flicking with our numerous remotes, Lori finds an episode of the Kevin Masters show that we haven't yet seen. As we sip our tea in silence, I hope that his verbal assassination of a 'gritty' cheesecake might perk her up, but no, she remains morose and apparently unaffected.

'Lor,' I venture, 'are you okay with Nadia and her kids coming to our thing on Sunday?'

''Course I am,' she declares, gaze fixed on the TV. 'I suggested it, didn't I?'

'Well, yes,' I say hesitantly. 'I know you did. I thought that was lovely of you. But you just seem a bit—'

'I'm all right, Dad. Really.' She pulls up her bony knees and hugs them to her chin.

As we fall back into silence, I glance at her. I thought it was odd, actually, her asking them along; almost as if she was overly keen to show how absolutely *fine* she is with everything. She can be unfathomable sometimes.

'You don't mind me going away with Nadia, do you?' I venture, as Kevin Masters makes a gagging motion when appraising a contestant's lemon tart. 'I mean, you would say, wouldn't you, if you didn't want me to?'

'Why would I mind?' she asks sharply. 'You've been away plenty of times before, haven't you?' Without her, she means.

'Um, yes, I suppose so.' It's true; a bunch of us went to Prague for Fergus's fortieth, and to Berlin last October for no reason in particular. My ex Zoe and I had a terrible week in Croatia when she shunned my suggestions for exploring the area, insisting instead on frying herself on the beach. I've never been a lying-on-the-beach kind of person, but went along with it while Zoe chain-smoked, grinding her cigarette butts into the sand and ignoring my warnings that she was burning. 'I'm slathered in sunscreen, Mr Health and Safety Man,' she retorted. 'Relax, live a little . . .'

A few hours later, she was lobster pink and vomiting into the washbasin in our tiny apartment. 'Don't you dare say I told you so,' she raged as I held back her hair.

Now Kevin Masters' round, profusely sweating face has filled the screen as he announces this episode's winner. Usually, Lori has a strong opinion on his choice, but tonight she seems preoccupied. 'You can phone or text me any time, you know,' I remark, as the show's credits roll. 'When I'm in Barcelona, I mean. Even when I'm abroad you can still—'

'I do know how phones work, Dad,' she snaps.

I glance at her. 'Okay, love . . . So, um, are you looking forward to *our* trip?' I ask, referring to the week in Majorca we have planned for late August.

'Yeah, of course I am.'

'Just the two of us this year!'

'Uh-huh.' She clicks off the TV and we sit in silence for a few moments. I knew better than to quiz her on why her friend Shannon didn't want to come this year,

205

as she has previously, but I gather it's because she has a boyfriend now, and his parents have invited her on *their* holiday. How can poor Lori compete with a boy with oddly swept-over hair (she has shown me photos) who somehow manages to be a DJ who's 'mainly known for techno' at fifteen years old? I mean, how can he be 'mainly known' for anything when he's not even old enough to buy a lottery ticket?

It's slightly disappointing, and I'm worried that Lori will be lonely or bored, trapped with me for a week, even though Shannon came armed with so many bottles and potions last year that we had to check in her case to the plane's hold. She'd brought fake tan, for goodness' sake – at thirteen years old! Over the following week I'd kept spotting evidence of her presence around the apartment: some kind of sparkly brown powder scattered all over the beige rug, and what looked like a spider sitting on the side of the washbasin, but which turned out to be a strip of false eyelashes. But then, Lori and Shannon had fun, giggling away on the beach and in their shared room, while I hung back, trying to give them their space.

'Dad, can I ask you something?' Lori sits up straight and turns to me, with the poise of an interviewer.

'Yes, what is it, love?' I ask lightly.

'Um . . . after your holiday . . . I mean the one with Nadia, not *our* one . . .' Christ, she's making it sound as if I have about fifteen holidays a year . . . 'D'you think you might move in with her?' she blurts out quickly.

I stare at my daughter. 'Is that what you're thinking? That me and Nadia are planning to live together?'

'Well, I just wondered if you might be.' She shrugs dramatically, affecting casualness as she gets up.

'Oh, darling – no,' I say firmly. 'There are no plans for

that at all. We haven't even mentioned it as a possibility . . .' I stand up and place my hands on her shoulders. 'Lor, I knew something was bothering you. I could just tell—'

'It's just, if you do move in with Nadia,' she cuts in, refusing to meet my gaze now, 'I guess you'll sell this place and I'll have to stay with Mum the whole time, won't I?' It all tumbles out in a rush.

'No, love! I'm *not* selling this place. It couldn't be further from my mind. It's your home as much as it is mine. But what's this about? Is it Mum? Is there something—'

'No!' she snaps.

I pause as she lowers her gaze. 'Look, honey – Nadia and I are having a good time together, and who knows where it's going to lead? I have no idea at the moment. It's still quite early days and we'll just have to see . . .'

'Yeah, I know that.'

'And anyway, I have you, and she has Alfie and Molly, and you're always going to take priority for us . . .'

'That's not fair, though, is it?' she asks, frowning.

I step back and study her face. 'What d'you mean?'

'Well,' she says, assuming an airy tone now, 'I'm practically an adult, and they actually *are* adults. They don't even live with her.'

'It looks like Alfie does for the time being,' I remark.

'Yeah, but what about you and *your* life? You're getting older, Dad, and—'

'Cheers, love,' I say, attempting a joke. 'Are you suggesting I should settle down properly before I croak it?'

She tries, feebly, for a smile. 'Sorry.'

'Oh, Lori, sweetheart. I wish you'd said you were worried . . .'

'I'm *not* worried.'

'You are, I can tell.'

'How?'

'Because I'm your dad,' I say, 'and I know when you're upset . . .'

'I'm not upset!' We look at each other, and I squeeze her hand. It's a wobbly smile that flickers across her lips, but at least it's there now, and she lets me hug her.

'Darling, look,' I say firmly, 'I can promise you, things aren't going to change, okay? I mean, there are no plans that you don't know about, none at all.'

She nods.

'You would tell me, wouldn't you, if something was happening with Mum?' I add. 'I mean, you've been spending more time here, and that's great. You know it's always fine with me. But you really must tell me if something's worrying you or stressing you out—'

'Of course I would,' she says quickly, turning away to slurp the cold dregs of tea from her mug, then she saunters off towards her room to signal that there's nothing more to say on the matter.

Chapter Twenty-Six

'Bloody teenagers,' Nadia murmurs, late the following night, when we are lying together in the semi-darkness. Yes, we are actually in bed, at her place. Molly greeted me with a grin and a brief hug, and Alfie managed a restrained sort of half-smile – at least I *think* it was a smile. Maybe he was trying to suppress a sneeze, with him just having got over his cold and everything.

Anyway, it was certainly better than a sneer or a blank stare. The four of us sat around and chatted for a while – well, for about three and a half minutes – and I managed not to mention the weather or university or which Scottish city might be the wettest/most northerly. Basically, I just came out with a lots of 'Phew, that was a busy week'-type stuff. Then Molly went out, perhaps to anaesthetise herself with booze after being subjected to my prattlings, and Alfie drifted off to his room.

All of that might sound unremarkable, but I am regarding it as a huge step forward, in terms of being able to see Nadia with her family around. When Nadia suggested we come to bed, Alfie didn't leap from his room and try to stop us. No one has claimed to be ill, or switched on a deafening electric toothbrush or shoved a chilli in their eye.

The 'bloody teenagers' reference was made because Molly apparently nicked Nadia's £40 bottle of gin a couple of nights ago, to take to a gathering, blithely saying that she would replace it when her mother 'needed' it. 'What she actually said,' Nadia says, 'is, "Tell me when you really need gin and I'll go out and get some for you." Like I have a drink problem and she – the martyr – will supply me with booze if I'm absolutely desperate. When in fact she stole my special gin with the Orkney botanicals!'

'And she'll replace it with Gordon's – if you're lucky,' I suggest with a smile.

'More like supermarket own brand. And a half bottle at that,' she says, and I smile and stroke her hair, realising what an idiot teenager I've been myself lately, with all my Danny Raven googling, huffing over them all going out for some bog-standard noodles and even slightly resenting the fact that she has been busy looking after her ill son.

'I've been so short with Alfie too,' she continues in a hushed voice. 'It sounds awful but I have this finite amount of patience with all the moaning and sodden tissues dropped everywhere, and once that's run out . . .'

Personally, I'd say she's been *beyond* patient. 'Does anyone actually not mind looking after sick people,' I remark, 'apart from nurses?'

She laughs. 'But we're not allowed to admit that, are we? As parents, I mean. We're supposed to tend them without complaint or resentment. Oh, and weirdly, he relaxed his "no honey" rule . . .'

'Do vegans avoid honey?'

'I think it's a shady area,' she says, 'but he decided it was okay to have it in a hot toddy with lemon juice, hot water and a big glug of whisky.'

'Sounds like it did the trick, the honey-with-alcohol method.'

'Yeah.' She smiles, her wonderful, expressive face illuminated on one side by the street light eking in through her cream curtains. Although I'm pretty sure nothing will 'happen' tonight, it's lovely just being in bed together, even if we are just catching up on each other's lives. No one could ever accuse me of being too sex-focused when I am perfectly happy to lie here and update her on my party preparations; specifically, that my freezer currently houses one hundred and forty sausage rolls and, yes, several quiches. Seems like I am Quiche Man again.

She rests her head on my chest as I update her on the Pancake situation (he's still missing), and give her a thrilling, doubtlessly libido-stirring account of how I raked through the hoover bag's contents with my bare fingers in an attempt to find Jean Cuthbertson's wedding ring. I also mention that Mags left me a box of Black Magic in the back room. However, I don't tell her what Sally said about Mags's alleged crush on me (or whatever it is), as you can't say, 'One of the volunteers is apparently in love with me,' without sounding ridiculous. Nor do I mention Lori bringing up the totally hypothetical issue of Nadia and I moving in together, because how would I do that without it becoming an actual thing, to be discussed as a possibility 'one day'?

Instead, I bask in pleasure as she tells me that her night out with Danny, his girlfriend and the kids was 'a bit shit actually. Kiki's convinced I need some kind of deep treatment to prop up my face before everything subsides . . .'

211

'What?' I exclaim.

'And Danny moaned about the price of the green juice Molly ordered . . .' I listen sympathetically, trying to hide my delight. 'He thinks the juice thing's ridiculous,' she adds, 'when it's just some pulverised veg.'

'I suppose he has a point,' I say, magnanimously.

'Or is it centrifuged?' she asks, and I agree that that's probably the correct term, although my attention is wavering now as she is caressing my inner thigh. On and on, her fingers go, whirling and stroking in that lovely slow and sensitive way she has, rendering me incapable of continuing our conversation about juice-pricing policies. And then, my God, we are kissing and then actually doing it, with a young, impressionable person under the same roof, capable of crashing through her bedroom door with an axe, or at least filing an official complaint to some official body or other for impacting negatively upon his mental health. And although we are *quieter* than mice – or maybe because of that, and the way the sound limitations seem to heighten our every breath – it is possibly one of the most thrilling experiences I can ever remember.

And as we lie there afterwards, in a fuzz of amazement at having managed it at all, it strikes me – for perhaps the thousandth time – that I am extremely glad that I chose to buy Christmas presents in Lush during my lunch break on December 20.

Chapter Twenty-Seven

Nadia

What a relief it was to have Jack stay over on Thursday night, and for it to happen, to reassure us both that we can be together, and even get down to it when one or both of the kids are at home. However, I was *slightly* relieved that neither Molly nor Alfie had surfaced as Jack and I had coffee and bagels, before he shot off to work.

Still, it feels as if we are over a slight hurdle, and over the next couple of days, I allow myself to feel cautiously optimistic about Jack's gathering. Of course it'll be fine, I tell myself, whilst trying to plough through my work. It's a long time since I had to worry about how the kids would 'behave' whenever I took them along to something special.

Sunday arrives, and after much deliberation I opt for a dress I bought in last year's sales. It's bias cut and loose-fitting, a beautiful cobalt blue with a tiny white flower print. I blow-dry my hair and apply light make-up, and decide on flat pumps. 'Not too dowdy?' I ask Molly, as I dither about in our hallway.

'It's *so* not dowdy,' she enthuses. 'You look lovely, Mum. Really pretty.'

'Oh, thanks, darling. So do you.'

She looks down, having swapped her usual jeans and baggy T-shirt for an actual dress – vintage red and black spot – without having even been asked to dress smartly. 'Aw, this old thing,' she says, laughing, tugging at the hem. Meanwhile Alfie has shaved and washed his abundant dark hair, and looks remarkably presentable in clean jeans and a black T-shirt, admittedly ironed by me – swiftly – in the hope that Molly wouldn't see. She did, though.

'Why d'you do Alfie's ironing for him?' she asked, rounding on me.

'Because if I didn't he'd go out in a crumpled one.'

'Well, let him!' She groaned in exasperation. Molly hasn't let me iron anything of hers since she was about fifteen.

And now, admittedly, I'm feeling rather edgy as we set off in my car, just after two p.m. Molly is in the passenger seat, Alfie in the back, along with a bunch of mixed flowers, a cheery combination of lilacs and lime greens wrapped in cellophane and secured with brightly coloured twine. I popped out and chose them this morning, taking care not to go for anything ostentatious. The last thing I want is for us to arrive, all three of us new to Jack's family, with a whacking *ta-daaaah!* kind of bouquet.

As we make our way across town on this blue-skied afternoon, I figure that it's perhaps not ideal, meeting Jack's parents for the first time at a family event. But then, he did say it was just a little gathering, a few drinks and snacks, nothing formal. I suppose I'm just horribly out of touch with the 'meeting a boyfriend's parents'-type scenario, because to get to that stage, you have to have reached proper relationship territory. I was hardly going to meet Ryan Tibbles' mum and dad.

214

As we arrive at Jack's flat with our wine and our flowers, and Jack greets us at the door, I can tell immediately by all the chatter and laughter that chilly formality won't be an issue today. Jack kisses and hugs me, and greets Molly and Alfie warmly. I glance at Alfie, delighted that he's scrubbed up so well. Perhaps he's on the way to getting himself back together, and recovering from the Camilla episode. Maybe he won't notice if that blasted onesie 'accidentally' finds its way into Jack's charity shop. He might even find a job to see him through the summer, and even agree to go back to uni . . .

I've never been one of those smug mothers who brags about her children's achievements. In fact, on occasion, I've probably focused too much on the stuff I've done wrong instead of allowing myself to think, 'C'mon, Nadia – you haven't cocked up *too* badly. Look at these lovely young people you helped to create.'

Right now, though, I *do* feel proud of Molly and Alfie, just for being here really, all smiles and pleasantries as we step into Jack's flat. 'They're all keen to meet you,' he says with an apologetic grin as he leads us along the hallway, through the kitchen and out towards the block's shared back garden, where everyone seems to have gathered.

'Really?' I ask.

'Yeah. Mum's taken up painting, and I made the mistake of telling her you're an illustrator. Sorry if she foists her sketchbooks on you . . .'

'Oh, that's okay,' I say quickly as we step outside. 'I'd love to see them.' I pause. 'Is Iain here?'

'Nope, he called off,' Jack says. 'Reckons he's coming down with something. I think he liked the *idea* of coming, but when it came down to it, nerves got the better of him.'

I nod. 'Well, at least he knows he was invited.'

'Yeah.' Jack smiles. 'Anyway, let me get you some drinks . . . Lori, could you help, please?'

'Sure,' she says, all smiles when she sees Molly.

'I love your top,' Molly says, and Lori looks down.

'Aw, thanks. Got it from Dad's shop.'

'You're so lucky that he runs a charity shop!'

'Yeah, I know.' Lori beams.

'I told you, I'm coming over as soon as I get a day off. Get all the best stuff.' Lori laughs, and I sense how much she has warmed to Molly already: this cool older girl, wearing not a scrap of make-up, hair worn loose and tumbling casually around her face. Alfie is holding back a little, but I'd expected this. At least he's come, I reflect; the way things have been recently, that's a breakthrough.

As Lori and her startlingly tanned friend go off to fetch everyone drinks, Jack introduces us to his mother, Pauline, his father, Brendan, and an assortment of aunts, uncles and family friends, whose names I try to remember as we are greeted warmly.

'Lovely to meet you. Jack's been telling us all about you . . .' This is Brendan, who Jack has told me is sixty-nine years old. Tall and rangy, with a light tan and sparkling pale blue eyes, he looks at least a decade younger.

'Good things, I hope,' I say with a smile, liking him immediately.

'Oh, yes, of course, love. Nothing but good stuff!' He beams at Alfie, Molly and me. 'You're like peas in a pod, you three . . .'

Alfie smiles politely.

'Oh, what a handsome boy you are,' Pauline enthuses, when she's been introduced.

'*Mum*,' Jack scolds her good-naturedly as my son shuffles uneasily, unsure of what to do with the compliment.

Pauline laughs. As a farmer's wife, I'd imagined her to be the homely, scrubbed-cheeked sort, but in reality she is startlingly elegant with enviable cheekbones, expertly applied subtle make-up, and a chic silvery bob. 'So, you're at university, Alfie?' she asks as Lori returns with our drinks, and Jack wanders off to greet a cluster of new arrivals.

'Well, er, I've just sort of—'

'Alfie's just finished his first year,' I cut in, knowing it's wrong to answer for him, but I'm less than keen to discuss the whole dropping-out issue right now.

'How about you, Molly?' Pauline asks.

'I'm at Edinburgh uni,' my daughter replies.

'What're you studying, love?'

'Neuroscience.'

'Oh, my goodness! You've got it all going on, girl. Good for you . . .' She grins and pats Molly's arm, and I glance at Alfie and want to hug him. 'So, Nadia,' Pauline adds, 'I hear you're an artist . . .'

'Yes, well, an illustrator really . . .'

'Jack says you've worked for John Lewis!'

'Oh, yes, I did a stationery range for them . . .' I can't help feeling flattered that Jack has mentioned this to his mum.

'Mum worships at the altar of John Lewis,' Jack remarks with a smile as he passes with a plate of sandwiches.

And now one of Jack's aunts – Hilary, I think, I'm hopeless at remembering a whole raft of names – has beetled over to ask, 'You work for John Lewis, Nadia? Lucky you! I hear they offer a brilliant discount . . .'

217

'Oh, I'm just a freelancer,' I start to explain, but she isn't having any of it as a tall, ginger-haired man joins us. The aunt introduces us: 'This is Drew, my husband. Drew, this is Nadia. You know – the one who works for John Lewis?'

'Lovely to meet you,' he says, shaking my hand warmly. 'See that cake over there?' He indicates an impressive creation that has appeared amongst the sandwich and sausage roll platters on the table. Shaped like a ship, it's smothered in white fondant icing with numerous windows painted on.

'It looks lovely,' I say.

'Hilary made it,' he announces with pride, 'didn't you, love? For Brendan and Pauline's send-off—'

'Really? It's so professional.' I glance around the garden, aware of checking up on Alfie, who looks a little stranded now, hovering close to Molly and Lori but not really joining in.

'She does them for birthdays, parties – any occasion really,' jovial Drew goes on, taking a big swig from his wine glass. 'You should stock them.'

I look at him, momentarily confused. 'Sorry, I don't—'

'Seriously,' he says, 'you should sell them in John Lewis.' He pauses. 'They do sell cakes, don't they?'

'Er, no, I don't think—'

'In the cafés, then? They all have cafés, don't they?'

'Yes, as far as I know . . .'

He beams at me. 'There you go then!'

I smile, deciding it's a little too late to explain that I only designed a small range of children's party stationery for the company, and hold no sway whatsoever when it comes to the restaurant menu. Not that it matters, as the general talk soon turns to Brendan and Pauline's

218

forthcoming cruise, which will take them from Portsmouth to South Africa, Gambia and Mozambique. Jack's parents are clearly thrilled about their trip.

'First proper break we've ever had in all our married life,' Brendan tells me, leaning close to my ear.

'Really?' I gasp. 'That's incredible. I'm sure you deserve it.'

'We're very lucky,' Pauline concedes. 'Jack's big brother Craig insisted it was time for us to do something like this, and of course he can run things perfectly well while we're away.'

'We've been saying it for years,' Jack says as he arrives with a plateful of sausage rolls.

Brendan laughs. 'Anyway, they ganged up, the two of them . . .'

'So we're off,' Pauline says with a smile, 'for fifty-two days!' Drinks are replenished – as I'm driving I'm sticking to water – and as the talk of the cruise continues, I notice now that Lori's tanned friend is wearing astoundingly lush false eyelashes. You can virtually feel the gust whenever she blinks.

Alfie is starting to look more relaxed now, and I wonder how much booze he's knocked back already. He's positioned himself by an ice bucket filled with bottles of white wine, and I've spotted him helping himself a couple of times. At least he seems to be enjoying himself, I reflect, aware of over-fretting again.

'Would you like to see my sketches, Nadia?' Pauline asks now, clearly a little giddy herself from knocking back several glasses of wine in the sunshine.

'I'd love to,' I say, and off she dashes. Spotting me standing alone momentarily, Drew reappears, with a different aunt-and-uncle pairing.

'Lovely son and daughter you have,' the woman says.

'Thank you,' I say, genuinely delighted. Is anything more pleasing than someone complimenting your offspring?

'Jack said they're twins,' she marvels. 'What a gift!'

'I guess so,' I say, glowing with pleasure now as I allow myself to think: maybe we're all going to get along after all. Jack, Lori and my family, I mean. Of course, it's ridiculous to think I need my children's approval to be involved with someone, but it'll be a whole lot easier if they can all rub along reasonably happily. And now, as the afternoon tips into a glorious evening – it's unusually warm, even for early June – I start to wonder about Jack and me, and where we're going. I don't mean in a place sense – we're off to Barcelona next Sunday – but after that, as the summer stretches on.

I turn to see Alfie laughing loudly at something his sister has said. Lori and her friend are chuckling too. Alfie looks a little tipsy, but then, he is nineteen, he's allowed to drink; I'll just wander over in a minute and quietly suggest that he takes it easy.

Despite not drinking, I'm still finding the convivial atmosphere infectious. When Pauline returns with a leather-backed sketchbook, I am all revved up to say kind things about her drawings, whatever they're like – because why wouldn't I? She is my boyfriend's mum, and she's rather tipsy and excited about flying down to Southampton and boarding that Africa-bound boat.

'Please be honest,' she says with a nervous smile as she hands the book to me, as if I might review it unfavourably.

I turn the thick pages. Clearly, she has a natural talent for watercolour landscapes; the scenes she's captured, of

Perthshire hills and villages, are quite beautiful. 'These are lovely,' I exclaim.

Brendan reappears at her side, clutching a plate bearing a wedge of ship-cake. 'Aren't they! Isn't she talented?'

'Oh I don't know about that,' Pauline says, flushing as other guests cluster around.

'No, you really are,' I say firmly, studying more sketches of the family's Perthshire farm: the stout, proud house, numerous outbuildings and the surrounding lush landscape, all lovingly depicted in subtle colours. 'You've even made a stone wall look beautiful,' I add.

As Molly and Alfie wander over, I hold out the open sketchbook for them to see. 'Oh, that's lovely,' Molly exclaims, peering more closely at a sketch of a sheepdog stretched out in a yard.

'Thank you,' Pauline says with a self-deprecating smile. I turn to Alfie. 'Isn't it gorgeous?'

'Yeah, that's really nice. Where is it?'

'That's our farm,' Brendan explains, wiping a cake crumb from his mouth. 'Plenty of subjects for Pauline to draw, we've very lucky . . .'

'You're farmers?' he asks.

I turn and look at him. 'I told you that, Alfie. I mentioned that Jack grew up on a farm, and this is his parents' first proper holiday in—'

'Did you mention it? I can't remember.'

'Yes, Alf,' I say firmly as he drains his wine glass. I have told him this, I'm sure of it, but then often, when I try to communicate with Alfie, I'm aware that I might as well have opted for Morse code for all he's taking in.

Pauline turns the page. The next sketch is of several cows dotted about in the shade of a tree.

'Is that your farm too?' Alfie asks.

'Yes,' Pauline says, beaming proudly. 'We have thirty-six acres . . .'

'And you have *livestock*?' my son exclaims.

'We have a dairy herd, yes,' Brendan replies.

Alfie clears his throat, and I catch his sister – who's always been acutely attuned to his moods – giving him a sharp look. 'Don't you have a problem with that?' he asks, turning to Brendan now.

Brendan frowns, clearly puzzled, but seems to recover his joie de vivre quickly. 'God, yes, we've had our tricky patches, haven't we, love?'

'Oh, yes,' Pauline says as I hand her back her sketch-book, which she holds close to her chest.

'That's why they started diversifying a few years back,' adds Drew.

'Into vegetables?' Alfie asks.

'No – into cheese, love,' Pauline explains. 'Small batches at first but things have grown slowly and steadily. We're delighted, actually. We'd never imagined it would take off like it has. You should try some . . .' She indicates the table where Jack is busily setting out more food.

'I'm vegan,' Alfie announces, rather tartly, 'so I don't eat cheese.'

'Well, no one's forcing you, son,' Brendan chuckles, 'although I have to say you're missing out. Sure you don't want to try our new batch?'

'I don't eat it,' Alfie reiterates.

'Okay, Alf, you've made your point,' I murmur, sensing my stomach tightening.

Alfie frowns at me, briefly, and I start to enthuse again over Pauline's sketches. 'You really should exhibit some of these,' I start. 'I'm sure a local gallery would show them . . .'

'That's so nice of you to say,' she says, beaming now. 'But it's just a little hobby really . . .'

'I have to say,' Alfie observes now, 'the dairy industry is just as bad as the meat industry.'

'Sorry?' Brendan says with a frown.

'Alfie, just leave it please,' I say, throwing him a quick warning look, and wrangling the topic back to Pauline's sketches. 'I bet these would sell, if you wanted to do that.'

'You really think so?' Her blue eyes are glinting. 'You've really made my day, saying that, you being a proper artist.'

'Nads?' I turn to see Jack beckoning me over to the table, and hesitate over whether to leave the group. It's fine, I tell myself; Alfie's drunk a little too much, but Molly's here too, and hopefully, now he's made his statement, he'll let the matter drop. I think of Danny's words: *You worry too much. What did it matter that he chucked in the tuba?* He's right, I decide; I've fussed over him way more than Molly, who wouldn't have allowed it anyway. From the age of eight she was insisting on assembling her own packed lunches – raggedy jam sandwiches, Monster Munch and a token tangerine – and I wasn't allowed to even glimpse her UCAS application before it was submitted.

'Hey,' I say, joining Jack at the table where a selection of cheeses and oatcakes have been laid out beautifully, accessorised with grapes and figs.

'How're you doing?' he asks.

'Great,' I reply, sensing the knot of tension in my stomach unravelling a little. 'Your parents are lovely. I'm sorry to say Alfie's being a bit opinionated . . .'

'Oh, I'm sure he's fine. He's obviously very passionate about the cause.'

'Yeah, I guess so.' I smile, taking in Jack's handsome

face. He has an ease about him that's terribly attractive; there's something extremely appealing about a man who's relaxed around his parents, and a whole gang of uncles and aunts. I remember Danny resorting to an awful lot of huffing and eye-rolling whenever we visited his mum and dad. *Tinned ham again,* he'd mutter, looking pained, *with the jelly still stuck to it.* I was always seized by an urge to hiss at him to grow up. My parents had had a particular fondness for tinned meat too, and I'd wished they were still around to offer it to me.

Jack squeezes my hand. 'You're a big hit with them, I can tell. And . . .' He leans towards me and whispers: 'You look gorgeous today.'

I smile. 'Oh, thanks.'

'Will you wear that dress in Barcelona?'

'I'd sort of planned to.' I pause. 'Can't wait, can you?'

'God, no.' He laughs. 'I'm counting the days actually.'

'Ooh, I must try these,' Drew announces as he wanders towards us, smiling his thanks as Jack refills his glass.

'I think you should,' Jack says.

'All made on the McConnell farm, I assume?'

'Of course,' Jack says, with notable pride. 'Their cheddar was the category winner at last year's National Cheese Awards.'

'I'd better try some too,' I say. As Jack cuts me a sliver, I glance back across the garden where Molly and Alfie are still chatting with his parents. A few others have gathered around now, and the atmosphere seems to have lightened again. Alfie is a fully grown adult, I remind myself. This is a perfectly lovely, grown-up gathering – not nursery. I don't need to be on watch as if a fracas might break out at the sandpit.

'Oh, this is delicious,' I enthuse, nibbling at the cheese. 'So different to your supermarket stuff . . .'

'Takes fifteen months for it to mature,' one of the aunts explains as she arrives to top up her glass.

'Hmm. It's so . . . *rounded*.' I pop another sliver of delicious, densely creamy cheese into my mouth. Oh, wow. I adore cheese. I'm in awe of people who make it and have the willpower to leave it sitting around for months, slowly ripening, without scoffing the lot. Even when making the kids' favourite lasagne back in the day, I'd find myself guzzling chunks of industrial orange cheddar before I'd even managed to get it in the oven.

Now Jack is cutting a slice of a different variety for me to try. 'This is softer and creamier . . .'

'Sweet talker,' I chuckle as he smears it onto an oatcake for me. I take a bite. 'That is sensational!'

'Yeah.' He laughs.

'Do they always bring a selection for you?'

'Yep, emergency rations, as if I'm a starving student . . .'

Then Alfie's voice rings out across the garden: 'No, but what I'm saying is—'

'Let's not talk about this right now, son, okay? Can we just leave it?' That's Brendan, who sounds firmer now, and somewhat less cheery. I stand still, the cheese-smeared cracker held halfway to my mouth. Molly has hold of Alfie's arm, and she's scowling at him. The atmosphere has changed drastically from when we were chatting about John Lewis and Pauline's sketches.

'Oh, Christ, Jack,' I murmur.

'Nads, I'm sure it's fine,' he says. 'Don't worry—'

'It looks like he's lecturing them,' I say, poised to rejoin the group.

'They can handle it,' Jack insists. 'Honestly, they're

225

tough people. They're not going to be upset by a teenager telling them—'

'So you're saying it's fine,' Alfie bellows suddenly, 'to keep cows in an almost constant state of lactation?'

Jack winces. 'Oh.'

'God, I'm so sorry . . .'

'Nads, it's all right,' he starts, touching my arm.

I pull away, sensing my cheeks flaring. 'Hang on.' Horribly aware of the gathering storm, I dump my plate next to the now-ravaged ship cake and hurry across the lawn.

Chapter Twenty-Eight

It doesn't seem so bad when I land back at the assembled group. Alfie has stopped shouting, and if Brendan and Pauline were taken aback by his sudden outburst, then they seem to have recovered themselves with admirable speed. Perhaps they even found it amusing – youthful indignation and all that. After all, they have brought up three sons of their own, and lost one – their youngest boy. I can't begin to imagine how anyone would cope with something like that.

'Hi,' I say, a tad too brightly, beaming around at everyone. 'I've just been sampling your cheeses, Brendan. They really are delicious.'

'Thank you, love,' he says warmly. 'You should take some home with you. We always bring Jack a hamper full.'

'Oh, I will,' I say, sipping my glass of sparkling water and wishing now that it was wine and I wasn't driving. Still, it's probably best that I have my wits about me. More fool me for assuming I could bring the kids along to such an event, and just kick back and relax . . .

At least Jack's parents seem like lovely people, I decide. I have already warmed to Pauline, and Brendan seems quite the charmer with his lean, weathered face, glinting eyes and shock of fading auburn hair. I am always terribly impressed by proper artisan types, people who make delicious things with care and love, and I plan to quiz them all about it so Alfie can't get a word in. *Anything* to prevent him from haranguing them on their special day . . .

'Who d'you sell your cheeses to?' I ask.

'We have a shop on site at the farm,' Pauline explains, 'and there's an online business too. We have a couple of local youngsters who help with that. Then there are delis in Crieff and Pitlochry that stock the full ranges. We've even had interest from Waitrose.'

'That's amazing,' I enthuse, making a mental note to keep conversation on the cheese track. This is good, I decide. Let's *cheese* our way through the rest of the afternoon . . . A pause settles over us. 'D'you eat much of it yourself?' I ask, aware of Molly throwing me a quizzical look, meaning: *Mum, could you stop going on now, please?* But I can't. Naturally, I know my children intimately, and I can sense Alfie drawing himself up for another attack.

'We do, love, but . . .' Pauline pats her slightly rounded stomach. 'We need to limit ourselves, don't we, Bren?'

'Oh, I can eat whatever I want,' he says, grinning. 'When you work like I do, up at five in the morning for milking—'

'Up at five!' I exclaim, aware of Alfie's gaze boring into him.

'We're well used to it,' Brendan explains. 'It's all we've ever known, isn't it, love?' Pauline nods. 'It was my parents' place,' he adds. 'It's in our blood.'

'We're very proud of it,' his wife asserts, still cradling her sketchbook. 'We grow our own feed and we're very careful about animal welfare . . .' I catch her smiling indulgently at my son. 'So, you've nothing to worry about there, Alfie.'

'Hmmm,' he murmurs.

Please, Alf, I will him, keep your opinions to yourself. This is Jack's family. I love Jack, and it's been brilliant, these past few months. Please don't screw it all up by making a show of yourself and, by association, of me.

I shoot him a pleading look, which I'm hoping he'll interpret correctly. Meanwhile, one of the aunts is enthusing over the garden, which is shared between six flats. For a communal space, it really is lovely; I know Jack tinkers about here, weeding the border by the craggy brick wall, hauling out the lawnmower and trying to keep things tidy. He told me that he and Lori always have a competition to see who can grow the biggest sunflower. God, I *love* this man. I glance over towards the table, where he's chatting to an elderly lady in a floral frock.

'We grow all our own vegetables,' Pauline is saying now. Ah: now we're on safer territory. Homely, nutritious, non-controversial veg. We've done cheese, so perhaps we can move on to potatoes now? *Okay, so they're dairy farmers*, I try to communicate telepathically to Alfie. *However, they are clearly thoughtful, decent people too, enjoying a family gathering before the trip of their lives. So don't you bloody well dare spoil it.*

'It sounds like a lovely place,' Molly says.

'Yes, but it's still farming, isn't it?' Alfie starts. I give him a warning look, which seems to silence him momentarily.

'Of course it is,' Brendan says mildly.

229

'And basically, that means using animals as a commodity,' my son remarks.

'Alfie, this isn't the time,' I say firmly, catching Molly's exasperated look.

'I'm just saying,' he starts.

'Alfie!'

He blinks at me, and I sip more water, wishing we could browse through Pauline's drawings again, and that Alfie would drift away from this group and perhaps offer to help, the way Lori is, touring the garden with her spray-tanned friend, offering platters of sandwiches and cake.

'Look,' Brendan says, rather wearily, 'farms are always going to exist as long as people eat meat . . .'

Yes,' he concedes, 'but if we all adopted a plant-based diet—'

'Alfie, please,' I start.

'I don't think *that's* going to happen,' Brendan says, shaking his head.

'Why not?' Alfie crows, seemingly impervious now to my interjections, or my hand clamped on his arm.

He shakes me off, and I catch a hazy look in his eyes. Christ, he must have knocked back even more wine than I realised. He looks pretty drunk, at four in the afternoon. How have I allowed this to happen?

'That's not the way the world works,' Brendan says firmly, glowering at Alfie now.

'Couldn't you have an arable farm?' Alfie counters, at which Brendan actually splutters, which seems to incense my son even further.

'Right, so we ditch our sixty-strong dairy herd and, what . . . plant a few carrots? Or a couple of rows of rocket?'

'You said you grow vegetables!'

'Alfie!' I snap. 'Please, stop this now. It's not your place to—'

'We do grow veg,' Pauline cuts in, throwing her husband a worried glance, 'but they're just for the kitchen . . .'

'Well, do it on a bigger scale, then,' Alfie barks.

'Oh, Christ,' Brendan groans, and I'm aware now of the various aunts and uncles melting away from our group, and Jack landing beside me.

'Hey, Alfie,' he says with a tight smile. 'Everything okay here?'

Molly looks at him, and then me, and slopes off towards the table to refill her glass. 'No, it's not,' I say coldly. 'I'm so sorry. I think we'd better go . . .'

'Oh, really?' he asks, looking crestfallen.

'No need to do that,' Pauline adds.

'Alf,' I murmur, touching his arm again, 'can you just drop this subject?'

He frowns at his empty glass. To their credit, Brendan and Pauline have stuck with us, and seem to be waiting patiently to see what will happen next. 'All I was trying to say,' he starts – is that a glimmer of humility I detect now? – 'is that veganism is the only way to go if you care about animals, and view them as being equal to human beings, instead of just existing for our convenience . . .'

'We all care about animals,' I say firmly. 'Look at how we spent hours the other evening, looking for Pancake . . .'

'Pancake?' Pauline asks, brightening now.

'A volunteer's dog,' Jack says. 'He escaped, took off in shock when—'

'But we don't *respect* them,' Alfie thunders, for some reason directing this at Pauline now. 'If we farm them,

231

we don't. If a child dies, then it's terrible – but why is it so different for animals? I mean, why are they regarded as lesser species just because—'

'Alfie!' Brendan cuts in sharply.

'If a kid is killed by a car,' my son rants on, 'then it's a huge tragedy, isn't it? But if it's a bird or a badger it's just left lying in the road as if it never mattered at all . . .' Alfie gazes around at his stunned audience. A few moments ago, I'd started to think we *could* stay for a while, if I banished him to the bottom of the garden where Molly is chatting to Lori and the spray-tanned girl. But now, with a sickening dread, I realise that won't happen. Pauline is staring at Alfie, with her mouth open and tears rolling down her cheeks, and Brendan and Jack are comforting her. I try to apologise, but Jack silences me with a wave of his hand before turning back to his mother.

'It's okay, Jack,' Pauline says, choking back sobs.

'Mum, shhh, please . . .' He turns to look at me, and I see something in those blue eyes, something I have never seen before: a kind of hurt that I'd do anything to heal.

'Jack,' I start. 'I'm so sorry. Maybe we'd better leave . . .'

'Yes, I think you should go now,' he says, with a calmness that crushes my heart. 'Please, Nadia. Please just take your kids and go.'

Chapter Twenty-Nine

Jack

Mum is crying, just like she was crying back then, all those years ago. A tough, no-nonsense farmer's wife in tears. The very sound fills me with dread and memories.

'Have you heard from Sandy?' Mum had managed to choke out when she'd called. 'Have you any idea where he could be, Jack? You must know. He talks to you. He *never* talks to us anymore . . .'

'Mum, I don't know what you mean,' I said blearily, clutching the phone and surveying the cans, bottles and ashtrays all dumped haphazardly on my kitchen table. I was twenty-nine years old, but still capable of acting like a teenager myself. We'd gone to a party last night, my flatmate Nick and I, and that girl had been there – the one who worked in the Spanish restaurant, who I had the hots for. For a while I'd thought she might have been interested in me. She'd quizzed me about Gander Books, where I worked, and was telling me about the poetry she wrote and did I think they'd be interested?

'It's worth a try,' I told her. 'Send it to me and I'll

make sure someone reads it.' In truth, I had no influence whatsoever and actually, Gander rarely published poetry. But Christ, I was a bit drunk and eager to impress.

I went to the loo at the party, and when I came back, she and some six-foot-five giant with a bushy red ponytail were locked in a snog, his hands clamped firmly on her bum.

So that was that. Announcing to Nick that the party was 'crap', I suggested that a few of us should debunk to our place, and that's what we did. We sat up drinking and smoking and talking rubbish until dawn crept into the kitchen.

'He set off yesterday afternoon,' Mum was telling me now, 'and he promised to phone me when he arrived in Glasgow. Haven't you heard anything at all?'

'Mum, I didn't even know he was coming!' I exclaimed. 'He wanted to, but I said he couldn't. Not this weekend . . .'

'But he told me you said it was fine!' I could sense the panic rising in her voice.

'He was lying then,' I said, wondering if it was my hangover that was making me feel jittery now, or a growing fear that something bad had happened to him. Of course it hadn't, I told myself. Sandy was sixteen and sharp as anything. 'I told him it wasn't the best time,' I added, aware of another sensation washing over me now: shame, that's what it was. 'I've, um, had loads of stuff on . . .'

'Well, I tried to call you last night,' Mum went on, 'but you didn't answer. I left you a message on that machine . . .'

The answerphone, she meant, and I knew she hated

'talking into it' as she always put it – so she must have been pretty het up to leave a message. Back then, I hardly knew anyone who had a mobile.

I glanced across the debris on the table to where the phone cradle sat; the red light was blinking. Nick and I were terrible for picking up our messages, and Mum was now saying, 'I left a couple, actually, and another this morning.'

'Sorry, I've only just got up,' I muttered.

'I thought you'd think I was being silly and that the two of you had probably gone out somewhere—'

'Mum, he'll be fine,' I cut in. 'You know what he's like. He might have set off to see me, but he probably ran into some mates, and they all decided to go off somewhere else instead.'

'But where?' she asked. 'We've called everyone we can think of. No one's seen him. I think he must have taken a bag – I can't find that khaki rucksack of his . . .' She started crying again. 'And Craig's been all over the place this morning, driving around looking for him, checking all the fields, the woods, *everywhere* . . .'

'Mum, it's okay,' I murmured, aware of a tightening in my throat. We hung on in silence for a few minutes. The kitchen smelt disgusting, of stale smoke and beer and something burnt. I remembered then that Nick had decided to make cheese on toast, and I'd spotted it under the grill, its edges blackened, the cheese blistering, and we'd turfed it into the bin.

'Shall we phone the police, or what?' she asked, and I heard Dad's voice, deep and powerful, always seemingly in control, in the background. I grabbed a dented lager can, took a swig and nearly choked. It had a cigarette butt in it.

'Jack?' Mum prompted me. 'What d'you think we can do, love? I'm frantic here. I just want to know he's safe . . .'

'Let me see if he's left me a message, Mum,' I said. 'I'll call you right back.'

Chapter Thirty

Nadia

'It's good that they're not afraid to speak up,' Danny had declared once, after we'd been told at parents' evening that both of our children were prone to shouting out in class. 'Who wants biddable kids who accept everything at face value? Wouldn't you rather they were bold and outspoken, and had the courage to stand up for their beliefs?'

Actually, no, I wouldn't! Not if it means Alfie coming out with a torrent to an elderly couple whom we'd never met before, at a gathering hosted by my boyfriend (or is he my ex-boyfriend now?). In fact, I'd rather they were biddable. Terrible word, admittedly – it sounds namby-pamby and spineless – but how about we substitute it for 'polite', or maybe 'sensitive to other people's feelings'?

'Mum?'

This time, as we drive home, Molly is installed in the back seat, and Alfie is hunched sullenly beside me.

'Mum!' she repeats, more sharply this time.

'Yes?' I snap, which is unfair of me, as she wasn't the one to make Pauline cry.

'You're driving a bit . . . erratically.'

'Oh, am I?' No bloody wonder. I'm having to muster every ounce of willpower not to stamp down on the accelerator really hard.

'You're going round corners a bit too fast . . .'

'Molly, I do know how to drive, thank you!' I shout. Again, utterly unfair.

'All right, all right,' she murmurs. 'Never mind me. Just crash the car then. Write it off and kill us all . . .'

Oh to have biddable young offspring, perhaps from the Victorian era, who'd be so happy to spend time with Mama – having been raised by nannies – that they'd simply sit quietly and beam at me in delight.

I glance at Alfie who is studiously picking at his finger-nails. He apologised, but too late, and to the wrong people. 'Sorry, Mum,' he muttered under his breath as we left Jack's flat – but what good was that? I ushered him out quickly as if he were a confused person who'd wandered into a ladies' knitting evening and started shouting sexually inappropriate comments. Molly followed closely behind.

'I really am sorry,' Alfie adds now.

'I told you, it's Jack's parents – and Jack – who you should be apologising to.' He flinches as I clip our wing mirror by careering too closely to a parked car.

'Well, I will, then. I'll do it as soon as I can.'

I flick him a quick sideways look. 'How are you going to do that?'

'Uh . . . I don't know.' He pauses. 'I could write them a letter . . .'

'I thought sending a letter was a logistical nightmare?' I remark tartly.

'No, I could probably manage it,' he says, as if we are talking about white water rafting in Nepal.

238

I jam my back teeth together, unable to trust myself to continue any kind of conversation with Alfie without braining him. And now, as we drive towards home, my anger morphs into something more akin to . . . *desolation.* I'm picturing Jack's face, and his wide, bright smile as we arrived with our flowers and wine, and how welcoming everyone was, and how much I was enjoying browsing through Pauline's sketchbook and sampling the cheeses, just being part of Jack's world.

I'd felt honoured that he'd asked not just me, but my kids, too, because he is a kind and generous man, and – I like to think – he wanted us to be there together, as a couple. I'd never imagined we'd leave, the three of us, amidst expressions of shock and disapproval, or that I'd be wiping tears from my face as we pull up in our street.

I let us into the flat. Molly disappears into her room, and Alfie to his. Thankfully, there is wine in the fridge; half a bottle of cheap Pinot that's being lying open for God knows how long. I pour the lot into a huge glass, noting that it tastes slightly off – but what the hell. I'd guzzle anything right now.

My mobile rings, and I snatch it from my bag, praying that it's Jack to say it's okay, don't worry – they were a bit shaken up but everyone's fine now.

It's Danny. I let it ring out and stuff it back into my bag. A text follows: *Kiki says she has a cancellation for Mon, that facial thing at 12. Fancy it?*

'Oh, fuck off,' I mutter, taking a big swig from my glass. So I really 'need' one, do I? She's probably right. But I suspect it would only help if she could actually get *into* my brain, and work her pokey fingers around in there – and somehow, miraculously, erase my shame.

*

Despite my tentative texts and call next day, it seems that things are far from okay with Jack and me. Yes, he said, his parents headed off for their flight to Southampton.

'Alfie knows he was out of order,' I told him, aware of concerned looks from Corinne and Gus in the studio. I've been trying to throw myself into my latest commissions, but am aware that my work isn't quite right. There's a flatness about it, mirroring the way I feel inside.

'There's no point in going over it now,' Jack said. 'Look – I'd better go. I'm in the shop . . .'

'Don't suppose Pancake's turned up?' I asked.

'Oh, yeah. He was found late last night.'

'Really?' I exclaimed. 'You didn't let me know!'

'Um, I didn't think to . . .' he said, and I was shocked. The kids and I had been involved in the search! Couldn't he have texted the good news? 'Someone found him,' Jack added, 'wandering around their garden just across from Kelvingrove. Looked like he'd been hiding out in their shed.'

'Well, that's good,' I said, trying not to sound put out.

'Yeah. Anyway, sorry. Mags is just asking me to price up some stuff . . .'

I wanted to add, 'We are still okay, aren't we? We're still going away together?' But he'd gone. Clearly, stock pricing was far more urgent than talking to me.

And now, on this rainy Monday afternoon in the studio, I figure that of course we'll be okay, once the dust has settled. I'm truly sorry for Alfie's bolshiness, but it's happened; I've learned from it. I won't take him to any social gathering until he's at least forty years old, and even then I'll gaffer tape his mouth shut. Hopefully, Alfie has learned from it too. He mooched around the flat last night, applying for casual work: bar shifts at a racecourse, flogging pies at a football match. Pies, stuffed with meat?

'I really need a job,' he said, tapping away at his laptop.

'I guess you could wear industrial gloves,' I remarked, 'for handling them.'

'Mmm. Yeah.' He thought I was serious, and I was startled by a sudden wave of sympathy for him – over his broken relationship, his uncertain future and the fact that he hasn't yet fathomed out who he is.

'But, if you do find yourself working in that kind of environment,' I added, 'you can't start haranguing strangers.'

'No, I realise that,' he says, gaze downcast.

'You can't shout at some massive Celtic supporter for eating the meat pies you've just sold him.'

'I know that, Mum!'

'Do you, though, Alfie?' I asked, really worrying for him now. 'You did go to a party for dairy farmers and shout about lactation.'

He looked up at me, his eyes filled with sudden tears. 'Oh, Mum. I'm sorry . . .'

I put down my paintbrush now, not caring that I've splashed paint where it shouldn't be.

'Nads?' Gus calls across the studio. He and Corinne don't know about yesterday's disaster. They've been immersed in their work, and I haven't been able to face going into it anyway. At least, not yet.

'You okay?' Corinne asks, frowning as she looks round from her desk.

'Oh, I'm fine,' I say briskly, but of course it all tumbles out.

'Silly bugger,' Corinne says, handing me a mug of tea. 'I know . . .'

241

'Oh, sod it,' Gus says, draping an arm around my shoulders now. 'It's not that bad. He's nineteen, and if you can't act like an opinionated git at that age, then when can you?'

I can't help smiling at that, and thinking yes, he's probably right. Alfie's still a kid, really, seemingly incapable of flushing the loo or making a sandwich without carpeting the kitchen in crumbs. However badly he's behaved, he didn't mean to upset anyone. He's my son and I love him to pieces. And nothing will ever change that.

Chapter Thirty-One

Jack

Nadia wasn't to know why Mum was so upset – and neither was Alfie. However, pretty much everyone else knew, so last night I found myself in the weird position of defending Alfie when he'd been a sanctimonious goat.

Is it okay to feel that way about the son of the woman I love? Fuck it – I *do* feel that way. I might be of the opinion that his mother is the most gorgeous woman I've ever met, but that doesn't mean I have to be friends with her son.

After Nadia and her kids left last night, the do was pretty much over. Mum gathered herself together, but everyone kept fussing around her and the atmosphere was hardly celebratory. 'That was pretty insensitive,' Drew remarked later, when we'd all drifted inside and my parents had retired to bed.

'Yeah,' Lori exclaimed, all indignant. 'Poor Gran!'

'Well, he wasn't to know,' I said.

'Imagine, someone coming out with something like that, after what your mum and dad went through,' muttered Aunt Hilary, who loves a bit of intrigue. 'D'you think it'll ruin their holiday?'

'No, absolutely not,' I murmured, just wanting everyone to leave so I could get some kip on the sofa bed – my parents were sleeping in my room – and for them to head off for their flight to Southampton in the morning. I wished I'd never had the damn party.

And now, as I price up bone china crockery in the shop's back room, I remind myself that Alfie was just being 'passionate about the cause', and that he had no way of knowing that shouting about dead children and roadkill was possibly the worst thing he could do in front of my parents.

I've never told Nadia that I started volunteering at a charity shop because Sandy had been obsessed by dogs. It might have seemed weird or maudlin and, anyway, I have never felt the need to explain it to anyone. It was just something I wanted to do – for me and for him.

Sometimes we'd have a dog on the farm who wasn't up to much, but Sandy wouldn't allow him to be re-homed. The most clueless, erratic collie would end up being his pet – allowed to sleep on his bed – and he was brilliant with them. He wanted to work with animals, like at a rescue centre, or training guide dogs or police dogs, something like that. He'd planned to visit all the dog rescue centres in Glasgow to see if he could volunteer over a summer. He was always desperate to get to the city. So desperate, in fact, that he made up his mind to come, even when I said he couldn't.

Alfie didn't know any of this, so it's not really his fault, and it's not Nadia's either. After all, it's not as if she could have lassoed him and dragged him, still shouting about lactating cows and why my dad should grow carrots, out of my garden. It's going to make things difficult, though, with me and Alfie. I think it's safe to say that we're probably not heading for the beers-together scenario I'd envisaged at some point down the line.

Chapter Thirty-Two

Nadia

Although we still haven't seen each other since Sunday, I can sense the chilliness emanating from Jack. I understand why, of course. No one wants to see their mum reduced to tears. But I've apologised over and over, and even suggested I call his mum, or write her a note – but of course she's at sea for fifty-odd days (I have a mad vision of sending, I don't know, an albatross or something with an airmail letter) and anyway, he doesn't want me to. *It's fine, it'll blow over,* he said on the phone, rather brusquely. And now I'm at a loss as to how I can make things right.

At least we've been in touch sporadically, and our trip is on the horizon; that's sure to smooth things out. I've texted to suggest he stays over on Saturday night, as our flight is early Sunday morning from Glasgow airport.

Okay, he replied.

U sure? I texted back. *We are okay, aren't we?*

Sure, talk to you soon, xx. Well, a couple of kisses at least. I decided to try to amuse him:

Off to clinic with Corinne this afternoon. She's having

*coil removed, bit nervous. Says it's been there since Blair
was Prime Minister and she's built it up to a massive thing.
Well, not really massive. I think they're pretty tiny . . .*

Installed at the kitchen table, I sip my first coffee of
the day on Thursday morning and pause before sending.
Pre Alfie's outburst, I'd have just pinged it off without a
second's thought, knowing he'd find it amusing. Jack likes
Corinne, finds her scatty and fun and entertaining. Now,
though, I wonder if it's a bit much.

Still, I press send.

Half an hour later he replies: *Hope all goes well.*

He's just busy, I tell myself, figuring that he might have
gone to open up the shop early, as he does sometimes,
when there's a backlog of donations to sort out.

And now Molly emerges from her room, a little dozy
but at least *up* – in contrast to her brother, who's never
appeared before I've set off for the studio.

'Hey, Mum.'

'Hi, sweetheart.' She pushes back her tangled hair and
smiles. I've enjoyed having her around, although I glimpse
her rarely. Most evenings she's been catching up with her
old friends. Sometimes she's hauled Alfie along, after
nagging him to 'tidy yourself up a bit', and off they've
gone, tumbling back in way after I've gone to bed.

At least he's out and about, I've told myself. It has to
be better than lying about in that wretched onesie.

'How's work going?' I ask her, pouring her a coffee
from the jug.

She smirks. 'It's crap, Mum. Totally crap, but it's money.'

'Oh, really? Why's it so bad?'

She slurps her coffee and tips a mound of muesli into
a bowl. 'The greenhouse is roasting, even when it's not
that hot outside. The trolleys with plants on are impossible

247

to move without crashing into things, and customers keep coming in with plants they've killed – sometimes ones they haven't even bought from us – blaming it on us . . .'

'Oh, God,' I say, laughing.

'Yeah! They'll go, "Look at the state of this jasmine. Totally wilted and dead!" And it'll still have its IKEA label on.'

'The *cheek* . . .'

She spoons cereal into her mouth. 'But you know the worst thing?'

'No?'

'Kids,' she exclaims, 'running about, riding on trolleys, kicking over geraniums . . .'

'Oh God, I can imagine,' I murmur, remembering the one time Danny and I took her and Alfie to such a place. I'd had a notion of planting herbs in our shared garden for all the residents' use, and needed pots, compost and plants. *Jesus wept,* Danny wailed, as our pre-schoolers careered about, knocking over a concrete Buddha and cracking his head.

'That's what they think of all that mindfulness shit,' some bloke announced, laughing.

'This is seven degrees of hell, Nadia!' Danny blasted. 'Fuck the compost. Get in the sodding car, you lot – right now!'

Garden centres joined a list, which already included IKEA, Clarks shoe shops, DFS sofa stores, department store china departments and all the tea rooms in the world as Places The Ravens Would Never Go To As A Family Ever Again. 'You can go on your own next time,' Danny thundered, while I protested, 'I just thought it'd be nice to have fresh herbs. The ones in packets always go off.'

248

'I'm never having kids,' Molly declares now.

I glance at her, all slender and lovely in her vest top and jeans, her skin genuinely radiant, as opposed to the sort of radiance promised by the way of extortionate creams. 'I felt the same,' I tell her, 'when I was your age.'

She tips her head and looks at me. 'So what changed your mind?'

'Um . . . meeting Dad, I guess?' It feels a little odd to admit this, given our circumstances now.

'Huh.' She seems to digest this like some kind of interesting but rather odd-tasting sweet.

'I'm never going to change *my* mind,' she declares. 'I always thought babies were lovely, but not now, not after working at that place.'

'A few shifts at a garden centre have altered the whole course of your future . . .' I smile.

'Well, yeah!'

'Aren't there any parts of the job you enjoy?'

She wolfs the rest of her muesli and dumps her bowl in the sink, for those ever-obliging washing-up fairies to attend to. Whilst she doesn't cause quite the levels of devastation that Alfie does, I really need to establish a few house rules. 'I quite like arranging the seed packets in alphabetical order,' she decides.

'Sounds therapeutic.'

'It is! It's soothing. It should be offered as a treatment for people who are under stress.'

'Maybe Alfie could do some shifts there?' I suggest, not entirely joking.

She shakes her head and pulls an expression of mock-horror. 'No way am I working with him.' She hugs me briefly, stuffs her hair into a ponytail band, and is gone.

Before leaving for the studio, I alert Alfie to the fact

249

that I am off to work, and perhaps he could get up soon and follow up his job applications?

'Mmm, yeah,' he drawls from his room. My phone rings as I stride towards the subway; it's Danny.

'Hi,' I say. 'Everything okay?'

'Um, Kiki wants to know about that facial?'

'Are you the messenger now?' I ask, faintly amused.

'Looks like it,' he says. 'Can you just agree to a time slot?'

'For God's sake, Danny! I don't even want one. This is crazy, that you're haranguing me about it just to get her off your back . . .'

'Uh, she just seems to think you'd benefit from it. Look, I've got to go to a meeting in a minute. We're just starting casting; it's mental at the moment . . .'

'You called *me*,' I remind him. Is anything more annoying than someone phoning, then implying they're too busy to talk?

'Yeah, I know.'

'Okay, can I just ask, does she do those facials on herself?'

'Huh?'

'I mean, does she put her own fingers in her mouth and massage them about?'

He splutters. 'Jesus. I've no idea . . . Okay, look – she said how about Saturday, ten a.m.?'

'All right.' Hell, why not? I am intrigued, and if it'll help to erase a few crevices from my face in time for Barcelona, then why not?

'Brilliant. Oh, and there's something else . . .'

'No, just a facial,' I say quickly. 'I don't want any kind of acid peel, or my epidermis sanded off. There's too much potential for things to go wrong.'

'No – I mean for the auction thing,' he explains.

At the subway's entrance now, I stop and frown. 'What auction?'

'Your boyfriend's celebrity auction thing? For the charity?'

'Oh yes. I'd forgotten about that!'

'Well, I have something for him,' he says, adopting a brisker tone now.

'What is it?'

'A denim jacket,' he replies. 'Just an old thing, Levi's I think, covered in rusty old badges, looks like it's been lying in the corner of a club having beer sloshed on it since about 1995. But if he wants it . . .'

'Whose is it?' I ask, stepping into the station now, expecting some industry bod I've never heard of.

'Seb Jeffries.'

I stop again. '*The* Seb Jeffries?' Christ, I know they're mates, sort of – at least he's appeared in several of Danny's films. 'Danny, that's amazing!'

'Well, it's all I could get,' he mutters.

I hear voices in the background, someone calling his name. *Danny, can we get things started now, please?*

'Just a minute,' he says distractedly, then to me: 'I hear there was some kind of fracas at a party for your boyfriend's parents?'

'Yeah, it was all pretty awful.'

'Well, Alfie feels terrible, you know. Look, Nads – we know what he's like, thinking he bloody knows everything, but he's not all bad, is he? I mean, he has a good heart, underneath all the bullshit and bluster.'

'Yes, of course he does,' I say quickly.

'Mmm. Yeah. Well, he called me, nagging about that bloody auction, said we *had* to help Jack out. Went on about some face-of-waffles woman's gloves . . .'

251

'Mittens,' I correct him, my stomach beginning to fizzle with excitement now.

'Gloves, mittens, whatever, and I said yeah, I'd try and come up with something. So, Seb said he could have the jacket . . .'

'This is way better than an apron or mittens,' I gush now, barely able to contain myself. This will make everything all right. Jack will be delighted, and Alfie forgiven, and . . .

'Well, okay,' Danny says, 'I'll get Kiki to bring it along to the salon on Saturday and you can pick it up then.'

'Great, thank you,' I say, overwhelmed with gratitude now. 'Thank you, Danny. I can't tell you how much . . .'

'Okay bye,' he barks, switching back into professional mode now, and he's gone.

We're in the sexual health clinic waiting room, Corinne and I, although we're not behaving in a terribly clinicy sort of way. While the only other person here – a man in his early twenties – looks decidedly glum, we are giddy over the thought of Seb Jeffries' jacket, and the fact that on Saturday my mouth will be probed by Kiki's fingers – and, on top of all that, Corinne is determined to 'get a good look at that coil when it comes out'.

'Why d'you want to?' I ask, trying to keep my voice low. I don't wish to traumatise the young man.

'Because it's interesting,' she declares. 'I haven't seen it since it went in, and I'm pretty sure that was pre-decimalisation.'

He slides his gaze towards us and he shuffles on his plastic chair.

'It'll be like being reunited with an old, long-lost friend,' I murmur. 'Like that programme with Cilla Black . . .'

252

'*Surprise Surprise*,' she reminds me. 'It'll be like a ship-wreck, covered in barnacles, being dragged up from the seabed . . .' She shudders. 'I should donate it to some-where.'

'Jack's auction?' I suggest, and we both splutter. 'Actually, he does have some crazy things donated to the shop,' I add. It strikes me now that it's been a while since he sent me a picture of a quirky donation, to amuse me: a jigsaw depicting the Blue Peter tortoise, a box of plastic knickers. Perhaps nothing funny has been handed in – although I realise it's more likely that we're not in a 'sending amusing pictures' phase just now.

'I was thinking more of a museum,' Corinne adds. 'Oh, thanks for being here with me. I was freaking out last night, but it really has to come out. It's way overdue.'

'If it were a library book,' I whisper, 'you'd owe thou-sands.'

The young man's name is called, and he stands up with a barely perceptible smile, before disappearing around the corner. And then Corinne is called. Thankfully, she hasn't asked me to go in with her, so I'm left to mull over the good news I'll be able to tell Jack, when we speak.

I have already decided to hang back and wait until the jacket is actually in my possession – post-facial – just in case it doesn't actually happen. The last thing I want is to promise something wonderful, and then not deliver. But I still fiddle with my phone, fighting an urge to text Jack.

Corinne emerges remarkably quickly, all smiles. 'It was easy,' she reports. 'There are two little strings, I'd forgotten about those . . .'

'Like a light pull? That's handy!'

253

'Yeah. The nurse just told me to cough and it pinged out.'

'Well, that's good.'

'It nearly hit her in the face,' Corinne chuckles as we step out into the late afternoon sunshine. We continue in this vein, discussing mid-life sex as we wander towards the city centre and find ourselves occupying a table at one of the pop-up bars in the busy street. Just across from Lush, as it happens.

'She wanted to talk to me about contraception,' she adds, after we have ordered a glass of white wine each, 'as if I'm twenty years old. Christ, I'm nearly fifty, Nads! I've been single for three years, I'm not looking for a serious partner – and if I fancy a fling, then obviously, condoms are fine . . .'

'Keep your voice down,' I chuckle as the waiter heads over. 'Fancy some wine?'

'Oh my God, yes,' she declares, grinning. 'After today, I fancy *all* the wine.'

Chapter Thirty-Three

Jack

There should be a celebratory atmosphere in the shop, what with Iain showing up for his shifts again following Pancake's return, and it being Mags's birthday on this sunny Thursday. But there's a kind of tension in the air, and I'm getting a sense that Mags preferred it when Iain was off, Pancake-hunting. Then she could tamper with his books and hover around me far more than usual, as if in his absence I needed 'extra help'. It was all, 'Like a coffee, Jack?' 'Can I get your lunch when I'm out? Doesn't Iain always get you the wrong thing?' And now he's here again, she seems to be sulking, eyeing the supermarket cake I brought in and saying merely, 'Thank you, is it lemon or plain sponge?'

There's still no sign of that wedding ring, much to Jean's consternation when she pops in again. And Dinah has called to tell me that the Dumfries shop has managed to get hold of a diamanté tiara donated by some model-cum-TV-presenter, who has also agreed to come to the actual event.

'I'm working on it,' I told her. 'I'm sure we'll manage

to get hold of something.' Hmm. Ratty old T-shirt donated by the drummer of a Glasgow band no one's heard of? Realistically, it might come to that.

As I lock up the shop, I wonder – with a prickle of shame – whether the flatness in the shop today might have been down to me.

It's later, when I've been home and changed into my running gear, that Nadia calls me. 'Hey, how's it going?'

I can tell immediately that she's had a few wines, and I'm a little envious; I'd far rather go out for a drink than a run tonight. 'I'm good,' I reply.

A small pause. 'I'm out with Corinne. We've ended up having a couple of drinks after that, um, that thing she had done – you know?'

'Oh, yeah,' I say.

Nadia chuckles, and I'm overcome with a snag of sadness. She's so . . . buoyant and alive. From that first night we went out, I've felt as if the world around me has had a filter applied. Not one of those crappy Instagram ones that Lori always scolds me for using – 'They're awful, Dad! Here, give it to me!' – but a subtle brightening, entirely natural and filling me with joy.

'Corinne says to tell you,' she adds, 'd'you think that thing she had removed could be donated somewhere? To a museum, or displayed on the fourth plinth in Trafalgar Square?'

In the background, Corinne barks with laughter.

'Haha,' I say dryly.

'Jack?' There's concern in Nadia's voice now.

'Yeah?'

Another pause. 'Look, I wasn't going to say anything,' she starts now. 'But after Sunday, Alfie must've felt pretty awful – I mean, genuinely sorry – because he rang his dad—'

'Look, we've talked about it,' I say firmly. 'I don't think we should go on about it anymore, okay? There's nothing else to say, really.' I inhale deeply. I am standing outside my block, poised to go for my run. 'They're on their cruise now,' I breeze on, 'and by the time they come back, they'll be full of all that, so it's fine.'

Although I can hear the chatter and laughter from a bar somewhere, Nadia doesn't speak for a moment. 'Jack, I know Alfie's a bit of a disaster at the moment. There's stuff that's gone on at uni – I don't know whether it's with his girlfriend, or the course, or what it is. I'm just hoping that he gets himself together this summer, you know? And finds a job, like his sister has – anything to give him some structure, a sense of purpose . . .' She tails off. 'Are you doing anything right now? Why don't you come into town and meet us for a drink?'

'Oh, I can't right now,' I mutter, knowing I should see her really, to explain precisely why Mum was so upset. But she's with her friend, and they've had a few wines, and I can imagine how it'd turn out: a flood of emotions and gushing apologies that would do no good at all.

'What are you doing?' Nadia asks.

'I'm just about to go for a run.'

'Ah, right . . .' She makes some kind of noise, and perhaps I misconstrue it, but it sounds like an exasperated sigh.

'So, I'd better go,' I add.

'Oh, please come out,' she exclaims. 'I'd love to see you. I'm sorry it's been so weird since Sunday. It's like we're not communicating the same anymore. Maybe it's me, and I'm just being paranoid . . .'

257

'Let's talk another time,' I start.

'Things'll be a lot better when he has a job,' she reiterates.

'Well, maybe his dad can help him out?'

There's a lull in the background noise. Perhaps she has stepped outside. 'What d'you mean?'

'You know,' I say, hating the coldness that's crept into my voice now, 'with a job or something. You mentioned he's casting for a film. There must be loads of work for—'

'You mean his dad could put him in the film?' she asks tersely. I'm cursing myself now for leading our conversation down this road. 'It was just a thought,' I say now, aware of a dramatic change of mood as Nadia clears her throat.

'The film industry doesn't work like that,' she says coldly.

'Well, I just wondered, seeing as Danny often uses people off the street, who have no drama training or anything . . .'

'You think he'd just stick his son in a film?' she gasps. 'How would that look? Alfie isn't even interested in acting – not remotely. He'd *hate* it . . .'

We fall into an ill-humoured silence. It's a lovely, warm evening, and the tiny park across my street is filling with groups of students sprawled out on blankets, drinking from plastic cups. There's a whiff of weed in the air.

'Jack?' Nadia's voice jolts me.

'Yeah?'

'Are you . . . okay?'

'I'm fine,' I reply, over-emphatically. 'I was agreeing with you that it might be good for Alfie to do something, to see what working is like,' I mutter, aware that I'm spinning off now down an ill-advised direction, but unable to pull myself back.

'He *has* been working,' she says levelly. 'He's a student. He studies English Lit.'

'I know.'

Then: 'You think, because he's not up milking cows at five in the morning, then he's not really working?'

'Oh, that's nice!' I snap.

'Well, what d'you mean, then?'

I exhale, my heart quickening now. Before I met Nadia, I guess I knew there was something missing in my life, but I didn't know what it was. I'd had my years with Elaine, which ended pretty disastrously when I found Charlie Gillespie's wallet sitting on the side of our bath (they'd had a sodding bath together, in our house! He'd dried his arse on one of our towels!). It had all come out, how he'd made her feel special and young and really cared about her (yeah, for a couple of months after she and I had split up, and then he ended it). And later on there was Zoe, and a couple of others, people I thought I cared about but it was never right, because there was something missing.

Well, maybe that's the way life is, I figure now, as Nadia politely asks me not to tell her what's good for her own child, adding, 'I'd never tell you how to be a parent to Lori. I just wouldn't, Jack. It's out of bounds.' Maybe there is always something missing, and we learn to adapt to that, filling the space with other things, like, uh – well, *stuff*. Because no one can have everything, can they? I have a brilliant daughter, and a job I love – well, like, at least. It's okay. *I* am okay.

I open my mouth to try to express all of this, but she's off again: 'Look, Jack, can we stop this, please? I wasn't calling to argue with you. I phoned because I was happy. Okay, I'm a bit drunk, but Corinne and I have had a laugh and I had great news to tell you—'

259

'Nadia, please stop,' I say curtly.

'You're still in a mood with me, aren't you? You're still mad about Sunday . . .'

'I don't want to go over and over this.'

'He'd had too much wine. He didn't mean it . . .'

'Nadia,' I cut in, although for that split second it could be Elaine I'm talking to, who'd call, drunk, when she was on a night out, even after we'd broken up, and after the Charlie Gillespie episode was over. *I made a mistake, Jack. We all do that, don't we? Can't we get together and talk?*

'What?' Nadia says sharply now.

'I'm sorry,' I say before I can stop myself. 'I can't do this right now. I'm not coming to Barcelona with you.'

Part Three

The key to a successful holiday with one's grown-up child

- Accept that they will have a 'museum limit' (which might well be 'just the one', or even 'none') and it is unlikely to match yours.

- Do not force your itinerary on them.

- Do not expect them to walk anywhere.

- Be prepared to spend roughly half of your holiday finding places where they will happily eat.

- Do not expect them to keep in touch constantly as if they are twelve years old.

- Be ready to pay for everything.

Chapter Thirty-Four

Nadia

It's Sunday morning, and something incredible has happened.

Alfie is up and properly dressed, without complaint – jeans, T-shirt, even shoes – *at 5.20 a.m.* It's not even light yet. I find myself glancing at him, awestruck, as he goes about his business, drinking coffee, zipping up his wheeled suitcase. I'd be no more mesmerised if I'd spotted an Arctic fox was pottering around my flat.

I decided not to wake Molly at this hour; we said goodbye last night. She was fine about Alfie coming to Barcelona with me. 'Oh God, he needs it, Mum,' she said. 'Get him out of the flat – out of Glasgow for a while. Put a smile on his face. Anyway, I'm working all next week and Thomas'll kill me if I don't show up, after he went on at his dad to take me on.'

With twins, there's a certain kind of pressure to treat them fairly. Every Christmas, I'd count all their stocking presents to make sure they had equal amounts. Danny thought I was being silly, and he was probably right; they never compared their loot. But better to play safe, I always thought. Gift allocation was one aspect of parenting that they couldn't tell me off about.

Perhaps I've always shied away from confrontation, because on Thursday evening, after that heated conversation with Jack, I didn't call back, or text, or try to persuade him to change his mind. I was pretty upset, and after a couple more wines with Corinne I headed home, feeling annoyed with myself for drinking too much and screwing things up so badly.

Molly and Alfie came in around midnight and found me having a little cry on the sofa. As I heard the front door opening I'd tried to blot my face back to something resembling normality, but they knew immediately that something was wrong. 'Jack says he's not coming away with me,' I explained.

'Oh, Mum!' Molly swooped down beside me and gave me a hug. 'Why? What's happened?'

I glanced at Alfie, who was now sitting on my other side, and had placed an arm rather awkwardly around my back. 'It's not 'cause of what I said, is it?'

I shrugged. 'We just had a bit of a heated conversation.'

'Oh, shit, Mum. I'm so sorry.'

'Alf, it doesn't matter,' I said quickly. I couldn't face raking it all up again. 'Sod it. Sod him. I just won't go.'

'You've got to go!' Molly insisted. 'It's all paid for, isn't it? I bet you wouldn't get any of it back.'

She had a point. Why shouldn't I go? And why shouldn't I take someone else?

By the following morning it had been agreed that Alfie would come. I worried that it might seem as if I was 'rewarding' his terrible behaviour at Jack's, but then, I wanted company. The idea of roaming the streets of Barcelona alone, trying not to miss Jack, was hardly appealing. I didn't want to be that solo traveller who'd find herself tippling back cava alone in a bar.

I'd also started to figure that, with some time alone, just the two of us, I might be able to convince Alfie that flouncing out of university after just a year was pretty foolish and mad. And perhaps my generosity – he was pretty chuffed to be asked – would lend me some bargaining power. 'If you're coming with me,' I ventured, in a face-off in the kitchen, 'you've got to promise to stop acting like such a slob around the flat. I can't stand it, Alf. The wet towels, the loo roll thrown on the floor, the kitchen devastation . . . It's doing my head in. I'm just not used to this anymore, and I can't stand having to do a deep-clean every time you've buttered a cracker or peeled a tangerine.'

'Okay, okay,' he said briskly.

'I'm just saying . . .'

'I hear you, okay? You've made your point!'

I clamped my back teeth together. Was it going to be possible for us to exist together in a tiny apartment in Barcelona without me murdering him? Well, I'd committed to it now – having paid to change the name on Jack's flight, and shoved Jack's half of the Airbnb money back into his bank account, despite the fact that, during our curt text exchange late on Thursday night, he'd been adamant that he didn't want any kind of 'refund'.

No, no, I'd decided, rather sanctimoniously – and, okay, a little drunkenly too. *I will owe you nothing. My conscience will be clear.*

I spent Friday working from home, taking breaks to pack, carefully folding my most attractive dresses, which (I hoped) would lend me an air of elegance as Alfie and I wafted around the city. Perhaps, I mused, a couple of photos of me not looking terribly awful might make their way onto Facebook, for Jack to see. Not to make him miserable or anything, or even regret his decision, even if now, almost a week since his gathering, I do wonder if the whole thing was blown up out of all proportion.

After all, it's hardly unusual these days for a teenager to shun animal products (I'm always slightly shocked whenever I see Molly tearing into a steak), and to be blinkeredly opinionated, as if everyone else – particularly the 'older generation' – is thick and uncaring, concerned only with pensions and holidays and double-locking their front door. Alfie was wrong, I know that – but he does seem contrite, and if Jack can't see that, then maybe he's really not right for me after all?

Admittedly, I can't imagine Lori behaving that way. Whilst not shy exactly, she's more timid, less sure of herself. Even at fourteen, Molly and Alfie were bolder and more opinionated – which is a positive thing, surely? Although no one wants a kid they can't take out in public, in case they start mouthing off and making old ladies cry.

I'm wondering now, did I screw it all up, this mothering thing? Was I not firm enough? I was angry about the smashed Buddha in that garden centre. Danny and I marched them back to the car, and they were sharply told off and sent to bed early. But maybe I should have made them glue him back together, then scrub our entire home – with toothbrushes – in order to do penance for their crime.

Does *any* parent ever know if they've done a decent job?

On Saturday morning, the day before our trip, I took myself down to Kiki's beauty salon, as agreed via Danny, where she greeted me with a brisk hug and a waft of her light floral fragrance. 'Perfect timing for your holiday,' she said, whisking me into the back room, which was painted a restful warmish grey. She draped me with a rustly black cape, held back my hair with the aid of a soft elasticated band, and directed me to sit on a reclining chair.

'What've you been up to?' I asked over the gentle vocal music. It sounded like angels singing softly, and I decided I was pretty safe in her hands.

'Oh, this and that,' she replied, squirting lotion onto her delicate hands and applying it to my face with featherlight strokes. The stroking became a little firmer in a lovely, soothing, rhythmic way. We hadn't specified the kind of treatment I'd have, but I figured I'd just leave it to her. She was the guru after all, and so far, I had to admit, everything smelt – and felt – wonderful.

'You're harbouring an awful lot of tension in your jaw,' Kiki murmured.

'Mmm, no wonder,' I replied. 'Jack's not coming to Barcelona tomorrow.'

'Why's that? Is he ill?'

'No. We've had a bit of, um . . .' I tailed off, wondering how much to share with her. It's not as if we're mates – but then, it felt oddly intimate, the two of us alone together in this quiet, deliciously scented room. As her fingers glided across my forehead – 'this is a soothing cleanser, with mallow extract' – I found myself opening up and telling her everything that had happened between Jack, Alfie and me.

'Oh, God, you poor thing,' she said, her sympathy clearly genuine.

'Well, poor Jack's mum, really.'

'Yeah, but it must've been terrible for you too. Even worse in some ways, feeling responsible . . .' Now my face was being wiped with something cooling that smelt vaguely of cucumber. I inhaled it slowly, wishing this treatment could go on all day and night. It felt *wonderful*. 'I'd imagine everyone would feel sorry for an older lady in tears,' she added, 'and of course they should – but no one would consider how *you* felt in that situation.'

'Never mind me,' I murmured. 'It was just awful for Jack's mum and dad.'

'Well, I think you're a fantastic mum,' Kiki declared, which stunned me slightly.

'Really? That's kind of you to say . . .'

'No, I do,' she said rather quickly. 'You have a lovely family, Nadia. I've always thought that. Those kids are a real credit to you – and to Danny too, of course, but let's face it, you've done the lion's share of the work.' She cleared her throat hurriedly and turned away, ostensibly to reach for a pot of cream. However, I sensed that something had upset her.

'Close your eyes please,' she instructed, returning her attentions to my face. 'You'll feel more benefit that way.'

Obediently, I closed my eyes, and wondered if perhaps she and Danny had had a row too, and she was still in the fragile aftermath. I've never known them to argue, but then, I wouldn't expect to be party to the ups and downs of their relationship. 'This is a deep, enriching moisturiser,' she explained. 'It'll help to soothe away fine lines and create a soft, springy texture.'

'It smells lovely,' I said, pushing away an unwelcome memory of peddling those skincare products to Jack in Lush.

She sniffed, and I opened my eyes. 'Are you . . . okay?'

'Oh, yes . . . I suppose so.' Her voice wavered. 'You know. Just life. Just . . .' I closed my eyes again. Something was definitely bothering her, and it felt wrong to observe her at such close quarters. 'I wanted children,' she blurted out. 'I probably shouldn't say that, and you're meant to be relaxing. I don't normally chat to clients during treatments but . . .'

'I'm not really a normal client.'

'No.' She paused. 'And you know Danny, what he's like. He's great, of course: full of energy and life and spontaneity.' She laughed dryly. 'Too much spontaneity sometimes. But when the kids issue came up . . . well, he was adamant we wouldn't have any, that he had his family already, and that he'd made that clear when we first got together. I was fine with that – it felt like there was tons of time . . .'

'Time to change his mind?' I suggested gently.

'Mmmm. Yes. And he did, eventually, after years and *years*.'

I was poised for her to continue, but not quite sure that I wanted to hear the nitty-gritty of baby-making between Kiki and my ex.

'I had one very early miscarriage,' she added, 'and he said that was that, our one chance. So I went back on the Pill . . .'

I was stunned by this. I'd always thought Danny ran around after Kiki, tending to her every need. 'Only I'm not really taking them,' she said.

'You mean, this is now?' I exclaimed. 'You're not taking your pills *now*?'

'That's right,' she said levelly. 'I had the miscarriage in February, so just four months ago. Still not pregnant, though.' She paused. 'D'you think I'm doing a terrible thing? I know I'm forty-two. I'm ancient . . .'

'You're not ancient.' Christ.

So Danny might become a dad again, in his fifties, without even being aware of her plans? It's unlikely, I suppose. While I'm not familiar with the statistics, I can't imagine that conceiving at her age is a given. No, she's *not* ancient – compared to me she's pretty youthful – but is it even wise, given the risks? And what if she does become pregnant, and Danny's appalled? Would he insist on a termination? I can't imagine that, but still . . . might her subterfuge break them up? Would she really relish being a single mum in her forties?

All of these questions were whirring around my head, jarring with the angel music. Should I tell him? No, of course not, I decided, my eyes still firmly closed. It's none of my business . . .

A sharp snapping noise halted my racing thoughts. I flicked open my eyes just in time to see that Kiki was now wearing blue plastic gloves. 'Open your mouth, please,' she said. I opened up, just like at the dentist's, and her fingers slipped inside.

What a weird thing, I found myself thinking, more to distract myself from her pokey movements than anything else. Kiki telling me all that stuff . . . I mean, why? Was it because she thought I 'understood' Danny, or had she simply needed to confess?

Ow! She delved around, sort of massaging my gums and cheeks from the inside – *agh!* She was working deeper into the tissue now, pulling at my cheek linings, twanging at the tender parts under my tongue. Christ, it was painful, but it was *good* pain, surely? She'd already told me Kate Moss has this done – not by Kiki herself, but one of her 'skincare inspirations' – and hopefully, this horrendous treatment fell under the 'no pain, no gain' banner . . .

Tears sprang from my eyes. Perhaps she was trying to unscrew my back teeth? I gagged and worried I might vomit in my mouth. I imagined Kiki's fingers swilling about in a sort of sicky soup, and wondered if she'd carry on, politely pretending it hadn't happened, like when someone has food stuck to their lip and you decide not to embarrass them by pointing it out.

I gagged again loudly, like a frog, and tried not to think about a terrible oral sex episode from my youth. I was eighteen years old and unprepared for what Wayne King was expecting me to do with his appendage. This was worse. Far worse. A young male – even a rampant teenage one – has only one penis and it felt as if thirty-five fingers were at work now, jabbing and thrusting, and no matter how hard I tried, no amount of picturing Kate Moss's cheekbones (perhaps Kiki was rearranging my bone structure?) could stop the pain.

The angel music had finished. I was going to die, I decided. Kiki regretted telling me about wanting to be pregnant. She was mortified, and scared I'd tell Danny, and the only way she could see to deal with it was to kill me.

Chapter Thirty-Five

I didn't die, obviously. Red-eyed and traumatised, I staggered after Kiki into the reception area where I fumbled with my purse, trying to pay her. She reminded me that it was her 'treat'.

'Oh, and the other thing!' she announced, bobbing down behind the counter. 'I almost forgot.' She reappeared clutching an M&S carrier bag.

'The denim jacket!' I croaked, having forgotten too.

'Yeah.' She winced. 'What are you going to do with it, now you and Jack have had a row?'

'Still give it to him, I guess,' I replied, pulling it from the bag and holding it up. As Danny had already described, it was a classic Levi's denim jacket, covered in badges: The Stone Roses, The Smiths, Pearl Jam. A musky whiff was coming off it, and I stuffed it back into the carrier bag.

Kiki grinned. 'You could sell it on eBay. I would!'

I chuckled, as much as my violated face would allow. 'I'll think about it. Will you tell him thanks?'

'I will,' she said. 'Oh, hang on – there's a note with it

too . . .' She bobbed down again and rummaged about, then stood up and handed me an envelope. I pulled out the small white card, and read: *Hope this rank old thing rakes in a few pennies. Fantastic charity, happy to help. Love, Seb xxx.*

'Wow,' I murmured.

'Pretty good, huh?' Kiki smiled. 'Sorry if you found the massage a bit painful. It really does work wonders, though. You're glowing, actually.'

Hmmm. I very much doubted it. But perhaps my blood was so traumatised, it was trying to flee to the surface and burst out of my face? 'Well, thanks for your time, Kiki . . .'

'No problem,' she said, touching my hand. 'Thanks for listening to me, warbling on. I shouldn't have really . . .'

'You didn't warble.'

'No, really.' She smiled, and her pale blue eyes moistened. 'Sometimes you just need to get things off your chest.' She paused. 'You won't say anything, will you?'

'No, of course not,' I said truthfully. As if I'd blab to Danny about any of this.

'It's just . . .' She smoothed back her copperish hair. 'These days, everything revolves around Danny, with his *career* and all that. Everyone wants him. It's all *his* friends. I hardly get time to see my women friends anymore . . .'

I studied her lightly freckled face, overcome by a wave of pity for her, despite what she'd just done to me. To think I had always slightly envied her beauty, and that fancy coffee machine of theirs with its many levers and knobs.

'I worry that they're all falling away,' she added quickly.

273

'I'm sure they're not,' I said, 'but please, don't worry about anything you've told me today. I promise I won't breathe a word.'

Post-facial, I needed to decompress a little, so I wandered around town in a blurry haze, aware of a wave of sadness sloshing over me as I passed 'our' branch of Lush. Although I pointedly looked in the other direction, I still caught a whiff of it, wafting out through the open door, taunting me with its pungent fragrance.

Never mind that, I told myself, a plan already formulating in my mind. I would drop off the jacket at Jack's shop – I already knew this was one of his Saturdays off, the *last* thing I wanted was to see him – and then I would go home to pack, and prepare for my trip.

The shop was busy, milling with customers all browsing, chatting, trying on hats and clustering around the curtained changing area. It was Mags who took it from me, examining it from all angles, as if I might have been trying to flog her a designer knock-off. 'Are you sure this is genuine?'

'Yes, of course!'

'So it really belonged to Stan Jeffries?'

'Seb,' I corrected her. '*Seb* Jeffries. He's very famous . . .' She shrugged in a 'whatever' sort of way.

'And yes, it really belonged to him,' I added, catching a glimpse of Iain through the open door to the back room. He grinned, and I waved. At least he seemed happy to see me. 'My ex-husband knows him,' I went on. 'They've worked together. And look, there's a note with it . . .' I delved into my shoulder bag and handed her the envelope. She scrutinised it, even checking its blank side, as if still suspicious of its authenticity. Why was she being so frosty with me? I couldn't understand it, and hoped that Jack hadn't been saying bad stuff about me, or Alfie, to the volunteers. Surely he wouldn't do that?

'You will keep it safe, won't you?' I added.

'Yes, of course,' Mags retorted. 'We have a safe in the back room. I'll put it in there. Now, I'd better get on.'

Perhaps I *should* have flogged it on eBay, I reflected as I travelled home on the subway, my face still tender from Kiki's ravages. But it was done now, and hopefully it would rake in a huge amount at the auction.

Would Jack even text to say thank you? I doubted it, but at least he'd know I cared, and that I love him and want to make things right.

And now, on this hazy Sunday morning, I decide that it doesn't really matter what Jack thinks, because Alfie and I are driving to the airport on our first holiday together in four years.

Going away with teenagers just became too grim to continue with. Although they got along pretty well at home, trapped on holiday together, Molly and Alfie tended to bicker perpetually, and I seemed to get on their nerves simply by being there – even though I had paid for it all. For our last trip, I said they could bring a friend each, and booked an apartment sizeable enough for all of us in Majorca. As the lone adult – amazingly, none of my friends had fancied joining us – I felt utterly outnumbered.

Although I tried to be perky and jolly and pretty much stay out of their way, what woman really wants to go away with *four* fifteen-year-olds, including two who don't even belong to her? Corinne, Gus and I have had some pretty raucous city breaks, to Amsterdam, Paris and Berlin, but I haven't had a 'couple holiday' since Danny and I

275

split up. Ryan Tibbles kept referring to our four days together as 'our holiday', but the furthest we ventured was to the shop at the end of my street for bread.

Anyway, who needs holidays to be romantic, loved-up affairs? Not me! I have my son at my side now, and we shall re-bond during our time away, and figure out how to be together as adults. We have arrived at the airport and settled ourselves into a café for a breakfast consisting of coffee and cake: vanilla sponge for me, and a hefty-looking vegan brownie for him ('Delicious,' he says unconvincingly). As he munches away and sips his soya latte, I sense him letting down his guard a little. 'I hope things are all right with you and Jack when we get back,' he says.

I look across the table at him, surprised that he seems to be considering my needs – and by extension regarding me as an actual human being. 'Well, let's see.' I pause. 'It's fine, love. It'll be nice for you and me to have some time together.'

He bites his lip and peers at me. 'You haven't split up, have you?'

I shrug, to demonstrate that I am not remotely troubled by the possibility. 'I'm not sure.'

'Oh.' He winces, as if not knowing how to respond. 'Was it because of—'

'Don't worry about it,' I say quickly, turning to check the departures on the monitor. 'It probably wasn't going anywhere anyway. Look, we'll be boarding pretty soon. We'd better go to the gate.'

As we stride along to departures, and then settle into our seats on the plane, I make a firm resolution to put Alfie's lactation outburst behind us. It wouldn't be fair to heap more guilt upon him. And now, as we take off, emerging through clouds to the bright sunshine above, I'm thinking: maybe it really is for the best.

It was lovely, the thing Jack and I had, from Christmas Eve until just a week ago. I felt fully alive again, and blazingly happy; it felt as if my days and nights were filled with fun and joy and about a zillion orgasms. But maybe everyone has a certain quota of orgasms allocated to them for life, and I'd had the rest of mine in those heady five months.

Now it looks like it's over, I can focus on other, equally important aspects of my life – like work. More commissions have been coming in, and I'm aware that I'll need to crack on as soon as we're back home. Just as well, then, that I won't be having sex with anyone! Boyfriends are time consuming, I tell myself now, and I was managing perfectly fine without one. So many of my friends – well, Corinne and Gus – are single, and they function perfectly well. Even the supposedly rock-solid couples, like Danny and Kiki, clearly have their difficulties too.

I glance at Alfie. As he's dozing now, he doesn't see the tears trickling from my eyes. And by the time he wakes up, and we are descending towards Barcelona airport, my eyes are perfectly dry, my face has just about recovered from Kiki's assault, and I just know we're going to have a brilliant time.

Chapter Thirty-Six

Jack

Nadia will be in Barcelona by now – on her own. She'll be fine, I tell myself. Without me distracting her, she'll be able to mooch around the city, taking photos, making notes, gathering inspiration for her maps.

In some ways, it'll be better for her. It was supposed to be a working trip, after all.

Early on Sunday afternoon, when Nadia has probably just arrived at that apartment we chose, I decide to head out for a run. It'll clear my head, I reason. The haze has lifted, and the sky is light blue streaked with transparent clouds. I started running a couple of years ago, egged on by my brother, who does marathons and Iron Man challenges and all kinds of mad stuff that guys are often drawn to at a certain age. It's like men suddenly realise they're heading for fifty and panic. They can't just start jogging around the park, or having the odd game of badminton. It has to be seventy-five-mile runs, triathlons, cycling across China and sleeping in huts.

While I've never been the sporty type – unless you

count a few brief spells of gym attendance – doing something outside, as opposed to grappling weights in a sweaty room, was vaguely appealing. I thought it might be a sort of antidote to spending so much time in the shop's back room, sifting through dusty old books and shoes bearing the imprints of strangers' bunions.

Gradually, running stopped being torturous and became almost pleasurable in a weird kind of way. However, today it fails to make me feel better about anything. In fact, I just feel like a sweaty, middle-aged bloke trying to fill in some time. Two-thirds of the way round my usual route, I start walking, and when I'm almost home I call Lori, just to say hi.

'I thought you were going away?' she says.

'Yeah. Well, I sort of had a change of heart . . .'

'Why?' she exclaims.

The TV is blaring in the background. I can picture the living room, with Elaine watching telly, maybe a drink on the go – but that's not fair. I shouldn't jump to conclusions. 'Nadia and I just, um, had a bit of a chat, after the thing last Sunday,' I explain. 'The thing with Gran and Grandad, I mean.'

'Oh, Dad . . .' The TV noise fades, and I gather that Lori has wandered into the kitchen.

'It's okay. I'm sure we'll work things out.'

'Alfie probably didn't mean to upset them,' Lori adds.

I unlock my front door and step inside. 'Yeah. I'm sure he didn't. So, what're you up to today?'

'Nothing much.'

'Is it just you and Mum in?'

'Er, no – Harry's here . . .'

'The guy Mum's seeing?'

'Uh-huh.'

279

In the kitchen now, I unlace my trainers and kick them off. 'Is he around a lot, then?'

'Quite a bit,' she replies, doing her usual thing of supplying minimal information.

I clear my throat, grab a glass from the cupboard and fill it with water. 'D'you like him?'

'He's all right,' she murmurs, and now I hear a deep male voice calling out, 'Grab us a Strongbow from the fridge, would you, Lor, love?'

Lor, love? I bristle. 'Was that him?'

'Yeah,' she says, with emphasis, meaning: who else would it be?

'Hmmm.'

'I'd better go, Dad.'

'Right,' I say, regretting the tetchiness that's crept into my voice. 'Better get him his cider, eh?'

We end the call on an oddly irritable note, and I'm ashamed now for reacting like that. After all, it's not as if he told her to help him inject heroin. He only asked her to fetch him a cider from the fridge.

I head out again, having decided to buy some new running shoes as mine are feeling all flat and done in, as if all their bounce has gone. Or maybe that's just me? The shop is staffed by cheery young men and women, and a blonde ponytailed girl fetches numerous shoes for me to try. They have gel soles, cushioned insoles and extra buoyancy in the heel, and the girl points out all the 'quirks' of my running style as we watch a video of me pounding along on the shop's treadmill.

Having bought some ruinously expensive shoes, I'm at a loss as to what to do next. I have no plans to meet anyone, and nothing I really need to do on this sunny Sunday afternoon – because I'm supposed to be in

Barcelona. What am I going to do about work this week? Go into the shop and have to explain the whole ruddy thing, or not go in and pretend I'm in Spain? But then, what if I'm spotted out and about? Glasgow is a huge city, but I rarely go out into the centre without bumping into someone I know, even if it's just one of our regular customers. Oh, and the volunteers will expect me to bring back some kind of interesting treats for them from my holiday, as I do normally. Will I be able to buy Spanish sweets online?

Sod it, I decide. I might as well come clean tomorrow, and tell Helen I won't need her to look after the shop this week after all. The alternative – to spend the week in hiding, with nothing to occupy myself – doesn't bear thinking about.

Chapter Thirty-Seven

Nadia

Our top-floor apartment is possibly the cutest place I have ever stayed in. It's beautifully furnished in mid-century style, with a collection of art books and elegant glassware and ceramics, and filled with light from the tall, shuttered windows. There is a balcony overlooking the street of quirky shops and cafés in this ramshackle but delightful area of town, and Alfie and I are standing on it, gazing down.

'We should get out and explore,' I suggest. 'Fancy a stroll down to Barceloneta? It's the beach area.'

'Uh, okay,' Alfie says.

'It's not too far,' I add.

'Yeah, let's go,' he says, clearly having decided to be on his best behaviour as we trot down the steep, narrow stairs. From our neighbourhood, we make our way through the Gothic Quarter. After almost an hour, due to our gentle ambling and the fact that we've got lost several times, we still haven't arrived at our destination. Yet, incredibly, Alfie hasn't moaned about this.

'Yeah, cool,' he said, when I suggested stopping to

browse in a bookshop crammed with lavish art books, many dumped in teetering piles on the floor. He didn't seem to mind that I spent twenty minutes in a tiny shop that sold only hand-made soaps, or that it took me an equal length of time to choose an ice cream flavour.

It's early evening by the time we reach the waterfront, and it's buzzing with buskers, strolling tourists and skate-boarders. Hungry now, we start to explore the streets a little further back from the water. Happily, Alfie seems pretty relaxed about the fact that this is Barcelona, and Catalan people love their hams and cheeses, and haven't converted their splendid city to veganism just for him.

Installed at a café table in a pleasantly shady side street, he orders spaghetti with tomato sauce – I reckon this'll be his default choice – while I go for a couple of tapas comprising marinated mushrooms and sumptuously cheesy croquettes. We have a glass of wine each, and I notice with relief that my son is already looking less pallid and drawn. We chat about our plans for the week: 'I'm happy to just go along with things,' he says. I wonder whether it's the debacle at Jack's that's turned him all pleasant and amenable so suddenly, or if he genuinely doesn't mind what we do.

'I won't drag you to hundreds of museums,' I add.

'You can if you like . . .'

'Oh, come on,' I say, smiling. 'I know you have your cut-off point and it's no fun looking around them with someone who's dragging their feet . . .'

'I'm nineteen, Mum,' Alfie reminds me, laughing now, 'not six.'

I smile at him, figuring that this isn't remotely how I imaged my trip to pan out, but perhaps it really will help to bring us closer. It's painful when your kids, who once loved you to pieces and cried if you left the room, start to regard you with sneers as if you smell terrible and exist solely to ruin their fun. No one warns you that this stage starts when they're about twelve and goes on until . . . well, this morning, actually. That's seven years of being mildly disliked! Even Molly, who's pretty sunny these days, had a tendency to regard me as a nuisance when she hit her teens.

But never mind that now, because the atmosphere is convivial as Alfie and I tuck into our supper. 'D'you honestly not miss cheese?' I muse, having devoured my croquettes.

'Everyone asks that,' he reminds me. 'It's actually addictive, did you know that?'

'Really?' I ask with genuine interest.

'Yeah. The dairy proteins are really concentrated and act as sort of opiates.'

'That makes sense. Once I get started, I find it almost impossible to stop.'

'I've noticed,' he says, chuckling. We finish our supper, and amazingly, Alfie doesn't exhibit any concern over the fact that I'd like us to walk back to our apartment, via a couple of bars.

We stop off for coffee, and another wine, and by the time we're back at the apartment and say goodnight – me heading for the double room, and Alfie to the single-bedded box room *without complaint* – it strikes me that I am one truly lucky woman.

Okay, so things have gone wrong with Jack and me. But right now, as I slip between the cool white sheets, I figure that there are worse situations I could have found myself in than to be in this glorious city, with my son.

Chapter Thirty-Eight

Jack

'This is amazing,' I exclaim on Monday morning when I show up at the shop.

'It's all right, I s'pose,' Mags says as I examine the denim jacket.

'Mags, this'll fetch loads!' I tell her. 'He's really popular, you know. D'you know how Nadia managed to get hold of it?'

Mags shrugs, then mumbles, 'Something about her ex-husband knowing him . . .'

'Oh, right. Of course.' Christ – so she actually asked him for me, and he came up with this. It's far better than a pair of sheepskin mittens or a grubby apron. 'That's Danny Raven,' I add. 'Have you seen any of his films?'

She looks blank and shakes her head. 'Are they musicals?'

'No, they're not musicals,' I say, trying not to smile. 'They're quite gritty really, very British . . . about ordinary people having struggles, trying to make something of themselves.'

'Who wants to go to the cinema to see stuff like that?'

285

she retorts, tailing me to the back room. 'There's enough of that in real life.'

'Well, I s'pose he likes to reflect real life.'

'I don't want it reflected.' She eyes the jacket with what I can only describe as mild distaste as I fold it carefully and place it on the counter. 'I want to be transported somewhere. I want fun and music like in *Mamma Mia!*' She brightens. 'Have you seen either of them?'

'Er, bits of the first one – Lori had it on DVD . . .'

'Seen the end bit?'

'Um, no, I don't think—'

'I have it,' she announces. 'You could come round and watch it with me. You need to see the whole thing, or you'll never know how it turns out.'

To think, I muse, *I have reached the age of forty-nine without finding out which of the three men Meryl Streep had a kid with!*

'It's not massively my kind of thing,' I say, at which her expression falls; Mags's moods are always clearly displayed. 'But . . . thanks anyway.' I turn to busy myself by unpacking a box of children's books. One of them is one of those touchy-feely kinds with panels of fur and Velcro. When I flick through it to check for marks or rips, a piece of cooked bacon drops out.

'So, are you back in all week, then?' she asks, her tone cooler now.

'Um, I'm not sure. I've had a chat with Helen and she said she'd been looking forward to spending some time here. So I might just drop in now and again, but take some time off too . . .'

'Right.' I can sense Mags mulling this over, itching to ask the real reason why I didn't fly to Spain yesterday. So far, I have brushed off everyone's queries with a rather vague, 'Oh, Nadia decided to make it a working trip.' Whether they believed me or not is up to them.

Right now, with Mags beginning to sort a large bag of shoes rather huffily, going into any more detail about my lamentable love life is the last thing I need.

At least Iain is impressed with the jacket, as he keeps removing it from the safe in the back room, where it's being stored until Dinah drops by to collect it for the auction. 'Have you heard of Seb Jeffries?' he keeps asking customers as he rushes out with it to show them.

'No,' retorts Jean Cuthbertson when she comes in that afternoon. Jean seems no more impressed than when Mags told her 'we' (I seem to remember that she just stood and watched) sorted through the hoover bag's contents in our search for her wedding ring.

'He's really well known,' Iain says loftily. 'He's in all these dark, depressing films where people hang about on patches of grass and nothing much goes on. You know, the ones Danny Raven makes?'

She narrows her eyes at him. 'Who?'

'He's a film producer. I mean director. He's a mate of Jack's . . .'

'Still don't know who you're talking about . . .'

'Well, he's an actor!' Iain exclaims.

'Seb Raven?'

Iain groans. 'No – Seb *Jeffries* . . .'

'What would I want with his jacket?' Jean asks, frowning at it. 'It's for a man.'

'You could, uh, wear it over a dress, or casually toss it over your shoulders,' Iain offers, suddenly the style expert.

'I have a perfectly good coat, thanks,' Jean retorts as she strides out of the shop.

287

All through Monday and Tuesday – I've accepted I might as well come in after all, extra pair of hands and all that – the jacket is paraded about and shoved in customers' faces. A delicate-looking woman with a small child reels back in surprise. 'Could it be washed?'

'Oh, yes – denim's very hard wearing and washable,' Iain replies, 'but you'd have to take the badges off and not let your little girl play with them.'

'I'm a boy,' the child shouts.

At one point, Iain models it, twisting and turning so it can be viewed from all angles, and striding back and forth as if our rather worn shop floor were a catwalk. The other volunteers and I are all in hysterics. Even Mags cracks a grin. I'm so grateful to Iain for shaking me out of my gloom that I offer to take him back to that pizza place once we've closed for the day.

We wait until everyone else – well, Mags really – has gone home, and we sneak off.

And here, as we tear into our pepperoni pizzas and cheese-laden garlic bread, I find myself knocking back a couple of beers and telling Iain what really happened between Nadia and me. Of all the people I could confide in, I choose him – perhaps because I know his response will be straightforward and honest, a knee-jerk reaction to the mess.

'That's awful, Jack,' he murmurs with genuine concern. 'She's a lovely lady. I like her a lot.'

'Yeah, I do too,' I say.

'After she brought in the jacket as well!'

'Yes, well, I told her before that . . .'

'But why?' he asks.

I inhale deeply. 'I've explained, Iain. My mum got upset at the party, and then afterwards Nadia and I had a bit of a tetchy phone conversation – a row, I suppose, the first one we've had. She was out with a friend, and a bit drunk, and it sort of escalated. Before I knew it I'd said I couldn't go away with her.' Christ, what possessed me to do that? I reflect now. It seems so trivial and stupid.

Iain tuts and shakes his head. 'Aww, that's bad.'

'Yeah. I know.'

He munches thoughtfully on his last scrap of pizza, and we fall into silence for a few moments. 'You know what, though?' he adds.

'What?' I ask.

'You didn't really mean to break up, did you? I mean, you just said it because you were mad.'

'Erm . . .' I take a sip of my beer. 'No, I suppose I didn't mean it. At least, I didn't plan to say what I did. It just sort of . . . fell out.'

'And now *you've* fallen out,' he exclaims, seemingly pleased at his word usage. 'Which is silly, really, 'cause you want to be with her. I can tell.'

'I do,' I murmur. 'I really do.'

Iain nods. 'So, you might as well phone her, say sorry, and just go . . .'

I can't help laughing at that.

'What's funny?' he asks, looking crestfallen.

'Because . . . I can't do that, Iain.'

'Why not?'

'Because it's too late. She's already gone.'

'Why can't you just go out and join her?' he asks.

I consider how best to explain it. 'I can't tell her I'm not going and then, two days later, call her up and say, "Hi, Nads! Look, I was a bit of an arse the other day and I'm really sorry. So, what I've decided is, I'm coming out to Barcelona with you after all."' I look at him, and he frowns.

289

'I think that sounds pretty good,' Iain remarks. 'That's exactly what you *should* say. Why don't you write it down to make sure you get it right?'

Oh, Jesus. 'She'd just think I was messing her around, not going one minute, going the next . . .'

'It's not minutes,' he insists. 'It's *days*. Tell her you've had time to think things over. Go on – add that in . . .'

I smile and drain my beer glass.

'D'you want me to phone her for you?' he asks.

'No!' I exclaim. 'No, thank you. Anyway, you don't like using the phone . . . '

'Oh, I'd do it for you, if it'd help. I could pretend it was to thank her for bringing the jacket in,' he says, raising a brow, as if this counts for real subterfuge.

'Iain. I'm not—'

'You shouldn't just give up,' he interrupts, looking quite disappointed in me now. 'I bet, if you phoned her, she'd be really pleased. She'd much rather be with you than wandering about on her own, lonely and upset . . .' I watch as he licks a finger and whirls it round his plate in order to gather up the crumbs. Iain Harrison, who has never had a partner as far as I've been able to gather, is dispensing relationship advice. And pretty sensible advice at that . . .

'She might be enjoying the peace,' I remark.

'You don't really think that. I can tell when you don't mean something, Jack. You're a terrible liar. I can tell by the shape of your mouth.'

'But I don't know how she's feeling,' I add, uneasy now at the way he's scrutinising my face across the table. 'And she mightn't be on her own anyway. Perhaps she's gone with a friend instead? I just don't know, Iain. And even if she hasn't, she'll be pretty pissed off with me right now.

290

She seemed to think I was making a comment about the kids having a famous film-director dad, and how he could give Alfie a job, just like that . . .'

'Did you say that?' Iain wants to know.

I wince. 'Kind of. At least, it came out that way.'

'Apologise then, in person!' he says. I open my mouth to protest, but he's off again: 'You know when Pancake went missing?'

'Er, yes . . .'

'Well, you told me not to give up, didn't you? You said I had to keep looking, stay positive.'

'I'm not quite sure it's the same thing, Iain,' I murmur with a smile.

'It is,' he insists. 'I love Pancake. You love Nadia . . .' He blinks at me. '*Don't* you?'

'Yes, of course I do,' I reply.

'Then go get her.' He beams across the table at me. 'Go to Barcelona and say sorry, and don't forget to thank her for the jacket.'

Chapter Thirty-Nine

Nadia

Yesterday we strolled around the Picasso Museum and gazed in awe at the Sagrada Família (at least, I did; Alfie prodded at his phone). We pottered around Parc Güell and browsed the incredible stalls in the Boqueria food market. Alfie didn't even complain about the prevalence of cured hams dangling from hooks, and enormous, succulent sausages piled up everywhere we looked. However, I noticed that as time went on, his phone-poking increased, and by the time we emerged from our apartment this morning, it had welded itself to his hand. He seemed to have slipped back into a rather listless frame of mind, murmuring that it was 'hot', and showing rather less enthusiasm at my suggestions of what to do.

When I probed him about what was wrong, he just muttered that he'd 'had some texts'. From Camilla, I assumed, although naturally he wasn't prepared to tell me. Anyway, I guessed they hadn't exactly filled him with joy.

'What would *you* like to do?' I ask now as we meander through the Gràcia quarter, with the intention of doing some shopping.

'Don't mind,' Alfie replies.

I glance at him. 'Maybe, if you have a read of the guidebook . . .'

He throws me an incredulous look, as if I'd suggested consulting tarot cards. I suppose it does seem rather quaint to him. But I like an old-fashioned guidebook, with pictures and everything neatly organised into sections: food, entertainment, trips out of the city. So much less confusing than consulting hundreds of online travel guides where no on can agree on the best things to do.

'It's so hot,' Alfie announces for about the fiftieth time.

'Well, it is Spain,' I remind him.

'I'm just saying. I didn't think it'd be this hot in June.'

I glance at him as we stroll. 'I did say bring some shorts, didn't I? You must be roasting in jeans.'

'I am,' he says in a pained way. 'But I told you. I don't have any shorts.'

'I'll buy you some then,' I say.

'Oh, I don't want to go shopping for shorts with you . . .'

Roast, then! I think, irritated now that he's not appreciating being here enough. Perhaps we should have gone to Greenland instead? But that wouldn't have been much help for my maps, and in fact, our explorations here have given me loads of ideas for imagery and colours. So thank you, Jack, I think bitterly; it's proving to be a useful research trip after all.

I'm about to suggest to Alfie that we choose a hat for him, but think better of it.

'I could give you some euros,' I venture, 'and you could go and buy shorts and we'll meet up later. How does that sound?'

He twists his mouth into a frown. 'Where would I go?'

'C'mon, Alf,' I say. 'Use your initiative. There are thousands of shops.'

It's wrong to compare my kids, I know that, but Molly would jump at the chance to shoot off and do a bit of shopping. My daughter and I have been texting daily, and all's fine at home; she's been working hard, and seemingly partying hard too, judging from her Instagram feed.

Alfie and I stop off for lunch in a shady square, after which I press a wad of notes into his hand with the instruction to meet at Café Opera on the Ramblas in a couple of hours' time. He lopes off, looking a little bewildered. And now, as I wander around the streets alone, I find Jack sneaking into my thoughts. He could have at least texted to say thanks for the jacket, or even a simple, 'Hope you're having nice time'. I stop walking with the intention of checking my phone – and discover it's not in my bag.

With a sickening jolt, I realise I've left it on the café table. I can picture it sitting there, next to the zinc ashtray. I charge back, but by the time I reach the square, an elderly couple are already sitting at the table. No, they haven't seen my phone, and none of the staff have either. Someone must have wandered by and grabbed it. 'Oh, Jesus,' I mutter, my initial thought being: what if Alfie needs to contact me? But then, we're meeting at three, and he's only buying shorts. I can use his phone later to let Molly know I've lost mine.

Slightly soothed – it's insured, after all, and I will *not* let this mishap ruin my day – I stroll onwards to the shops, with the intention of perusing dresses. Bright colours and zingy prints abound here. Last year, I'd fallen into the habit of wearing so much black – hence fitting in so well with the Lush staff – that I'd almost forgotten which colours I liked. But then I met Jack, and my confidence soared and I started to think: yes, of course I can wear red or pink or emerald! Almost instantly, I fell back in love with colour, specifically prints, which I'd loved when I was younger. And now my wardrobe is filled with the cheery colours and patterns I'd worn pretty much every day as an art student.

I upgraded my underwear, too. My old, saggy articles haven't seen the light of day since I met Jack; I've taken to wearing 'girlfriend undies' in black or cream lace, and my previously squidgy belly has flattened a little, probably due to our 'activities' and being wildly, deliciously, in love.

I stop with the intention of heading into a shop, but am whacked with a wave of sadness. God, I miss him. We'd so looked forward to this trip. I'm picturing his face, his lovely blue eyes and wide smile, and the way we lie together, our legs tangled together in bed, after sex. I miss his voice, his laugh, the way he smells when he pulls me close to him. I'm not even angry with Alfie anymore because it's not just about him; it's about the row Jack and I had afterwards, when I'd got drunk with Corinne. It's a fuck-up, that's what it is. I don't want to be shopping alone. I'm no longer interested in dresses. But I have no phone, and there's over an hour to fill before I meet Alfie at Café Opera.

I pace the streets, passing glorious Gaudí buildings – all swirling curves and glinting mosaics – but I'm unable to appreciate them fully. I want to grab Jack's hand and say, 'Look at that! Imagine designing a block of flats with no right angles, just swooping curves and those crazy turrets!' But I can't do that, because Jack isn't here, and when I arrive at Café Opera just after three, Alfie isn't there either.

*

Two hours I spend, worrying myself senseless: an hour in the café, and another prowling the nearby streets and repeatedly popping in to see if he's turned up yet. I keep spotting tall, gangly, dark-haired boys in grey T-shirts and thinking they're him. I even consider calling his mobile from a public phone – if they still exist – but I'm not confident I could make one work, and anyway, in my agitated state, I'm not sure I can remember his number. Why are we all so dependent on mobiles? In the olden days, we used to arrange a time and somewhere to meet – 'Boots Corner', it was in Glasgow – and that would be that. Now, if someone's running late, they just phone. It's stopped people being on time for anything. No one *cares*.

Of course nothing's happened to Alfie, I keep trying to reassure myself. He's nineteen, he'll be fine; he's probably waiting at the wrong café, he never listens to me. Perhaps he thought I meant the Opera House? I check its foyer, just in case – but there's no Alfie.

At just after five p.m., convinced that he's been attacked down some shadowy alley, I consider telling a policeman what's happened. However, they are large, intimidating men with huge guns. My son ducking out of coffee with me hardly seems like the sort of issue they'd involve themselves in. At 5.35 p.m., I decide to head back to the apartment to see if there are signs that he's been back too; perhaps he dropped off his shopping? Maybe a pair of shorts were just too heavy for him to lug around, in this heat? And – bloody hell – there he is, lolling on the sofa in his pants!

'What're you doing here?' I ask, aghast.

'I was just awfully hot,' he replies. 'I was sweating buckets, Mum. It's cooler in here.'

I'm so mad at him, I have to take a moment to calm

down slightly before I can speak. 'It *is* hot,' I snap, 'but what did you expect? Polar bears sitting on glaciers?'

'Uh?' he says, looking baffled.

'Never mind. But we did say we'd meet at three, and I've been worried senseless.'

'Sorry,' he says, yawning. 'I did try to phone you.'

'Well, I've lost my phone, left it in the café where we had lunch . . .'

'Aw, Mum!' He pulls a sympathetic face.

'So, when you couldn't get hold of me, wouldn't it have been a better idea just to turn up at Café Opera, like we'd arranged?'

'Yeah. Sorry.' He nods contritely.

I exhale. No point in going on at him now, even though he's pretty much ruined my afternoon. With my head thumping and the beginnings of a blister having formed on my heel, I wander through to the kitchen.

I had intended to just fetch a drink of water, but instead, I stop and stare. There was a rectangular glass chopping board on the worktop. Now – mysteriously – it has shattered into tiny pieces, like a windscreen. 'Alfie!' I call through. 'Alfie! What's this?'

'Uh?'

'Come here a minute, could you?' I know it's only a chopping board; it's not as if he's set the sofa on fire or smashed the toilet. But right now, after worrying about him for well over two hours, I'm hardly capable of keeping things in proportion.

'What is it?' He leans casually against the doorframe. I point at the broken glass. 'How did that happen?'

'Oh, erm . . .' He winces. 'Sorry about that. I was just peeling and cutting up an apple.'

I stare at him. 'But you've smashed it! Why did you—?'

297

'I don't like the skin,' he says mildly.

Oh, for crying out loud. 'I don't see how you managed to smash it, Alf.'

Alfie shrugs. 'I dunno either.'

I glare at him. 'Did you take a hammer to it?'

He splutters in disbelief. ''Course not!'

'Jesus,' I say, my headache cranking up a notch now. 'Well, you can clear it up.'

He frowns at me, then steps towards the broken glass, looking bewildered as to how he might dispose of it. Envisaging him managing to get glass fragments wedged in his skin, I snap, 'Just leave it to me. You go and relax. You've obviously had a really *shattering* day.'

'All right. Thanks, Mum,' he murmurs, shuffling back to the living room where he clicks on the TV. A terrible pop song, possibly sung by a nine-year-old, bellows out. I brush the broken glass into a carrier bag, then set about tidying the apartment. This is just like being at home, I reflect. During his time back here this afternoon, he has managed to dirty three mugs and several plates, all of which have been dumped in the sink.

In the bathroom, his socks, a T-shirt and a pair of boxers are lying on the floor, and he's somehow managed to daub the washbasin with toothpaste. In keeping with tradition, he has also left the loo roll strewn on the floor.

As music belts out of the TV, I sit on the closed loo lid and ponder the prospect of another four days, in this city, with my son.

It'll be fine, of course. I'm just agitated after losing my phone, and spending the rest of the afternoon searching for Alfie. But the thought of another day spent mooching around together – with him becoming more and more listless, and perpetually moaning about the heat – makes me feel quite desolate.

Perhaps we simply aren't designed to go on holiday together anymore. These days, we parents of teenagers like to think we're pretty much the same as our kids – just a little saggier, and more likely to lock our windows and borrow library books. After all, we enjoy lots of the music and TV shows that they do. We buy our clothes from the same shops, we borrow each other's shoes and can enjoy a glass of wine together; our tastes seem to have blended into one giant, for-all-ages pot. But it's an illusion really. We are probably just as different as our parents were to us; we just *think* we're hipper, more down with the kidz. And now I'm getting the feeling that Alfie only agreed to come with me – his tedious protein-obsessed mum – because he felt bad about what happened at Jack's gathering.

Should I have come on my own? Possibly. But perhaps it's not a complete disaster. I could have a day to myself tomorrow. Clearly, Alfie wouldn't be averse to being left alone for a while. He could lie about here, where it's cooler, nibbling skinless apple slices. If he closed the shutters he could even pretend he's in Glasgow! And I could head out of the city – visit somewhere that would hold little interest for him.

I fetch my guidebook from the bedside table, and spend an hour perusing the 'trips out of the city' section. 'Alf, I think I'll go to Figueres tomorrow,' I tell him as we tuck into a makeshift supper from bits and bobs we bought at the Boqueria. I simply couldn't face hoofing around in search of a restaurant with exciting vegan options tonight.

'What's that?' he asks.

'It's a town, about an hour or so by train. It means "fig trees". It's where Salvador Dalí lived.' He nods, and for a moment it looks as if he'll say he wants to come too. With his eccentric moustache and surrealist style, Dalí is the kind of artist Alfie is drawn to. But shamefully, I realise I don't want him to come with me. I need a break, that's all. A few hours where I'm not trying to gee him up, or feeling cross about the way he drags his feet along, like a four year-old enduring a trip to the supermarket. I don't want to be wondering where the hell he's wandered off to, or what he's going to eat for his meals. He has already started to mutter, 'Pasta with tomato sauce – *again*,' whenever we've perused a menu. As if the restaurants of Barcelona have put it there merely to irk him.

'I don't think you'd like it,' I say now.

'No, I *do* like Dalí, Mum. He was pretty mad, wasn't he?'

'Seems like it, yes.'

'He used to paint his whole body blue, and drink cocktails made from his own blood!'

'Wow,' I say, smiling.

'And he used to sit in his chair, falling asleep with a spoon in his hand, and when the spoon clanged onto the floor he'd wake up, and that's the time he had his best ideas.'

'Amazing.' Christ, this is the perkiest he's been since we arrived.

'So, is it his actual house you're going to?' he asks, interest piqued.

'Um, no – it's a museum.'

'With his paintings in?'

I nod. 'A few, I think. It's just a building with a few bits of stuff,' I say, without enthusiasm. In fact, from what

300

I've read, the Dalí Theatre-Museum is an eye-popping structure painted pinkish-red with golden croissants stuck all over it and enormous white eggs perched on its roof. It houses the largest collection of Dalí works in the world, including bizarre moving sculptures and an audacious sofa shaped like lips.

'Would I like it?' Alfie asks.

'You'd probably find it a bit dull, to be honest.'

'Oh.'

'And then there's the train journey, in this terrible heat . . .'

He winces. This clearly tips it for him. 'God, yeah. Okay then. I'll probably just have a rest day here. Sure you don't mind going on your own?'

'No, I'll be fine,' I say.

'Okay.'

I perch on the sofa beside him. 'Did you buy yourself any shorts, by the way?'

'Nah, I couldn't face the shops.'

It occurs to me that I should ask for my euros back. But I must be feeling a smidgeon of guilt at not wanting to spend tomorrow with him, so I decide to let him keep the cash – and even hug him – before I head off to bed.

Chapter Forty

Jack

Hey, where are you right now? Fancy a coffee? As the plane touches down at Barcelona airport, I rehearse in my head what I'll say when I call her. *Hi, darling. Guess where I am!*

No – not that. That's a sure-fire way to make a person feel extremely uneasy. My parents did it once, shortly after I'd moved to Glasgow. They'd called me from a phone box when I'd woken up on my sofa one Saturday morning, unwashed and hungover, having blundered home horribly drunk just a few hours before. *Guess where we are, Jack! We're at the end of your road. We decided to drive down and surprise you. So . . . surprise!*

'Great!' I enthused, while the voice in my head screamed, 'What the fuck?'

So I know better than to ever say that. The trouble is, though, it will be a surprise (or shock?) to Nadia when I show up. My decision not to tell her I'm coming seems rather rash now, but I figured there was too much potential for her to say, 'No, please don't!' Or, worse: 'I've met someone else. It all happened so quickly, and actually, he is here with me now.'

The other possibility is that she decided not to come to Barcelona after all – perhaps she didn't fancy mooching about on her own – and has forfeited the flight and Airbnb apartment. But I think that's unlikely. She's not the kind of person who'd freak out at the prospect of travelling alone. No, she'll be here, I decide. Perhaps she's brought a friend: Corinne or Gus, maybe. But that'll be okay; there's a tiny second bedroom, as far as I can recall. The place we hired is actually meant for three. Although I don't have the address – as she booked it – I'll phone her as soon as I'm in the city centre, and she'll be thrilled.

Or at least, quite pleased. Of course, there is the very real possibility that she'll be extremely irritated that I've schlepped out here after her, with no warning. Will she think it's presumptuous of me to just show up, expecting to stay with her as if nothing's happened? Should I get a hotel instead, or would that just seem weird?

Jesus. What the hell am I doing here? This is all Iain's fault!

I lift my wheeled case down from the cabin locker and join the line of passengers as we all begin to shuffle off the plane. Right now, I'm wondering whether I'm quite the adventurer, having flown out to make things right with the woman I love, or if I'm raving mad.

So desperate am I to speak to Nadia, it's all I can do not to phone her as the train hurtles from the airport towards the city. But I manage to resist. I'll leave it until I'm actually there, when I've had a little more time to think things through.

That way, I can do it properly. All I have to do now is figure out precisely what 'it' is.

Chapter Forty-One

Nadia

'It's just a building with a few bits of stuff in,' I'd told Alfie, as if I was describing a branch of B&Q. But in fact the Dalí Theatre-Museum is stunning, filled with crazy artworks – melting clocks and eerie portraits – and bizarre inventions. I am transfixed by a grotesque portrait of Picasso with a giant spoon protruding from his mouth. There's a golden nose sculpture, various voluptuous statues and a vintage taxi in which rain falls on the inside. The museum doesn't even *slightly* resemble a large DIY store.

The fact that it's milling with visitors doesn't spoil it for me. There are numerous rooms and courtyards to explore, and although I'd have loved to have Jack here with me, I'm determined to absorb as much of this bonkers museum before I catch the train back to Barcelona this evening.

Alfie might grumble on about 'people of your generation', as if we are one faceless mass, obsessed with vitamins and adequate house insurance, but there are people of all ages here, including the extremely elderly and delightfully eccentric. I spot a lady in a yellow sundress, a green satin turban and baby blue suede thigh boots. Thigh boots, in this heat! Another woman is strutting about in a sequinned leotard and a tutu made of netting, plus red patent platform shoes. A towering man in a sort of catsuit – which appears to be made out of bubble wrap – struts by me and shouts, 'Hi!'

In this wondrous museum, exhibits and visitors seem to merge, and it's all so fascinating I actually stop wondering whether Alfie is okay (of course he is. He'll be lying in the apartment, in darkness), and if all's fine with Molly at home (why shouldn't it be? She doesn't even live with me anymore). While I'm pretty sure that Alfie would enjoy the spectacle for half an hour or so, I have to admit I'm relishing having hours to spend here, with no one yawning ostentatiously and demanding a snack and a drink before we've even had a chance to look at the artworks.

Three hours drift by in a Surrealist haze, and I'm wondering what to do next when a woman's voice, with a strong Scottish accent, cuts through the air. 'Obviously he was genius, but barking mad,' she exclaims to the small group who seem to be with her.

'Obsessed with sex,' another woman adds, 'although he couldn't actually do it . . .'

'His wife was crazy,' a man interjects. 'She had tons of affairs. Always at it . . .'

'Poor Dalí!'

'Yeah. And he built her a grand secluded house, up in the mountains . . .'

'She lived in it on her own . . .'

'Wouldn't let him visit!' Someone taps my shoulder. 'Did you know she tried to poison him . . .' The woman breaks off. 'Oh, God, I'm sorry. I thought you were Fran!'

'That's okay,' I say, smiling.

The woman beams. 'Whereabouts are you from, then?'

'Glasgow. How about you?'

'Paisley,' she replies. 'So, what d'you think of this place?'

'It's pretty mind-blowing,' I admit.

'Sure is. We couldn't decide on the Prado or here. It had to go to votes and I'm so glad this won. So, are you staying in Figueres?'

'No, Barcelona. Just a few days with my son.'

'Aw, lovely! Is he with you today?'

'Um, no,' I reply with a smile. 'He fancied . . . a rest day.'

She chuckles, clearly understanding the subtext, and I sense a kind of kinship with her. 'How about you? Are you all family or friends?'

'We're an art group,' she replies. 'Just amateurs – an old bunch of mates really. Art's our excuse to come away together. A common interest, so we can say it's a hobby trip – like a golfing holiday . . .'

'But without the golf,' says another woman with a laugh.

'We drink and we draw,' the first woman adds.

'More drinking than drawing really,' says a bald man in a striped T-shirt.

'That sounds fun,' I say.

'You should join us,' the first woman says, turning to the man. 'She's left her son in Barcelona!'

'Teenager?' he asks.

'Yes,' I reply, and the man laughs.

'Teenagers in museums. Bloody nightmare! Well, you're welcome to come around with us, unless you prefer to be by yourself. I know some people do. We won't take offence.'

It's Danny who springs into my mind now; specifically,

how he would have reacted to a middle-aged man – or any stranger – inviting us into their group on holiday. When the kids were little, we went on a few package holidays to Spain and Majorca where apartments were all stacked up around the pools. All around us, adults on sunbeds would be chatting away, befriending each other while the kids splashed about in the water. By the end of the week, I'd notice that many of these families had merged into big, boisterous gangs, drinking and eating together, taking group photos, the children playing en masse. *Please, Nads,* Danny declared one evening, *never expect me to make friends with other people on holiday.*

'Why not?' I asked. 'Don't you like meeting new people?'

'"I like meeting new people!"' he'd teased, mimicking a Miss World contestant. 'No thanks, sweetheart. Because I have plenty of friends already – at home,' he retorted, as if his quota had been filled, and that would satisfy him for life – or perhaps, more accurately, he'd surmised that none of those holidaymakers would be his 'type'. Perhaps they might not be au fait with the lesser-known Hitchcock films, or maybe he was scared they'd quiz him mercilessly when his profession came to light: 'Have you met anyone famous? Go on, you must have! Tell us all their dirt!'

But unlike Danny, I wasn't semi-famous, and even if I had been, I'd never have been like that. Surely being open to 'meeting new people' is one of the great joys of life?

I look at the group, whose joie de vivre is oddly infectious; since the row with Jack that's something that's been lacking in my life. 'That would be lovely,' I tell the bald man. 'Thank you.'

'Great! So, I'm Rico . . .'

307

'I'm Nadia.'

'And this is Fran . . .' Ah, the one I was mistaken for.

'Hi,' I say with a smile.

'This is Gerri, and Elsa . . .'

'Welcome, Nadia,' Gerri says, clutching at my arm, 'to the Wasted Artists. Now, how about a lunchtime drink?'

Chapter Forty-Two

Jack

There are certain signs that someone isn't into you anymore, and not answering your calls has to be one of the clearest. I tried calling Nadia as soon as I arrived in the city, emerging into the muggy heat from the station. Almost immediately I felt engulfed by the chaos of the Ramblas with its garish fast food outlets, the numerous kiosks cluttering the central pavement, and the street sellers flogging cheap sunglasses, handbags and trashy toys.

Normally, I love finding myself in a big, brash, glittering city like this one. As a kid I was always itching to leave the farm behind, and for my real life to begin. However now, with Nadia's phone simply ringing through, I don't quite know what to do with myself.

Find a hotel, I decide. It feels like a safer option than expecting to stay at the apartment, and if things go well and everything's patched up, then I can always move over to the flat. It's probably best to choose somewhere pretty close, I reason, remembering that 'our' Airbnb is in El Raval, an area that used to be considered rather shady, apparently – a keep-your-wits-about-you kind of place. But now it appears to be buzzing with cool coffee shops, boutiques and bookshops amongst the seemingly longer-established ethnic grocer's stores, junk shops, barbers and workaday cafés.

As far as I've gathered so far, Barcelona is an in-your-face kind of city: show-offy and grand, with a comfortingly scruffy edge, like the fancy dress costumes Lori used to wear when she went through a mercifully brief princess stage. In contrast my hotel is dark and cave-like, squished between a newsagent's, with sun-faded guidebooks crammed in its window, and a shop selling what looks like flammable nightwear for ladies of a certain age. I like the look of the hotel, though. It seems more befitting my 'mission' than a faceless chain, and the fancier places are way above my budget.

I check in by way of a grouchy receptionist – squat and stocky, her hair in a bun – and head up to my room, which is pleasantly spartan and undeniably clean, and I dump my bag on the light green candlewick bedspread. 'You're here now,' I tell myself. Which begs the question: *what next?*

After that last conversation with Nadia, I'd explained to Lori that 'plans had changed', that Nadia 'wanted to focus on work' and I wouldn't be going to Barcelona after all. And then, suddenly, I *was* going: 'But what about Nadia's work?' Lori asked, not unreasonably. 'Doesn't she mind?'

'Of course not,' I'd replied, jovially, but now, my worry is that she will mind, very much. Still, I decide, I can enjoy this city, and have fun and see interesting things! Feeling more positive now, I shower quickly and pull on a fresh T-shirt and jeans. And now, as I head out into the clammy afternoon, I've convinced myself that that's what I'll do. I shall explore this city, soaking it all in, *immersing* myself, like she would. Surely that's a more attractive proposition than having someone say, 'I've just sat miserably, in my hotel room and cafés, thinking about you'?

So that's what I do.

Is there a cathedral in Aberdeen? Christ, I think, cringing at the memory. It's a wonder Nadia even wanted to keep seeing me after that. And now, as I gawp at the awesome Sagrada Família – which looks more melting wedding cake than cathedral really – I wish she were with me, so I could remind her of that conversation and we could laugh about it.

I meander the streets, loving the feel and vibrancy of the city immediately, but feeling slightly out of sorts, as if something's missing. No, not something. Some*one*. And this is oddly guilt-making as I know I should be appreciating being here. After all, I'm very lucky. I picture Lori's face, if she were here with me, and decide I really must make the most of it.

To ward off my lingering sense of unease, I march around at quite a pace, stopping for a beer at a lovely art deco bar, which I bolt down too quickly. Then it's onwards again, into the Gothic Quarter with its tangle of dark, narrow streets and looming buildings, beautiful and fascinating but also rather oppressive.

By the time I emerge into bright sunshine, I am gasping for more liquid, sweating profusely and regretting my choice of clothing.

Who wears jeans in this weather? No one, it seems, apart from me. A quick scan confirms that, while there's the odd pair of chinos being worn in the crowds around

311

me – and naturally, the heavily armed police are in their uniform trousers – mainly it's shorts. I'll have to buy some today, as I cannot face another day hoofing around in my Levi's.

As there don't seem to be any regular high-street-type stores in this area, I wander further towards Barceloneta, down by the water, figuring that there are bound to be beachy-type clothing shops close to the waterfront. And indeed there are, and the clothes inside them appear to be truly terrible.

I am not a vain man, I remind myself as I flick through rails crammed with T-shirts in jarring designs. However, I know what I like, and it tends towards the basic: non-shouty colours, no logos if possible. I search through horrific shorts in cheap, rustly material and wonder what would Nadia make of me showing up to meet her in a banana-coloured nylon pair. As she has yet to call me back, it's not an issue I need to trouble myself with now.

I move onwards to another store. Again, it favours the loud and brash, only here the shorts all seem to be patterned with smiley faces and Pokémon characters, both of which I'd have assumed would have slipped into extinction. My charity shop has a more wearable selection than this. Where are the kind of shorts that roughly ninety-five per cent of adult males in Barcelona – basically everyone who isn't a guard or a businessman – are strolling about quite happily in?

I'm in the wrong part of town, I decide, turning to leave. I need to go to a normal shopping district and find the Catalan equivalent of Gap, or perhaps actual Gap. And that's what I'm about to do, when a tall young man emerges from a curtained changing room – wearing a T-shirt and shorts.

I cast the latter a quick look. They are a dull khaki green, baggy and roomy and perfectly acceptable attire. In the periphery of my vision I'm aware of him shuffling about, head bent, back towards me. 'Uh, *habla Iglesias por favor?*' he mutters. *Iglesias* – like Julio Iglesias.

'*Sí?*' the male shop assistant says.

'Erm, d'you have more shorts just like these ones? 'Cause I think I'm gonna need two pairs . . .'

I know that voice. The last time I heard it, it was spouting on about bovine lactation in my back garden. And as he turns towards me a stupid question pops out of my mouth: 'My God, Alfie. What are *you* doing here?'

Chapter Forty-Three

As I explain that I decided to fly out and 'surprise' his mother, Alfie looks at me as if I am completely mad. 'So . . . she actually doesn't know?' he asks, frowning.

No – because that is what I mean by a surprise. 'Erm, no,' I reply. 'I've tried to phone her a few times since I arrived, but it's just ringing—'

'Oh, yeah,' he says, picking up his chunky white coffee cup – we're now installed at a pavement café – 'that's because her phone's lost. She left it on a café table yesterday.'

'Oh, Christ. Any chance of getting it back?'

Alfie shrugs, as if it's of no consequence to him. 'Don't think so.'

We fall into silence, and I gaze around the pleasingly crumbly square, trying to pretend that we are sufficiently at ease with each other for the lull to feel comfortable. Perhaps anyone wandering by would surmise that we are father and son? However, as it is, the lull feels anything *but* comfortable. For one thing, Alfie has already explained that Nadia is out of town, having gone off to Figueres for the day, and he seemed not entirely enamoured with my suggestion that we have coffee together. But I had to ask, and in fact, I wanted to, if only to try and shift things onto a better footing with him, and, ultimately, with Nadia. I have no intention of bringing up his anti-dairy-farming rant today, if ever. The last thing I want is more hostility from him – although a proper apology wouldn't go amiss.

Still, he's young, I remind myself: the age I was when I flew the coop and landed in Glasgow. And, although I thought I knew it all, I was an idiot back then.

Probably still am, I reflect, conscious of Alfie checking me out from time to time across the table. He's placed his phone next to his coffee cup. Its screen is cracked, the whole thing held together with badly administered yellowing Sellotape, all bumpy and curling up at the ends.

'So, why did you tell Mum you didn't want to come?' he asks.

'Because, erm . . .' I stir my coffee. Of course, I am not about to go into the row we had on the phone, particularly as it was triggered by him, and nor do I want to explain that I behaved like a complete and utter arse to his mother.

'She said you had, erm . . . a kind of thing,' he prompts me, 'on the phone.'

'Yes, we did,' I murmur. 'And I regretted it and changed my mind and . . .' I shrug. 'And, well, here I am.'

Although he's been tending to avoid my gaze, his eyes meet mine now. He's so similar to his mother, his eyes the same intense green, his nose and mouth echoing the face I've grown to love seeing. She is so unaffectedly, naturally beautiful, and I'm overcome by an intense wave of missing her.

'Seems a bit weird,' Alfie remarks, not unreasonably.

'Um, yeah, I suppose it must do.' Of course it's weird; after all, I was urged to fly out here by a man who thinks it's okay to boil an entire butternut squash in a pot. 'So, how's it been so far?' I ask, twiddling a teaspoon now, the lactation issue hanging over us like a murky cloud.

'Huh, all right,' Alfie says.

'Are you enjoying it?'

He rakes at his mop of dark hair. 'It's okay. It's very *hot . . .*'

'Yes, but it's a great city, isn't it?' I remark, gazing around the square again as if to demonstrate how much I am appreciating its beauty.

'Yeah, it's all right.'

Just *all right*? I sense my jaw clenching. 'What kind of things have you been doing?' I ask, aware of sounding oddly formal.

'Uh, just walking around and stuff.' Jesus, is this the most enthusiasm he can muster? He might as well be in Hull – not that there's anything wrong with Hull. In fact, I've never been there, and I'm sure it has tons to offer, but possibly not incredible Gaudí architecture with crazy mosaics and white, curvy roofs like melting icing . . .

I picture Lori, who was thrilled when we went to Paris together, just the two of us, last Easter. I'd found us a cheap last-minute deal, a twin room in a grubby hotel near Gare du Nord; but it was brilliant, exploring with her, seeing her eyes shining with excitement as she photographed everything within sight: the bridges, Notre Dame, the iconic Metro signs, the portion of fries that came with her steak in a little silver bucket.

This probably sounds as if I think I am a better parent than Nadia is, in that at least my child *appreciates* a trip.

And I don't at all. I have messed up in countless ways. Although I've worried about Elaine's drinking, and Lori's attitude towards school, and why certain teachers seem to dislike her (i.e. not allowing her to the Christmas dance), I have never managed to get to the bottom of what's really going on.

In short, I haven't been able to fix things. And isn't that what a dad is supposed to do? Make his child feel secure and safe and cared for? I'm not sure if I have managed to do that at all. But yes, Lori *was* thrilled to be somewhere exotic and wholly different from Glasgow. And now Alfie's hand keeps twitching towards his phone, as if pulled by a powerful magnetic force, and he's barely managing to resist it. At least he has manners, I suppose. I know some kids would sit there prodding away at it, even if they were out having coffee with their mum's boyfriend (or, rather, *ex*). And maybe Lori will be like this in five years' time – dull-eyed and listless, picking at a sugar packet the way Alfie is now, until it rips and the white grains scatter all over the table. Although I can't imagine it, that doesn't mean it won't happen, and if it does it'll serve me bloody well right.

'So, um, how's your mum doing?' It feels weird, referring to her that way – and also as if she is ninety-seven years old and in hospital.

'She's all right,' Alfie concedes.

'Well, I imagine the Dalí place will be very good . . .' And now I am speaking as if I am not fully au fait with the English language. He has this effect on me, this boy. I like to think I'm a normal, reasonably functioning man, but a few minutes in Alfie's company turn me into a complete weirdo. *Is there a cathedral in Aberdeen?*

'It does sound good,' Alfie mumbles. Well, we're agreed on that then!

I drain my coffee. 'D'you know when she's heading back?'

He shakes his head. 'Sometime later on. Not that late, she said. We were going to have dinner . . .'

'Ah, right. I wonder if she meant dinner like you'd have at home, at seven or eight, or much later like they do here?'

Alfie gawps at me.

'They eat very late, don't they?' I remark, sweating a little now.

'Um, yeah, I suppose so,' he says, and now he's looking at me as if he would very much like me to pay for our coffees and fuck off and leave him alone, instead of chattering on weirdly to fill the silences.

'I don't think I could sleep if I had my dinner at eleven at night!' Oh, for Christ's sake. Shall we talk about my digestive system now?

'Well, er . . .' Alfie's hand closes around his phone.

'I'll get the bill,' I say quickly, checking my own phone for the time. 'It's just gone six. What're you up to now?'

He opens his mouth to answer, but is distracted by a text. He picks up his phone and peers at it. 'It's Mum.'

'Is it?' I bark, managing to restrain myself from reading it.

'Yeah.'

'I thought she had no phone?' That sounds accusatory and wrong.

'She's used someone else's.'

'Really? So she knows your number, then? I'm impressed! I don't know anyone's off by heart—'

'Oh, yeah.' He rolls his eyes. 'She memorised it so she can always keep tabs on me . . .' He holds it out so I can read it:

318

Mum here – I borrowed a phone. Hope all's ok love? Met some lovely people, going for drinks, will catch a late train back. Any probs call this number – his name's Rico. Love Mum xxx.

'Who's Rico?' I ask, frowning.

'No idea.'

'Right.' I smile tightly and pay the bill. As we get up, each of us clutching a carrier bag containing our identical shorts – there was nothing else remotely wearable in the shop – an idea occurs to me.

Alfie is alone, probably without too much money and will more than likely be hungry pretty soon. And I am alone too – and, I realise, starving now. 'D'you fancy finding somewhere to eat?' I suggest.

'Um, I don't really know where to—'

'I'm sure there are plenty of places that have great vegan food,' I cut in, feigning both knowledge and enthusiasm.

He nods, taking this in.

'My treat,' I add. 'C'mon – let's go stuff ourselves . . .'

His expression changes then, from a blank flatness to the slightest hint of a smile. I watch him, fascinated by the facial development, like David Attenborough observing a platypus chipping its way out of an egg.

'I'm pretty tired,' he adds. 'I might go back to the apartment, have a nap . . .'

Christ, what's wrong with this boy? He's in the flush of youth!

'Okay,' I say carefully, 'so how about we swap numbers and meet up in a couple of hours, after your sleep?'

He pushes his hair out of his eyes. 'Yeah, okay,' he says, albeit reluctantly.

'Shall we meet here – on that corner – at, say, eight?'

'Yeah. Sounds good.' We exchange numbers and make our way back to the main street, where we part company. I glance back to see him loping off at a slight forward slant. Whilst I'm not madly enamoured with spending hours in Alfie's company, I need to try to make things right between us. So that's what I intend to do. We'll have a fun evening somehow. I will not rake up the fact that he made my mother cry, and I will do my best to befriend this boy if it ruddy kills me.

Chapter Forty-Four

Nadia

If Jack's mother favours pretty sketches of rural scenes, this group favours a different approach. 'This is why we call ourselves the Wasted Artists,' Gerri says with a throaty laugh as the barman at their hotel knocks up a second round of margaritas for us. By 'us', I mean Gerri, Rico, Elsa, Fran – and me. We had a late lunch at a lovely Moroccan place down the road, then strolled around Figueres, chatting and gazing at the shuttered houses in weather-worn pinkish stone. We wandered from the grand main avenues to narrow, tucked-away streets, until Gerri decided we all needed a restorative cocktail . . . or several.

She has a mane of crinkly light brown hair and is wearing a lime green linen shift over black leggings and flat red pumps, plus a chunky necklace of multicoloured beads. She drinks fast, finishing her cocktail first, as if afraid that the barman might run out of ingredients. 'So, what kind of art d'you all make?' I ask, looking around the table in the corner of the bar. 'I mean, how does this group of yours work?'

'Clue's in the "wasted",' chuckles Rico. 'We get

together once a fortnight, have a few drinks, bring along stuff we're working on, or start portraits, do collage, make things with our hands – whatever we feel like really . . .'

'Where d'you have your meetings?'

'Fran has a studio,' he explains.

'Top floor of my house,' she says. Although I'd put the rest of the group at around mid-fifties, Fran is oldest: rangy and elegant in a simple blue dress, with a sharp, silvery crop from which her animated face seems to shine.

'So, is there a *lot* of drinking?' I ask, sipping my potent cocktail.

Elsa, who seems a little quieter, nods and laughs. 'Oh, yes. We play records and have a bit of a night.' She indicates Fran. 'She has quite a record collection . . .'

'Sounds brilliant,' I remark, wondering what the well-behaved life drawing groups I've modelled for would make of such a set-up.

They quiz me further about my own work, my upbringing, my kids, and the fact that their father is Danny Raven – not that I've name-dropped. By the time we'd sat down for lunch they had already managed to wheedle that little factlet out of me. They even know about Kiki Badger and her torturous facials, and Gerri announces loudly, 'Well, if it'd make me look as good as Nadia, I might give it a shot!'

'No, don't,' I say quickly. 'You feel like someone's trying to remove your face, from the inside.'

'No pain, no gain,' she chuckles, and I smile that she's come out with the very phrase I'd used to reassure myself when Kiki's fingers had been inside of my mouth.

'Another round?' Elsa suggests.

'I'd really better go and catch a train,' I say quickly. 'I

322

should make make sure Alfie's okay.' I look at Rico. 'Has he replied to my text yet?'

He fishes his phone from his pocket and checks it. 'Nothing yet, love.'

'C'mon, stay a bit longer,' Gerri urges me. 'You're one of us now, Nadia.'

'But he might start to worry.'

Fran laughs, deeply and throatily. 'How old is he again?'

'Nineteen,' I reply.

'Does he have any cash,' Rico asks, 'or at least access to some?'

'Erm, I left him some euros, yes . . .'

'And you honestly think,' Elsa chuckles, 'that a nineteen-year-old boy, who's been left alone in Barcelona – with money – is going to be pacing about, wondering where the hell his mother is?'

Everyone laughs and I have to agree she has a point. 'The thing is,' I add, 'he's a little fragile right now. He's split with his girlfriend and looks like he's dropping out of uni. He's a bit of a lost soul . . .'

Rico taps my shoulder. 'Another margarita while you think about it? We should probably have some tapas too. They do amazing ones here. Shall we just have a selection?' As everyone murmurs in approval, Rico catches the eye of the barman. He is clearly on friendly terms with the Wasted Artists already as, with a nod and a hand gesture, Rico manages to communicate that another round of his excellent cocktails and an array of dishes are required.

'He reckons the secret is to put the ice in the glass first,' Gerri says.

'I'll remember that,' I say. 'They're absolutely delicious.'

And so we have another round, and tuck into a vast

323

selection of tapas, while everyone shows me pictures of their art on their phones. Fran creates enormous splashy abstract canvases, favouring shimmering colours that seem to dance. Rico, who often works in collaboration with his boyfriend, is primarily a sculptor with a passion for reclaimed debris found on demolition sites. Gerri paints on sheets of parachute silk, and Elsa incorporates mosaic into her stunning portraits.

At just before ten, Fran announces, 'I think you should forget about going back to Barcelona tonight and stay with us instead.'

'But I don't have a room booked,' I protest.

'Yes, but my room's a twin – one of our group had to drop out at the last minute. So you can stay there.'

I pause for a moment and look around at my new friends. Rico is making the barman laugh, and Gerri is chipping in to persuade me to stay. It's so tempting. Fran and Elsa are looking at me expectantly, so I smile and say, 'Okay, if you're sure – why not? I'll just let Alfie know . . .' Rico hands me his phone.

Decided to stay over in Figueres, I write. *Hope that's okay. Text me back please? And call if you need anything. This is Rico's phone.*

Minutes later, a reply comes: *All fine here Mum just out.*

'He's out!' I exclaim, frowning.

Fran hoots with laughter. 'Of course he's out. What else would you expect?'

'Yes, but where? And who's he with?'

Rico grins. 'He'll have just found people . . .'

I let this idea settle: that my son might not have spent my absence lying in the apartment in semi-darkness, getting up only to break things occasionally, but has thrown himself out there, into the delights of a Barcelona night.

'Anyway, you're with us tonight,' Fran says companionably, patting my arm, 'so you don't need to worry about Alfie right now. Just relax and think how great it is for him to have some space, away from his mum, out on the lash with people his own age.'

Chapter Forty-Five

Jack

'Are you sure you don't want me to tell Mum you're here?' Alfie asks.

'Just leave it for now,' I reply.

'Why?'

'I just . . . don't want to unsettle her,' I say.

Alfie frowns at me, clearly confused. 'Why would it do that?'

'She might feel the need to come straight back,' I say, realising how unlikely this is, now she's with Rico. *Bloody Rico.* As we finally found somewhere where Alfie thought he might like to eat – after he'd rejected something like twenty-five places – she texted Alfie again, with the announcement that she is staying in Figueres overnight. 'Or maybe,' I add, trying for a joke, 'she'd be horrified and never come back, and stay in the Dalí Museum forever.'

Alfie manages a nod, and I look at him as he picks at a kind of flatbread adorned with scorched black bits and a meagre scraping of tomato sauce. It seems almost criminal, when we're in a city famed for its food, that he finally selected what is possibly the worst restaurant – not just in Barcelona, but in the whole of mainland Europe.

'Can you imagine,' I struggle on, 'what that would do to a person's brain? Being trapped in the Dalí Museum for your whole life?'

'Huh, yeah,' Alfie murmurs, clearly wondering why I am talking like this, as if he is seven years old.

'So, how's your food?' I ask.

'Okay,' he replies. 'How about yours?'

'Fine,' I reply gamely, although I suspect some mean-spirited individual from somewhere like Slough decided: *sod those Catalans with their mouthwatering tapas, seafood, cheeses and hams. What I'm going to do is cash in on this vegan explosion, and dish up substandard flatbreads and a few gloopy alternatives, because they'll eat anything as long as we put a big, leaf-covered sign outside and call it 'Veg-Life'.* It sounds like some kind of 'tonic' you'd find languishing at the back of a health food shop.

We are sitting outside, in a nondescript courtyard with a few half-arsed fairy lights strung around the potted, leafless trees. The grubby white plastic tables and chairs are of the kind you might spot on a bungalow's weed-infested patio. There is actual moss growing on them.

Like Alfie, I am working my way through some sort of flatbread. I'm okay with the charred base, and even the grated 'cheese' (reconstituted nut matter? Who knows?) that's been scattered upon it. But there is also a carrot element; par-boiled, slightly softened on the outside and hard within. Basically, it's a carrot pizza.

Even more unsettling is the fact that Nadia is having a holiday fling with her hot Spanish lover in the birthplace of Salvador Dalí. (Well, not *in* the actual museum – at least I'd hope not. But close enough for it to be completely thrilling for her.) And now, as I hack away at my dinner, I'm picturing this Rico: tall, devilishly good-looking, a local who spied the beautiful tourist wandering around the Dalí Museum and swooped in, expertly offering to show her round.

They toured the museum together, I've decided. Then it was dinner – of course, he knows the best places, hidden and exquisite where only the locals go – and then they had drinks in some delightful courtyard bar, under the stars. By now she might even be back at his apartment, overlooking some achingly beautiful square. And they'll be in his bedroom, with the cool white sheets, shutters open, warm breeze wafting in . . .

Maybe the fact that his mother has gone off and met someone new, just like that, is unsettling for Alfie too. He doesn't look unsettled, though, as he shovels his food in wordlessly, as if to get this evening over as quickly as possible. The staff, I've noticed, all seem mildly depressed; a girl with a pierced eyebrow is roaming the tables, giving them a perfunctory wipe with a greying cloth (perhaps she could tackle the moss on our chairs?). An elderly couple are sitting opposite each other, looking rather stunned by the platefuls of various mush that have been placed in front of them.

'What's yours then?' the woman asks in a strong Yorkshire accent.

'I think it's . . . a grain?' her companion ventures.

'A brain?' she exclaims.

'No, *grains*,' he replies hotly. 'Like barley or something . . .' He glares at her, and it strikes me that few scenes are more dismal than a couple who are clearly having a terrible time together, on holiday.

328

'Jack?'

My God, did Alfie just address me by name? 'Sorry, what did you say?'

He fixes me with a steady gaze. 'I said, I s'pose running a charity shop is quite a cool thing to do really.'

So he appears to be initiating a conversation with me. This is a good sign, surely? 'It's fine, you know? It has its challenges but—'

'You're not working for a big, horrible organisation that wants to screw its employees, are you?' he suggests, sipping his beer.

'Well, no, there is that.' I sip mine too. We are on our second, which I hope is okay, but then, he is nineteen. I'm hardly going to suggest that he switches to lemonade. 'But we do have sales targets,' I add, 'and our area manager keeps a close track on our takings. It's all compared, year-on-year, we have aims and objectives, it's actually very closely monitored . . .'

His eyes begin to glaze and I realise I'm in danger of anaesthetising him with tedious facts. What's wrong with me? Whenever we're forced together in a situation where we at least have to try to communicate, I end up spouting inanities. *Aberdeen's the most northern city in Britain, isn't it? Now, shall we talk about its annual rainfall?* It's odd because it's not as if I am unused to being around teenagers. Lori's always spent half the week with me. When she first started getting spots, we went to the chemist together and got someone to talk us through how to deal with the oiliness and outbreaks. I'd bought Lori what she needed when her periods started when she was staying at mine. It wasn't a big deal. We've talked about puberty, bodies, sex – all that. Yet put me in close proximity with Alfie and I start saying things like 'sales targets', 'aims

329

and objectives' and, of course, 'cathedrals'. I must stop this, or the poor boy will end up trying to impale himself on his knife.

'I do enjoy it, though,' I continue. 'It's fascinating, the kind of things we have handed in.'

This perks up his interest. 'D'you get much weird stuff?'

'God, yes,' I say with a knowing chuckle.

His eyes are on me now. 'Like what?'

'Like, uh . . .' And now, despite the fact that there must be something that falls under the Weird Stuff category every day, I cannot think of a single thing. Oh yes, there *was* something – but I don't feel entirely comfortable with the idea of Alfie announcing to Nadia: 'Jack was saying he was handed in a glass dildo at the shop. Why would he even tell me that, Mum?'

'What kinda things, then?' Alfie prompts me.

'Um, er . . . like a knitted Womble . . .'

'A what?' He peers at me through his hair.

'A Womble. It's a character from a kids' programme from years ago. You wouldn't know it.' *So why the hell are you telling me then?* his flat expression says. 'They used to go around collecting litter,' I barge on, 'and make useful things out of it.' I pause, wondering how to make this even remotely relevant to today's world. 'They were pioneer recyclers,' I add, catching our waitress's attention and requesting a couple more beers. 'That okay with you?' I ask Alfie.

'Oh, yeah! Thanks.' And then: a smile. An actual raising of the mouth corners suggesting that *drink* is the only way to proceed here. Another beer or two, then we can part company and he can go back to his apartment, and await Nadia's return tomorrow – that is, if she comes back then, and hasn't decided to spend the rest of the trip shagging Rico in Figueres. As for me, I'll head back to my hotel and then wake up and explore more of this fascinating city all by myself. Or I might just find a bar to hide in (perhaps I'll make notes on my sales targets?) until it's time to go home.

But right now, the waitress is tossing a laminated dessert menu onto our table as if it's a court summons. I am smiling politely and saying 'No, thanks', then paying our bill, dusting off a mossy smear from the leg of my shorts and suggesting to Alfie: 'D'you fancy another beer somewhere before we call it a night?'

He shrugs and checks his phone. 'Yeah, why not?' Twenty minutes later, he is perched on a high stool in a rowdy bar with tears spilling from his eyes.

Chapter Forty-Six

He's trying to hide it, of course, wiping his face with his hand, and turning away from me as if something terribly interesting is happening across the room.

'Alfie?' I venture, frowning.

'Yeah?'

'What's wrong? Are you okay?'

He nods, lips pressed tightly together. Surely it can't be the booze; he's only had three small beers with dinner, plus half of the one I bought him in here. Nineties music – The Strokes, I think – is blasting out; the average age is probably about twenty-two. I'd spotted this place, and thought he might like it. Now I wish we'd gone into the bar two doors down, a more sedate place with a guy playing tinkly piano.

'Has something happened?' I ask, conscious of a wave of responsibility for this distraught young man.

He nods. 'Ummm . . . yeah. Kind of.'

'Something . . . today? What is it, Alfie?'

He exhales loudly and I try to figure out how to be of any use to him at all when we barely know each other. 'Is it . . . something you can tell me about?'

He shakes his head mutely. A couple of guys jostle past us, knocking against Alfie's shoulder. A splash of beer from a glass hits the front of his T-shirt, and he winces. 'Not really,' he murmurs, rubbing at his face again.

'Okay,' I say, 'but if you do want to tell me . . .' I pause. 'It's so noisy in here. D'you fancy a walk?'

'A *walk*?' he gasps, as if I had suggested a bungee jump, whilst fire-eating.

'Just a stroll,' I say quickly. 'We could find somewhere quieter to sit, or if you just want to head back to your apartment, that's fine, of course.' He looks at me, and I sense him sizing me up.

'Yeah, all right,' he mutters. 'I would like a walk. But not miles, okay?'

'No, not miles, just a wander about . . .' I stop. 'Or we could find somewhere, like a bench or something. It's still lovely and warm out there. We could just sit.'

And that's what we do, turning off the main thoroughfare and following the narrow side streets until we find a stone arch, which leads to a small square, bordered on all sides by high buildings in softly worn creamy stone. There are a couple of antique shops, now in darkness, and a single café with just one young couple sitting outside. There are benches beneath spindly trees in the square, and we sit down.

I glance at Alfie, who seems to have recovered himself now. He's a handsome boy, with angular features: a strong nose, full lips like his mother's and heavily lidded eyes. For a few minutes, neither of us speaks. It doesn't feel awkward now. Every now and again, a lone person or a couple strolls through the square, and then it's deserted again. Even the people from the café have left.

333

'Um . . . Jack?' Alfie says finally.

'Yeah?' I glance at him, but look away again. I have a hunch that he might be more inclined to talk if he feels I'm not watching him intently.

'I, um . . .' He clears his throat. 'I'm sorry about that . . . *thing*. With your mum and dad, I mean. I shouldn't have said it.'

'Oh.' I ponder this for a moment, taken aback that he's brought it up at all. 'It's all right,' I say. 'You went into one a bit, but it's okay—'

"Cause I really feel strongly . . .'

'Yes, I can tell you do,' I cut in. 'That's fine. Of course it is. You're an adult, you can follow your own principles and lead your life how you want to. I respect that.'

I sense him studying me in surprise. 'You do?'

'Of course I do! Why wouldn't I?'

'Well, I upset your mum, I probably said too much . . .'

'Look, Alfie,' I say, more firmly now, 'you're entitled to make your own choices about what to eat and how to live. But I do think, when you're trying to persuade people into a different way of thinking, there's no point in lecturing or haranguing them—'

'But I didn't mean—'

'Because when you do that,' I continue, thinking what the hell now, 'you just push people away. D'you see what I'm saying? They feel bullied and their natural response is to reject what you're saying outright.'

I glance at him. He is picking at his nails, but clearly listening. His phone has remained in his shorts pocket.

'Look, Alfie,' I add, 'you had no chance of persuading my parents to stop dairy farming and grow lettuce. It's their way of life – a huge part of who they are. But,

334

y'know, maybe some people can be persuaded to think about things differently.'

'To stop eating animal products, you mean?'

I hesitate. After that carrot flatbread I could actually murder a steak and chips. 'Yes – if you're *gently* persuasive, but give them the chance to make up their own minds . . .' I stop, hearing myself telling him – a bona fide young adult – how to communicate with other humans. But amazingly, he appears to be listening. 'It's like in the shop where I work,' I continue. 'We try to make things seem appealing by presenting them as best we can. Say a customer walks in and starts browsing. We might suggest a certain top, or jacket, might suit their taste, but we don't foist a pink floppy hat on them and then, when they say they're not sure, bash them on the head and snatch their purse.'

Alfie laughs. My God – an actual laugh, as if we haven't been thrown together, awkwardly, in our matching shorts (there really were no other acceptable ones in the shop). 'I get what you're saying,' he says with a nod.

'Sorry if that sounded a bit lecture-y . . .'

'No, it didn't at all.' He smiles. 'And, look . . . I'm sorry if you and Mum split up 'cause of all that.'

'Oh, I don't know what's happening there,' I say quickly, keen to switch the focus back to him. 'Look, Alfie, you were upset just then, in the bar. What's going on?'

He sighs loudly, and I can sense him weighing up whether he feels he can tell me. 'It all went wrong with Cam – with Camilla,' he mumbles.

'Right. Yeah. Your mum mentioned that. You were meant to be going travelling, weren't you?'

He nods dolefully.

'Did she decide she wasn't going, at the last minute?'

335

Like I'd done, I realise, ducking out of this trip. What an idiot.

'No, it was me,' Alfie says carefully. He turns to look at me straight on. 'Turned out she'd been seeing someone else. I saw stuff on her phone. Texts and stuff . . .'

'Oh, that's not good.'

He inhales as if mustering the courage to tell me more. 'She'd been sending him nudes.'

I frown at him, not getting it at first. 'What d'you mean?'

'C'mon, *you* know.'

'No, I really don't . . .'

'Everyone does it,' he says, rather sharply.

'You mean when people send naked pictures of themselves?'

Alfie snorts in disbelief, as if he can't quite believe I'm so ill-informed. 'Yes, that's what I mean. You must know that.'

'Well, I have heard it's a thing,' I say. 'I read about celebrities having theirs stolen off the cloud or somewhere, but do normal people do it too?' He nods. 'Christ, Alfie. I've only just got my head around the fact that everyone photographs their food!'

He laughs dryly. 'We didn't feel the urge to photograph our flatbreads, did we?'

I smile. 'Er, no. I must admit, I didn't feel compelled to.'

'That place was pretty bad, wasn't it?'

'Yeah.' I nod. 'So, anyway – you found out about this other person . . .'

'Uh-huh. And it turned out Camilla had only been seeing me because she's into drama – she wants to be an actress – and she thought she could meet my dad and get to know him—'

'You mean she *used* you?'

Alfie nods resignedly. 'She thought she'd get a part in his next film. One of her friends told me.'

'But that's ridiculous,' I splutter. 'Is she really so confident to think that? That it'd be a done deal just because you two were together?'

'She's used to getting pretty much everything she wants,' Alfie says with a shrug.

He stands up from the bench and rotates his shoulders, as if to get his body properly working again. I get up too and, slowly, we wander together towards the archway.

'Didn't you spend Christmas with her family?' I ask, remembering seeing Nadia by the river on that cold December night. Alfie had just told her he wouldn't be coming home for Christmas. She couldn't compete with the girlfriend, Nadia had said.

'Yeah. And she was probably acting then too.'

Poor kid, I reflect as we start to make our way back to his apartment and my hotel. I suppose it's a hazard of having a famous parent. I know from my frankly ridiculous googling sessions that Danny Raven is known for plucking kids from obscurity, giving them virtually free rein with the loosest of scripts, and changing their lives forever.

'And I did a stupid thing,' Alfie goes on, 'when I was with her.'

'What?' I ask, alarmed now at the prospect of some kind of confession.

He grimaces. 'I can't stop thinking about it. It's on my mind all the time. I was thinking about it when we were eating just then . . .'

'Think about what, Alfie?' I ask.

He blinks and looks at me. 'Will you promise not to tell Mum if I show you?'

337

'Show me *what*?'

'This.' He lifts his T-shirt sleeve slowly. At first I think: Christ, he's been self-harming and it's gone septic and I'm going to have to figure out how to help him . . . But it's not that. It's actually a small tattoo of a woman's face; she has Cleopatra eyes, a mane of indigo hair and, I have to say, although I'm no expert, it's probably not the world's finest tattoo.

'Oh,' I murmur. 'And your mum doesn't know?'

'Nope, not yet,' he replies.

I frown and peer at it more closely. 'Is it . . . Amy Winehouse?'

'No!' he exclaims. 'Why would I want a tattoo of Amy Winehouse?'

'Erm, I just thought, you know – the hair, the eyes—'

'It's Camilla,' he retorts. 'Look . . .' He points at the hair region to indicate the lettering semi-concealed within: CAMILA.

'Oh, yes. I see it now.'

'It's even fucking spelt wrong.'

'Um, yeah. I see that too.' Even I know better than to suggest that perhaps they could insert another 'L'. 'Well, I guess it's done now,' I say as he tugs his sleeve back down.

'Yeah.' He slides his gaze over to me. 'I was drunk when I had it done.'

'Right.'

'They shouldn't have done it when I was like that, right? It wasn't a good place . . .'

'Um, no, it doesn't sound like it.' We amble onwards in silence for a few moments. 'Alfie,' I say tentatively, 'is this why you were upset just now? Because of the tattoo?'

He shoves his hands into his pockets and nods. 'Because of all of it, I s'pose.'

338

'And is that why you don't want to go back to Aberdeen?'

'It's just such a fuck-up,' he says. 'I'm a laughing stock, basically. Everyone knows I had it done. I've had texts about it since I've been here.'

'So it's not about your course, or not liking university . . .'

'Can we just forget it now?' he says firmly.

'Yes, of course we can.'

'Our apartment's just along here,' he adds when we reach a corner dominated by a brash bar, its illuminated sign pulsing.

'Okay. My hotel's just a few minutes away too.' It seems a rather abrupt ending after the revelations tonight, but then, what can I do? It's his parents he needs to talk to about this, not me.

We stop, and Alfie says, 'Please don't say anything about the tattoo, will you? To Mum, or anyone else . . .'

'Alfie, I don't even know if or when I'm going to see your mum. But no, I won't say a word to anyone.'

He nods, mouth set grimly. 'I'd better tell her myself.'

'Yeah.' I want to give him a hug and say it'll be all right, but I'm not sure how he'd respond to that. 'Good luck, then. And you do know she'll be fine about it, don't you?'

'You reckon?' He laughs dryly.

'I do, actually, once the initial shock's worn off.' I pause. 'Look, it's not that bad, honestly. At least it's pretty small.'

Alfie smirks. '"At least it's pretty small." Things not to say when someone shows you their new tattoo.'

'Christ, yes . . .' I wince, remembering Nadia and I chuckling over the issue of anti-compliments: *I once went*

339

to the kids' school concert, she told me, *in a short red dress that I loved. I mean, mid-thigh short. Not knicker-flashingly skimpy. And some woman bustled over and said, 'Ooh, you're brave to wear that!'*

The thought of how she made me laugh triggers a fresh wave of longing, and I quickly clear my throat. 'Alfie, listen – it's not that big a deal. Really. You can probably have it removed, or turned into something else, and even if you can't, as time goes on it really won't seem so terrible.' I break off, realising I'm probably saying completely the wrong thing.

'People of your generation *always* say that,' he remarks.

'Do we? Well, I've never said it before. I suppose what I mean is . . .' I pause, wishing we'd gone to that quiet bar with the tinkling piano so we could sit down and talk, instead of it all coming out on a busy street corner.

Alfie is looking me expectantly. I am almost waiting for him to say, *You're not my dad.*

'I mean, you're young, Alfie,' I continue, thinking: sod it, he'll probably hate this, but I'm going to say it anyway, 'and this is a precious time in your life. What I'm trying to say is, there's no point in ruining it by worrying about things you can't change, and then making rash decisions about dropping out of university.'

'Is it, though?' he asks sharply. 'I mean, is it a precious time? 'Cause it doesn't feel like it right now.'

'Yes, of course it is!'

He thrusts his hands into his shorts pockets. 'I know people think that. But *why* is it? I mean, people like you – people of your age – think, "Oh, being young is all about being free and having fun, being able to do whatever you like with no responsibilities . . ."'

'Well, I didn't quite mean—'

340

'But it's not like that,' he charges on. 'It's tough. Really tough! We have so much pressure heaped on us. There's our parents, our friends, all of that. All those expectations. We're supposed to be happy and realise how lucky we are – but people let us down, and uni's not all about having fun, you know. Did *you* go?'

'To university? Er, no, I didn't. I did a college course. But what I'm saying is—'

'And actually,' he says firmly, 'it's quite patronising to be told, "These are precious years."'

We stare at each other as a boisterous group of lads – a stag group, probably – pass by, singing and cheering. 'They are,' I murmur. 'Honestly, they are.'

'But no more so than any other years!' Alfie exclaims. 'I mean, if you look back over your life' – Christ, he's making it sound as if I'm about to topple into a grave – 'would you honestly say that your teenage years were the best?'

'Um, not necessarily, but—'

'So, what are you basing this on, then? I mean, *what*?'

He sighs irritably. His eyes are hostile now, and pink patches have sprung up on his cheeks. 'Alfie,' I start, 'I'm sorry if that sounded patronising. I didn't mean it to be. But there's this thing I want to tell you about . . .' I look down the street where there are more cafés and bars, perhaps less boisterous than the one we're standing outside. 'D'you mind if we go get a coffee or something? It's still not too late.'

He shrugs. 'If you want to, yeah.'

And that's what we do, this boy who doesn't belong to me and I. We find a quiet café, virtually deserted apart from a small group of elderly, smartly dressed men who are chatting companionably with the barman, and we take a corner table. I look at Alfie as he settles in his seat; just nineteen years old, an age my brother Sandy never got to see. 'I want to tell you about my little brother, who died when he was sixteen,' I say simply.

Alfie's face falls, and he looks at me properly, all traces of belligerence sliding away now. 'Oh, right. I'm sorry. I didn't know.'

'No, well, you wouldn't. I don't talk about it very much. I haven't even told your mum the details. But these *are* precious years, Alfie, and I only mean that because life is so fragile, and a wrong thing can happen and . . .' I pause and swallow, aware of Alfie looking at me now with a mixture of concern and alarm. 'I know things seem bad at the moment,' I continue. 'Maybe you feel like you've been made a fool of, with Camilla sending those, those *pictures*, and you're angry at yourself for getting the tattoo—'

'What happened?' he asks, frowning.

'All I wanted to say is, none of that matters because you'll be okay, you know? You'll get through this, and maybe Amy – I mean Camilla – can be made into, I don't know, a symbol or something, some kind of *design* . . .' Shit, how drunk am I on those three little beers? I stop and look at him, aware that my own eyes are wet.

'Jack,' Alfie says, leaning towards me now, 'what happened to your brother? *Tell* me.'

Chapter Forty-Seven

So Mum had called me in a real state. Sandy had set off to visit me and never turned up. No one knew where he was. He was terribly wilful and independent; I tried to convince her he'd just be hanging out somewhere with friends, but she wouldn't listen.

'Go see if he's left you a message,' she said. I told her I would, and promised to ring her straight back. But even before I'd pressed the answerphone button, I knew there wouldn't be a message from him. Sandy wasn't a leaving-messages kind of boy. He just roamed around, skipping school whenever he wanted to, nicking our parents' booze and heading off for camp-outs in the woods with his mates.

Although I was long gone from home by this point, I had a pretty clear idea that these 'camp-outs' didn't exactly involve knot-tying or stick-whittling or any other Scouting-type activities. And now, as I played the answerphone messages – the ones from Mum, plus a couple of older ones from mates inviting me and my flatmate Nick to things that were long past – I convinced myself that that's what he'd done. He'd been pissed off with me, and instead of badmouthing me to Mum and Dad, who hated any of us to bicker, he'd got together with a bunch of pals, and they'd set up camp somewhere and had a bit of a party.

'That's what he'll be doing,' I told Dad, as he answered the call when I rang back. 'He'll be out somewhere, and they'll have drunk too much, and they'll all be lying in some ratty old tent, sleeping it off . . .'

'But it was a cold night.'

'They'll have built a fire, Dad. You know how he always comes home reeking of woodsmoke.'

'But it's gone ten o'clock!' he exclaimed.

'Dad, not everyone gets up at five in the morning like you,' I said, trying to lighten the mood. 'He'll be fast asleep, I guarantee you. You'd better give him hell – from me, as well – when he gets home.'

But he never came home. My little brother had decided to hitchhike to Glasgow; perhaps he thought he'd get a cheap hostel, as I'd said he couldn't stay with me, and he'd wanted to save money for that.

He must have been standing at the roadside when he was hit by a car. It was a hit and run, and his body was discovered two days later, knocked into the gorse just a few metres from a bend in the A9. No one was ever caught. Somehow, the driver was able to go on with their life without handing themselves in to the police.

And life went on for my family, too – what other choice was there? But despite the two decades that have passed since we lost him, I still hear Sandy's voice:

I won't be any bother. You won't need to look after me.

Chapter Forty-Eight

It seems natural that we meet up in a café next morning. *Desayuno:* it sounds so much better than breakfast. Alfie has some kind of spicy beans on toast, and I go for eggs and hash browns. He has the good sense not to lecture me about hens being used as a commodity.

'Has your mum been in touch?' I ask as we finish our coffees.

'Yeah, she texted this morning from . . . that phone.' I catch him checking my reaction. 'God knows what's going on with her,' he mutters. 'She was only supposed to go and look at some Surrealist art for a few hours, and she's been gone a whole day and night now.'

'Oh, she's probably just having a really good time,' I say brightly. 'Any idea when she might be thinking of heading back?'

'About lunchtime, she said.' He pauses. 'I didn't tell her you're here.'

'Thanks,' I say, fiddling with my cup. 'So, um, d'you fancy hanging out for a bit? Seeing some sights? Or maybe you've had enough of me tagging along . . .'

345

'No,' he says with a shrug, 'we can do stuff if you like. So, where d'you wanna go?'

I ponder this, knowing I should be able to think of something, having a teenager of my own. But then, I know Lori, and she'd enjoy the whole experience: going for coffee and ice cream, buying a few daft bits of tat. She'd even tolerate the odd museum, as long as we didn't linger too much. But all I really know about Alfie is that he's vegan, he is/was studying English at Aberdeen university, had a posh girlfriend who screwed him over, and is currently sporting a terrible tattoo.

While he sips a second coffee, I consult various city guide websites on my phone, and realise that whole categories of attractions might be met with disdain: for example, parks or gardens. Parc Güell looks incredible with its madly eccentric buildings, like fairytale castles or hobbits' houses, but Alfie says he's seen it already.

We finally decide on the Miró Foundation, which involves a huge walk – far steeper than I'd anticipated. Although we chit-chat on the way there, we don't touch upon the matter of Camilla, or university, or any of that, and I'm wondering now if he regrets showing me the tattoo. I'm also reeling a little from what I told him about Sandy. I hadn't planned to do that at all. It just . . . fell out, entirely by accident. Oh, Christ.

As we wander through the light-filled galleries, marvelling at the intensity of the paintings, I start to relax a little. Alfie even seems to be enjoying himself. At least, there's no moaning or grumbling or going all floppy, the way kids can tend to do when subjected to art.

Plus, Nadia will be back in town soon. Perhaps the three of us could have lunch? I know there's been this

346

Rico situation but, well, maybe I've read too much into that? From that first text Alfie showed me, it sounded as if there was a group of them last night. Perhaps I just panicked, and it's not the hot-Spanish-lover-type situation I've been imagining? So things might be okay between us, after all.

From the gallery, Alfie and I head back down to the Gothic Quarter. As we wander past shop after shop, all crammed with the kinds of things I'd usually find interesting – old books, antiques, paintings and curios – I'm aware of a sense of anticipation growing in me: I want to see Nadia, and apologise.

We stop off for coffee, and I ping a message to Lori: *Hey love how's things?* But there's no reply. We stroll down to the waterside, and I try to appreciate the long, wide promenade, and the huge, glinting structure at the end of it – a coppery fish – whilst wondering if things *are* okay at home, and how Nadia will react when she sees me.

'Fancy sitting on the beach for a bit?' I ask Alfie.

'Uh, I'm not that keen, to be honest.' Maybe he's scared I have swimming trunks on beneath my shorts, and will strip off to reveal them? So we perch on the edge of a concrete block, like a couple of old curmudgeons who are afraid of sand. I check my watch: just gone one, and still no reply from Lori, or any indication from Nadia about whether she's on her way back. Alfie and I make our way to the Picasso Museum – but of course, the queue is vast, and we can't face standing in line in the baking heat. Instead, we wander back towards the Ramblas, and finally, Alfie's phone rings.

'Mum? Hi.' He glances at me, and we stop. I try to adopt a casual stance and wander away a little to give him privacy. 'You what?' I hear him murmur. 'You mean . . . you actually had all your clothes off?'

I fix my gaze upon an unremarkable shop selling all manner of souvenirs – bags, hats, beach towels – emblazoned with crude interpretations of the notable Gaudí buildings. I really can't understand who buys this stuff.

'But why?' Alfie gasps. 'I can't see why you had to . . .'

I try to focus on the souvenirs dangling from hooks and revolving stands, but I'm not really seeing anything properly.

Then: 'God, Mum. Have you gone completely mad?'

Chapter Forty-Nine

None of the other stuff matters, I reflect as the plane touches down at Glasgow airport. There was the call from Iain who, sounding quite hysterical, babbled, 'Veronica sold it! She sold it for £1.50, Jack! I'm so sorry. It was locked up in the safe, I promise you. I don't know who took it out. I think it was Mags. She kept saying we should steam clean it or something, make it smell a bit better in time for the auction. I said, no, leave Jack to deal with that, when he gets back. He knows best . . .'

Veronica is one of the older volunteers; a quiet lady who goes about her business in an efficient way, pricing up items, tidying shelves and manning the till when required. She'd seen it lying about and thought it was just a normal jacket, apparently.

Anyway, that's not important, and neither is the revelation that Nadia did some life modelling for that art group in Figueres. Who knows what was going on there, and what does it matter anyway? She's waited long enough for her freedom after bringing up twins, mainly on her own, by all accounts as Danny was often away working.

What she gets up to now is her business, as she and I are clearly over.

And now, all I want to do is get home, because Lori finally responded to my text, with a call.

'Dad, I'm really sorry to call you but Mum's had an accident. She's in hospital.'

Imagine: apologising because she needed me. I was having a coffee across the road from my hotel when she phoned. I left in a blur, grabbing my stuff from my room, checking out when the woman with the bun finally appeared at reception – I had to ring the brass bell on the desk three times – and heading straight to the airport. Luckily, I managed to get on the next flight to Glasgow.

Elaine had had a fall, apparently, and I hadn't been around to look after my daughter. Instead, my brother Craig had driven from Perthshire to Glasgow to take care of his niece, when I should have been there, reassuring Lori that everything would be okay.

Well, I will be now.

Chapter Fifty

Nadia

'For God's sake, Alf, why didn't you tell me Jack was here?' I ask, no longer caring about the state of our apartment. There are crumbs everywhere, a puddle of orange juice on the kitchen floor, and various items of his clothing deposited all over the place.

'He told me not to,' Alfie replies, huddled on the sofa with a coffee.

'But why? Didn't he think I'd want to see him?'

He shrugs. 'He just . . . I don't know. He wasn't sure how you'd react, I suppose.' He pauses and I see the flush spreading across his cheeks. 'He thinks you've kind of . . . met someone.'

I frown at him. 'Met someone? You mean, a man?'

He nods. 'Yeah.'

Any thrill I might have experienced over Jack flying out here, presumably to make everything right with us, has disappeared as it's all so bewildering. 'Who?' I exclaim.

'Someone called Rico,' Alfie murmurs with a shrug.

'Oh, Alf. For goodness' sake.' I pace across the living room. 'They're a bunch of lovely people, that's all, from

Paisley. They're huge Dalí fans and it'd been a big deal to them, to come on this trip. We had a real laugh last night and—'

'And then you did some life modelling for them this morning?' Alfie remarks with a frown. 'How did that happen?' I fix my gaze on his face. His accusatory expression transports me right back to that moment, all those years ago, when he and Molly found out that 'my' kind of modelling involved removing all my clothes, and they were disgusted with me.

'Gerri had this beautiful room in the hotel,' I explain, 'all ornate, with amazing antiques, and a gorgeous carved fireplace and a chaise longue, and they thought it would make a great setting for a sketching session. And Fran was saying, "I wish we had a model" and, well, I just thought, why not help them out when they'd been so lovely and welcoming to me?'

Alfie eyes me levelly. 'Because . . . you were in a *hotel* with these people, and not at your normal kind of drawing class?'

'But it was the same kind of thing,' I insist. 'I've told you before, Alf. I'm not a body in a situation like that. I'm just a collection of curves and angles, like—'

'Like a bowl of fruit. Yeah.' He nods grimly, and we slump into an uneasy silence.

'So, where's Jack now?' I ask, trying to sound casual. He shrugs. 'Dunno.'

'But . . . you said you've spent time with him?'

'Yeah.' A hint of a smile then. 'It's been all right, actually. I mean, *he's* all right . . .'

'Of course he is. I'm glad you've been getting along.' It strikes me now that all the things I've nagged Alfie to do repeatedly, like flush the loo after use, he pointedly ignores. Yet Jack asks him to do one simple thing – i.e. not tell me that he's here in Barcelona – and Alfie *obeys* him. Is it a man thing? Are young men wired to follow instructions solely from fellow males?

'Alfie,' I start, 'could I borrow your phone, please? I'd really like to call him.'

'Sure.' He hands it to me, and it gives me a small glow of pleasure to see 'Jack' stored in Alfie's contacts. However, he doesn't answer, and when I try again, as we head out into the muggy afternoon, he still doesn't pick up.

'D'you think he's annoyed?' I venture, as we stroll down through Barceloneta towards the beach.

'Why would he be annoyed?' Alfie asks, airily.

'Well, me staying overnight in Figueres . . .' I stop. 'Honestly, Alfie, it was nothing.'

'Mum, please,' he says firmly.

'Rico is gay, actually.'

'Right, okay.'

I glance at him as we reach the waterfront. Does he believe me, or not? Of course, I could show him Rico's website, where there's plenty of info about his artistic collaborations with his husband Luke, but I'm not sure that's what Alfie's being so prickly about.

'I wish I'd known Jack was here,' I add, as we follow the steps down onto the sand. 'I'd have come straight back, you know.'

'I don't really want to sit on the beach, Mum,' Alfie says quickly, as if I hadn't spoken.

'Oh, come on, hon. Let's just chill out here for a while. Take your T-shirt off – get some sun on your body. You're so lucky, you always tan so easily, unlike me.' I stride onwards, then look round to see him hanging back.

'Mum, I don't really want—'

'I have towels in my bag, and sunscreen,' I say with a smile. 'Don't worry, it's only factor ten. Not the thick stuff, the kind you used to call "bandages" . . .'

He blinks at me, and seems to gather himself as he makes his way towards me, and we find a clear patch of sand.

Here, I pull off my T-shirt; I'm wearing my swimsuit underneath. I look at Alfie, hoping he'll at least take off his own T-shirt, and expose his skinny torso to the sun. He looks at me, and then I see him inhale deeply as he grabs at the bottom of his faded pinkish T-shirt, and hoists it up over his head. 'That's better,' I remark.

'Is it?' He gives a curious look.

I frown. 'What d'you mean?'

He turns then, and points to his upper arm, and now I see it.

It's a horrible tattoo marring my beautiful son's arm, badly drawn and ugly. And is that Camilla's name entwined in the hair, wrongly spelt? He looks at me nervously, checking my reaction. I try to dredge up something positive – or even just neutral – to say about it, but nothing comes. But in a way, perhaps it explains a lot. 'Oh, Alf,' is all I can say.

'Mum, please, don't go on.'

'I'm not going on! All I said was . . .' I stop, because what's the point of saying anything now? Instead, I just look at it for a few moments longer, and then we hug, tightly; amazingly, he allows it. I can't remember the last time we held each other like this.

'Maybe,' I venture as we pull apart, 'you should keep it covered for a while?'

'It's awful, isn't it?'

'It is, but you know that anyway, and that's not what

354

I mean. It just looks a bit sore, love.' As he grunts and pulls his T-shirt back on, I fish out the sunscreen from my bag. 'I just don't want it getting sunburned,' I add. 'They probably said that, when you had it done, and they gave you a talk about after-care . . .'

Alfie looks at me, and for a second I know he's weighing up whether or not to lie. 'Mum,' he says, wincing, 'there wasn't a talk about after-care. I just . . . left.'

355

Chapter Fifty-One

Jack

When I arrive at the Royal Infirmary and find Lori and Craig sitting with Elaine in the busy ward, it seems that the 'fall' is just part of the story.

'So, *here* you are,' she says, with a trace of snideness that hardly seems justified, given the circumstances.

I hug Lori and my brother, grateful when he offers to take Lori for a coffee so Elaine and I can 'have a bit of time'.

I pull up a plastic chair and sit down. 'So you've broken your arm and collarbone,' I say, and she nods.

'Look, Jack, please don't lecture me.' Her face is pale and sweaty, her hair matted and unwashed. I can tell she's been crying. She's wearing a sling, her forearm is in a plaster cast, and she doesn't seem to be able to move without wincing.

'The last thing I'm going to do is lecture you,' I murmur.

'Well, yeah, but you might as well know what happened.' She clears her throat, and I hand her the glass of water from the side table. 'Me and Harry had a bit of a sesh last night.'

'Right. So that's how you—'

'Look, I don't know exactly what happened,' she says quickly. 'I must've blacked out. When I came to, in this place, they said I'd had my stomach pumped . . .'

'Oh, God, Elaine!'

'Yeah, I know.' Her eyes brim with tears and she blinks rapidly. 'Crap, isn't it? I thought I was getting on top of it, Jack. I've tried, you know, but I'm not going to go to meetings, all that stuff, with a load of people who sit around, sharing their innermost thoughts, confessing the worst things they've ever done in some mass spilling out of emotions.'

I touch her unbroken arm. She feels cool and clammy. 'I don't think it's always like that,' I say gently.

'I thought I could do it by myself,' she goes on, 'for Lori, you know? And I was doing really well. I really was. I was only drinking moderately. I mean, okay, maybe a doctor wouldn't call it moderate, but things were fine, honestly!' She stares at me, eyes defiant now. Of course, things weren't really fine. But if she'd made a good job of kidding herself that that was the case, then maybe I had too.

'Elaine,' I say, 'all that matters is you getting well, okay? No one's going to judge you. No one'll give you a hard time for—'

'Yes they will,' she says gruffly.

'Who's "they"? Who are you talking about exactly?'

She shrugs. 'Well, your parents always made it pretty clear what they thought of me . . .'

'Oh, come on. They liked you.'

'You know that's not true,' she says. I exhale, not really wanting to rake over all of this again – not because it's untrue, but because it's in the past.

357

In fairness, my parents never quite knew what to make of Elaine, who was a bit of a new-ager back when we were together, a mass of flowing red hair, little vest tops and hand-made batik skirts that she'd tie around herself haphazardly; one fell off in Tesco once, leaving Elaine shrieking with laughter in her top and knickers in the nappy aisle.

And yes, there were frequent drinking injuries – her 'little mishaps', as she called them – like the time she toppled off a bar stool and split her head. 'I only popped in for one after work,' she retorted. '*You* often go out after work!' Yes, I said, with the guys from the Gander offices, and generally, that didn't end up with someone having to have their head stitched.

'People are so well meaning,' she mutters now, 'when they talk about drinking. It's always, "Let's look at your patterns. How many units of alcohol would you say you have in a week?"' She narrows her eyes at me. 'We all know the rules, don't we, Jack? You halve it. Anyone who doesn't is lying.'

'Elaine,' I say, 'that's fine, we can talk about all of this later, when you're out of here. But in the meantime, Lori will come and live with me.' I pause. 'I mean, for the foreseeable future, okay?'

I almost expect her to argue that too, but she just nods. 'Okay. I s'pose that's the best solution for now. She's been good, you know.'

'I know, she's a great girl.'

Elaine blinks at me. 'She helps out when I'm, uh . . . not too well. She's so supportive.'

'It's supposed to be the other way round,' I murmur, regretting it instantly as she glares at me.

'Yes, well, it might not have been the drink last night

anyway,' she snaps. 'We'd had a curry earlier, and the restaurant was so stuffy. So was the pub actually. Maybe it's my hormones – a kind of hot flush – and I fainted?'

But you've just told me you had your stomach pumped. What were they trying to get out of there – naan bread?

'Or maybe it's low blood pressure?' Elaine's eyes widen at this sudden idea. 'Better to be low than high, right?'

'Yeah, I guess so!' I remark, feigning positivity.

She grunts. 'I just want to get out of here, Jack. Everyone in here is mad, drunk or out of their heads on something. Apart from the medical staff, obviously.'

'Yeah, well, I'd hope that's the case . . .'

'But they're all rushing around, mad busy, being shouted at by people who should be saying thank you instead of abusing them . . .'

'I'm sure they're all doing their best,' I say, 'and you'll be able to come home as soon as they decide you're ready.'

'Hmm.' She rolls her eyes, and now I'm starting to realise how it's been for our daughter, pretending things were okay, perhaps taking time off school to look after her mum, when things have lurched to the wrong side of chaos.

Why didn't Lori tell me how bad things really were? It makes sense now: her poor attendance at school, her supposed inability to concentrate. Perhaps that's why she didn't go to the Christmas school dance; because she was needed at home.

With a stab of shame I realise I should have known that things were escalating out of control. The signs were all there. I should have been stronger, more forceful, and insisted that Lori moved in with me full time. Now it's clear that she has been carrying way too much for a girl of her age – for anyone really. She's been brave and loyal to Elaine, and has been trying to look after her and not rock the boat.

Well, she won't have to deal with all of that on her own anymore.

Chapter Fifty-Two

Nadia

We speak on the phone once I'm back home and I've got myself a replacement mobile. 'I wish you'd just let me know you were in Barcelona, Jack,' I say. 'It's crazy, us two rattling about in the same city and not being together.'

'You weren't *in* Barcelona,' he remarks.

'Yes I was.' I frown. 'I only stayed in Figueres one night.'

'Yeah, well, anyway.'

'What does that mean?'

'Nothing,' he says, rather hotly. 'Maybe I shouldn't have come . . .'

'Why d'you say that?' I ask. There's an awkwardness now that we never had before. We're both holding back, that's obvious; I texted him from Alfie's phone as soon as I found out he'd been in the city, to a blunt response. As soon as I heard about Elaine, I assumed that was why. But speaking to him now, I decide that if Jack believes I was off having some rampant fling in Figueres, then bloody well let him.

'You were doing your own thing,' he says now, sounding distracted. 'I shouldn't have just rolled up, foisted myself on Alfie . . .'

'He loved you being there!' I exclaim. 'Look, Jack – I'm grateful to you for taking care of him . . .' I break off at the sound of Lori's voice in the background. 'You sound busy,' I add.

'No, no, it's fine. I'm just in Lori's room. We're packing up her stuff . . .'

'Is Elaine out of hospital now?'

'Yeah, and she's . . . um . . .' He lowers his voice. 'She's getting help.'

'That's good,' I say. 'So, Lori's moving in with you?'

'Uh-huh.' He can't talk now, that's obvious, and so we say a stilted goodbye. So that's that then, I decide. At this point in our lives, there's just too much going on.

I take a deep breath as I chop up peppers for the lasagne I promised to make tonight, just for Molly and me. 'Please, Mum,' she begged, 'can we have a proper lasagne with cheese? I'm feeling penalised because of Alfie's veganism!'

As I make the sauce, I'm remembering how wonderful it was to feel as if something new was starting for me – the sense that life was opening up again. I read a feature in a magazine on the flight home from Barcelona, all about HENs. Happy Empty Nesters, in other words – a new generation who might have dreaded their kids leaving home, and feared that they had been slung on the scrapheap. Not today's HENs, the article said. We are just starting, the writer was keen to assert; the world is ours for the taking. We have so many opportunities, and numerous youth-making treatments at our disposal if we want them (Kiki's pokey fingers in my mouth? No thanks!). It's our time to burst into life.

362

But can I 'burst'? Do I actually have the energy? Sure, I loved being with Jack, feeling that finally I was an actual woman again, and not just a collection of angles, lumps and other bits. God, it was great. But I'm with my family now, and surely they have to come first?

'Mum,' Alfie says after dinner that evening as he settles beside me on the sofa.

'Yes, Alf?' I say. It's just the two of us tonight. As usual, Molly is out with friends.

I hear him inhale, and I glance at him, trying not to express concern. Clearly, he wants to tell me something, but I also know that paying full attention is the quickest way to scare him away; perhaps I'm learning.

'Mum,' he says again, 'when we were in Barcelona, and I hung out with Jack a bit, he told me what actually happened to his brother.'

'Really?'

'Yeah.' He nods, and although I want to ask, *So what did happen?* I know better than trying to probe him when he doesn't want to talk. So I leave it there and, just like when the kids were younger and I wanted to talk about stuff, I get on with something else.

It's when I have gathered together my sketchbook and pens, and started to draw, that my son tells me what happened to Sandy, and to Jack, all those years ago.

Chapter Fifty-Three

Jack

I'd assumed the possibility of the two of us having a beer together was virtually nil. But here we are, Alfie and me; he called about the charity auction and we arranged to meet. We've been keeping in touch sporadically via text, and I happened to mention that Seb Jeffries' jacket had been sold. And now, apparently, the brother of one of Alfie's uni mates is a rising star on the Scottish comedy circuit and said of course he'd donate something.

'What kind of thing?' I ask as we settle at a table in the pub.

'He's saying a mountain bike . . .'

'A bike?' I exclaim. 'Is he sure about that?'

Alfie laughs. 'It's probably held together with bits of tape and string – but yeah. He sounded pretty sure.'

'Well, I'm really grateful for that,' I tell him. 'Did your dad ever hear what happened to Seb Jeffries' jacket?'

Alfie shakes his head and laughs. 'Nope, I thought it was best that he didn't. Not that he'd be bothered really. But it'd be a bit embarrassing if Seb found out . . .'

'Yeah.' We have another beer, and then I suggest we have food and, thankfully, despite it being a rather old-school pub, there are plenty of vegan choices on the menu.

As Alfie tucks into his veggie burger I catch him eyeing my macaroni cheese. 'D'you miss cheese?' I ask, then catch myself. 'I bet everyone asks that,' I add.

He grins. 'I do actually, but don't tell anyone.'

'I won't.' A conspiratorial look passes between us and we fall into silence as we eat.

It's only when we're leaving that I sense that Alfie didn't just want to meet up about the charity auction today. There was no need; he could have just texted or called. We step out into the warm evening, and we're about to part company when he stops and looks at me.

'Thanks, Jack.'

'Oh, it was only a burger,' I say.

'No,' he says quickly, 'I mean spending that time with me in Barcelona. For, you know . . . not judging me.'

I frown. 'Why on earth would I judge you?'

'Well, for being a jerk, for saying that stuff in front of your parents . . .'

'You weren't to know about Sandy. How could you have?'

Alfie shrugs. 'I told Mum. About your brother's accident, I mean. I hope you don't mind.'

I open my mouth to say no, I don't mind – although I do a little. Now I wish I'd had the chance to tell her myself. I shouldn't have kept it from her, I realise that now. I should have explained why Mum was so distraught that day. If we'd talked it through, perhaps Nadia and I would still be together now. Instead, I had a stupid row with her on the phone.

365

And I'm meant to be a full-grown adult?

'I said you'd always felt responsible,' Alfie adds, 'and that you blamed yourself for what happened. Mum couldn't believe it, she said she wished she'd known—'

'Alfie,' I cut in quickly, 'd'you mind if we don't talk about this now?'

'Oh. Of course.' He pauses. 'I think you should call Mum, though.'

I frown. It's a warm evening, late in June, and the bars are starting to fill up. 'D'you think she'd like me to?' I ask.

'I don't know. Probably. Why not just phone anyway?'

I consider this for a moment. I seem to be taking relationship advice from the unlikeliest sources these days – but I'm not sure I trust Alfie's judgement. 'Just say hi to her from me,' I say.

Alfie nods. 'I will. I'll tell her tonight. And also, um . . .' He clears his throat. 'I'm going back to university, Jack.'

I stare at him. 'Really? Are you sure?'

'Yeah,' he says, raking at his hair with a hand. 'When I told you that stuff in Barcelona, about Camilla and the photos, all that, even the tattoo . . .' He pauses. 'It didn't seem quite such a big deal after that. After getting it all out there, I mean.'

The gist of what he's telling me sinks in. 'So, you hadn't told anyone before then?'

'No.'

'Not even your friends?'

He shakes his head. 'So, thanks for listening to me.' He grins now. 'You're not weird after all . . .'

'You thought I was weird?' I exclaim.

'A bit.' He grins and nods. 'But actually . . . you're all right.'

366

I can't help smiling at that. 'So are you, Alfie. You really are all right.'

We stand there, a little awkwardly now with the evening sun on our faces. 'Well, I'm off home then,' he says briskly. 'I'd better go and tell Mum.'

Chapter Fifty-Four

Iain

I prop open the cookbook against my spice rack. Maybe it's wrong to describe it as a cookbook because it's way more than that. There are tips on healthy stuff, how to stay well, how to live until a very old age – which I fully intend to do, like Una upstairs, who's eighty-three. And there's nothing in the book about examining your poos. Maybe Jack made that up because he wanted to put me off trying these recipes and force his soup idea onto me?

Anyway, Una said she thought it was a good idea, when I told her my plan. Luckily, I had Nadia's phone number stored in my contacts from when we all looked for Pancake together. It was important to keep in touch that day, in case anyone had a sighting. So I called her, and I told her all about the denim jacket, and how reasonable Jack had been, considering.

I also told Nadia that he hasn't been his normal self since he's been back from his trip. Like something – or someone – is missing. I think she understood what I meant, and she seemed to still care about him. I didn't want to be too obvious, though. Jack always says, when you want to sell something you don't bash them over the head with the idea. You don't wave the thing in their face and shout, because that way, they'll feel pressurised and run away.

It's much better, he always says, to try to make it seem appealing – in a subtle way – and leave the customer to make up their own mind. And that's how I wanted Nadia to feel: non-pressurised. So I've made all this food, and bought wine from the shop down the road. I wasn't sure what to get; it's pretty confusing, choosing wine, as I don't normally drink it unless I'm out. Una often offers me something, but that's generally sherry. Anyway, in the end I went for red.

'Just what I need,' Jack says when he arrives and I hand him a glass. He peers at it, and I can see now that there's sediment at the bottom of it.

'Sorry,' I say, frowning.

'Oh, I'm not worried about that. We've all got to die sometime, haven't we?' He laughs and takes a sip.

'I'll show you what I'm making,' I say, leading him through to the kitchen where I've set everything out.

There's a soup – I hope he approves of that! 'It's lentil and spinach, with raisins in,' I explain. 'Very healthy.'

'It looks great,' he says with a nod. 'Unusual, but I can't wait to try it.'

'And for the main course there's a bake in the oven . . .'

'A bake?' He raises a brow.

'Yeah – that's what it's called. With beans, brown rice, leeks, herbs and spices.'

'Right. Sounds delicious . . .' I see his gaze flick to the three wine glasses I've set out on the worktop, each filled with canned mandarin segments. 'And they're . . .'

'They're our dessert,' I say, and it's clear now how

369

impressed he is. 'So – three courses! D'you think you can manage all that?'

'Uh, yeah, I'm sure I can . . .'

I pause and look at him, because now his expression has changed and he looks, I don't know, quite emotional.

I frown. 'I'm sorry the pudding isn't a recipe from the book. I'd planned to do something proper but I'd kind of . . . run out of steam by then. It's pretty tiring, isn't it, all this cooking?'

'It really is!' He pulls a wide smile.

'But I thought fruit would be fine. It's healthy, isn't it?'

Jack nods, his mouth pressed tightly shut. It looks as if he wants to say something, but can't.

'Is it . . . all right, d'you think?'

He looks at me, my boss Jack, who's so much more than that. He's my friend – more than Una, even. He's always listened to me when no one really does, and never treats me as if I'm stupid. He's right up there with Pancake for me. I never thought I'd be as fond of an actual human as I am of my dog.

'It's wonderful,' he says finally. 'Honestly, Iain, I'm so impressed you've done all this by yourself. I can't believe you've gone to all this trouble for me.'

'Well, I just thought, after all you've done . . .'

He nods, and points to the desserts. 'Is the spare one for Una?'

'Er, no. Not exactly.'

'Right.' He gives me a confused look, but doesn't press it further. I clear my throat and take him through to the living room where there's a table I found in the street and thought might be useful.

'Nice piece of furniture,' he remarks, stroking its top.

'Yes,' I say, smiling, 'but look.' And I show him that

the table top actually opens, and there's a sewing machine hidden inside.

'Wow,' he marvels.

'I know! A secret sewing machine. D'you like it?'

He chuckles. 'I do. I like secrets. I think everyone does.'

God, I hope so, I think, feeling my nerves getting the better of me now, because what if he's annoyed at what I've done?

My buzzer sounds. 'Someone's at the door,' I say unnecessarily, rushing to answer it. And as soon as I open it, I can see why Jack hasn't been the same lately, because she really is just the right girlfriend for him. So why did he just let her go?

Nadia smiles as I beckon her in. 'Hello, Iain. Hope I'm not late . . .'

'Hello, Nadia,' I say, overcome by shyness now, and aware of Jack behind me. 'No, you're right on time.'

'Nadia?' Jack sort of laughs, and so does she, and they step towards each other and hug. I stand back a bit, not quite sure what to do with myself, because they're still holding each other as if they never want to be apart. They go through to the living room, and sit on the sofa I found round the back of an old warehouse, and managed to drag home all by myself.

And that's when I decide to call Pancake, because I think we'll just go for a little walk now, around the block. The thing in the oven shouldn't burn, I don't think. I consider telling them we're going out, as I clip on Pancake's lead in the hallway, but then decide not to. They seemed so happy to see each other, I bet they won't even notice anyway.

That's fine, because that's what I wanted really: the two of them back together again. And now I'm out in the street, I have something else to do. I suppose I should have told Jack as he's the boss, and he should get to do all the important things. But this time, I've decided to keep it to myself.

I found those horrible old trousers of Jean Cuthbertson's under the sink in the back room of our shop. They'd actually been chopped up into four pieces – two from each leg. Someone must have thought they'd do as an old cleaning rag. I mean, no one was going to buy them.

Round the corner from my block now, I pull out the slip of paper from my pocket, with Jean's phone number on it, and I make the call on my mobile. A sharp voice answers. 'Hello, Jean?' I start, glad I'm making the call standing up. Una once told me it makes you sound more important.

'Who's this?' Jean mutters.

'It's Iain. Remember Iain from the charity shop? We've spoken a few times.' I don't like using the phone normally, but this is going well.

'Yes, I remember you,' she says.

There's a pause as I turn into the patch of waste ground where we started our search for Pancake. He's pulling on his lead now, sniffing at clumps of grass. I can tell Jean is waiting for me to say something, and I can't help smiling at that. I knew what she said about me in the shop – Mags took great delight in telling me – but I don't want to keep her waiting too long.

'Well, I'm ringing with good news,' I say, feeling the smile spreading across my face now. 'I'm very happy to tell you I found your ring.'

Chapter Fifty-Five

September

Nadia

It feels funny driving with Alfie in the back, and Jack beside me. Not awkward exactly – just different and new. The three of us are on our way to Aberdeen, and Alfie seems unusually perky, like a child on his way to a sleepover. I guess that's not too far from the truth. Being thrown together with friends and a load of rubbish food, with no parent on hand, suggesting that they really should start thinking about getting some sleep now or they'll be *shattered* tomorrow . . . a student flat-share is a sort of extended sleepover with the addition of booze and cigarettes.

I don't blame my son for being delighted at finally getting out from under my feet – especially as, for a short while there, it looked as if we might be trapped together permanently. He has that gleeful giddiness about him, as if he has narrowly averted disaster: like the time I forced him to come shopping with me, and a bird chose to splat its business on *my* head, and not his.

Jez and Ned won't mock him for bringing his 'footed pyjamas' from home. I suspect they will barely notice if a chopping board smashes, if the bathroom floor is strewn with loo roll or the sink heaped with dirty dishes to be done 'later' (that is, if they fail to self-clean). My son is more than ready to live his own independent life and, naturally, I am delighted that he made the decision to return to uni.

Molly headed back to Edinburgh a week ago, and admittedly, I am looking forward to reverting to the space and peace of a teen-free flat. I loved the time Jack and I had together – those early months of it just being us. Perhaps I didn't fully appreciate how special it was, and how lucky we were to have found each other. Naturally, Jack came back to my place after that lovely evening when Iain had gone to such trouble over the soup with raisins in, the mysterious 'bake' and the tinned mandarin segments served in wine glasses. I've always loved the way Jack is with Lori, and he's kind of similar with Iain; just caring in his own, easy-going way. He's not even aware of it. He's a good person, and I can't believe we almost blew it over something that could have been fixed if we'd talked.

Instead, we acted like teenagers. Does anyone ever truly grow up?

'Any interesting Aberdeen facts then, Jack?' Alfie asks now from the back seat. When I glance in the rear-view mirror I can see that he's smirking.

'I can tell you it's *not* the most northern city in Britain,' Jack replies.

'No? Really?' Alfie asks with exaggerated interest. 'So, which one is? I hope you've researched this . . .'

'I have. It's Kirkwall on Orkney.'

'Oh. 'Cause it's got a cathedral?'

'It does, yes,' Jack says. 'It's called St Magnus and it's about eight hundred years old. I can tell you all about it if you like.'

'Nah, save it,' Alfie sniggers. 'Put it in an email or something. Or write me a letter.' The two of them chuckle. Although I know Alfie confided in Jack in Barcelona – and of course, Jack told Alfie about Sandy's accident – they seem to have bonded way more than I could ever have hoped for. After all, it's only four months since Alfie narrowly missed walking in on us romping about on my sofa. Back then, I'd have been delighted if they'd managed to sit and have a cup of tea together and talk cordially. But now it's constant chit-chat, often with Alfie gently ribbing Jack about aspects of his personality that my son associates with being 'of your generation' (i.e., ancient). He had Jack's sports watch properly programmed and working efficiently within five minutes. He couldn't believe Jack hadn't heard of the rising-star comedian who donated a bike to the charity auction – but at least the assembled audience at the auction clearly had. The gleaming mountain bike (bought on a whim and barely used, apparently) raised by far the most money of all the celebrity-owned items.

'What am I bid for these mittens?' Dinah's strident voice rang out at the auction in the Assembly Rooms in Edinburgh. 'They're very, um, fleecy inside, super-warm, and they've been kindly donated by our favourite soap star, Miranda Ford . . .' On and on she banged about the snugness of the mittens, while everyone clapped and Miranda Ford beamed and shimmered from her table at the front. She was extremely pretty in that blonde-hair-pink-cheeks kind of way, like a child's drawing of a princess.

375

'Please,' Jack murmured into my ear, 'someone bid . . .'

'C'mon, folks!' Dinah called out. 'Let's get the bidding started!' This was becoming embarrassing. Kevin Masters' apron had gone, and the mountain bike, plus various other lesser items that other shop managers had managed to rake in. Dinah had clearly been holding back Miranda's mittens as the star item. 'Folks!' she cried again, a smudge of desperation creeping into her voice now.

'Poor Miranda,' I whispered to Jack.

'I know. Christ.' He winced and looked around the room.

I looked at Alfie, who didn't seem remotely concerned, and why should he? He's never watched a soap in his life. He's barely capable of empathising with his parents or sister, let alone an embarrassed soap actress whom he has never seen on screen. I glanced at Iain, who was sitting opposite Jack; the only volunteer who had wanted to come, despite Jack's offer to everyone. I'd have thought Mags might have wanted to, but I get the sense that she's a little offish whenever I'm around.

'I think she has a thing about you, Jack,' I'd teased him.

'Don't be ridiculous!' he exclaimed, and I laughed. Of course she has; I could tell the first time I saw them together in the shop.

'Jack, you should bid,' Iain was saying now.

'Why me?' Jack exclaimed.

'Because no one's bidding. It's embarrassing.' He looked at Alfie. 'What about you?'

'No way,' Alfie said, cringing.

'They're sheepskin,' Molly added. 'He doesn't wear it.'

'Doesn't wear sheepskin? Why not?' Iain scoffed, as Dinah's voice rang out again:

'Do I have a starting bid of just ten pounds?' She

looked around the room with a hopeful expression. Her face brightened. 'Fantastic. The young lady here . . .'

We all turned and stared at Molly, who grinned. 'No more bids?' The room fell quiet, and everyone seemed to be staring at my daughter. 'Sold!' Dinah announced. 'To the young lady in the red jumper. And that brings our auction to an end today.'

'I can always use a pair of gloves,' Molly murmured, as Dinah launched into her thanks at the end. Alfie pretended to be mortified to be mentioned personally; obviously, Jack had asked Dinah to include him.

'I only asked my mate to ask his brother,' he hissed.

We have arrived at the outskirts of the city now. It's a bright, warm morning, and the sky is a clear, cloudless blue. It feels the right kind of day for a fresh start. 'So, your stuff'll definitely be at the flat, will it?' I ask my son.

'Yeah, the guys have got it. They picked up the keys yesterday . . .'

'Can you direct me now?' I ask.

'Huh?'

'You said you know the way, Alf. I need you to tell me where to—'

'Yeah, yeah,' he says, as we make our way through the suburbs: austere, proud houses with immaculate gardens, gradually making way for shabbier modern bungalows.

'Turn left!' Alfie shouts suddenly, in the manner of someone who has never driven a car and doesn't understand that a driver needs more than a millisecond's notice in order to perform a manoeuvre.

'Christ, Alfie!' Jack exclaims.

'I need more warning than that,' I mutter.

'You've gone past it,' Alfie complains with a sigh. I

glance over to Jack, catch his eye and smile. I'm so glad he came today, not that Alfie and I need any help really; it's just good to have him here. He had offered to drive us, but his old banger finally gave up the ghost last week (my brother-in-law could hardly disguise his glee when he heard, and immediately offered to source an excellent bargain for Jack at auction). Naturally, Danny is away again. So we are in my car, which also contains several large bags of household items; a starter pack for living, if you will. Yes, Alfie left home officially last year, and I bought him all the kitchen stuff for that, plus towels and bed linen, all the essentials. However, he confessed that pretty much everything had broken or disappeared during his year in halls, and could he start afresh?

His dad had a moan about it, unsurprisingly. 'Bloody millennials,' he started, at which Alfie piped up: 'Yes, Dad, I know. What we need is a bloody war.' This is the man who complains about the price of green juice in a noodle bar, after all. Well, he doesn't seem to be baulking at spending a few quid now, not now they're fitting out a nursery to Kiki's specifications.

She was pregnant, it turned out, that day she trauma-tised the inside of my mouth with her fingers. She claimed she didn't know then, but I'm not so sure; perhaps she'd been testing me, to see if I could shed any light on how Danny might react? Nothing to do with me, of course, but I'm happy for them, and although Alfie and Molly were a little freaked out when the announcement was made, I know they are delighted. 'Having a baby at his age?' Alfie sniggered to me, once the news had sunk in. 'It'll knacker him.'

The boys' flat is in a rather unlovely concrete block, but it seems bright and clean enough as we help him carry in his belongings. This time, we are actually allowed into the premises and even offered a cup of tea by Jez, Alfie's cheery flatmate. Then it's back south for us, as we have decided to drop in on Jack's parents in Perthshire.

We are greeted warmly by Pauline and Brendan and given an enthusiastic account of their cruise, and Craig and his wife Jill join us for coffee. Later, I am given a tour of the farm, including the shop, and the barns, which have been given over to cheese production. 'I recognise this,' I tell Pauline, as we wander off together through a small glade, 'from your sketches. Have you been drawing much lately?'

'Yes, I did feel quite inspired after meeting you,' she says. 'Encouraged really. You were very kind.' We make our way through an orchard adjoining the yard. There's a gentle breeze, and one of the sheepdogs is pottering along at our side. 'I'm so sorry about what happened that day,' I add. 'At Jack's place, I mean.'

'Oh, don't mention it,' Pauline says quickly. 'We didn't give it another thought.'

I glance at her, suspecting that this isn't entirely true, but I'm grateful for her generosity.

Then it's just us: me and Jack, having said our farewells and now heading back home to Glasgow. At least, I'd assumed that's what we would do, but now he's saying, 'Could you just turn off here? It's a lovely village and there's a little hotel I wanted you to see . . .'

'A hotel?' I ask, glancing at him and grinning. We arrive at the village, which is little more than a cluster of cottages and a couple of old-fashioned shops – a general store and a grocer's – arranged around a bend in the shallow river. It's astoundingly lovely in the golden light of the late afternoon.

'Like it?' Jack asks as we park up and stroll towards the hotel.

'It's lovely. It looks so cosy. Wouldn't you just love to spend the evening in that lounge, looking out over the hills?'

'Well, we could,' he says, smiling. 'You know Lori's at Shannon's tonight, and there's no work tomorrow, is there?'

I stare at him. 'They might not have any rooms.'

'But they might have,' he says, taking my hand. 'We could go in and ask.'

I'm laughing now as we make our way to the worn stone steps that lead to the front door. 'It'd be crazy to stay here when we're so close to your mum and dad's.'

Jack shrugs. 'But wouldn't you rather stay here?'

'Yes, of course I would, but I don't have anything with me. I didn't think we'd—'

'There are those shops just along the road,' he remarks. 'I'm sure we could get what we need . . .'

'Oh, I don't know,' I say. 'We could probably buy toothpaste, but what about knickers and—'

He laughs. 'You're worried about knickers?'

'I just mean . . . ' I tail off.

'Actually,' Jack says, 'I sort of brought an overnight bag for us. I hope you don't mind.'

I stop and look at him, realising now that we can do this; we can just stay the night, on a whim, because why shouldn't we? We're not answerable to anyone now. It's just us two.

'Of course I don't mind,' I say, kissing him.

'Well, that's good,' he says as we step into the hotel where the young woman on reception looks up and smiles.

'Can I help you?' she asks.

'Yes, I'm Jack McConnell,' he says, making my stomach flip as he squeezes my hand. 'I reserved a room for tonight.'

Minutes later, we are on the very top floor, poised to unlock our door. Jack pauses and looks at me. 'You *really* don't mind, do you?'

'Are you crazy?' I ask as I take his hand, my heart soaring with joy as we step into our room. 'I can't think of anywhere else I'd rather be than right here, with you.'

The End

Everyone has a last straw . . .

An unmissable novel from the voice of the modern woman!

What happens when The One That Got Away shows up again . . . thirty years later?

Forget about having it all. Sometimes you just want to leave it all behind.

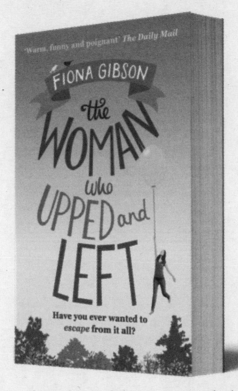

A warm, funny and honest read that's perfect for when you've just had enough.

Midlife crisis? WHAT midlife crisis?!

A hilarious read for fans of Carole Matthews and Catherine Alliott.